A POWERFUL EXPLOSION ROCKED
THE ISLAND AT THAT MOMENT

Bolan and Encizo glanced up in time to see the villa disappear in rolling smoke and flames. The small-arms fire had petered out, and Bolan took the compact walkie-talkie from his belt, keyed the transmission switch and spoke.

"Report."

The voices came back one by one, four members of the Phoenix team reporting in. With Raphael and Bolan both intact, that made it six, all safe and sound.

"Regroup as planned," the Executioner commanded, feeling mixed relief and disappointment as he led Encizo up the rocky hillside.

They had done their job, but only to a point. A number of their targets had escaped the trap, and it would take more precious time to verify IDs. When that was done, the hunt would have to start from scratch.

And this time they had to get it right.

Other titles available in this series:

DON PENDLETON'S

MACK BOLAN®

STONY MAN™

BLOOD DEBT

A GOLD EAGLE BOOK FROM

WORLDWIDE®

TORONTO • NEW YORK • LONDON
AMSTERDAM • PARIS • SYDNEY • HAMBURG
STOCKHOLM • ATHENS • TOKYO • MILAN
MADRID • WARSAW • BUDAPEST • AUCKLAND

First edition March 1995

ISBN 0-373-61899-9

Special thanks and acknowledgment to
Mike Newton for his contribution to this work.

BLOOD DEBT

Printed in U.S.A.

BLOOD DEBT

To the victims of terrorism and oppression
in Bosnia-Herzegovina

PROLOGUE

Paris

"Coming."

It was all the driver had to hear. He had the motorcycle's engine idling, nosed in against the curb, and any moment he expected a policeman to appear, demanding that they move along. Their luck had held, but every stationary moment multiplied the risk—of witnesses, a careless accident, potential failure.

"It's about time," Seamus muttered to himself, the words contained within the tinted bubble visor of his helmet. Scoping out his target on the Boulevard du Montparnasse, he raised the motorcycle's kickstand, shifted into gear and pulled out from the curb.

A taxi almost clipped him, swerving with a sharp bleat from its horn, and Seamus cursed his own stupidity. His passenger responded with a sharp slap to the driver's helmet, registering his displeasure at the sloppy start.

Downrange the target missed their little sideshow, self-absorbed as always, moving toward the diplomatic vehicle that waited to receive him. He was portly, balding, and the hair that still remained to him was streaked with gray. In short, the very model of a fat-cat bourgeoisie.

It would have been enough to kill him for his looks, in Seamus Taggart's view, but there was more. The bastard's diplomatic service had included time in Northern Ireland, where he had made the most of every opportunity to criticize the IRA. When three of Taggart's friends had been murdered on Gibraltar by the bloody SAS, this man had gone on television to proclaim the killers as heroes.

Only luck had spared his life this long. The move to Paris was conceived as a reward, and there were more-important targets back in Belfast, ripe and waiting to be plucked.

But Taggart and his mates had memories that never failed. No enemy or insult was forgotten in their endless war against the British crown. They only wanted opportunity, a wee bit of incentive to expand their hunting ground and let the bloody Brits know there was no safe haven in the world.

Nowhere at all for them to hide.

He had an automatic pistol tucked inside his belt, beneath the nylon jacket, but he did not plan to use it. Taking out the target was O'Leary's job, and he had drawn a Mini-Uzi for the job, complete with extra magazines. All Seamus had to do was put O'Leary close enough to nail the porky bastard, give him ample time to make the kill and shake off any hot pursuit.

No sweat.

He had been memorizing Paris street maps for the past two weeks, until the city felt like bloody Dublin to him, all the major landmarks and escape routes filed away for future reference in emergencies.

If all went well, it was supposed to be a simple drive-by, cruising east on Boulevard du Montparnasse to make the touch, then right—or south—on Boulevard Raspail, and on from there to drop his wheels close by the City University, where they would go unnoticed for a while. If things went as usual, the motorcycle would be stolen by some enterprising thief, while Taggart and O'Leary caught the Metro out to Pont de Neuilly and retrieved their car.

And it was all downhill from there, the drive north to Calais, where they would catch the ferry bound for Dover . . . but they had to get the job done first.

The target had a sluggish, awkward way of walking, age and weight combining to slow him down. That made it easy for O'Leary, but a drive-by had its problems: How much should he lead the target? Were there innocent pedestrians about, and did he care? If he should miss the first time, would there be a second chance?

He left O'Leary to concern himself with details, slowing down a fraction as the target came in range. O'Leary shifted on the pillion, lining up his shot, and then the Mini-Uzi's rapid stutter gave the motorbike some competition in the noise department, rattling off at least a dozen rounds.

It was a risk, but Seamus Taggart could not come this close and still deny himself a quick glimpse of the kill. He was in time to see the target reeling through a clumsy little dance, blood spouting from his chest like crimson streamers on a windy day, and then the street demanded all of his attention. Cranking on the throttle, he weaved in and out through traffic, watching for the flash of blue lights in his rearview mirror.

Nothing.

By the time they reached the Metro station, Seamus Taggart had begun to think about their mission as a job well done.

Toronto

AMAL FROWNED.

The Jewish pig was late again.

For someone who professed to represent Jehovah's "chosen people," he was singularly thoughtless, always keeping others waiting while he dawdled over meals or dallied with his teenage mistress at her flat on Dundas Street.

Of course, Amal expected no less from a Zionist. Their appetites and arrogance were legendary. Anything they saw and coveted was automatically assumed to be their property, a gift from their indulgent god. It made no difference whether they were lusting over women, foreign aid from the United States or territory in the Middle East. Jehovah would provide, with some assistance from the crack Israeli army and their allies who had dominated the United States for the past half century.

But that was changing, and Amal would strike another blow for change this very afternoon.

The pig was not a major player, in the universal scheme of things, but he was still a figure to be reckoned with in Canada. And back in Tel Aviv his death would send a message to the parasites who feasted on the lifeblood of Amal's people.

The trap was relatively simple to arrange, once they procured the address of the target's teenage whore. It was a residential district, west of Lambton Park, and while he might have rented an apartment for a sniper's nest, the getaway was also a consideration. The Israeli had security around the clock, two men with guns who sat outside and smoked while he was servicing his slut. It was imperative that neither one of them should be allowed to point the finger at a given window, thereby leading to interrogation of the landlord, a review of checks and bank receipts . . . the list went on and on.

The answer was simplicity itself. Amal arranged for one of his associates to steal a nondescript sedan in Hamilton and stash it in a small garage they rented by the month. He got the C-4 plastic explosives from a friend across the border, in Detroit, where life was cheap and high explosives were available on demand. It took an hour and a half to rig the bomb for maximum effect, loading the back seat with cartons of scrap iron procured from the dump.

Amal was cautious to a fault when he arranged for the delivery of the bomb. He hired a pair of local hoodlums and instructed them to park another car beside the entry to the whore's apartment house and leave it overnight, thereby securing a parking space. At ten o'clock next morning, they returned with Amal's hot sedan, picked up the first vehicle and replaced it with the car bomb.

When the target left his love nest, driving west, as always, toward his office, he would pass within a yard or so of the sedan. Amal would have the setup covered from a block away, the detonator in his pocket, waiting for the proper time to strike.

So he had planned the trap, and so it was arranged, without a hitch. The Zionists had missed him on their first pass, rolling toward the little bitch's flat, and they would never have another chance. Next time Amal laid eyes on them, he would be counting down the final seconds of their worthless lives.

The Palestinian commando checked his watch again and smiled. Five minutes, give or take, and it would be all over.

As if in answer to his fondest wish, Amal beheld the nose of the Mercedes Benz emerging from the driveway, pausing while the driver glanced up and down the street. There was an instant when he feared the target might betray him, turning east this time instead of west, but then the driver cranked his wheel around and aimed the German limo at Amal.

A few more seconds. Just another yard or so...

He pressed the button on his radio remote control, the box no larger than a pack of cigarettes, and even with the blast expected, its concussion made him flinch. The stolen car disintegrated in a flash, its detonation smashing windows up and down the block. Amal could feel the heat from where he sat, but he was well beyond the effective shrapnel range.

Not so, the Jew.

Amal would later wish that he had taped the blast to play back in slow-motion for his friends. One moment the Mercedes was sedately motoring along in his direction, peaceful and secure. The next it was a smoking hulk, tipped over on its side and burning in the middle of the street. Its window glass had fused or shattered, and the side of the Mercedes facing the blast was stripped of paint, bare metal scored and blackened by the high-explosive charge. No passengers in sight. No sign of life within the car that he could see.

The fuel tank blew a moment later, smothering the crippled limo in flaming gasoline. When no one screamed or moved at that, Amal was satisfied. He made a U-turn in the middle of the block and started back in the direction he had come from. At the blast site, dwindling in his rearview mirror, neighbors had begun to venture from their homes and flock around the funeral pyre.

He left them to it, driving carefully, avoiding any confrontation with police. His mission was success- fully completed, and his masters would be pleased.

Amal was looking forward to his next assignment.

Thinking of the terror he would spread among the Jew-pigs always made him smile.

Rome

IT WAS A WARM NIGHT on the Via Labicana, and the trench coat Giuliano wore was hot enough to make him sweat right through his shirt. He knew it made him look suspicious, standing on the sidewalk with the perspiration rolling down his face, but there was no alternative. His weapon would not fit inside a shopping bag, like the Beretta submachine guns Paulo and Vincenzo carried on the far side of the street.

It was Giuliano's lot to draw the worst part of the mission, packing the Schermuly multipurpose gun beneath his coat and sweating like a pig, while everyone around him dressed in shirt sleeves, walking hand in hand with loved ones for a last glimpse of the Coliseum after dark.

His target was inside there even now, absorbing "culture" as a part of his abbreviated stay in Rome. The purpose of his visit, which brought him all the way from the United States, had been an open secret for the past six days. The White House had dispatched this undersecretary to negotiate cooperation in a solid front against the brand-new wave of terrorism sweeping Western Europe. Another day or two at most, and he would fly back to the States, his mission a success.

Except that he would not survive another day or two. The Yankee's time had run out. He simply did not know it yet.

Giuliano's weapon was a single-shot projectile launcher, manufactured by the British firm of Webley and Scott, but marketed by Schermuly. Breech-loaded and chambered in 37 mm, it was theoretically designed for the delivery of nonlethal riot loads—CS or pepper gas, perhaps baton rounds—but the ugly gun was nothing if not versatile. The high-explosive rounds that Giuliano carried could have stopped an armored car.

Tonight, he thought, they would be called upon to do precisely that.

The gunners with their short Beretta SMGs were strictly backup, standing by to cover his retreat and guarantee that no one lived inside the target vehicle. But if Giuliano did his part effectively, the two of them would be superfluous.

And he counted on success, not allowing himself to dwell on failure, not with all the planning that had gone into this moment. He was ready; they had verified the target, and he knew their time was coming. Giuliano didn't have to check his watch to know the Coliseum would be closing to the public in another twenty minutes or so. Before that happened, the American would exit with his tour guide and bodyguards, climb back inside the Fiat limousine and start back toward his luxury hotel on Via Casilina.

In the process they would have to pass Giuliano's stand.

His weapon had a maximum effective range of some 150 meters, but the range tonight would be closer to thirty feet. The limousine had tinted windows, but he didn't need to see the target's face. It was enough to score a solid hit, and he would try for two or three if there was time.

So much depended on the time.

The Yankee's escorts would be armed with automatic weapons, pistols, anything they needed to defend his life. The armored limousine had gun ports, so they didn't have to step outside, but there would always be a crucial interval between the first alert to danger and a physical reaction. Giuliano had to make the most of that brief time and score his first hit while the guards were fumbling with their weapons.

Across the street Vincenzo raised a hand and seemed to swat at an imaginary fly. It was the signal Giuliano had been waiting for, and he could feel the perspiration flowing down his back and chest in rivers now. He wished that there was time to wipe his hands, but he was concentrating on the street, one hand inside the pocket of his trench coat, wrapped around the heavy weapon's pistol grip.

He saw the Fiat coming, nosing into traffic, merging with the flow. It turned in his direction, as he knew it must, remaining in the lane against the curb. Giuliano waited, stepping forward two more paces, narrowing the gap. A woman stepped in front of him, and Giuliano moved around her, biting off an insult as he focused on his prey.

The guards may well have noticed him, but he would never know for sure. Behind the tinted windshield, they were perfectly invisible as Giuliano brought the heavy weapon out from underneath his trench coat, grasped the foregrip in his left hand, twisting at the waist to help absorb the recoil with his upper body.

Sighting on that windshield as his index finger curled around the trigger, taking up the slack.

The Fiat seemed to lurch, as if the driver sought to swerve away from Giuliano's gun, but traffic in the middle lane prevented him from veering out of range. The 37 mm HE round went in on target, boring through the windshield like an ice pick penetrating plastic, seeking more resistance for the impact fuse.

And finding it inside.

The first shot was enough—he knew that much instinctively—but Giuliano still had two more rounds stuffed in his pockets, and he meant to use them both. Reloading automatically, ignoring everyone around him, he stepped back and fired the second HE round into the back seat of the limousine.

Beyond the mass of twisted, flaming metal, he could see Vincenzo moving rapidly along the crowded sidewalk, making his escape. Wherever Paulo was, he would be doing likewise, seeing that his services were not required.

Giuliano was about to load the third round when he realized that he was taking too much time. Instead, he dropped his weapon and took off running east along the Via Labicana, rudely jostling anyone who barred his path. Two blocks away, on Via Celimontana, he shed his trench coat, dropping it in a curbside garbage can, and kept on walking at a steady, undemanding pace.

The sirens did not trouble Giuliano. They were faraway and headed for the site of the explosion. Witnesses at the scene would give at least a dozen descriptions of the gunman, none of them accurate. The darkness had precluded any decent photographs without a flash, and Giuliano would have noticed any cameras at the scene.

When he had traveled half a mile, the young man let himself relax. Tomorrow or the next day, when he checked in with his comarades, they would give him all the praise that he deserved.

Tonight, though, he would bask in anonymity while watching the reports on television.

In his own way, Giuliano thought, he was a star.

Berlin

A DRIZZLING RAIN was falling on the Hohenzollern Damm as Werner Kraus stepped out of his VW station wagon, turning up the collar of his raincoat to prevent the water trickling down his neck. Gert Wessel joined him on the sidewalk, muttering a vain curse at the weather as he reached underneath his coat to hoist the submachine gun wedged beneath his arm.

Their driver kept the motor running, pale exhaust fumes curling from the tailpipe like a wisp of dragon's breath. The traffic had begun to thin along the Hohenzollern Damm, and that would ease their getaway.

The Palomino Club had been constructed with Americans in mind. Its very name was taken from a horse, for God's sake, putting Werner Kraus in mind of a saloon from one of those Clint Eastwood "Westerns" filmed in Italy and dubbed in broken English. It attracted tourists now and then, but the majority of drinkers at the Palomino Club were U.S. servicemen, accompanied by German sluts who sold their honor for the price of dinner and an evening on the town.

The servicemen were seldom in their uniforms these days, but Werner Kraus could spot them easily, regardless of their dress. They had a certain look about them, close-cropped hair and ruddy cheeks, too quick to smile and laugh at nothing. Kraus believed that he could pick out an American in any given crowd before the bastard even spoke, but there would be no challenge in the Palomino Club tonight.

The nightclub was itself a target. Everyone who patronized the bar or worked there had already chosen sides. That made it simple when the orders were received to stage a demonstration in Berlin against the U.S. war machine.

The MP-5K submachine gun slapped against his hip as Kraus led his companion through the rain and down a flight of concrete steps. The Palomino was a basement club, the entrance etched in neon. Heavy-metal music blasted at them as they crossed the threshold, Werner feeling grossly out of place among the beefy, redneck soldiers and Marines. He watched them swilling beer and fondling German tramps, behaving very much as if they owned the country where they had been stationed for a year or so. In fact, they were little more than glorified security guards, nearly superfluous now that the Fatherland was reunited and the Russian bear had crept away to lick its wounds in private, but their native arrogance was irrepressible.

They needed to be taught a lesson in humility.

He glanced at Wessel, caught his nod and brought the MP-5K out from underneath his jacket, leveling the stubby weapon in a firm two-handed grip. No fumbling with the safety or the cocking lever—he had done that in the car. His index finger curled around the trigger, tightening.

The submachine gun's magazine holds thirty rounds, enough to last for 2.25 seconds at the weapon's cyclic rate of some 800 rounds per minute. Werner Kraus had practiced with the piece for hours, learning how to milk short bursts at need, but there was no time for finesse inside the Palomino Club. He simply held the trigger down and let it rip.

Beside him, Wessel did the same, his Uzi nearly matching Kraus's rate of fire. They swept the bar and nearby tables, screams replacing laughter as the bodies started falling, smiles erased from chubby farm-boy faces in a flash.

Reloading swiftly, Kraus was backing toward the exit as his comrade reached inside his raincoat for a grenade. Sweet irony to think it had been stolen from a U.S. military base near Stuttgart, sold to the Red Army Faction by a sergeant more concerned with profit than his fellow man.

Kraus reached the doorway and fired another burst to keep their heads down while his comrade made the pitch. Gert Wessel was a step or two behind him when he reached the sidewalk, sprinting for the station wagon, laughing in the rain.

The blast was muffled by the nightclub's heavy concrete walls, but then the fire alarm began to clamor, music to his ears as Werner reached the car and slid into his seat. The driver could not help but chuckle to himself as Gert piled in behind them, banged his skull against the door frame, rasping out a curse.

All three of them were laughing as they drove away, the tears of heaven streaming down to wash the gutters clean.

CHAPTER ONE

Kasar, Greece

The island lay in darkness, with a layer of clouds obscuring the quarter moon. Mack Bolan looked for lights ashore, saw none and hoped their landing would be unopposed. If there were gunners waiting in the tumbled rocks behind the beach, perhaps with night scopes, they would catch hell going in. It might well be impossible to land, and Bolan didn't want to think about defeat when he had come so far to see the mission through.

His night goggles picked out nothing that resembled human forms on shore, but you could never be completely sure. No matter how a raid was planned, researched, rehearsed, the possibility of human error remained.

They could not see their target from the south side of the island, but he knew exactly where it was, the sprawling villa sheltered just beyond that craggy rise of ground away to Bolan's left. Approaching from the target's blind side was a calculated move, designed to minimize their risk of landing in the face of hostile guns. Still, there were drawbacks, chief among them the extended hike from landing zone to target, if they landed unopposed.

A thousand yards of rocky ground, and anything could happen on the march.

Kasar lay south of Samos, one of several hundred tiny islands seldom noticed by the tourists bound for Athens, Andros, Mikonos or Crete. In fact, it was privately owned by a Saudi Arabian sheikh who occupied his villa, on the east end of the island, for a week or two each spring. The other fifty weeks or so, he rented out Kasar to anyone with ready cash on hand. The list of tenants included movie stars, musicians, two bestselling authors, European royalty... and well-heeled Middle Eastern terrorists.

The latter were in residence tonight, and Bolan meant to drop in unannounced, together with the men of Phoenix Force, to welcome them in style.

Six men in all, Bolan and his men occupied two Zodiac inflatables. The rubber craft had set off from a fishing boat a quarter mile offshore, where Jack Grimaldi waited with the captain and his mate to guarantee their ticket home did not "get lost" while Bolan and his team were otherwise engaged.

It was a major exercise, from Hal Brognola's viewpoint, but their target justified the risk involved. Kasar was not a simple bivouac for Palestinian commandos resting up from forays into Israel or the nonstop fighting in Beirut.

Not even close.

In fact, according to the CIA, the island had been rented for the summer by an agent from Iraq, on personal assignment from Saddam Hussein. His mission: to coordinate and fund the efforts of at least a dozen terrorist assault teams spotted all around the world. Without dictating policy or otherwise insulting leaders of diverse—and sometimes hostile—groups, the agent was assigned to flatter, bribe and otherwise "encourage" actions aimed primarily at the United States, Great

Britain and their Western allies in the coalition that had crushed Saddam in Operation Desert Storm and maintained economic sanctions and surveillance over Baghdad since the war.

In short, Saddam was hungry for revenge and he had hatched a scheme to satisfy his appetite without exposing any individual Iraqi to suspicion. The Hussein regime could watch and gloat, pretending innocence, while gunmen from the Japanese Red Army, Shining Path, PIRA or Turkish People's Liberation Army executed Baghdad's dirty work. Saddam was picking up the tab himself, with arms and ammunition, gold or petro-dollars, anything his comrades might request.

And it was working.

Within the past three months, a string of unexpected terrorist attacks had rocked the world from Lima to Berlin. The targets were American and British for the most part, an Israeli here and there. At first it seemed to be no more than one of global terrorism's standard cycles, winding up to fever pitch before authorities responded forcefully and stemmed the tide.

The first hint of a difference had come when the Israelis jumped a band of Palestinian guerrillas in the West Bank four weeks earlier. The lone survivor broke tradition by responding to his captors' questions gladly, almost gleefully, describing how the great Saddam Hussein was pouring cash into a covert war against the Zionists and all their allies in the West. It seemed an idle boast at first, the kind of fantasy a young fanatic weaves to steel himself for suicidal combat, but the next report—from Belfast—changed all that.

A bare six days behind the West Bank operation, a paid informer in the IRA had tipped his British handlers to the rumor of links with Baghdad. Weapons, money, anything the Provos needed for their next offensive would be made available upon demand. The Arabs didn't even care to dictate targets, just so long as the guerrillas struck their common foe at every given opportunity.

It was a sweetheart deal, and by month's end informants from Peru, Colombia and Spain reported similar connections. Gunners from the Shining Path, the ETA and M-19 were all receiving gifts or "loans" from the Iraqi government, the timing of the contacts too remarkable for mere coincidence.

It took the brains at Stony Man Farm another seven days to collate information from a dozen sources, sketch the outlines of the plot and learn of a projected summit meeting scheduled on the rented island of Kasar. If Hal Brognola's information was accurate, representatives from a dozen or more terrorist cliques were expected to meet their Iraqi sponsor and discuss upcoming strategy.

Mack Bolan meant to crash that party with a few good friends.

In front of him the rocky beach was fifty yards away and closing fast.

YAKOV KATZENELENBOGEN scanned the rocky shoreline through his infrared goggles, clutching the AK-74 in his strong left hand, bracing himself against the Zodiac's hull with the metal pincers that replaced his right. There was no sign of life onshore.

When they were finished, there would be no sign of life around the villa, either.

Aerial reconnaissance by Jack Grimaldi had supplied the Phoenix team with photographs that covered every square yard of Kasar. There was no beach to speak of on the south side of the island, just a rocky inlet with a strip of dark sand large enough to ground the Zodiacs. A narrow path of sorts wound between the tumbled boulders, across the island's jagged spine, to their destination on the other side.

Geography could be a friend. In this case, while the island's southern face seemed inhospitable, that very aspect had prevented tourists or the Saudi owner from encamping there. With any luck at all, the new Iraqi tenants and their lethal houseguests would rely on secrecy and Mother Nature to protect their southern flank.

If there were guards on duty, Katz reflected, they would be the first to die.

Another moment brought them to the narrow, gritty beach, harsh gravel mixed with the sand. Bare feet would find rough going here, but Katz felt nothing through the thick soles of his combat boots. He helped Rafael Encizo and David McCarter ground the rubber boat and watched as their comrades came ashore in number two.

Six men against how many? Thirty? Thirty-five?

The odds based on numbers didn't matter. Katz would not have traded his companions for another force three times the size. If anything, he was almost inclined to feel a twinge of pity for his enemies.

They were a grim crew, dressed in camouflage fatigues, their hands and faces daubed with war paint. Half of them were carrying Kalashnikovs, the others packing MP-5 SD-3 submachine guns, the reliable Heckler & Koch man-shredders with their built-on silencers for quiet kills. They would be saving the grenades and Semtex charges for the main assault, when there was no more hope of a surprise. If any of their hardware was disabled or discarded in the firefight, there was nothing traceable to the United States, much less to a specific hardsite in the Blue Ridge Mountains of Virginia, where the crew of Stony Man was standing by for a report.

But they would have to wait.

The Phoenix team had work to do.

McCarter took the point, luck of the draw, the others falling into step behind him as he found the path and started climbing the ridge. Four hundred yards to reach the crest, then two hundred more downhill before they reached the villa where their enemies had gathered overnight.

Katz found his pace and started climbing, thankful for the path that had been cleared by goats or men in the fairly recent past. Sound footing let him keep the rifle in his good left hand instead of slinging it across his back. If they were jumped along the way, Katz knew, a crucial second might make all the difference in the world between survival and the long, cold night of death.

In time they reached the crest and started down the other side, more cautious now, a trifle slower, with McCarter feeling his way downhill. The night goggles helped, but they still might not reveal an ambush till the guns went off.

In that case, Katzenelenbogen knew, his men would be like insects on a tabletop, scurrying about in search of cover, desperate to avoid the killing blow.

Glimpsing the villa's lights below, he slipped the goggles off, allowing them to hang beneath his chin. The infrared became a liability when you were facing lights of any serious intensity. One flash was enough to blind a careless warrior, leave him helpless and surrounded by his enemies.

Better to face the encroaching darkness as is, than be caught by surprise and disarmed.

About one hundred yards above the villa, they split into two groups of three men each. Katz led McCarter and Encizo to the left, or west, flanking the enemy on one side, while Bolan took Gary Manning and Calvin James away to the east.

With any luck they would arrive at their respective destinations simultaneously.

And if their luck ran out...well, then, it would be every hunter for himself.

As a MUSLIM, Afif al-Takriti was theoretically forbidden to partake of alcohol, but rules were made to be broken, in daily life as in politics and war. He sipped his second glass of wine and listened as the others talked, recounting exploits, dressing up the action to impress a group of strangers whom very possibly they would never meet again.

The meeting on Kasar was most unusual—perhaps unprecedented in the history of modern terrorism. The Iraqi knew that representatives from different groups communicated now and then, exchanging arms or information as a form of mutual support, but he wasn't aware of any other gathering like this.

And it had all been his idea.

Saddam would get the credit, naturally, and that was only fair. The Father-Leader of Iraq supplied the cash and arms that had made the meeting possible, but it was still Afif al-Takriti's idea to solicit the various groups from abroad to assist in chastising the West.

He scanned the spacious parlor, mentally checking off the several groups in turn. The Shining Path from Peru was represented, along with Germany's Red Army Faction. Members of the Provisional Irish Republican Army sat side by side with spokesmen for As-Sai'qa, the Palestinian "Thunderbolt" group. Abu Nidal had refused to attend, but three of his lieutenants were present, acting on behalf of his Black June organization, the "corrective" wing of Al Fatah. Argentina's Revolutionary Workers' Party shared a table with the Basque ETA military wing. Italy's Armed Revolutionary Nuclei was present, along with some survivors of the Red Brigades. A trio from the Japanese Red Army sat apart and watched the others with suspicious eyes. The delegation from Colombia's M-19 faction was engaged in solemn conversation with delegates from the Turkish People's Liberation Army.

It was perfect. Seeing so much hatred concentrated in a single room made al-Takriti proud. To think that he had brought these hard-eyed men and women from around the world to join a common cause! When histories of this era were written, he would certainly be named as one who struck a telling blow against the Zionists and their collaborators in the West.

Afif al-Takriti was not deceived by his progress, however. He understood these men and women well enough to know that some of them were driven more by ego than by ideology. They yearned for recognition and the power that had been denied them in their humdrum daily lives. Dismissed and crapped on by the ruling class in their respective homelands, they had scoured college campuses and unemployment lines for other disaffected losers like themselves, adopting slogans, choosing sides. For some the choice of targets was en-

tirely cynical, while others took the cause to heart as
true believers, martyrs in the making.

Either way they were expendable. Their chosen life-
style left them vulnerable, constantly in need of money,
arms and ammunition, vehicles, places to hide. Their
revolutionary scruples often took a back seat to survival, all the more so when a paying job came swad-
dled in the trappings of a righteous cause.

The bait made all the difference in the world.

Afif al-Takriti set his wineglass aside and clapped his
hands softly. "If I may have your full attention for a
moment, please..."

The silent Japanese, two women and a man, leaned
forward in their seats. The others interrupted conver-
sations of their own and turned to face their host. None
of them bothered to return his smile.

"I want to thank you again," he said, "for taking
time out of your busy schedules to join me here. You've
introduced yourselves, I see. As promised, each group
represented will receive a token of appreciation from the
Father-Leader of Iraq for making time to hear me out."

Al-Takriti nodded to his officers, and they began to
circulate around the room, disbursing party favors in
the form of compact bundles wrapped in butcher's paper, bound with string. Inside each packet there was
currency, equivalent to fifteen thousand American dollars.

"This gift," al-Takriti said, "is yours to keep and
spend as you see fit, whatever may transpire from this
point on. Some of you have already helped the Father-
Leader of Iraq chastise his enemies abroad, and for that
you have been well paid. The purpose of our meeting is
to discuss future cooperation on a larger scale."

Several terrorists were smiling now, and all of them seemed interested. Of course, they had not traveled so far from their homes to turn al-Takriti down, reject the cash he gave away so freely, but he knew there were proprieties to be observed. He had to mouth the proper phrases, make the egocentric terrorists feel special, valued members of a team.

And such they were.

Where else would he find seasoned killers, innocent of any public link to Baghdad, willing to commit atrocities on his behalf?

There was much to be said for the free-market system, indeed.

"For those newcomers to our grand alliance, welcome. I am pleased to have you join us. Now, before we talk about the future, I would like to note the recent efforts of our veteran members. Our thanks to the Provisional IRA for the elimination of Sir Albert Smythe in Paris."

Smiles among the Irishmen at that. Al-Takriti waited while the Basques and Palestinians applauded. They were almost childlike, basking in the admiration of their peers.

"To the Red Army Faction, for the recent action in Berlin—"

Al-Takriti's train of thought was interrupted by a muffled burst of automatic-rifle fire outside the villa. In a heartbeat all of his assembled guests were on their feet, most of them drawing weapons, the remainder standing with their hands tucked under jackets, clasping polished steel.

It was a fact of life that this sort never traveled anywhere unarmed. Al-Takriti had made no attempt to take their weapons from them on arrival, trusting in his own armed guards to keep the peace among them, even as they staked out the perimeter.

Before al-Takriti had a chance to speak, there came another burst of automatic fire, from several weapons this time. It could only mean a raid in progress, and he felt his blood run cold.

"This way!" he shouted as the room exploded into Babel, thirty-seven mouths all jabbering at once. "With me! There is no time to lose!"

But even as he turned and fled the sitting room, al-Takriti understood that he might be too late.

THE FIRST IRAQI LOOKOUT died without a sound.

McCarter spotted him from twenty yards and lined the shot up with his MP-5 SD-3 submachine gun, squeezing off a silent 3-round burst that dropped the gunner in his tracks. His rifle clattered on the stony ground, but it wasn't the kind of sound that carried far enough to rouse his nearest comrade.

Moving in, the Phoenix Force warrior stooped beside his prostrate target, feeling for a pulse and finding none. Once he had verified the kill, McCarter instantly dismissed the Arab from his mind. The living were his problem now. The dead would have to take care of themselves.

Behind him Katz and Encizo were advancing through the darkness, following his lead. The lighted villa lay some forty yards in front of him, beyond a low retaining wall constructed out of native stone. From all appearances, the wall had been designed for decoration more than any real security. It stood chest high, and flowered vines had taken root among the mossy stones.

McCarter crept in toward the wall, taking care with each step to avoid kicking stones in his path. He moved in a combat crouch, the submachine gun braced against his hip, eyes tracking on an arc from roughly ten to two o'clock, examining each shadow for the vestige of a human form. He almost missed the second sentry, closing from his left. An awkward footstep gave the man away before McCarter saw him, spinning into confrontation with the threat. He stroked the MP-5 SD-3's trigger, caught the Arab with a rising burst that sealed his lips forever as it dumped him over on his back.

And that was where McCarter's luck ran out.

The guy was dead as hell, no doubt about it, but his finger clenched the trigger of his AK-47 as he fell, a wild burst rattling off toward outer space. Spent cartridges made tinkling music on the rocks before the gun kicked free and lost its voice.

But silence is a lot like Humpty Dumpty in the children's nursery rhyme. Once shattered, it can never be repaired. All the villa's lookouts were alert by now.

The time for stealth was past.

McCarter cursed the dead man even as he turned away and sprinted for the low retaining wall. He didn't need a glimpse of Katzenelenbogen or Encizo to be certain they were keeping pace, responding to the dictates of their training and experience.

Whenever any soft probe went to hell, the hunter had a choice of pushing on with all deliberate speed or running for his life.

Which, in the circumstances, meant McCarter had no choice at all.

He caught the mossy wall with one hand, vaulted over, landing in a crouch. Encizo landed at his right a moment later, Katzenelenbogen close behind. From somewhere between them and the floodlights mounted at the corners of the villa, startled voices told him guards were on the way.

And then the shooting started from the far side of the house. The other members of their team engaged.

Each had drawn specific targets based on recon photos taken from the air. McCarter's was the wide veranda at the southwest corner of the house, complete with deep-pit barbecue and swimming pool, in case the tenants tired of splashing in the blue Aegean Sea. He left the others to their own appointed tasks and struck off toward the main house at a run.

He took out the floodlights with a short burst from his SMG, advancing into shadows cast by lights still burning in the house. The men inside were at a disadvantage now, emerging into darkness, silhouetted by the very lights that left them blind to danger in the night. McCarter saw them coming, half a dozen of them grouped together, with an Arab in headdress in the lead. He chose his spot behind the bulwark of the barbecue and let them come.

The pointman would be an Iraqi, brandishing the standard AK-47, sliding back the tall glass door, stepping clear. The group that followed him, McCarter saw, included two more Arabs and three Japanese. Two of the latter were women, and all of them were armed.

So be it.

He had studied terrorism till the facts and raw statistics nearly clogged his brain. McCarter knew that women played a major role in certain revolutionary groups, the Japanese Red Army chief among them. They were ruthless killers, known for their brutality, which sometimes left their male comrades in awe.

To hesitate or shout a warning would only jeopardize McCarter's life for some misguided strain of chivalry. He knew exactly what he had to do.

When all of them had cleared the house, he found his target on the pointman's chest and held the submachine gun's trigger down, a long burst ripping through his human targets from left to right and back again. They fell together, arms and legs all tangled in the clumsy attitudes of death.

McCarter fed a fresh mag to his SMG and stepped around their tumbled bodies, moving toward the unprotected house.

CHAPTER TWO

Calvin James was ready when he met the enemy, his AK-74 cocked and locked, the selector switch set on full automatic. He preferred the M-16 A1, but the conversion of the new Kalashnikov to 5.56 mm was a compromise that he could live with. The AK-74 was lighter than the original, but preserved the classic AK-47's known reliability in harsh conditions.

Not that he expected any snow or sandstorms on the island where his enemy had gone to ground. For here and now it was enough to have a piece that hit what he was aiming at, delivering enough destructive energy to do the job.

James knew their fat was in the fire the moment he heard automatic fire erupting from the west side of the villa. There was no mistaking the report of a Kalashnikov original, which meant at least one sentry was alert enough to bring his comrades under fire. He offered up a silent prayer for all of them and pressed on toward the low retaining wall that ringed the property.

His first stop was a barn of sorts, where vehicles were housed. James knew that going in, because a couple of Grimaldi's aerial surveillance photographs had caught a sleek Mercedes pulling out of the garage. That gave his adversaries a potential method of escape, and Calvin James had been assigned to pin it down.

So far, so good.

Approaching the garage, he met a sentry coming from the opposite direction, running as if his life depended on it. Calvin fired a 6-round burst that knocked him off his feet and punched him over onto his back, unmoving where he fell.

There was no padlock on the motor pool. James flipped a latch and stepped inside, prepared for any challenge from a guard inside. None came, and Calvin counted four vehicles, including the Mercedes Benz, before the sound of shots and shouts outside demanded his attention.

No more time to waste.

He used a full mag from the folding-stock Kalashnikov, one measured burst for each vehicle in the motor pool. When he finished, oil and water, gasoline and radiator coolant mingled in a spreading lake that told him none of the four cars was going anywhere without a major overhaul.

Reloading on the move, he walked to the open door of the garage and peered outside. Two Arab-types were moving in on the garage, both armed with AK-47s. As they closed the gap, one broke off to the left, the other to the right.

Calvin took the left-hand gunner before he had a chance to circle out of range. A burst of 5.56 mm tumblers sent him spinning like a top and dumped him facedown on the villa's curving driveway.

His companion saw it all and looked in vain for cover, finally breaking toward the villa in a dead-end run to nowhere. Calvin tracked him for a few yards with the sights of his Kalashnikov, and nailed him with a 4-round burst between the shoulder blades. The guy was airborne for a moment, then he touched down on his face and slithered ten or fifteen feet before he came to rest.

James looked around for targets, came up short and listened to the sounds of concentrated firing from the villa. He couldn't see any members of his team, but knew approximately where they were—or where they should be if their plans had not been thrown off track.

James smiled. His own part in the raid was more or less complete. The motor pool and its guards were neutralized, one avenue of exit from the villa closed to those inside.

Which left the Phoenix Force warrior with some free time on his hands.

He checked the load on his Kalashnikov again, then went outside to join the killing game.

As HE CLEARED the low retaining wall outside the villa, Gary Manning knew the raid was bound to be a bitch. The slim advantage of surprise was lost, and their targets were bailing out of every door and window in a hectic dash for safety. Never mind that they were on a rocky island, with the nearest house a half mile distant. The assembled terrorists had not remained at large this long by meekly giving up when they were challenged.

They would fight until they died or found an exit from the trap, and that meant scouring the grounds— the whole damned island, if it came to that—for stragglers.

Manning's primary concern was pinning down the helicopter, making sure that none of their intended targets had an opportunity to fly away. The little chopper only seated six, but it had been decreed that no one must escape the trap.

Okay.

The bird was loading human cargo when he got there, two on board and nine or ten still waiting, wrangling over who would have to stay behind. Two Arab guards were covering their flank and glancing nervously toward the villa, where a major firefight was in progress.

Manning took the watchdogs first, a short burst from his silent submachine gun dropping one before the other targets even realized that they were coming under fire. The dead man's comrade heard his sidekick hit the deck and turned, gaping at the corpse, but he was not in time to save himself.

A second burst from Manning's SMG ripped through the Arab gunner's chest and pitched him backward. He flattened against the chopper's fuselage, then dropped to a seated posture, leaving crimson traces behind. Released by lifeless hands, his AK-47 dropped between his outstretched legs.

Manning turned to the helicopter and its would-be passengers. The pilot had him spotted now, mouthing silent warnings behind the Plexiglas bubble of his windscreen, turning to shout at the passengers already seated. He was going for a lift-off, and he might have managed it, except that Manning beat him to the punch.

The chopper had begun to rise when Manning fired another burst of parabellum manglers that shattered the windscreen and nailed the startled pilot to his seat. Instead of gaining altitude, the helicopter wobbled, nosing over toward the group of stranded terrorists, its rotors whipping flesh and turf before they came apart, the awkward airship settling on its starboard side. A heartbeat later flames erupted from the engine, spreading rapidly until the shattered helicopter and its occupants were all consumed.

Four men had been effectively dismembered by the rotor blades, and Manning found a fifth dragging himself toward the edge of the helipad, leaving a broad crimson trail from the stump of one leg. The wounded gunner glanced across his shoulder, crazed with pain, saw grim death pursuing him. He gasped what sounded like a curse in German, then a short burst from the MP5 SD-3 silenced him forever.

The tall Canadian reloaded, following the handful of survivors who had managed to avoid the helicopter's death roll. There were three of them, he saw, and they were running toward the southern property line, away from the villa. Manning didn't know if they had marked an exit in advance or if they simply hoped to slip away in the confusion.

Either way their time was running out as Gary Manning set off in pursuit.

He wondered who they were, these three in front of him and the dead he left behind. All terrorists, he knew that much, but it would take a set of Polaroids, reviewed at Stony Man, to connect the lifeless faces with names, specific groups and theaters of operation. For all he knew, some of the dead might never be identified.

No matter.

It was Manning's job to see that no one got away. A clean sweep was the goal, and nothing less would satisfy.

Ahead of him the runners disappeared into a stand of trees. Beyond that cover lay the wall, then a hundred yards of open rocky ground that sloped off to the sea.

Nowhere to hide.

It would be butcher's work from that point on, and Manning steeled himself, picking up the pace.

The quicker he was finished here, the sooner they could start for home.

AFIF AL-TAKRITI BELIEVED in being prepared. The raid was a surprise, of course, no doubt about it, and he cursed himself for that, but it did not have to be a *fatal* surprise. He had begun preparing for emergencies the moment he had set foot on Kasar, and he was not without resources now. At different points around the property, they had four cars, one helicopter... and the boats.

The boats were designed for speed, with inboard motors and official top-end speeds of sixty miles per hour. Having tested both of them himself, al-Takriti knew that they were capable of more—as much as seventy if they were hammered to the limits of endurance for a finite length of time.

And it would not take long to reach another island, dodging into cover at the first opportunity, waiting for dawn to plot a circuitous course toward the mainland. Getting off the cursed island in one piece was his priority right now, and if a number of his guests decided to accompany him, so much the better.

There was more security in numbers, and the terrorists he helped to save might feel a certain bond with Baghdad when the smoke cleared and al-Takriti tried to resurrect his master plan.

He might still salvage something from the plot, but first he had to save himself. When that had been accomplished, he could concentrate on picking up the pieces...and persuading his superiors that it had not all been a waste of time.

"This way," he urged the others. There was no one covering the hidden exit from his den, and it was only a short jog through the flower garden to a secondary path that zigzagged down the hillside toward the dock and waiting boats.

He had eleven people with him. Two were his personal guards. The others were three men from As-Sai'qa, two each from the ETA and M-19, plus a pair of mismatched stragglers from the IRA and Turkish People's Liberation Army. All were armed, but none appeared to draw much courage from the weapons in their hands. The Turk was clearly frightened, and the Irishman could barely take a step without a new curse falling from his lips.

"Be quiet!" snapped al-Takriti. "If they have not seen us yet, we must not draw attention on our way down to the boats."

Al-Takriti let one of his soldiers take the point, falling into step behind the rifleman, the others following him along the narrow trail. As with most of the others, al-Takriti was armed with a pistol, his personal choice being the reliable Browning BDA-9M. He gripped the double-action weapon tightly as he made his way downhill, his attention divided between the villa, where fighting still raged, and the dark path.

They were within fifty feet of the dock when a figure rose up in front of them, seeming to sprout from the ground, blocking their path. Al-Takriti's pointman took the first rounds from an automatic rifle in the stranger's hands. He pitched over backward like a rag doll.

Al-Takriti hurled himself to the left, facedown, skinning knees and elbows as general firing erupted on the hillside. There seemed to be no larger ambush party, just a single man, but he was standing fast and dueling with the gunners in al-Takriti's party, dropping two more where they stood.

Al-Takriti saw him pivot, following the Turk and triggering another burst that brought his target down.

Instinctively the Browning found its mark, and al-Takriti squeezed off three rounds in rapid fire. He saw the stranger jerk with each successive impact, reeling, going down.

"Come on!"

He rallied the survivors with a shout and sprinted toward the dock, all thoughts of stealth abandoned in the race to save himself. If no one followed him, al-Takriti would be forced to leave them all behind. He was a born survivor, and he didn't plan to die so far from home, on this accursed island.

Eight men reached the dock alive, four piling into each of the speedboats. Al-Takriti ended up with his surviving bodyguard and the pair from the ETA, who huddled in the stern and eyed their shipmates like potential enemies. The other boat held two Colombians and two survivors from As-Sai'qa, who had lost their comrade in the ambush. Al-Takriti had the engine of his own boat growling by the time one of the M-19 commandos figured out the mechanism on the second craft and brought it to life.

"Cast off and follow me!" he shouted. One of the Arabs waved a pistol at him in acknowledgment. Al-Takriti nudged the throttle, making off for open water.

He was safe! Unless the bastards had patrol boats waiting off the island, he had done it!

Even so, he would not feel secure until he found another hiding place in which to spend the night. Tomorrow he would have to risk the mainland . . . or perhaps strike off for Crete. If he could purchase more fuel there, it would be possible to make a run for Libya, two hundred miles due south.

Khaddafi's soldiers would not turn him back, not once he had identified himself. He would be safe in Libya, until he could arrange for passage home.

And there he would be called on to explain his failure to Saddam Hussein.

If he survived that challenge, thought Al-Takriti, he was capable of anything.

THE BOATS WERE BOUND to give him trouble, Rafael Encizo knew. A native Cuban, island born, it seemed that every hard-luck story of his life revolved around the ocean and a boat. His first trip to the States, in exile, was a nightmare Rafael would just as soon forget. In later years he had returned to Cuba more than once, on seaborne raiding expeditions, watching friends and comrades die in combat with the soldiers of Fidel. There had been other raids since he had joined the ranks of Phoenix Force, and every time he took to water there was trouble. In San Juan...

Encizo caught himself as his mind began to drift, lose focus on the here and now. He concentrated on the mental image of the recon photos he had studied while preparing for the strike. He knew exactly where to go and what to do. He had to cut off the enemy's retreat by water while his comrades mopped up at the villa.

Simple.

If the trap worked well, he would be watching empty boats until the all-clear signal brought him in. With any luck he might not have to fire a shot in anger all night long.

But that would be *too* simple.

The firing came ahead of schedule, telling him a sentry had surprised some member of the raiding party. Still a hundred yards from the dock, he hurried on and found himself a place among the rocks, where he could interdict the passage of escapees fleeing the villa. There was no time now to wire the boats as he had planned. He had to watch the trail instead and cut off any fugitives before they reached the dock.

It still might be all right, despite the loss of critical surprise, but Rafael was well aware of how plans had a tendency to come unraveled in the heat of combat. You could spend a month refining strategy and see it shot to hell in seconds flat, because some unanticipated problem reared its ugly head.

Like now.

He heard them coming down the slope before he saw the pointman, giving up the count before he hit the dozen mark. If all of them were armed—and Rafael assumed they were—it would be difficult, perhaps impossible, for him to pin them down.

Still, there was nothing for him to do but try.

He waited, hardly breathing, while his enemies trooped down the hillside. When the pointman came within ten paces, Rafael stood up and shot him in the chest, a burst from his Kalashnikov delivering sufficient force to slam the gunman over onto his back.

It went to hell from there as six or seven of his adversaries opened fire with handguns, scarcely bothering to aim. Encizo dropped two more while bullets whispered past his face on either side, chipped rock around his feet and swarmed above his head. He kept his nerve, kept firing, and his enemies began to scatter, breaking from the trail.

He picked one out at random, swung around to track the running target with his rifle, putting three rounds in the runner's back from twenty yards. The dead man belly flopped and gained a few more yards of ground, but he was going nowhere fast.

Encizo never saw the man who shot him, but he registered the muzzle-flashes from the corner of his eye, too late to duck and cover as the first round struck his chest, the second hammering his ribs. Round three was high and wide as Encizo plunged back and downward, clinging to his rifle as he fell.

The howling darkness opened wide to swallow him alive.

THE DYING SENTRY'S warning shots had done their job in terms of clearing out the villa. By the time Mack Bolan reached his destination, men were scampering around the grounds in all directions, looking for the nearest exit, some assisting wounded comrades, most intent on looking out for number one.

He met two Latin gunners, a suggestion of Indian blood in their faces, intent on escaping via the long, curving drive. At first glance they confused him with one of their host's bodyguards, but the confusion resolved when he shot both men dead in their tracks with his Heckler & Koch SMG.

Moving on.

Bolan heard the explosion and saw the eruption of flame as the chopper went down. Inspired, he palmed a frag grenade and dropped the safety pin along his line of march, holding the spoon in place as he searched for a target deserving of special attention.

There!

A jagged muzzle-flash erupted from a kitchen window of the villa, and he answered with the frag grenade, an easy pitch that dropped it through the window frame with room to spare. Three seconds later an explosion rocked the east side of the house, but he was out of range, already seeking other prey.

He never knew if it was fate, coincidence or pure dumb luck that let him hear the crash of guns downhill, from the direction of the dock. Split-second choices were the warrior's stock in trade, and Bolan didn't hesitate. The men of Phoenix Force could mop up any stragglers in the house or on the grounds, but if a part of the contingent got away...

He moved downhill with long, determined strides, following the sounds of combat as they peaked then sputtered and died away. A nagging sense of apprehension followed Bolan through the darkness, dogging his tracks. Encizo was a veteran warrior, but not superhuman. If outnumbered and outgunned, he still might not succeed.

Might not survive.

The narrow downhill path was strewn with bodies. Three dead men sprawled across the trail, and Bolan saw a fourth off to his right, a few yards distant, looking like a stranded diver with his arms flung out above his head. Sluggish movement on the rocks ahead sent Bolan forward, moving in combat crouch, his MP-5 SD-3 ready.

He found Encizo lying on the stony ground, still clutching his Kalashnikov. His camo shirt was torn, but Kevlar underneath had stopped the slugs that knocked him down from drawing blood. Their impact had been enough to stun the wiry Cuban, and it seemed that he had struck his head on falling, but he would survive.

The snarl of motors brought Mack Bolan to his feet.

The boats! *Damn* it!

Leaving Rafael on hands and knees, he raced downslope to reach the dock, already knowing he would be too late. The speedboats had a fair head start and they were fading out of range as Bolan arrived. He squeezed off a burst he knew was wasted even as he pulled the trigger.

Two boats, and he could only guess how many terrorists had been on board. Encizo should have some idea, but that would be no help in tracking them. Grimaldi and the fishing boat were on the wrong side of the island for an intercept, deliberately avoiding any show of force that would have tipped their enemies to an ambush in the making.

Bolan gave himself the luxury of one more curse before he turned his back on the Aegean and began to climb. Encizo met him on the slope, a grim expression on his face.

"I fucked it up," the Cuban said.

"No way. It's lucky you're alive."

"For who?"

The warrior let that slide. "How many in the group you met?"

"Eleven, twelve." Encizo shrugged, dejected. "I'm not sure."

A powerful explosion rocked the island. Bolan and Encizo glanced up in time to see the villa disappear in rolling smoke and flames. The small-arms fire had petered out, and Bolan took the compact walkie-talkie from his belt, keyed the transmission switch and spoke.

"Report."

The voices came back one by one, four members of the Phoenix Force team reporting in. With Rafael and Bolan both intact, that made it six, all safe and sound.

"Regroup as planned," the Executioner commanded, feeling mixed relief and disappointment as he led Encizo up the rocky hillside.

They had done their job, but only to a point. A number of their targets had escaped the trap, and it would take more precious time to verify IDs. When that was done, the hunt would have to start from scratch.

Because they could not leave the job half-done.

Not this time, with a global reign of terror waiting in the wings.

This time they had to get it right.

CHAPTER THREE

Stony Man Farm

On Tuesday morning, three days after the assault in Greece, Mack Bolan woke to the smell of coffee, fresh and strong. It took a second for him to recognize the room, its furnishings, but he had no such lag time with the woman bending over him.

"It's half past seven," Barbara Price informed him.

"Jesus. I've been wasting time."

"Excuse me?"

Bolan smiled and touched her hand. "I didn't mean last night," he told her.

"Or this morning?"

"Well..."

"Why, you—" She went to punch his shoulder playfully, but Bolan caught her arm and pulled her down on top of him.

"I bounce back fast," he said.

"I've noticed."

It was true enough. The preparations for Kasar had taken up nearly two days, immediately following his flight to Greece. Then had come the firefight and the mopping up, a brisk retreat to Jack Grimaldi on the fishing boat and several hours of island-hopping hide-and-seek with the authorities before they cleared security at Athens International. Another nineteen hours in the air, with Bolan napping fitfully, his private thoughts and noisy fellow passengers preventing any decent sleep.

The Farm had looked like home sweet home on Monday night when he and the bedraggled troops of Phoenix Force arrived. Brognola was expected in the morning for a recap of their mission and a look at things to come.

The Executioner was sure of one thing: they were still not off the hook. A fair part of the job—perhaps the worst part—was still to be finished.

"Hey!" said Barbara, poking Bolan's ribs. "No fair spacing out while I'm seducing you."

"Is that what you were doing?"

"I'm in trouble if you have to ask."

"A joke," he said.

"So funny I forgot to laugh." Her Gilda Radner voice made Bolan smile. "What's on your mind?" she asked.

"The job."

Of course.

The major problem with a never-ending war was, very simply, that it never ended. Even a "decisive" victory was transient in the long view, binding only on the enemies you killed or badly terrified.

A little time would go by, and there would be brand-new enemies to cope with, unfamiliar names and faces grafted on the same old ruthless, grasping attitudes and motives, pushing for the same time-honored goals.

Control and power.

Wealth and luxury.

Enslavement or destruction of the weak and helpless.

You could paint it any color, dress it up in any uniform, unfurl the banner of your choice—and it would all come out the same. Rhetoric aside, the main difference between Hitler's Germany and Stalin's Russia was a matter of endurance and the fact that one strongman had cracked, turning out to be a raving lunatic. Discarding accents and geography, observing only the behavior, an ambassador from Mars would be hard-pressed to distinguish between a Nazi and a Communist, a Brooklyn mafioso and a member of the Ku Klux Klan.

"I need your full attention, soldier." Slipping one hand underneath the sheet, she guaranteed exactly that.

"All ears," said Bolan.

"I don't think so," she said with a muffled laugh.

"Well..."

"We're not expecting Able Team for an hour and a half. The briefing won't start for another thirty minutes, give or take, once they touch down. So what's your hurry?"

"If you put it that way..."

"That's exactly how I put it."

"What was it you had in mind?"

"I've seen your file," she said. "You need some work on undercover tactics."

"Ah."

She stood beside the bed and peeled her jumpsuit off, revealing the familiar luscious curves. A moment later she was underneath the covers, next to Bolan, smiling impishly.

"Before we start," she said, "you need to limber up. Get down and give me twenty."

Bolan smiled. "We aim to please."

"I'M ALMOST FINISHED," Aaron Kurtzman, a.k.a. "the Bear," told Hal Brognola. "Two or three more snaps to correlate."

"We've got the time," Brognola answered, peeling tinfoil from a stick of gum and wishing he was still allowed the foul cigars of yesteryear. "Don't rush it."

Kurtzman always had a sour feeling in his stomach when it came to working with the dead. He didn't let the feeling interfere with business or compromise efficiency, but he was conscious of it all the same.

The last time he had fired a gun in anger, it had been the night a bullet took his legs away and left him in a wheelchair. He had never been a front-line soldier in the style of Bolan or the others, but the war came home sometimes, and then you had no choice. When it was do-or-die, you either did... or died.

These days he did his killing through directives, orders passed from Washington to agents in the field. On rare occasions Kurtzman watched a hit go down by tasking a convenient satellite to let him spy on action several thousand miles away, the eerie bird's-eye view and infrared projections giving him some needed distance from the down-and-dirty truth.

At other times, like now, he sorted photographs.

The stills prepared from Yakov Katzenelenbogen's video were grim. Close-ups of lifeless faces, where a face could still be recognized as such. In other cases, panning shots of bodies, hoping that a piece of jewelry or a clothing style could narrow down the field, at least provide a hint of where the dead men came from prior to finishing their wasted lives in Greece.

"We're getting there," he said.

Brognola nodded. "Take your time."

He started with a body count, aware that it was imprecise. They knew how many visitors had dropped in on Kasar before the raid, but there was still some doubt concerning hosts and bodyguards in residence. For safety's sake, he rounded off the speculative count at fifty, hoping that was high.

The visitors were easier to track because they had been spotted coming in. Surveillance cameras had caught them at the Athens airport, on the waterfront. A few remained anonymous, primarily the younger ones, but group affiliations were determined by examining the company they kept. If some young stranger turned up on a flight from Barcelona, traveling with two known members of the ETA, it didn't take a rocket scientist to guess his politics.

Kurtzman started out with video on twenty-seven kills. Communications with authorities in Greece, by way of Interpol and Langley, told him there were seven dead inside the house and three more in the helicopter, all so badly burned that any ultimate ID would have to come from dental charts—assuming terrorists had checkups and the records were available from something like a dozen different countries.

Kurtzman had decided that he would not hold his breath.

Of the twenty-seven bodies he could identify nineteen faces. Of those, he matched thirteen to the surveillance photographs of visitors, eleven of them known by name. The other six were definitely Arabs, part of the Iraqi team. House staff, perhaps, or bodyguards.

But not the leader.

Kurtzman wondered if the guy had bought it in the villa when the Semtex charges brought his rented palace down. It was a neat scenario, but he couldn't afford to buy it in the absence of conclusive evidence.

Assume the worst in covert operations, Kurtzman thought, and you were seldom disappointed. On the rare occasions when an educated guess proved wrong, it was always a pleasant surprise.

"All done," he said.

"What have we got?" Brognola asked.

"Six terrorists are unaccounted for," said Kurtzman, "plus al-Takriti, maybe other members of his team. We don't have film on all of the Iraqis, so I can't be sure."

"Well, shit."

"We've also got ten dead with no ID. Assume one pilot for the chopper, that leaves nine. Our problem could be taken care of as we speak."

"How many dead Iraqis are we sure of?" asked Brognola.

"Six."

Hal frowned, shook his head. "No good. I estimate no more than ten or twelve men on the island when the players started to arrive. Six dead around the house wouldn't leave enough to cover the contingent Rafael reported at the dock."

And he was right, of course. Whenever there were any doubts, you put your money on the worst scenario and started thinking in terms of damage control. This time around, the worst scenario meant six surviving terrorists and their Iraqi sponsor still at large.

"Besides our friend from Baghdad, who's still missing?"

Kurtzman rattled off five names, two each from Lebanon and Spain, one from Colombia. "We're short ID on one guy out of Bogotá."

"Three continents. That's quite a spread."

"We'll cover it," the Bear replied.

"As if we have a choice." Brognola's face was grim. "What's Able's ETA again?"

"They told me 0900 hours."

"Still an hour. Anything from Striker yet this morning?"

"Barb was taking him a cup of coffee."

"Ah." Brognola rose and stretched both arms. "I wouldn't mind a cup, myself. You coming?"

"In a minute," Kurtzman answered. "I just want to have these sorted out and ready for the briefing."

"Okay." Brognola hesitated on the threshold, turning back. "Don't sweat it," he advised. "We work with what we have."

"I know."

And as the door hissed shut between them, Kurtzman also knew that sometimes it fell short of being good enough.

AN OPEN JEEP WAS WAITING on the airstrip as the men of Able Team unloaded from the Piper Cherokee and stood again on solid ground. Carl Lyons took the shotgun seat, Hermann Schwarz and Rosario Blancanales piling into the back. After the flight from Illinois, it was a short drive to the house.

Chicago had been relatively smooth, as such things went. A major ghetto gang from California was expanding under the cover of the "truce" that followed riots in Los Angeles, consolidating turf while sappy pundits from the L.A. *Times* to "60 Minutes" rattled on about the so-called peace and harmony in gangland. Never mind the evidence that two large gangs were simply closing ranks, killing off their Latino competition in unprecedented numbers, moving nearly twice the weight in crack from twelve months earlier. The networks and the major dailies had their blinders on, committed to reporting happy news from black America at any cost.

Chicago was the latest outpost in a web of drugs and violence spreading from the Golden State, enveloping the nation by degrees. Able Team had spent the past week raining on the gang's parade. It would not solve the problem permanently, in Chicago or beyond, but it was one alternative to blissful ignorance.

And now they could look forward to a change of scene.

A summons to the Farm meant something heavy. Lesser missions were explained by scrambled phone calls, sometimes meeting in the field with Hal or his lieutenant, Leo Turrin. This time they were sitting down with Bolan and the Phoenix team, which had to mean a war with several theaters of operation. Able Team was normally restricted to the Western Hemisphere, including forays into South America, but Lyons never tried to second-guess the crew at Stony Man.

It was enough to know that they were needed here and now for some job no one else could do.

They rode in silence toward the farmhouse, each man busy with his private thoughts. Lyons knew his comrades, Schwarz and Blancanales, would be thinking along the same lines as himself, arriving at roughly the same conclusions. The three of them had functioned as a team for so long they had passed the point of merely understanding one another. Lyons had no faith in ESP or psychic mumbo jumbo, but he knew his partners inside out, and there were times he would have sworn that he could read their thoughts.

Glancing at "Gadgets" Schwarz, Lyons knew his friend was looking past their briefing, toward the mission, wondering what kind of gear would be required. Schwarz was a wizard when it came to anything electrical or mechanical—his nickname said it all. He and Blancanales had known Mack Bolan long before Carl Lyons joined the team, but they were all like family now.

Except that no one in his right mind would predict their living happily ever after.

Blancanales was another friend of Bolan's from the old days, dating back to Vietnam, where he was dubbed "the Politician" for his slick negotiating skills. He could relate to damned near anyone, go native, work a problem out on terms they understood... but when diplomacy broke down, he was a mean hand with a shooting iron.

Together they were Able Team, and Lyons liked to joke that they were able to resolve most problems on their own, without assistance, never mind the hostile odds. Of course, when trouble ranged too far afield and spread the troops too thin, revisions of the game plan were required.

Today, for instance.

Hal Brognola met them on the front porch of the farmhouse. His concession to the rural setting was apparent in the loosened tie, the collar button open at his neck. Aside from these, he could have been decked out to meet the President for brunch.

"Good flight?" he asked of no one in particular.

Schwarz fielded it. "We flew out of O'Hare. That says it all. What's happening?"

"I've got a little something going you may find interesting."

"I understand the gang's all here," said Blancanales.

"Maybe 'little' isn't quite the word I'm looking for."

"You wouldn't have a pot of coffee on, by any
chance?" asked Lyons.

"Absolutely."

"I could use some while we talk."

"I'll have it sent down to the War Room," Hal replied. "We may as well get started right away."

TWENTY BY THIRTY FEET, the basement War Room is
serviced by an elevator in the southeast corner, and its
central piece of furniture is an extended conference table capable of seating twenty-five. It has no windows,
but various screens allow the occupants to view their
world through slides or motion pictures, videocassettes
or live transmissions via satellite. In the event of an assault on Stony Man, the War Room may be sealed
against invaders. Those inside could hold out for up to
twenty-four hours—the room has its own generator and
bottled-air supply—while red alerts are beamed to the
White House and the Pentagon.

The room was filling up when Bolan got there. Hal
Brognola stood at the table's head, and the men of
Phoenix Force were lined up in seats along one side.
Immediately on Brognola's left, there was an empty seat
for Bolan, with Jack Grimaldi next in line and the Able
trio lining up beside him. Aaron Kurtzman manned his
console, several feet behind and to the big Fed's right,
and Barbara Price sat nearby on a folding chair. Her
eyes met Bolan's as he entered, and she flashed the bare
suggestion of a smile.

When everyone was seated, Hal began his pitch
without preliminaries. "Everyone but Able Team

knows why we're here," he said. "Bear with me while I bring them up to speed."

"You ought to read the papers," Jack Grimaldi said to Lyons.

"Hey, read this," Ironman answered.

"Sorry, small print hurts my eyes."

"Okay, you jokers, listen up."

Brognola touched on all the basics—the widespread terrorist attacks, his knowledge from reliable informants of a grand design conceived in Baghdad, the summit conference and the move against their adversaries on Kasar.

"We came this close," he told the room at large, his thumb and index finger separated by perhaps an inch, "but close won't do the job. We've still got hostiles unaccounted for, presumably already home or on their way."

The lights were dimming as Brognola spoke, the first of several faces showing, several times life-size, against the south wall of the room.

"We counted thirty-seven terrorists arriving," Hal informed them. "Thirteen definitely show up on the video Katz brought us, with another six presumed to be Iraqis. General stature and apparel seems to match eight more, but we're confirming through the Greek authorities with fingerprints. We've got ten more officially beyond all recognition at the present time, but one of them's the chopper pilot, and his passengers were probably a couple of the Germans. Gary?"

Manning glanced up from his folded hands and nodded. "Right."

"Okay," Brognola said, "I may be stretching here, but weapons, coins and whatnot taken from the bodies in the house suggest specific nationalities, if nothing else. I doubt we'll ever sort them out entirely, but I'm betting that we've narrowed down the field to six, plus one Iraqi sponsor.''

"Who's the pinup?" Lyons asked.

"Zuheir al-Qadi," Hal replied. "Mossad identifies him as a major player in As-Sai'qa. That's 'the Thunderbolt,' a group of hard-core Palestinian commandos based in Lebanon. Specifically they run their operation from the Bekaa Valley, do a little target practice on the Christians in Beirut from time to time. They mostly save their energy for Israel, though.''

Hal nodded, and another face filled the screen.

"Al-Qadi's number two," Brognola said. "Kahlil Hassan Salameh. He looks young because he is. If he survives to see another birthday, he'll be twenty-four years old. In Tel Aviv they estimate he's killed at least three times for every year he's been alive.''

"I knew his father," Katzenelenbogen said. "By reputation, anyway. He was a hardcase with Fatah.''

"The very same. It may be something in the blood.''

"It's in the blood, all right," Katz said.

Another nod, another face.

"Alphonse Gogorza," Hal informed his troops. "A honcho with the ETA in Spain. He's good for six or seven murders where police are sure he pulled the trigger personally, twice that number where he gave the marching orders. He's been in and out of jail a couple dozen times since he was seventeen. They have a problem getting witnesses to testify, if you can feature that.''

The next face up was younger, with a pale scar tracking from one eyebrow to the hairline. It appeared the young man had forgotten how to smile.

"Ramon Aguirre. He's Gogorza's chief lieutenant in the Pyrenees. The analysts at Langley were a bit surprised to see them both outside of Spain together. If I had to guess, I'd say it underscores the relative importance of the meeting."

The next face showed Indian blood in the cheekbones and straight jet-black hair. There was cruelty, as well, in the eyes and the set of the mouth.

"Manuel Jesus Vargas," said Hal. "Any resemblance between this one and another Jesus is strictly semantic, I promise. He's a leader of the M-19 crowd in Colombia. They don't catch all the headlines that they used to, nine, ten years ago, but they're alive and well, throughout the countryside. Some spin-off groups do dirty work for the cartel, but Vargas and his crew are hard-line leftist revolutionaries. Which brings us to Mr. X."

On cue a sixth face showed up on the viewing screen. Long hair, dark eyes, with brows that nearly met above the nose. His smile was like the grimace of a hungry predator.

"No name on this guy," Hal continued, "but he showed up with the M-19 contingent. We're assuming he's a member, double-checking through the DEA in Bogotá and Medellín, but it's a long shot. They've got people in the mountains who the cops have never seen, much less interrogated."

Number seven was another Arab, slender, with a thick mustache that overhung his lip.

"Afif al-Takriti," Brognola announced. "We're ninety-nine percent convinced he's Baghdad's mouthpiece on this deal, which means he'll be reporting to Saddam. Before this gig he was involved in the extermination of the Kurds, but mostly he coordinates with terrorists outside Iraq. A kind of Daddy Warbucks to the psycho set, spending Saddam's money where it will do the most harm.''

"We're going after them," Katz said, no question in his tone.

"I don't see any choice," Brognola said.

"Suppose you're wrong about the ones who got away?" asked Gadgets Schwarz. "We could be chasing shadows in the wrong part of the world."

"Our people in Colombia and Spain will pull every string they can to let us know when any of the stragglers come home. As far as Lebanon, we're trying to coordinate with the Mossad."

"It's worth a look," said Bolan. "If we have to change directions later on, the only thing we've lost is travel time."

"So how do we divide this up?" asked Calvin James.

Brognola smiled with obvious relief. "I thought you'd never ask."

CHAPTER FOUR

Barcelona, Spain

One of the oldest terrorist groups in Europe, the ETA—
Euzkadi Ta Askatasuna, or "Basque Homeland and
Liberty"—traces its origins to a split in the Basque Na-
tionalist Party in 1959. Heavily influenced by Marxist-
Leninist doctrines, the group fights to "liberate"
Basque territory in the Pyrenees from Spain and France,
with the ultimate goal of creating a separate socialist
nation. As with other violent groups in Europe and
around the world, personality clashes and doctrinal rifts
have caused dissension in the ranks, and in the 1970s the
group split into two divergent factions. One, the ETA-
Militar, or "Milis," pursues armed revolution through
a program of assassination, sabotage and terror. The
group's "moderate" wing, christened the ETA-Politico,
agitates for revolution at the ballot box, reserving armed
force as a last resort and necessary evil.

Outlawed since its first emergence under the tyran-
nical Franco regime, the ETA-Militar clings to life like
a mutating virus, fattening its Swiss bank accounts with
the proceeds from bank heists, ransom kidnappings and
a heavy "revolutionary tax" imposed on businessmen
and laborers alike, at gunpoint. So crushing was the
debt imposed by leftist gunmen on the very people they
professed to serve that the Basque province of Guipuz-
coa dropped from first to fifteenth on the scale of per

capita income, suffering a drastic exodus as businessmen and farmers grudgingly evacuated their ancestral
homes to start from scratch in other parts of Spain,
France, even Portugal.

Few outlaws advertise their whereabouts, but Bolan
had connections. When Brognola handed him the
Spanish beat, with Jack Grimaldi for his backup, the
assignment came complete with heavy dossiers ob-
tained from state security by Interpol and CIA, trans-
lated into English for analysts at Stony Man. By
Thursday night he knew his adversaries well enough to
spot the more notorious among them in a crowd, and he
was carrying a coded list of targets in the neighborhood of Barcelona, Monserrat, Pamplona, Huesca and
Gerona.

He was starting in the Spanish coastal city on a whim,
to get things moving with a bang.

Security in Spain had verified Alphonse Gogorza's
safe return from Greece, and while there was no word
on his companion, Bolan was prepared to take Aguirre's
survival on faith for the moment. Pinning down Gogorza's whereabouts would be another problem, but the
Executioner was putting first things first.

Barceloneta is the old quarter of Barcelona, fronting
the docks, a traditional home to laborers and fisher-
men. Away from the district's main thoroughfare, the
Passeig Nacional, many of the streets present a de-
serted and threatening front, but Bolan wasn't easily
intimidated.

"Coming up here, on your right."

"I've got it," Jack Grimaldi answered, looking for a
place to park the rental car. He found it two doors down
from Bolan's target, pulled in to the curb and left the
motor idling with the stick in neutral. It was dark, the

nearest streetlight two long blocks away. "You still don't want me in on this?"

"You're in right where you are. It's not a two-man job."

The warrior recognized Grimaldi's wish to join the action, but he had the target covered. Two doors down and three floors up was a loft maintained by members of the ETA-Militar as a kind of arsenal-cum-safehouse in the Catalan provincial capital. Police had known about the place for several weeks, but they were holding off on any moves until such time as they required impressive headlines for the sake of their appropriations or morale.

Mack Bolan was about to beat them to the punch.

He left Grimaldi in the rental, walked the half block to an unmarked door and pushed his way inside. The lobby smelled of urine, either cat or human, Bolan couldn't tell. The Mini-Uzi worn beneath his jacket on a shoulder sling was fitted with a custom silencer, and Bolan swung it clear as he began to mount the stairs.

Six flights, and he met no one on the way, which was a lucky break for occupants of the dilapidated tenement. In those surroundings, Bolan would have been hard-pressed to differentiate between an enemy and someone taking out the trash.

He reached the third-floor landing, checked for guards, found none. Moving toward the numbered door, he paused to listen, picking up on muted sounds of television from within. A game show, by the sound of it, complete with clanging bells and laughter from the audience.

He had considered knocking, but his Spanish was not up to scratch, and he preferred complete surprise to botched diversions. Stepping back, he put his weight behind a kick that snapped the door's cheap lock and slammed it back against the wall.

A gunner some years short of twenty bolted off the couch, eyes wide with sudden fear. He lunged toward a sawed-off shotgun lying on a coffee table. Bolan's Uzi gave a muffled snort, and parabellum manglers punched the young man through a clumsy barrel roll, his dead weight flattening the table as he fell.

The loft had once been open space, but thin partitions had been raised to give it the appearance of a dormitory, lacking only doors. The sound of Bolan's entry and the TV watcher's fall brought gunners spilling from two nearby rooms, confused expressions on their faces, weapons in their hands.

Bolan counted three and took the nearest of them first, a short guy with a double-barreled shotgun, twenty feet away and closing fast. The Mini-Uzi stuttered briefly, stitched a line of holes across the broad front of his T-shirt, and the shooter staggered backward, going down.

The next in line was taller, with a long face under a receding hairline, lining up a nickel-plated automatic pistol for a hasty shot. The Mini-Uzi got there first and disemboweled him with a rising burst that punched him through a jerky little dance before he fell.

The last contender looked to be the oldest of the four. He actually got a shot off from his snubby pistol, but excitement sent it high and wide. It was a different game entirely from the normal regimen of sniping, drive-by shooting, or the point-blank execution of a hog-tied prisoner. This time the prey was shooting back, and it had spoiled the gunner's aim.

He never got a second chance, as Bolan's SMG spit out a burst of parabellum shockers, spinning him around like some demented dancer. He went down in an ungainly sprawl, his face mashed flat against the concrete floor.

And it was over, just like that.

Almost.

Bolan tore off a portion of the TV watcher's shirttail and dipped it in a spreading pool of crimson, moving toward a blank partition that would face the next man coming through the door. Begrudging every second now, he wasted no time on the artwork, satisfied with plain block capitals.

The letters *ANE*.

He dropped the scrap of rag and put that place of death behind him, jogging down the stairs. The neighbors were deliberately hard of hearing, keeping to themselves, but he was betting one or more of them would place a call to the police.

And that was fine.

Outside he slowed his pace and walked back to the waiting rental car.

"Okay?" Grimaldi asked.

"So far, so good," the Executioner replied. "Let's see about that secondary target while we've got some time to kill."

Beirut, Lebanon

ONCE UPON A TIME the capital of Lebanon was famous as a playground for the rich and reckless jet set, catering to diplomats and wealthy businesspeople with a taste for luxury. All that changed with the outbreak of civil war between Christians and Muslims in 1975, transforming Beirut into a battered, burned-out slaughter pen. The country at large was reduced to a free-fire zone where the Muslim-Christian conflict was exacerbated by native Lebanese fighting Palestinian guerrillas. As well, different Muslim sects pursued internecine blood feuds, bandits and opium growers promoted their own private agendas, and foreign troops made periodic incursions from Israel to the south or Syria to the east and north. Throughout the nightmare, a pervasive hatred for the Zionist regime in Tel Aviv appeared to be the only common thread in a chaotic tapestry of death.

The men of Phoenix Force had been to Lebanon before, but it was never easy coming back. The tourist trade had shriveled to nothing, so they needed cover stories that would adequately camouflage their mission in Beirut. They could not travel as a team without attracting far too much attention from potential enemies.

Instead, Katz flew to Beirut on his own, from Frankfurt via Cyprus, posing as a German dealer in Middle Eastern art. Manning and McCarter made the flight from London and arrived six hours later, carrying the paperwork required of two investigators for a private Christian charity. Encizo and James were the last to arrive, making the hop from Alexandria to Sidon, driving north to Beirut in a used car they purchased for cash. If anyone asked, they were arms merchants "on vacation," enjoying the scenery that some of their shipments had helped to create.

Katz, Encizo and James booked rooms at the same hotel, Katz on the fourth floor, his friends on the sixth. McCarter and Manning checked into another hotel three blocks distant, and reached out by phone to their comrades, arranging to meet in a park where the snipers had lately been quiet. The five would not be seen together publicly until the time was right for them to move against their enemies.

As-Sai'qa was but one of several violent factions operating from a base in Lebanon. Its major installation was a compound in the dreaded Bekaa Valley—home to bandits, heroin exporters, Shiite fundamentalist guerrillas and a mixed bag of Palestinian refugees. In the Bekaa anarchy was never far below the surface, and the Lebanese authorities had long since given up on the pretense of keeping order. Any uniforms you saw around the valley these days would by Syrian, an occupying force with no apparent plans for going home.

Despite the Bekaa Valley's relative security for terrorists, As-Sai'qa also had an outpost in Beirut to keep in touch with gossip, politics and business where the action was. Its members took no sides officially in the religious war that had effectively dismantled Lebanese society. While the Palestinians were mostly raised as Muslims, die-hard warriors of the Thunderbolt had long since shed religion as a force with any concrete meaning in their lives, adopting hatred as an end unto itself.

As-Sai'qa's unofficial front had once been an athletic club, renowned for members boasting seven-figure bank accounts. Two bombing raids and some low-budget reconstruction left it greatly changed, unrecognizable to former clients if they ever gave the place a second thought. These days it was a social club of sorts, where left-wing Palestinians hung out and muttered dire predictions of a holy war against the Zionists in Israel. Regulars would disappear from time to time, and word would filter back that this or that one had been killed in Gaza, in Jerusalem, in Haifa, the Negev.

The Phoenix warriors had agreed on strategy before they left the States, selecting basic targets, plotting the course by which they would proceed. Beirut was pivotal, and Katz didn't intend to launch a strike against the Thunderbolt without examining its operation first, determining the most propitious time for an assault.

Katz took the first watch on his own, across the street from his objective, first dawdling along a row of tiny shops that somehow clung to life, several of them sporting battle scars. He purchased nothing, but discussed the general state of art and craftsmanship with owners who seemed glad of the diversion from their dreary lives. On one hand, they continued eking out a living from the streets, performing as their fathers had before them, courting drudgery. On the other hand, each knew he might be shot or blown to bits with a grenade at any time, by total strangers acting on a whim.

It was surreal, a nightmare city, but the gruff Israeli did not let it take his mind away from business. He had come on a specific mission, and he never let it out of sight.

At dinnertime he took a window seat in a café that offered a clear view of the "social club." He took his time and counted heads, foot traffic traipsing in and out with no apparent pattern. Katz had memorized the faces of a dozen ranking soldiers in the Thunderbolt, but none of them appeared while he was staking out the club. In roughly forty minutes he watched a dozen young men enter and another seven leave. He guessed that there were twenty Palestinians inside, with room for several times that many on the premises.

Two exits he was sure of, front and back, but they would also have to check the roof. As-Sai'qa's neighbor on the south was two floors taller, offering a view from windows facing north. If Katz could only get inside and make his way upstairs...

He paid his bill and left the small café, ignoring traffic like a native as he dodged across the street. McCarter would be picking up the weapons now, while Calvin James and Rafael Encizo waited to relieve Katz on his watch.

As soon as he was finished.

But first he meant to get himself a bird's-eye view of the establishment where members of As-Sai'qa passed the time when they were in Beirut. It was the first stop on his hit parade, and he didn't intend to blow the game from any lack of preparation.

He was looking for a local artist—that was all. A garbled address, a mistaken name, whatever. Anyone who looked beyond the cover story and attempted to get rough with Katz was in for a surprise.

The last surprise of a lifetime, in fact.

Sopetran, Colombia

THE TRICK, Pol Blancanales thought, was leaving one or two survivors, making sure that he or they were clear on the intended message, fit to spread the word. It would be easier to blitz the camp and drop a dime himself, try stirring up the pot that way, but Blancanales was committed to the plan.

Divide and conquer, right.

Or so he hoped.

Colombia was much like Lebanon in some respects, including the murder rate and the proliferation of competing, often hostile paramilitary groups. While M-19 was easily the most infamous of the lot, best known for its raid on the Bogotá Palace of Justice that left one hundred persons dead in 1986, it was forced to contend with five other leftist cadres and an estimated one hundred thirty-eight armed neo-fascist groups for control of Colombian hearts and minds. In such an atmosphere, anything could happen—and it often did.

It would be happening this afternoon, a mile outside of Sopetran.

The smallish town was thirty miles northwest of Medellín, in Antioquia Province, and despite the presence of a lumber mill, the town's main source of income was cocaine. The M-19 guerrillas theoretically opposed free enterprise in any form, much less the "narco-fascism" of the Medellín cartel, but they had long since given up on trying to cut off the drug trade. Insiders said the raid against Colombia's Supreme Court in November 1986 had been a contract job, sponsored by cocaine billionaires, but M-19 held itself aloof from the dealers these days, preferring to tap their huge bankrolls by means of extortion, hijacking and kidnappings for ransom.

The camp outside Sopetran was one of several that M-19 maintained between the Andes and the Cordillera Occidental, training warriors for a final push against the government that never seemed to come.

This afternoon the men of Able Team would do some pushing of their own.

Pol Blancanales had the south side of the camp, Carl Lyons on his left, approaching from the west, while Gadgets Schwarz moved in from the northeast. Each member of the team was carrying an M-16 A1, each rifle fitted with a 40 mm M-203 launcher underneath the barrel. Decked out in camouflage fatigues, with bandoliers of extra magazines, grenades and high-explosive rounds, the Politician almost felt that he was back in Vietnam, preparing for a strike against the Vietcong.

Search and destroy. Same game, same rules.

Any number could play.

Pol met a sentry fifty yards before he reached the compound, squeezing off two quick rounds from his silencer-equipped Beretta Model 92. The guy went down without a whimper, Blancanales moving past him like a forest shadow, gliding on toward his objective.

Ninety seconds left, according to his watch, and he was in position, waiting for the main event. The draw had gone to Lyons, leaving him to ring the bell. As Blancanales waited, counting down the numbers in his head, he wondered how Ironman would announce himself.

And he did not have long to wait.

The M-203 launcher made a kind of popping sound, which was immediately lost in the disintegration of a prefab hut that housed the compound's generator and communications gear. The blast sent chunks of corrugated metal flying like unwieldy Frisbees, crashing into trees and clattering to earth.

Pol Blancanales had marked his target before the Ironman opened fire, and he lost no time squeezing off a 40 mm round at the mess tent, scoring a direct hit on the Primus stove and touching off a secondary blast from ruptured propane cylinders. A flaming scarecrow staggered from the wreckage, flapping wings of fire, and Blancanales dropped him with a mercy round between the eyes.

The M-19 guerrillas had begun to scramble now, recovering a bit from the initial shock, but it was far too little and too late. Triangulated fire sliced through their ranks as Gadgets joined the turkey shoot, each Able warrior picking targets on the run, occasionally lobbing 40 mm rounds downrange to keep the heat on.

Blancanales shifted his position twice as gunners in the compound tried to pick him off, but daylight robbed them of a muzzle-flash to sight on, drifting smoke and forest shadows playing tricks with vision. When they tried to break for cover, it was gone before they got there, high-explosive rounds erupting in the camp like thunderclaps, demolishing the barracks, CP hut and motor pool.

There had been twenty-five or thirty soldiers in the compound when it started, barely half that number standing after one minute. The guerrillas were losing ground inch by inch, and some were looking for an exit from the trap. Pol saw a couple of them edging toward the forest on his right, and instinct told him there was no time like the present.

Crouched behind a fallen tree, he shouted to be heard above the din of combat. *"¡Viva el Frente Armado!"* he bellowed. *"¡Viva el FAP!"*

He fired a burst at the runners, aiming high to miss them by a foot or so. A moment later they were lost among the trees, and Blancanales let them go.

Two runners were enough to carry word. The rest were on their own.

He fed the M-16 A1 another magazine and shouldered it in time to catch two gunners rising from the muck of the latrine and breaking for the tree line on his left. Pol could have let them go, as well, but he had used up his quota of daily good deeds.

He led the pointman by a foot or so, allowing for the distance, squeezing off a 4-round burst that dropped his running target in a heap. The second gunner dodged and swung around to spray the trees with wild fire from his carbine, but he had no target, no fixed point of reference.

No way to save himself.

The Politician fired another burst and watched the young man stagger, going down on one knee, finally pitching over on his face. He fell across his gun and didn't move again.

A sudden, eerie silence fell across the compound. Blancanales braced himself, suspecting that his enemies were preparing for a final charge at the perimeter, a breakout...but it never came. Long moments later static whispered at his hip, and he retrieved the compact walkie-talkie from its canvas pocket.

"Able Three," Carl Lyons said from somewhere in the bush. "I'm out of targets."

"Able One," said Blancanales. "Ditto."

"Able Two confirming," Schwarz replied. "I'm going in."

They met beside the smoking wreckage of the former CP hut and solemnly surveyed the carnage they had wrought. Pol didn't bother with a body count. Statistics were irrelevant from this point on.

"I hope those runners got the message," Lyons said.

"They'll spread the word," said Blancanales, "but I've got a feeling they could use some help."

"Suits me," said Schwarz. "Who's next?"

"We've introduced ourselves to M-19," Pol said. "I think it's only fair we pay a visit on the FAP."

The Ironman grinned. "My mother always told me it was best to share," he said.

CHAPTER FIVE

Lerida, Spain

Driving west from Barcelona, Bolan and Grimaldi reached Lerida in an hour. Their first glimpse of the city featured a mighty, ruined building perched atop a hill beside the Rio Ségre. Bolan recognized the tower of the ancient La Seo Cathedral, long ago deconsecrated and converted to a fort, then burned and pillaged when its tenants backed the losing side in one of Spain's innumerable wars.

Another war was coming to Lerida, but the population didn't know it yet.

Aside from local industry, including textile mills, and streets closed off to traffic so pedestrians could mob the picturesque boutiques, Lerida was a stronghold of Acción Nacional Española, a neo-fascist movement bitterly opposed to Basque separatism and the ETA-Militar. The two groups clashed with bitter frequency in Catalonia, and Bolan meant to take advantage of their blood feud if he could.

His first step had been to leave the ANE's initials at the scene of attack upon the ETA in Barcelona.

Now he was about to turn up the heat.

"We're almost there," Grimaldi told him, slowing for a left turn at a major intersection, pulling off the main street of Lerida and encroaching on a neighborhood that had seen better days. Tourists who veered this far off track would not linger here. The shops were more utilitarian than trendy, and the homes ran more toward drab apartments than the classic Spanish style.

The ANE maintained a front on Calle Hermosillo, where the Spanish National Party occupied a second-story office fronting on the street. Grimaldi found a parking space directly opposite and kept the engine running for a speedy getaway.

Siesta time had passed, and there were several patrons in the bakery downstairs from Bolan's target. Other shops on the street were doing slow but steady business, and he considered the potential risk to innocent civilians as he eyed the office, noting independent stairs that served the second floor.

Grimaldi seemed to read his mind. "You want to pass?" he asked.

The Executioner considered it, then shook his head. "There shouldn't be a problem."

Part of that was wishful thinking, Bolan realized. There were potential problems during any armed encounter, and they went beyond the obvious. A stray round or a ricochet could find civilian flesh outside the line of fire, and Bolan had enough ghosts on his conscience as it was.

"I'll use the Glasers," he decided, reaching into the athletic bag between his feet, extracting several Uzi magazines containing blue-tipped cartridges.

The Glaser Safety Slugs had been specifically designed for situations where a shooter needed stopping power, but feared wounding passersby. The bullets were unique, consisting of a plastic case and number 6 shot suspended in a Teflon gel. They exploded on impact, whether striking human flesh or any other medium. The Glaser's power punch was such that few survived a single wound, and none had lived to boast about a head or torso shot. Conversely, when a Glaser struck a wall, door, window—anything at all, in fact, aside from flesh and bone—it vaporized, incapable of causing more than superficial scratches to an unintended target.

Bolan switched a magazine of Glasers for the clip of armor-piercing rounds already loaded in the Mini-Uzi's pistol grip and tucked the little weapon back inside his jacket. His Beretta's magazine was filled with parabellum hollowpoints. If he had to fall back on his side arm, Bolan knew that he would be in desperate straits.

"Ten minutes, max," he told Grimaldi as he stepped out of the rental.

"Happy hunting."

Bolan crossed the street, ignoring shoppers on the street, and they returned the favor. On the stairs he hesitated long enough to bring the Mini-Uzi out from underneath his jacket, flicking off the safety with his thumb. He didn't know exactly what to expect inside the party office, but he meant to be prepared.

The door was frosted glass, bronze letters spelling out the party's name and listing office hours. Bolan turned the knob and stepped across the threshold, following the Uzi's lead.

A young man seated at a desk glanced up and lost his smile before it really had a chance to form. He stiffened at the sight of Bolan's SMG, recoiling with a muttered oath. The warrior raised a finger to his lips and motioned with his weapon for the man to rise.

He did as he was told, retreating past a mimeo machine and water cooler with his arms at shoulder height, toward an unmarked door. At Bolan's nod, he knocked and waited for an answer from within.

The Executioner was good enough with Spanish that he recognized the summons, following his captive through that door and into the inner sanctum of the Spanish National Party.

It was a disappointment overall. A short man in his thirties sat behind a cluttered desk, file cabinets ranged along the wall behind him. A younger man was standing on his left, bent forward, palms flat on the desk as Bolan entered, studying some sort of document.

The two men caught sight of Bolan and his weapon simultaneously, but they reacted in distinctly different ways. The seated man gave out a squeal of fright and dropped behind his desk. His companion straightened, stepped back and reached inside his lightweight jacket, apparently for a gun.

The Uzi stuttered, Glasers ripping through the target's chest, propelling him against a filing cabinet. He had reached his pistol, but it would not save him now, the Astra automatic slipping from his lifeless fingers as his legs turned into rubber and he buckled to the floor.

The young man from the outer office gaped and gagged, his lunch returning in an aromatic spew. He wound up on all fours, still retching, while the Executioner went looking for his boss. And found him huddled underneath the desk, resembling a weasel trapped inside its lair.

He snapped a short command in Spanish, punctuated with a gesture from the Mini-Uzi, and the party spokesman scrambled clear, reluctantly stood up to meet his fate. The hour's drive from Barcelona had provided ample time for Bolan to rehearse and memorize his single line.

"Por Barcelona," he informed the trembling man, *"y mis amigos muerte."*

Fishing in his pocket, Bolan palmed a small gold-plated pin that bore the letters *ETA*. It was a recognition sign of sorts, and had been lifted from a prisoner in custody, relayed through many different hands before it reached his own. Without another word, he reached across and pinned it on the office manager's lapel...and clubbed him with the Uzi, dropping him across his littered desk.

Grimaldi had his window down, a pistol in his lap, when Bolan reached the car. "I used to be a Boy Scout," he remarked. "You know the motto."

"Right. Well, you can get us out of here. We're done."

"Next stop?"

"Let's have a look at Renteria," Bolan said.

Jack grimaced. He put the car in gear.

Fredonia, Colombia

A PHONE CALL did the trick, Pol Blancanales tapping out the private number on a pay phone in the marketplace and rattling off his message, hanging up on the demand that he repeat himself and state his name. Considering the climate of pervasive fear and mayhem, cryptic anonymity would make his warning that much more believable.

Or so he hoped.

The private number was a gift from Hal Brognola's contact with the DEA in Medellín. It rang through to the local honcho of the Frente Armado Patriótico—the Patriotic Armed Front—a far-right paramilitary group that battled home-grown leftists when its members were not running errands for the Medellín cartel. If there was any single group the FAP despised and dreamed of wiping off the map, it would be M-19.

"All set," he told his comrades as he settled in the back seat of their car. "Let's roll."

It was a short drive from the teeming center of Fredonia to the outskirts, where a strip of two-lane blacktop slashed through wooded hills en route to Medellín, some twenty miles to the northeast.

The targets, when they came, would not be bound for Medellín, but for a nearby ranch, where members of the FAP hid out sometimes to practice their guerrilla exercises in seclusion. Blancanales had informed the honcho, one Luis Otero, that the troops of M-19 were massing for a raid against the ranch. Unless he missed his guess, Otero would dispatch a scouting party, at the very least. With any luck at all, he might commit substantial reinforcements to defend his hideaway.

There was, of course, no raid impending at the ranch...but there would be an ambush waiting on the highway, courtesy of Able Team.

They left the car a hundred yards beyond the point selected for their trap, concealed within a stand of trees, and walked back with their weapons to the cut where steep bluffs rose on each side of the road. Carl Lyons took the left, or western, side, with Schwarz and Blancanales on the east.

Some fifteen minutes later Blancanales saw the convoy coming with his Zeiss binoculars. The cars were nothing special, station wagons and sedans, but they were running in a tight formation, half a dozen men in each, and guns were showing in an arrogant display of power and contempt.

Pol keyed his walkie-talkie and pronounced a single word for Lyons.

"Contact."

"Roger that," the Ironman's voice came back.

Pol had the fat LAW rocket launcher on his shoulder as the point car came in range, the others running close behind. Schwarz had the high ground to his left, well clear of any back-blast from the throwaway bazooka, sighting down the barrel of his M-16 A1. Across the highway Lyons would be lining up his own LAW rocket on the tail car, ready to complete the trap.

Pol waited, counting off the seconds, lining up the perfect shot. The rocket launcher had no kick at all, since its design unleashed a blast of flame behind the weapon, scorching grass and leaves. The armor-piercing rocket rattled downrange on a tongue of fire and struck the point car's grille a foot or so above the bumper.

The results were startling.

Blancanales watched the car stop dead, enveloped in a ball of flame, as it attempted the impossible—a nose-stand, with momentum bringing up the rear. A body catapulted through the windshield, rolled across the flaming hood and struck the pavement several yards in front of the demolished car.

Whatever he had been in life, the human cannonball was nothing now.

The second missile, from the Ironman's launcher, was already airborne, striking the tail car with a shattering broadside before the driver could react to the destruction of his friends. The fuel tank detonated in a secondary blast that bathed the two-lane road in flaming gasoline.

Two cars in the middle of the sandwich were trapped by twisted steel and walls of leaping flames. The passengers were bailing out, unleashing bursts from automatic weapons toward the bluffs on either side, without a solid target they could isolate. Schwarz dropped the first two with his M-16 A1, and by the time he lined up number three, the Politician had his own rifle shouldered, searching for targets.

It was almost too easy, dropping panicky runners before they could get to the tree line, leaving those on the west side of the road to Lyons. Once, when two of them retreated to their vehicle for cover, Blancanales primed his M-203 launcher with a high-explosive round and lobbed it down on them. The blast nailed one inside the car and spit his comrade out onto the pavement, writhing in a haze of smoke. He tried to stand on fractured legs, but Blancanales dropped him with a 5.56 mm tumbler through the chest.

With his rifle set on semiautomatic to save ammunition, he lined up the targets from a range of sixty yards or so and tagged them like silhouettes in some demented shooting gallery. Several survivors returned fire with SMGs and pistols, coming closer with their hasty rounds, but they were running out of time. The Able warriors had the high ground, breathing down their necks, and there was nowhere for the neo-Nazi terrorists to hide.

The last car blew a moment later, one of Lyons's HE rounds impacting on the hood. A gunner who had tried to hide beneath the car came wriggling out, his clothes on fire, and broke in the direction of the trees. Pol Blancanales was about to nail him with a mercy round when Lyons fired a burst that spun the runner through a smoke pirouette and dropped him onto his back, flames dancing up and down his corpse.

Another moment saw it finished, no more moving targets on the road below. The Politician keyed his walkie-talkie, spoke a single word and got the Ironman's confirmation.

They were pulling out.

Not finished yet, by any means. They intended to continue their strategy of divide and conquer, stirring up the pot to see what surfaced.

Unless Pol missed his guess, the FAP and M-19 would soon be at each other's throats in an all-out shooting war. In the confusion Able Team might just be able to complete its mission and withdraw unscathed.

At least, that was the plan.

But even best-laid plans were prone to drastic alterations in the hellgrounds, Blancanales knew, and he would have to stay alert at every step along the way. The first false move could be a killer, and Colombia was not his notion of the perfect place to spend eternity.

Beirut, Lebanon

THERE WAS a skylight on the roof of the As-Sai'qa "social club," but Katz decided that it would not make a viable escape route since there seemed to be no staircase granting access from inside. That understood, he planned to hit the club with two men from the front and two in back, the odd man out assigned to drive the car.

Their weapons were provided by a contract agent of the CIA, with plausible deniability in mind. The assault rifles were standard AK-47s with folding metal stocks, backed up with SIG-Sauer P-220 side arms and Egyptian-manufactured frag grenades.

Encizo won or lost the draw, depending on your point of view, and wound up waiting in the car, with the motor running, across the street from the As-Sai'qa hangout. He had dropped Calvin James and Gary Manning two blocks farther back to let them circle in behind the club on foot. Katz marked four minutes on his watch to give them ample time, then tucked the AK-47 underneath his floppy coat and exited the car.

McCarter joined him from the shadows of a nearby alley, and they crossed the street together, checking left and right, but no one seemed to notice them. The shops along this street had closed at sundown, and the small café where Katz had eaten lunch was running out of customers. The stragglers who remained would soon be treated to an unexpected dinner show.

McCarter had been standing watch across the street from their intended target, counting heads, reporting to the team by walkie-talkie. Eight persons had arrived within the past two hours; none had left. There seemed to be no coded knock or password. New arrivals simply entered from the street, but Katzenelenbogen had no doubt there would be guards inside to check them out.

They reached the sidewalk, both men drawing automatic rifles as they stepped up to the door. Katz held the AK-47 in his good left hand and gave the door a shove with his metallic claw. McCarter followed close behind as Katz stepped into an entryway that smelled of perspiration and tobacco smoke.

The guard was young and slender, with a pockmarked face and sweat stains at the armpits of his khaki shirt. He had his chair tipped back against the wall, boots dangling, a vintage automatic shotgun standing in the corner close at hand. As Katzenelenbogen entered, he was munching on a sandwich, something stuffed in pita bread. He forgot about the food when he beheld the AK-47 pointed at his face.

The young man had a range of options, and he chose the obvious, if not the wisest, course. His sandwich hit the floor, and he was groping for his shotgun, fighting to maintain his balance, when a burst from the Kalashnikov tore through his chest. The chair bucked out from under him, and he went down, a splash of crimson dribbling down the stucco wall.

No time to waste from that point on. Katz shouldered through a beaded curtain, found himself inside the main room of the "social club," a bar immediately on his right, with tables filling the remainder of the room. Directly opposite the entryway, another curtain—cloth, this time—closed off a second room in back.

The circumstances gave him no time for a head count, but he estimated eight or nine men in the main room as he entered, every face turned toward the unexpected sound of automatic-weapons fire. As Katz appeared, McCarter close behind, the Palestinians were galvanized to action, tipping tables, two men dropping out of sight behind the bar, another breaking for the private room in back.

Katz hit the runner with a rising burst that snapped his spine and punched him forward through the curtained doorway, ripping the shabby drape down from its rod. As he hit the floor, a crash announced that James and Manning had arrived to join the party, gunfire popping as they met resistance in the other room.

Katz dropped into a fighting crouch and kept his back against the wall as he searched for living targets. In the middle of the room, two Palestinians were firing blind around their table barricades, unloading semiauto pistols while they kept their heads down.

But not completely out of range.

Katz stitched a burst across the nearest, his 7.62 mm slugs drilling cleanly through the wood in search of human flesh. A strangled cry of pain told Katz that he had scored, the hit confirmed a heartbeat later as his target's boots protruded from behind the table, toes toward the ceiling.

Number Two saw what had happened to his comrade and panicked, breaking cover in a mad dash toward the rear. He kept firing as he ran—one bullet whizzed close by Katzenelenbogen's head—then the slide locked open on an empty chamber and his luck ran out. The guy was screaming, fear and anger mingled in his voice, when Katz unleashed a burst that dropped him in his tracks, his body twitching on the floor.

McCarter lobbed a frag grenade behind the bar, and waited with his AK-47 as a chunky Palestinian sprang into view, attempting to evade the blast. A short burst from McCarter's rifle slammed him over backward. Then the frag grenade went off, exploding above the Arab's dying scream.

Three Palestinians had tried to hide behind a single table, but it wouldn't work, and two of them were running now. Katz tracked the runner breaking to the left with the AK-47, squeezing off a burst that jerked out his legs and dropped him on his face. Defiant to the end, the Arab tried to rise, but too much blood was streaming from his back and side, a drain his system could not tolerate, and he collapsed to rise no more.

McCarter took the other rabbit with a burst that spun him like a giant top. He went down in a heap, twisting and thrashing, until a second burst snuffed out the final spark.

The last Palestinian, holed up behind his capsized table, bellowed with rage as he emerged from cover, bullets streaming aimlessly from a stubby Skorpion machine pistol. Converging fire from two Kalashnikovs ripped into him before the Arab had a chance to find his mark, and he was dancing like a jerky puppet, twisting, stumbling, finally going down.

"All clear in there?" came the voice of Calvin James.

"We're done," McCarter told him.

James and Manning entered from the club's back room, reloading their Kalashnikovs. Grenade smoke swirled between them like early-morning fog.

"I'd say they're out of business," James remarked as he surveyed the carnage at his feet.

"This lot, at least," McCarter said.

"We've barely scratched the surface," Katz reminded them.

"So let's keep scratching," Manning said.

"The Bekaa?" asked McCarter.

Katz considered it and answered, "Not just yet."

CHAPTER SIX

Renteria, Spain

It was a gamble, carrying the fight to Bolan's enemies in the heart of their own territory, but the Executioner had never put his trust in odds. Renteria, near the French frontier, had suffered untold bloodshed since 1978, when the ETA declared its "permanent offensive against the forces of public order." Neither the demise of General Franco nor the institution of democracy in Spain had quenched the revolutionary thirst for blood in Basqueland, where policemen were routinely murdered, bombings scarred the landscape, and successful businessmen lived in constant fear of being kidnapped for ransom.

It was Bolan's kind of place, in terms of shaking up the enemy and driving home a message to the terrorist elite. Established law might not be able to contain the radicals, but cops and courts in a democracy were bound by certain rules.

The Executioner preferred to make his own rules as he went along, and he wasn't concerned with legal evidence convicting anyone beyond the shadow of a doubt.

The ETA was everywhere in Renteria, offering a wealth of targets. Bolan merely had to choose, and he was starting at the top.

Jorge Altube, a.k.a. "Peixoto," was acknowledged as the leader of the ETA in Renteria. Bolan knew of him further as a close friend of Alphonse Gogorza. They had come up through the ranks together, killing traffic cops and taxi drivers who were branded as "oppressors of the people," knocking off the odd bank here and there. Today they lived in hiding, more or less, except that Jorge Altube enjoyed his reputation as a Basque celebrity of sorts. It had not taken long for Stony Man to track him down and beam his latest address to the Executioner.

The safehouse lay a quarter mile outside of Renteria proper, fairly isolated from its neighbors in the middle of the foothills of the Pyrenees. Excluding air drops, Bolan's only hope of an approach was overland, and he would have to exercise the utmost caution all the way.

Grimaldi wanted in on this one, but the Executioner was firm. A two-man team would double the inherent risk of being spotted by their enemies, and Bolan wanted someone covering their wheels out here in hostile territory. Tagging his initial target would be fruitless if they wound up stranded in the Pyrenees, on foot, surrounded by the opposition.

Jack agreed with Bolan's logic, but he didn't have to like it, and he did his share of muttering as Bolan stripped for action in the darkness, picking out his gear. He chose the skintight blacksuit, all-black military webbing, the Beretta 93-R as his side arm. He replaced the Mini-Uzi with an FA MAS, the standard-issue assault rifle of the French military service. Constructed in bullpup design, the thirty-inch weapon resembled a sawed-off M-16 in some respects, except that its 25-round magazine was seated behind the trigger group. That aside, it mimicked the M-16 in using 5.56 mm ammunition, logging a respectable cyclic rate of 900 rounds per minute in full-auto mode. The short barrel sported a factory-standard grenade launcher, and Bolan carried several HE rifle grenades in a bandolier across his chest. He didn't plan on leaving anything behind, but if he was forced to ditch the piece for any reason, it would point his enemies toward France instead of the United States.

They parked the car a half mile past his target, and he used his compass for the first leg of the journey, trusting night goggles to keep him from tumbling into gullies or slipping on hillsides of loose shale. He kept to the natural cover where possible, striding boldly over open ground when there were no convenient trees or boulders on his route. The last three hundred yards were critical, and Bolan covered most of that stretch on his belly, thankful that the crescent moon was hidden by a layer of clouds. No one had farmed the acreage in several years, and knee-high weeds helped cover his approach to the Altube hideout.

He scanned the farmhouse and outbuildings through his night goggles, getting the lay of the land as he laid out four rifle grenades on the ground, where he could find them by touch and in haste. One each for the house and two cars parked out front, with a fourth for the barn if it showed signs of life.

He was attaching number one to the muzzle of the FA MAS when the front door of the farmhouse opened, spilling lamplight, and a short man emerged. He didn't have Altube's beard or balding skull. Bolan tracked him to the outhouse, gave him time to drop his pants and settle in.

He sighted a window of the farmhouse, going for the path of least resistance, lining up the shot. At sixty yards there would be no drop off the mark to speak of, but he still aimed high, at the upper pane of smoky, unwashed glass. His index finger found the trigger, curled around it, taking up the slack.

The FA MAS bucked once against his shoulder, recoil minimized by its design, and Bolan was reaching for his second rifle grenade as the first one sped home. He estimated five or six seconds to retrieve a new grenade and mount it, find his mark and fire. No more than half a minute for the four.

Number one went in on target, punching through the windowpane, exploding when it found a solid wall or heavy piece of furniture. The Executioner would never know exactly and he didn't care. For now it was enough to see the farmhouse burning, bright flames visible inside, smoke pouring from its shattered windows.

Bolan used his second grenade on a four-year-old Citroën, igniting the fuel tank on impact, unleashing a wide lake of fire. He could have let the flames devour the second car, a Volvo, but he took no chances. He lined up his third grenade and slammed it directly through the driver's door.

The late-night rambler staggered from the outhouse, hoisting baggy trousers with his right hand, brandishing a pistol in his left. Bolan shifted toward the latest target, squeezing off two rounds in semiauto fire.

The 5.56 mm tumblers struck his human target squarely in the chest, explosive impact slamming the dead man back into the outhouse. The door swung shut behind him, slamming with a note of grim finality.

Crapped out, thought Bolan as he took the last grenade and mounted it, seeking a target by firelight. In the doorway of the burning house, a man rose up, bright flames behind him, catching him in profile as he turned and shouted something to his comrades inside. The bristling beard was clearly visible, his bald pate glinting red and orange from the reflected fire.

It was Jorge Altube, all right.

The fourth grenade was an extravagance, but Bolan saw the opportunity and took it, lining up the shot and squeezing off before his target had a chance to move.

It is not every day you see a human being vaporized.

Sort *that* for dental records, Bolan thought. And he began the hike back to his car.

Sidon, Lebanon

DRIVING SOUTH along the coast, Beirut behind him, Yakov Katzenelenbogen put the final touches on his plan. As-Sai'qa's operation in the Bekaa Valley was their master target for the strike in Lebanon, but Katz wasn't prepared to take his men there in the middle of the night, with barely one day in the country to prepare them for the master stroke of the campaign.

Instead, he meant to cause a bit more trouble for the bastards first. Add more confusion to the formula and keep them guessing for a while, glancing nervously over their shoulders in Beirut and Sidon, expecting the next blow to fall on the coast.

When they were jumpy and distracted to his satisfaction, then the wrath of Phoenix Force would fall upon As-Sai'qa's jealously protected sanctuary in the Bekaa.

One step at a time.

They traveled in two separate cars. Katz drove Calvin James and Rafael Encizo, while McCarter and Manning hung back a mile or so, bringing up the rear. Short of finding a car for each man and thereby drawing more attention to themselves, it was the next best thing to life insurance Katzenelenbogen had been able to devise.

"You know our cover's shot, if anyone comes looking for us," James remarked.

"Of course," Katz answered. "But they have to find us first before they can deport us."

"Deportation wasn't what I had in mind." The black man's smile was almost brilliant in the moonlight streaming through the small car's windshield.

Encizo poked his head between them, leaning forward from the back seat of the compact. "Tell us more about Jamal Marraq," he said.

"There's nothing more to tell."

Their target in the port of Sidon was a ranking captain in As-Sai'qa, known to be a close friend of Zuheir al-Qadi. In his younger days he had survived at least a dozen raids across the border into Israel, while his comrades from Fatah were killed or captured. He was named by the authorities in Tel Aviv as a prime mover of several terrorist attacks that spanned the past three years, including the massacre of nine schoolchildren at Zefat.

Marraq lived with a price on his head, but Katz was prepared to kill him for free.

All in due time.

"You think he'll lead us back to al-Qadi?" James asked.

"He might," Katz said. "If nothing else, at least we have another chance to rub their noses in the dirt."

"Or something similar," said James, chuckling.

"I'll take what I can get," Katz told his friends. "I want to shake them up some more before we try the Bekaa on for size."

"You think our tagging him will put Zuheir al-Qadi on the run?" Encizo asked.

"I wouldn't go that far," said Katz, "but it should help distract him, at the very least."

"The Bekaa's bound to be a bitch," said James.

"And then some," Encizo agreed.

Katz knew exactly what they meant. The place was no-man's land, where contending warlords carved out their own preserves, defending them with private armies. Meanwhile the Syrian invaders operated as a strange kind of police force, mounting armed patrols on major highways, stepping in when internecine warfare went too far—by Bekaa standards—sometimes executing those who did not have their paperwork in order or produce sufficient bribes. Once they set foot inside the valley, Phoenix Force would have to deal not only with their chosen adversaries, but with hostile peasants, Palestinians from half a dozen different cliques, the Shiites, opium producers and the Syrian "peacekeeping" force.

Five men against how many thousands?

Many valiant soldiers would have shunned the Bekaa mission as a pointless trial by ordeal and potential suicide. Katz happened to believe his men could pull it off and return to Stony Man intact.

If he was wrong...

"We'll stake him out first," he informed the others. "See if he's got any kind of schedule we can follow. There's an outside chance we might find al-Qadi in the neighborhood."

But even as he spoke, Katz knew that it was not to be. Zuheir al-Qadi was a creature in the shadows. He had put his border-raiding days behind him, serving now as one who sent subordinates to do the dirty work. It was a bit surprising, when Katz thought about it, that the Palestinian had strayed beyond the limits of his sanctuary to attend the meet in Greece. The near miss on Kasar would only reinforce Zuheir al-Qadi's impulse to surround himself with bodyguards and stay on full alert against attack.

It was peculiar, Katzenelenbogen thought, how warriors sometimes lost their nerve. But then, a terrorist who preyed on women, children and the elderly would hardly qualify. He was a killer, surely, but the same was true of countless psychopaths locked up in jails and mental institutions. Simply spilling blood did not make one a soldier, any more than carrying a gun made one a man.

Still, Katz had listened to the rationale before: I kill, therefore I am.

The act and state of mind were frequently confused by moral cripples looking for a way to justify their aberrant behavior. In their own minds they were heroes, liberators, saviors of a world gone wrong.

It all came down to killing for a cause...or sometimes for the hell of it, if no excuse could be devised.

There would be no excuses this time, when Zuheir al-Qadi and his troops came face-to-face with Phoenix Force. Their tab was overdue, and Katz had brought his warriors to collect.

In blood.

"I see the lights," sang Calvin James, his voice a pleasant baritone. "I see the party lights."

Katz saw them, too. The lights of Sidon several miles ahead, like fire glow in the desert night. To him they did not look like party lights.

They looked like hell on earth.

Medellín, Colombia

THE SECOND-LARGEST CITY in Colombia has been a war zone for almost two decades now. With ten murders a day on average, Medellín boasts a per capita homicide rate nine times higher than New York City's. Most of the killings are drug related, some are political, but anything goes on the streets of Medellín. Young hit men, dubbed *sicarios*, will take a life on demand, charging as little as two hundred dollars American. If a paying customer is skeptical of their ability to do the job, some volunteer to execute a freebie on the spot, killing a random stranger while their client watches, to demonstrate their machismo.

It was, in short, the Ironman's kind of town.

Picking up Eduardo Gaviria's trail was the easy part. As the commander of a major drug cartel, he lived in lavish style despite the fact that he was technically a fugitive. What bribes could not accomplish in Colombia, a bomb or bullet often would, and Gaviria managed to maintain his life-style in the face of pending warrants, extradition orders from the States and a substantial bounty placed upon his head by rival dealers. In the aftermath of death and prosecutions that had ravaged the Ochoa family, Eduardo was a prime contender for the bloody throne. His generosity included judges, politicians and police commanders, newsmen…and the FAP, which had been subsidized with narco-dollars for the past five years.

It was a handy setup when you thought about it, using radicals to execute a bombing or a rubout now and then. A phone call from the killers, claiming credit for the FAP or some such group, and homicide investigators shifted their attention from cocaine to crazy politics. It was a tried-and-true technique in Medellín. Eduardo Gaviria had refined it to an art form, paying the neo-fascists well for their efforts.

Gaviria didn't reside in Medellín, of course. That would have been too obvious, an unnecessary challenge to the myopic authorities who took his money with one hand, while pledging with their other to defend law and order. His sprawling estate was situated half an hour from town by car, perhaps ten minutes if Eduardo used his private helicopter.

Lyons and the other men of Able Team would not be calling on Gaviria tonight, but they were sending him a message all the same.

Eduardo's home away from home in Medellín was an apartment two floors up from an expensive restaurant and gambling casino that he owned through paper fronts, a fact known both to Colombian authorities and agents of the DEA. The latter had delivered dossiers to Stony Man that gave the Able warriors leads on where to strike.

The nightclub had been christened La Paloma, but there were no doves in evidence tonight. The women wore expensive low-cut gowns, their escorts evenly divided between tailored dinner jackets and silk shirts open at the collar, showing off enough gold chains to handcuff Hercules. With the casino on the second floor, Gaviria's apartment had a decent buffer layer, presumably with ample warning if the cops or armed competitors came calling unexpectedly.

Still, every castle has its weak point. In Eduardo's case the soft spot was complacency, engendered by the ease with which he bent Colombian officials to his will.

Carl Lyons felt a bit uncomfortable in his tux, although the jacket had been cut a size too large, allowing room for him to hide the MP-5K submachine gun and its swivel mount. The custom silencer meant three more pounds of metal strapped beneath his arm, and Lyons half expected to be stopped by some hawk-eyed bouncer before they reached the elevator.

As it was, the Able warriors passed inspection by the maître d' and tipped him well enough to rate a pass to the casino. Once inside the elevator, though, Schwarz worked his magic on the wiring, thirty seconds with the box enough for him to bypass Gaviria's private code and send them past the gaming tables and on to the third floor.

Eduardo wasn't home. They knew that going in, but they had time to kill, and dropping by to say hello might pay them later dividends.

The car eased to a stop, and all three Able warriors had their weapons drawn before the door hissed open on a foyer green with potted plants. The guard on duty was lounging with his shoes off, thumbing through a nudie magazine, when he was startled from his reverie by their arrival. Fumbling for the automatic in his shoulder holster, he was too slow for a game where everything was riding on the first roll of the dice.

Carl Lyons hit him with a short burst to the chest and slammed him backward, bouncing off an easy chair and staining it with blood before he hit the floor facedown. The deep-pile carpet was a greedy sponge, absorbing blood from the unmoving gunner's wounds.

In seconds flat they had it covered, Lyons drifting past the empty dining room and kitchen toward the master bedroom, Schwarz and Blancanales veering toward the spacious parlor. Two slick gunsel types were watching television there, oblivious to the demise of their *compadre* on the front line of defense, both of them stunned to find themselves confronting hostile weapons in the master's house.

Gaviria had trained them well, and they obviously feared his anger more than death at any stranger's hands. Both men wore pistols and they made their move in concert, bailing out on each side of the couch and hoping for the best.

So much for hope.

Schwarz nailed the left-hand target with a burst of parabellum shockers from his SMG. The guy was halfway through a turn, and the momentum kept him going, arms outflung as if attempting to embrace the reaper. When he fell, he lost his nickel-plated pistol, lifeless fingers giving up their grip.

The gunner on the right was quicker, but it didn't save his life. Pol Blancanales stitched a tidy line of holes between his armpit and his hip, the impact throwing him off balance to sprawl on the short arm of the couch. He balanced there for two heartbeats, teetering. Then gravity took over, and he landed in a heap beside the sofa.

Done.

Carl Lyons found the doorway to the master bedroom standing open, muffled voices audible within. He crossed the threshold, found a dark-haired beauty riding bareback while the skinny guy beneath her clasped her hips and growled instructions in a raspy voice.

Their first hint of a problem was a rain of plaster dust in Skinny's face as Lyons fired a burst into the wall above the headboard. His companion never missed a beat, dismounting with a squeal of panic and dropping out of sight beyond the bed. The Ironman was prepared to nail her if she came up with a weapon, but the lady was intent on looking out for number one.

Her boyfriend, meanwhile, did his best impression of a candle melting underneath a heat lamp, swiftly losing his enthusiasm as he blinked the dust out of his eyes and stared at Lyons, paying more attention to the MP-5K in the gringo's hands.

"Eduardo wouldn't like you messing up his sheets," said Lyons. "But I guess you know that, eh?"

The naked man was glaring daggers at him, breathing through clenched teeth, afraid to move.

"No sweat," the Ironman said. "We'll let it be our little secret, 'kay?"

He had to give the gunner room. Carl let his submachine gun's muzzle droop a little and turned toward the open door as if he meant to leave. The naked shooter saw his chance and lunged for a compartment on the headboard, whipping back a little sliding door to reach inside.

Too late.

The MP-5K stuttered, opening his bony chest with all the delicacy of a chain saw. Skinny did a little break dance on the mattress, twitching through his death throes, while the sheets turned brilliant crimson all around. Another moment and the tremors passed. Carl Lyons left the dead man and the weeping bareback rider, checking out the empty bathroom on his way back to the elevator.

"Done?" Pol asked him.

"Clear."

"We need to leave a sign," said Gadgets, opening a sturdy pocket knife and stepping toward the coffee table. When he finished carving, Lyons saw a single letter, followed by two numbers, etched in crude block fashion: "M-19."

"We're out of here," the Politician said to no one in particular, retreating toward the waiting elevator car.

"Eduardo won't be pleased," the Ironman said as they descended to the street.

"I'm counting on it," Blancanales answered. "Anger breeds mistakes."

Lyons smiled. "I'll make a note."

CHAPTER SEVEN

Gerona, Spain

There were days when Pablo Lozaro devoutly wished he didn't have to get out of bed. On such mornings, the newspaper headlines and the early radio reports were full of blood and pain, more names of murder victims, their surviving relatives and orphaned children.

For a time when he was younger, Pablo had tried to memorize the names of victims killed by terrorists in Basqueland as a kind of personal memorial. Before a year was out there had been too many names for him to carry in his head, and he'd begun to list them in a diary, with their ages, date of death and brief observations of his own. Lozaro had been working on the second volume of his death book when he gave it up and burned the diaries, finally understanding that the best way to remember wasted lives was to alleviate such problems as he could around the neighborhood.

The rest, as someone said, was history. Lozaro never ran for public office, but he had supported candidates with all his energy, and some had even won. It never seemed to help, but he kept trying, giving speeches, writing pamphlets, hosting rallies where the moderates of Basqueland learned that it was not a criminal offense to speak your mind. Not now, with Franco in his grave and civil rights available to all.

Franco's death should have been the end of terror in the Pyrenees, but it was only the beginning. First the ETA announced that it considered any government reforms a sham and an attempt to rob the people of their birthright. Nothing short of revolution would suffice.

The ink was barely dry on that communiqué before assorted neo-fascists raised their voices to condemn the new democracy and call for a return to Franco's policy of ruling by executive decree. All members of the ETA were traitors, to be shot on sight, and anyone collaborating with the separatist cause must share their fate.

The war went on from there, Pablo Lozaro listening to both sides, hearing only hate behind their empty words. Suggestions of reform or compromise were instantly rejected by both sides, as if the thought of giving in on any minor point was tantamount to unconditional surrender. On the whole Lozaro got more death threats from the ETA than from their opposition in the ANE, but either group could find him if they felt a sudden urge to kill.

Five days a week Lozaro left his home at half past seven in the morning and walked four blocks to reach the small bookstore he operated downtown. He made a living at it, writing pamphlets on the side, collaborating with a handful like himself who loathed the killing and were not afraid to say so in the company of strangers.

Within the past two weeks Gerona had been witness to a bombing and a pair of drive-by shooting incidents. Miraculously no one had been killed, but that was *this* time, in a single town. Throughout the Pyrenees a week did not go by without some new atrocity committed by fanatics of the left or right. Lozaro was himself the target of sporadic threats, repeated every time he spoke out publicly against the violence that plagued his native land.

This morning, when he set out from his house, Lozaro had no intimation that the day would be unusual in any way. The early news was bad, with violent deaths reported out of Barcelona, Renteria and Lerida—probably the worst outbreak in months—but these things came in cycles. The fanatics schemed and plotted for a while, working themselves into a frenzy of anger, until nothing could contain their rage. Some times were worse than others, granted, but a single death depressed Lozaro. He didn't need scores of corpses to produce another speech or pamphlet calling on the killers to disarm.

Lozaro was rehearsing certain phrases in his mind, deciding how he ought to launch his latest broadside, when a car sped up behind him, ran a few yards past and veered up on the curb to block his path. Perhaps he should have seen it coming, but he was distracted, turning words and phrases over in his mind, momentarily oblivious to his surroundings.

And Lozaro knew he wouldn't have a second chance.

It was the standard tactic here in Basqueland. Four men leaping out of the sedan with weapons drawn, their faces hidden under ski masks or distorted by the hacked-off legs of women's panty hose. Lozaro was surrounded in an instant, pistols pressed against his spine, a submachine gun leveled inches from his nose.

"You come with us," Ski Mask demanded.

"It would seem I have no choice." Lozaro was amazed to hear his own voice, strong and firm, without a tremor.

"Hurry up!"

The order came from one of those behind him, and a pistol barrel gouged his back before Lozaro could take a step. He moved toward the car, surrounded by his captors, two of them retreating as the other two brought up the rear. Lozaro thought it must be a peculiar sight to any passer-by, but there was no one near enough to notice.

Wait! There was a tall man, window-shopping on the far side of the street, but he didn't appear to notice what was happening. Lozaro recognized the studied nonchalance that comes from living in a climate of pervasive fear, the grim determination to avoid involvement with the violent men at any cost.

He wished the stranger well and stooped to pull himself inside the waiting car.

Lozaro didn't hear the shot, but he experienced its impact in dramatic style. One moment he was leaning forward, toward the open back door of the car, a gunman clutching at his elbow. Suddenly he heard a wet sound, like a melon bursting, and the right side of his face was splashed with crimson, thick and warm. The gunner on his right collapsed against the car, blood dripping from beneath his ski mask. In another heartbeat he was on the ground. Lozaro heard his pistol clatter to the sidewalk.

Glancing up, Lozaro saw the tall man from across the street, but he was standing in the middle of the roadway now, a pistol held in front of him as if to aim. Indeed, while Pablo watched, astounded, he fired two more shots, their sound no louder than a muffled sneeze.

The masked man with the submachine gun staggered, gasping out a curse in Spanish as he fell, a hand clasped to the sudden geyser spouting from his chest.

The two surviving gunmen turned to face their adversary, and Lozaro hit the deck, facedown. He had been living in a war zone long enough to know the basic moves of self-defense.

A gun went off above his head, not muffled this time, and an empty cartridge danced across the pavement inches from Lozaro's nose. He heard the muted answer from the tall man's weapon, almost felt the bullets smacking into human flesh. One dying gunman lurched toward the street, collapsed there, while his short companion sat down hard...directly on Lozaro's back.

The impact cleared Lozaro's lungs of air and left him struggling to free himself. In the chaos of the moment, he barely heard or saw the car reverse itself, tires smoking, as a fleeing gunman grappled with the steering wheel and tried to save himself.

Too late.

A burst of slugs in rapid fire shattered the car's back window. Crimson sprayed the inside of the windshield as the wheelman died.

And left Lozaro all alone, except for one man who had just killed five.

Another moment and the stranger stood above him, offering his hand.

"We ought to get the hell away from here," Mack Bolan said.

Sidon, Lebanon

McCARTER WISHED he could have cracked open a frosty can of Coca-Cola, but he settled for a sip of water. It was warm and tasted of the plastic bottle that he carried, but it was the best that he could do right now.

The morning was already hot, his armpits damp with perspiration, and McCarter knew it would get worse before he was relieved at noon.

There was no shade on the roof he occupied, across the street from the apartment house whose tenant list included one Jamal Marraq. McCarter hadn't glimpsed the Palestinian as yet, but he could see the windows of Marraq's third-floor apartment, facing the street. The drapes were closed, and there was nothing he could do but wait until they opened or his target appeared on the street below.

They had reports confirming that Marraq was still in Sidon, but McCarter would require at least a glimpse before he was convinced. Too many "sightings" in the past had come up empty, where elusive targets were concerned. Still, there was hope.

As if on cue, the drapes on one of Marraq's windows parted to reveal a slim young woman standing in a sparsely furnished living room. McCarter studied her through his binoculars, pronounced her average in looks and concentrated on the room behind her. There was someone just appearing through a door to the woman's left. She turned to face the new arrival, and the man stepped closer, clearly visible.

McCarter smiled.

It was Jamal Marraq. His mustache had been sacrificed since he was photographed the last time, by a contract agent of the CIA, but there was no mistake. The pale scar on his forehead was a giveaway, if nothing else. The single wound Marraq had suffered in his border-raiding days, and rumor had it that the bullet came from one of his own men, a sentry scared enough to fire at shadows.

It was too bad that the youngster's aim was poor, McCarter thought. How many lives had this one stolen since his own near miss with death? Katz might have known the stats, but it wasn't important. For the moment all that counted was confirming their intended target's presence in the flat.

McCarter raised his walkie-talkie, keyed the button for transmission and pronounced a single word: "Contact."

There was no answer from the other end, and he expected none. The plan was to observe Marraq before they struck, select the perfect time and place for maximum advantage. Now that they were certain of his whereabouts, the final planning could begin.

It would have been a relatively simple thing to snipe him through the window where he stood, but Katzenelenbogen wanted something more dramatic to unnerve al-Takriti and the other leaders of As-Sai'qa, send them scurrying for cover in the Bekaa Valley, if they weren't already there. If Phoenix Force could catch them all together, there would be a better chance of wiping out the high command, while the alternative—a string of hit-and-run attacks all over Lebanon—increased the odds against survival, much less ultimate success.

Marraq and his companion stepped back from the window, disappearing from McCarter's line of sight. His different altitude prevented him from sweeping the entire apartment with his glasses, but he had the door well covered. There was no way for Marraq to slip away unseen, unless he cut a passage through the wall of an adjoining flat.

McCarter settled back to wait, removing a pack of roasted cashews from his pocket and eating them slowly, shifting his eyes from Marraq's small apartment at regular intervals, checking the street below.

Another thirty minutes had elapsed, and he had finished off the nuts, when three young Arabs climbed the stairs to reach Marraq's apartment. One of them knocked on the door while his companions waited, bookends flanking him on either side.

Marraq responded after a moment, beckoned them inside. They huddled in the living room, chairs drawn into a circle, two of the new arrivals visible from McCarter's perch. He wished the flat was bugged, but there had been no opportunity. Perhaps if he spoke Arabic and was proficient at the art of reading lips—

A scuffling sound behind him froze McCarter where he sat. It could have been a pigeon landing on the rooftop, but he didn't think so. Did Marraq have spotters in the neighborhood? If so, would they attempt to take McCarter prisoner or simply gun him down?

No point in taking chances either way.

He had a hand inside his jacket, fingers wrapped around his automatic pistol, when he heard another sound. Much closer now. The muzzle of a handgun pressed itself into his ear.

"You may survive or die." It was a male voice, speaking English with an accent, totally impersonal. "The choice is yours for now."

"And later?" asked McCarter.

"That," the faceless stranger said, "depends on who and what you are."

Medellín, Colombia

THE PROSECUTOR WAS A LADY. Slim, attractive in the Latin style, although she did her best to hide it with a business suit and minimal cosmetics. Meeting her in other circumstances, Blancanales never would have guessed her occupation, much less that she had survived the past two years with a reported million-dollar open contract on her life.

It was the price of honesty in Medellín, where judges, cops and politicians either sold their offices for silver or were paid for their integrity with lead.

Three different assassins had tried to collect the bounty on Veronica Guzman since April. Two had died in the attempt, shot down by bodyguards. The third had been convicted and sentenced to a prison term of forty years. But he had served a mere ten days before a jailer paid to look the other way allowed him to escape from custody.

It hardly mattered in a city where assassins and assassin wanna-bes hung out in bars and on the streets downtown, soliciting potential customers at bargain rates. A million dollars meant a lifetime of security in Medellín.

Guzman's escort to the secret meet with Able Team was an American, Brent Favor, representing DEA. His office was in Bogotá, but Blancanales had resisted the diversion from their target that a trip across the Andes would entail. The Fed did not object, and Guzman joined him in the hope that their cooperation with the Able warriors might produce some benefits for all concerned.

"You understand this is a most unusual suggestion," said the lady prosecutor, frowning over coffee in a rented room. They had avoided borrowing an office from the local prosecutor or the DEA, aware that the cartel would soon be made aware of any meeting on official turf.

"We're dealing with a most unusual problem," Blancanales answered. "If it was a straight drug operation, we'd be happy to defer, of course."

Carl Lyons almost choked on that one, doubtless thinking of the other times when Able Team had operated in Colombia without a by-your-leave from any local politicians, but the Ironman managed not to laugh out loud.

"The terrorist connection is our first concern," Schwarz added, filling in the momentary silence. "We can always go for the Iraqi sponsors, but we need to clean up everyone involved."

"My country has been plagued with violence since I was a child," Veronica informed him. "My own brother was a victim of La Violencia when I was only four years old. Assassins shot him down outside our home in Cali, and I watched him die. My life has been devoted to preventing such atrocities, but now you ask me to participate."

"Not quite," said Lyons.

"You have asked me to do nothing while you start a war in Medellín," she said. "My oath of office calls upon me to oppose such violence, even at the risk of death."

"The war's already here," said Blancanales. "All we want to do is wrap it up and minimize the innocent civilian casualties."

"By killing men." Her voice was stern.

"The men your courts and prisons never seem to hold," said Lyons. "I believe the guy who tried to kill you last served...what? Ten days on forty years' hard labor? You could use some help."

"We don't need any acrimony here," Brent Favor interjected. "As a federal officer of the United States,

I've also sworn to follow certain guidelines and restrictions, but we're not in Kansas anymore. The rule book doesn't always function when the other side holds all the cards.''

It was a mangled metaphor at best, but Guzman seemed to get the point. She nodded slowly, grudgingly, and squared her shoulders, staring back at Blancanales. ''You are after M-19, I understand.''

''That's right,'' the Politician said. ''Specifically Manuel Vargas and his cronies who are doing business with Iraq. I don't believe you want Saddam Hussein dictating policy in Bogotá or Medellín. We damned sure don't want his dispatching hit teams to the States.''

''What is it that you need from me?'' the lady prosecutor asked.

''Not much,'' said Blancanales. ''Any names we need can come through DEA, with Favor's help, if that's agreeable.''

''It's been approved,'' the man from DEA replied.

''Okay. Then all we really need is time and elbow room. Hold off the cavalry until we're done with M-19.''

''The cavalry?'' She looked a bit confused.

''Authorities,'' Brent Favor interjected. ''The police, the army.''

''Ah. So I should look the other way?''

''Not quite,'' Pol answered. ''When we're done, with any luck at all, Eduardo Gaviria's family and the terrorists he uses for his dirty work should be in disarray. I wouldn't be surprised if some of them rolled over, given half a chance.''

The lady glanced at Favor once again, awaiting his translation. ''Turn informer,'' he remarked, ''to save themselves.''

"Of course." She hesitated, frowning. "There would certainly be questions at the highest level of government."

"To which you would supply convincing answers, I've no doubt."

"I wish I shared your confidence."

"Such modesty." The Politician let her see his smile. "You were the youngest prosecutor in Colombia the day you got the job. Not just the youngest woman, but the youngest, period. You've had the top conviction record in the country three years running, and I think we can assume you've hurt the bad guys where they live, considering the price tag on your head. Nobody gets that far in government without political survival skills."

"If you succeed in killing Vargas and his cronies, someone will be called on to explain their deaths."

"No problem," Lyons told her. "Everybody knows the FAP and M-19 are at each other's throats, and that Gaviria supports the FAP. They take each other out, nobody loses. It's like Bugsy Siegel used to tell the papers."

"Bugsy Siegel?" Once again the lady prosecutor glanced at Favor for an explanation.

Favor smiled. "A gangster in America, before your time. He liked to court the press. When a reported asked about the gang wars during prohibition, Siegel said, 'We only kill each other.'"

"Right," said Lyons. "When they finish picking up the pieces, everybody figures Vargas and Otero had themselves a private little war, with Gaviria rooting for the FAP."

"It works for me," said Gadgets Schwarz.

The prosecutor faced them for a moment, silent, thinking. Finally she said, "God knows it would not be the first time that political opponents in Colombia resorted to the gun."

"We're in agreement, then?" Pol asked.

"I will not tolerate an injury to innocent civilians," Guzman said.

"That's not our style," the Politician told her. "You've got all the random killings you can handle as it is. If we don't have a clean shot at a target, we don't play."

"And your opponents? Do they automatically accept your rules?"

Pol shook his head. "No way. They act just like they always have, kill anyone they feel like killing any time at all. My point is that you've got that now. We can walk away, forget about it, and you've still got something like a dozen murders every day in Medellín alone. That's not about to change while you've got animals like Vargas, Gaviria and Otero on the prowl."

The lady prosecutor thought for another moment, frowning. "And how much time would you require before I send the cavalry?"

"Two days at the outside," said Blancanales. "If we haven't done the job by then, you'll know the reason why."

She blinked at that, surprised by the American's frank reference to his own potential demise. Somehow it seemed to do the trick.

"Two days," she said at last, "but not a moment more."

They shook hands like a pair of businessmen about to sign a contract, but the bargain they had made would never be committed to paper. Veronica Guzman was gambling her career, perhaps her very freedom, on the word of total strangers, and the Politician wondered why.

Perhaps, he speculated, she had simply seen too much since taking office for her faith in law-book justice to survive. Colombia was trembling on the brink of anarchy, and Guzman knew it. Maybe, Blancanales thought, she had decided that the war could not be won by sticking to the rules.

Whatever, she was holding back the bloodhounds for another forty-eight hours, time enough—with any luck at all—for Able Team to wrap up their mission in Colombia.

And if they failed...well, he had not been joking when he told the lady she would know the reason why.

Someone would have to come identify the bodies, after all.

But not just yet.

The Politician and his comrades hadn't lived this long by dwelling on defeatist thoughts or looking for the easy way around a problem. They had come to play for keeps and they didn't intend to lose.

It was the kind of game where only winners walked away.

CHAPTER EIGHT

Stony Man Farm

"It's falling into place," said Aaron Kurtzman, pushing back from his computer terminal.

"Seems so." Despite the vote of confidence, Barbara Price didn't sound convinced.

"Except?" The Bear glanced at Barbara, noticing her frown.

"I can't help thinking that they should have taken out al-Takriti first. For all we know, he's making new connections as we speak. I don't like trusting Baghdad to do nothing while our people mop up in the field."

"You know the reasoning," he said.

She nodded, but the frown remained. The logic was impeccable as Hal Brognola spelled it out. Al-Takriti and Saddam Hussein were bent on using non-Iraqi terrorists to seek their vengeance on the West. It was the only sure-fire way to keep the war birds out of Baghdad, with their smart bombs, laser-guided rockets and the 20 mm Gatling guns that fired a hundred high-explosive rounds per second. Dealing with al-Takriti's agents in the field disarmed him for the moment, while ensuring that the contract terrorists would not spin off on tangents of their own, beyond Saddam Hussein's control.

There would be time enough for punishing Iraq when Bolan, Phoenix Force and Able Team had finished mopping up the mercenary troops.

Or so they hoped at Stony Man.

Of course, a thousand different things could still go wrong on any front of their divided war. Barbara Price was the mission controller for Stony Man, which meant it was her job to fret and worry over endless possibilities for failure. She didn't expect the team—*her* team—to fail, but trouble had a way of lurking in the shadowed corners of her mind.

The day she didn't worry, Barbara told herself, would be the day it fell apart.

But not today.

The maps made everything impersonal, shrinking cities to the size of punctuation marks, reducing mountain ranges like the Alps and Andes to the point that Barbara could cover them with one slim hand. You couldn't smell the forest on a map or hear the sound of traffic flowing in the streets of Barcelona, Medellín, Beirut. When guns went off and lives were lost, the map remained unscathed.

Much like the scene at Stony Man, she thought.

For all the guns, security devices and military personnel disguised as farmhands, they were well removed from the incessant dangers faced by agents in the field. She knew that Bolan and the rest didn't hold that against her, any more than they would blame a general for remaining safe behind the battle lines, but there were days when Barbara Price held it against herself.

"Smooth sailing in Colombia," said Kurtzman. "We were lucky Favor had a friendly prosecutor on the line."

"Why shouldn't they cooperate?" she asked. "They're looking at a no-lose situation. At best, they get their house cleaned free of charge. At worst, some gringos bite the dust, and Bogotá can formally absolve itself with a complaint to the UN.''

''We can't expect the same in Spain or Lebanon,'' the Bear reminded her. ''Madrid is still recovering from Franco, even after twenty years. They're not about to get involved with anything that steps on someone's civil rights, officially or otherwise. As far as Lebanon, forget about it. It's a nuthouse with the inmates in control. The so-called leaders couldn't help us even if they wanted to.''

''I know.'' She forced a crooked smile, devoid of humor. ''Did you ever just get sick and tired of helping people who are too damned negligent, corrupt or just plain dumb to help themselves?''

''You mean, how many times a day?''

''I guess that's what I mean.''

He shrugged, broad shoulders rolling as he shifted in his chair.

''I used to think about it all the time,'' said Kurtzman, ''but it didn't get me anywhere. The way I see it, we're not doing it for them. I mean, we *are*, but that's just the smallest part, I think. The main thing is we do it for ourselves. Because we can, and knowing that, we couldn't live with sitting back and doing nothing while the whole thing goes to hell.''

''A born philosopher,'' she said.

''I wouldn't qualify for anybody's Ph.D.,'' he said.

''You need one sometime, you can borrow mine.''

''I'll take you up on that.'' The silence stood between them for another moment, then he said, ''You ought to get some rest. I'll call you if we get another bulletin.''

''Promise.''

"Cross my heart."

"All right, then."

It was coming up on forty hours since her head had touched a pillow, but she doubted whether she could sleep. She would go through the motions for her friend's sake, even if she had to lie awake in bed and count the perforated ceiling tiles.

Then again, she might get lucky.

Sleep was out there somewhere, waiting for her, but she hoped she wouldn't dream.

Olot, Spain

ALPHONSE GOGORZA flicked the curtain back an inch or so and closely scrutinized the men leaving the compact car outside the farmhouse where he had been hiding for the past six days. He recognized them both on sight, but he didn't surrender his grip on the Star Model Z-70 submachine gun, covering his friends on their short walk to the doorstep.

He was getting paranoid, Gogorza thought, but how else was a freedom fighter to survive in Spain? In his world paranoids were simply reasonable men who recognized "society" for what it was: a mechanism fabricated by oppressors to exploit the common people, bleed them dry and dump their desiccated bodies on the rubbish heap of history.

Gogorza knew the odds against him going in, but he was bound to keep on fighting with a true believer's zeal. No matter how the ruling class attempted to conceal itself behind the label of "democracy," he wouldn't rest until the greedy parasites were all destroyed.

If he survived to see that day, Gogorza thought, he just might take a crack at ruling on his own.

He opened the front door and waved his comrades inside. The taller of the two, Ramon Aguirre, was his second in command. Ramon's companion, Emilio Sanchez, was a decade younger than Gogorza, but he had a killer's nerves of steel.

"What news?" Gogorza asked Aguirre after he had locked the door and they were seated in the tiny living room. The farmhouse had no telephone, plumbing or electricity. When the sun went down, Gogorza lit a lamp. When nature called, he stepped outside. And when he needed updates on events beyond the scope of his five senses, he relied on trusted couriers.

"We missed Lozaro," said Aguirre.

"How?"

"The circumstances are unclear," Aguirre said. "Our men did not survive."

"Lozaro killed them?"

"It would seem that he had help from someone else."

"A bodyguard?"

Aguirre shrugged. "He's never used a guard before. There is a possibility, of course, if he was warned."

"Ridiculous!" Gogorza felt the angry color in his cheeks. "The only ones who knew about the plan were me, you and those we sent to bring Lozaro back."

"Perhaps it was coincidence." Aguirre's voice had sunken almost to a whisper, but Gogorza heard him well enough.

"Coincidence? What do you mean, *coincidence?*"

"The ANE despise Lozaro, too," Aguirre said. "He plays no favorites in his editorials. If they were watching him, they would have seen our men arrive."

"And intervened to snatch him for themselves?"

"It's possible."

"What happened to our men?" Gogorza asked. "How were they killed?"

"All shot, from what I understand."

"How many guns?"

Aguirre frowned and shook his head. "There has been no official statement. The police apparently believe our men were ambushed by a rival group. They have not linked Lozaro to the incident, at least not publicly."

"A gunfight on his doorstep, and the man is missing," said Gogorza. "Do you really think that all police are fools?"

"For all we know," Aguirre said, "Lozaro may be under lock and key. Protective custody. It would not be the first time the police concealed a witness out of fear."

"And what could he expect to tell them? All our men are dead. They can't be charged with any crime beyond the grave."

"Once they have been identified, the state can file indictments for conspiracy. And there are still the killers to be reckoned with. Perhaps Lozaro can identify them."

"All the more reason for finding him quickly," Gogorza replied. "We have sufficient trouble, as it is. First Greece, and now this business with the ANE. Silveira makes a grave mistake if he believes I will accept this insult sitting down. I want Lozaro found, no matter what it takes. I don't care if he's locked up in Gerona or if he was taken by the ANE. If he is still alive, I mean to hear him name the men who killed our comrades."

"I will try," Aguirre said.

"Don't try, Ramon." Gogorza's voice was razor edged. "A miserable failure *tries* to do his duty. Men succeed. You must not fail."

Aguirre nodded, opting not to speak. Gogorza took his silence for agreement, moving on to other business.

"We must not allow Silveira to believe that we are beaten," he declared. "Retaliation is in order. Something that will make him stop and think."

"A calling card, perhaps?" Aguirre said.

"Exactly. Just to let him know that we have not forgotten him."

"I know his brother," Sanchez interjected, speaking for the first time since Gogorza let him in. "He has a shop for tourists in Mataró."

For the first time in a week, Gogorza felt an honest smile tug at the corners of his mouth. "A tourist shop?" he said. "It's perfect. Sanchez, you must take a friend or two and bring me back a souvenir."

The young man grinned from ear to ear, anticipating blood. "A postcard at the very least," he said.

Gogorza nodded, satisfied, and turned back toward Ramon Aguirre. "Find Lozaro," he instructed. "Bring him to me. Do it now."

When they were gone, Gogorza poured himself a glass of wine and sat down with the submachine gun in his lap.

He might be paranoid, but even paranoids have enemies.

The time had come for him to teach those enemies the meaning of complete and utter fear.

Fredonia, Colombia

MANUEL VARGAS lit a cheroot, drew deeply and expelled the smoke in twin streams from his nostrils. "Once again," he said, "how many soldiers did we lose?"

"I make it twenty-six," his aide replied. "Two got away. They heard one of the sneaky bastards shouting '*Viva!*' to the FAP."

"Otero's people." Vargas spoke his rival's name as if it were a curse. "And yet you say he's having trouble, too?"

"Four carloads of his men were ambushed on the highway. I am told that none survived."

"Has no one claimed responsibility?"

"Not yet," his aide replied. "Otero will believe we are responsible."

"And so we should be," Vargas said. "In the meantime someone has done us a favor, Miguel. Who was it that said, 'The enemy of my enemy is my friend?'"

Miguel looked puzzled, finally shrugged. "I cannot say, Manuel."

"No matter. It is still the truth. Whoever harms Otero helps us in the end."

"Why would he suddenly attack us now?"

"He has no honor," Vargas answered. "Anyone who takes Eduardo Gaviria's money is a soulless pig."

Miguel was wise enough to overlook the fact that Vargas had accepted money from Gaviria on more than one occasion, executing contracts for the dealer when Gaviria was anxious to remain aloof from a particular assassination. That had been another time, before the rift between Gaviria and M-19. It was a rift that Vargas swore would never heal.

In fact, he had enough to do, promoting revolution in Colombia, without the aggravation of remaining at a smuggler's beck and call. The first time M-19 had worked for the cartel, in 1986, he should have learned his lesson. Everything the *narcotraficantes* touched turned into gold for them and shit for everybody else.

When M-19 agreed to raid the supreme court in Bogotá, seizing the Palace of Justice, it had seemed like a grand idea. They were striking a blow for freedom, getting well paid in the bargain, and what did it matter if the arrest records of various drug dealers were burned in the process? One hand washed the other, after all.

The raid had been disastrous, even with the free publicity that M-19 had gained around the world. The group's presiding officers were dead, their bodies stacked among the hundred who were slain before the siege was lifted. Granted, Vargas had advanced dramatically in rank, to lead a unit of his own, but rank could not replace lost friends.

Well, not at first.

He had continued working for the narco smugglers, on a piecework basis, for another eighteen months or so. Assassinations here and there, a bombing when he had the time and inclination to cooperate. The final break arose not so much from a sense of being used as from the understanding that Gaviria and others like him were in fact the die-hard enemies of revolution in Colombia. They sometimes hired a freedom fighter to perform their dirty work when they wanted to protect themselves, but all the plum assignments went to neo-Nazi cadres like the FAP.

Since then, his only dealings with the drug cartel had been on those occasions when the movement needed cash, and Vargas chose a pigeon for his men to kidnap, raking in the ransom payments, dodging hired assassins as he had learned to dodge the military and police. A life in hiding had become routine, but Vargas cherished hopes that he would someday walk the streets of Medellín again in triumph.

"Our friend is still with the police in Antioquia," said Vargas.

"*Sí,*" Miguel replied. "He has not been discovered yet."

"I want their views on who attacked Otero's people. We can always use another ally, yes?"

"Of course."

"As for the FAP, I want Otero found and punished. We have suffered his indignities for too long, as it is."

"*Sí, Jefe.*"

"It will be a valuable lesson for our other enemies. They will regard us in a whole new light."

"It shall be done."

"You have a place to start."

"We know his family, his woman," said Miguel. "It should be no great task to find him."

"Very well. I want our enemies on the defensive for a change. It is not right that we should run and hide from shadows while the fascists strut about as if they owned the country. All that must change."

"*Sí, Jefe.*"

"Leave me now. Next time we meet, I want good news."

Miguel looked doubtful, but he nodded, rose and left.

Good news. It had been so long since he had gotten some, Vargas wasn't sure that he would recognize good news if it came knocking at his door. The death of any adversary pleased him certainly, but there were always more lined up to take the dead man's place. The movement had been fighting for a dozen years, and Vargas for the best part of a decade, but he couldn't testify to any progress in that time.

Still, he had managed to survive, and that was something in a country where the whole machinery of government, along with the omnipotent cartel, was pledged to his destruction. Waking up each morning, drawing breath, must count for Vargas as a victory of sorts.

It would be different from now on.

His troops were taking the offensive, and his enemies would learn what it was like to live in fear.

Beginning now.

Baghdad, Iraq

AFIF AL-TAKRITI could have used some good news himself. He was still recovering from the debacle in Greece, his stormy meeting with Saddam when he got home, and now he was besieged with calls from Spain, Colombia, Beirut. All bringing news of fresh disasters, greater losses in the field.

A handful of his foreign lackeys had survived the meeting on Kasar. At least there were enough of them for him to tell the Father-Leader that their plan was still intact. The next phase would be unavoidably delayed, of course, but these things happened.

When he touched his cheek, al-Takriti winced, remembering Saddam's explosive backhand that had drawn blood from his nose and left him stretched out on the floor. Resistance or retaliation would have been tantamount to suicide, and he had seen the Father-Leader's private acid bath, the way his "special" victims writhed and screamed for what seemed hours before they found release in death.

Definitely not the way to go.

Al-Takriti had survived worse beatings—from his father, once or twice in military service, from his sergeants—and he could absorb one more without complaint if it meant life or death. A few kicks to his back and legs, before Saddam had run out of steam and ordered him to salvage what he could from the conspiracy.

Al-Takriti meant to do exactly that, and he wasn't about to risk the Father-Leader's fury with some more bad news, particularly when events halfway around the world were totally beyond his control. He answered each new call with promises of money, arms, whatever he could do to help... but help took time. He simply could not load a crate of weapons on a military plane and send it off to Bogotá or Barcelona. Lebanon was easier, since he had established contacts there, but even so, there were proprieties to be observed, restrictions on exactly what he could and could not do.

Al-Takriti was prepared to stretch a point if necessary, but the Father-Leader didn't always smile on initiative. Sometimes he punished it, in fact, if the results embarrassed his regime. Still, there were ways to hide one's tracks when dealing with a group of foreigners, and Afif al-Takriti knew them all.

In fact, he had invented some of them himself.

Beirut was his immediate concern. He felt a personal affinity for the As-Sai'qa freedom fighters, but there were more practical concerns, as well. Baghdad's involvement with the Thunderbolt had been more open than its dealings with the terrorists in Asia, South America and Europe. If the link was documented and exposed, it might provoke retaliation from the White House, and the last thing anyone desired was yet another air strike on the capital. Saddam could always strike his best defiant pose and bluster for the media, but each new bombing damaged his prestige, made him resemble a pathetic sideshow figure who defied the world but took no action in his own defense.

The global terror net had been conceived to change all that, and it had been successful in its early stages. Random incidents conceived by foreigners and financed by the Father-Leader had produced a spate of headlines from New York to Tokyo. It had been payback time for Operation Desert Storm and the embargo that was slowly strangling Iraq . . . until Kasar.

Al-Takriti still had no idea of how their enemies had penetrated his security. There were informers everywhere these days, and if a spy was not available, the Father-Leader's own intemperate announcements sometimes blew the whistle on a plan al-Takriti had been laboring for weeks to finalize. Of course, they scored a victory from time to time—the World Trade Center bombing was a case in point, a blind man and his lackeys taking all the blame—but triumphs had been few and far between.

Al-Takriti meant to change all that, but it would be an uphill fight. If it appeared that he was losing, he might be in danger from the Father-Leader, so he must be prepared to cut and run.

He had learned survival in the streets of Baghdad as a child, and honed his skills in the protracted war against Iran. His selection to create a global web of terror was a plum assignment, but it also came with built-in risks. Al-Takriti had been planning ways to save himself from the beginning, skimming money from the operation's budget for a personal escape fund, renting an apartment in Basra in his mother's maiden name. From there it was a short flight to Qatar or the United Arab Emirates, and on from there with doctored passports to the country of his choice.

But it would never come to that, al-Takriti told himself. He was a patriot, and he would do his utmost for the Father-Leader to redeem his country's honor and humiliate its enemies.

Still, it was good to know that if his plans fell through, he would not be required to go down with the ship.

That was the leader's job, and there could only be one leader in Iraq. Saddam would tolerate no usurpation of his own authority.

Al-Takriti would do everything within his power to fulfill his mission. Failing that, he would take steps to save himself. If Allah held that move against him, it would all be sorted out on Judgment Day.

Al-Takriti wished that he were home so he could smoke his hashish pipe, but that would have to wait. He still had work to do, long-distance calls to make. His foreign allies had been getting restless, and he had to put their minds at ease, if possible.

The Father-Leader's holy war had merely been postponed, but he would set it back on track as soon as possible.

The infidels would yet be made to pay their debts in blood.

CHAPTER NINE

Gerona, Spain

Once he had recovered from the shock of the attempted kidnapping, Lozaro had no end of questions for his unexpected savior. Bolan parried them with generalities until Lozaro finally relaxed a bit, directing him to the apartment of a friend who was away on holiday. Lozaro had a key to let him water plants and check the place from time to time. When they were safe inside, he put a pot of coffee on and settled in a chair across from Bolan's, in the living room.

"I do not wish to seem ungrateful for your help," Lozaro said in perfect English, "but I really must insist on knowing who you are."

"Let's say we have a common goal," the Executioner replied.

"Which is?"

"Restoring peace in Basqueland."

"From your demonstration on the street," Lozaro said, "I fear that we may disagree on what 'peace' means."

"I doubt it," Bolan said. "You can't have peace and terrorism, too. They're incompatible ideas."

"I would agree in principle, but your technique..."

"Some situations call for action," Bolan said. "I think you know what would have happened if I tried negotiating with the men who tried to snatch you off the street.''

''Of course, but—''

''Would you rather be with them right now?''

''I would prefer,'' Lozaro said, ''that no one should be harmed.''

''That's very noble, but it falls a few miles short of being realistic,'' Bolan said. ''The terrorists exist, they're killing people on a daily basis, and they're not about to stop because you ask them. I could have watched you die this morning, maybe hung around and given a statement to police. How would society have gained from that?''

''Who *are* you?'' asked Lozaro. ''Why have you selected me to rescue?''

''You needed help,'' Bolan said, ''and there are ways you could return the favor.''

''Ah.''

''It happens that I've picked up certain information on the ETA,'' said Bolan, ''and their obligation to a foreign power.''

''That is hardly news,'' Lozaro said. ''For almost twenty years they have accepted arms and money from the Soviets, the Czechs, Khaddafi. It is known that members of the ETA cooperate with Irish terrorists, the Red Brigades in Italy... the list goes on.''

''I don't mean last year's headlines,'' Bolan told him. ''A conspiracy in progress, sponsored by Iraq, that makes a mockery of any claim the ETA might have to seeking independence for the Basque minority.''

Lozaro frowned. ''It's interesting,'' he said. ''But why tell me?''

"Because you have an audience. The people listen when you speak. They read your editorials. I know about the work you did in Sabadell."

"That was nothing."

"Wrong. You put enough heat on the ETA for murdering a taxi driver that they finally broke down and paid a reparation to his family. The public pressure made them cave, but it began with you."

"I merely wrote—"

"Nine editorials," the warrior interrupted. "I know. I've read them." He paused for a moment. "Did you know they shot the triggerman for bringing so much grief down on their heads?"

Lozaro stiffened, going pale. "You can't know that."

"His name was Vincent Laxalt. Check it out. They found him in Manresa on the third of May."

"I know the case, but there was nothing to suggest—"

"I have my sources," Bolan said. "There was a note left on the body. The police suppressed it. Call and ask them if you like."

Lozaro glanced down at his folded hands and winced, as if imagining them stained with blood. "What is it that you want from me?" he asked.

"No more than you would do for any other story," Bolan said. "Review the information I provide, confirm the facts by any means you like, and if they check out, you spread the word."

"What word exactly?"

"That the ETA is selling out the very people they pretend to serve. The leaders—some of them, at least—have sold out to Saddam Hussein. They're taking odd jobs from the highest bidder, and that makes them no more 'freedom fighters' than the gangs who sell cocaine in Barcelona and Madrid."

Lozaro frowned. "You have specific evidence?"

"One phone call, and it's yours."

"I am obliged to verify my facts."

"I wouldn't have it any other way."

The Spaniard thought about it for another moment, finally nodding.

"Make the call," he said.

Antioquia Province, Colombia

THE JUNGLE ARMS DUMP was concealed from aerial surveillance by a camo net strung between trees. A clearing had been hacked out of the forest, but you wouldn't know it from the air unless you hovered low enough to let a helicopter's rotor wash make ripples in the netting. Even then, a spotter had to know what he was looking for or he could easily mistake the sight for leaves and branches blowing in the wind.

Pol Blancanales knew about the dump because a paid informer out of Medellín had tipped the DEA to escape indictment on his third cocaine beef in a year. The data had been verified by sending in a local creeper, after which the DEA had filed it for consideration as a future trade-off with the government in Bogotá. Since drugs were not involved, the Feds were not directly interested . . . until the CIA and Stony Man came asking for a handle on the troops of M-19.

Brent Favor passed the tip along to Able Team, and Blancanales carried it from there. A simple recon had confirmed the presence of a hidden compound in the jungle, but the rest of it—as far as group affiliation and matériel on hand—would call for hands-on scrutiny.

In fact, Pol didn't care whose weapon dump it was. The team was on a roll, and any ripples they could make from this point on would only help to agitate the enemy.

The dump was serviced by an unpaved access road that left the highway three miles from Barbosa, running east for half a mile before it curved back to the north. Pol found a turnout near the curve and drove their jeep well off the road, assisting Schwarz and Lyons with the chore of cutting brush to hide the vehicle from prying eyes.

When they were confident that it would pass inspection, they changed their street clothes for fatigues, retrieved their gear and struck off through the woods in the direction of the ammo dump. A quarter of an hour brought them to the fringes of a clearing where the trees had been cut back, replaced with tents and sheds constructed of corrugated metal painted green to help the camo nets conceal the site.

They had worked out their movements in advance. Schwarz circled to the left, Lyons to the right, while Blancanales counted off two minutes on his wristwatch. He was ready with his M-16 A1/M-203 when time ran out. The others would be in position now or else he would have heard their clash with sentries in the forest.

His target was a spacious tent with crates of weapons stacked inside. He couldn't read the stenciled legend on the crates from thirty yards, nor did he need to. Whether they were rifles, ammunition, rockets or grenades, they were about to blow.

He counted seven gunmen visible, at different points around the camp, but none of them was visibly alert enough to qualify as a sentry. Pol ignored them as he sighted on the tent and squeezed the trigger of the M-203 launcher.

Thump!

The high-explosive round went in on target, sailing through the open tent flap, plowing into O.D. crates that had been stacked chest high. The blast ripped canvas from its moorings, sent tent stakes flying and flattened two gunners who were near the tent. The others were seeking cover by the time a secondary blast ripped through the tent and hurled debris sky-high.

The spacious camo net was burning, adding smoke to the already hellish scene, as Schwarz and Lyons opened fire from their respective vantage points. Pol fixed a moving target in his sights and dropped the guy before he made six loping strides toward the forest, running for his life.

Too late.

Another HE round came in, this one from Lyons, opening the east wall of a corrugated metal hut. Grenades or something were stashed in there, judging from the way they detonated in a stunning chain reaction, like a giant string of fireworks going off. The Politician's ears were ringing from the rapid-fire explosions, and he watched as a pair of gunners were swallowed by the rolling fireball.

Bingo.

Schwarz nailed the last two, scared or dumb enough to run straight toward him from the clearing, more afraid of what was happening behind them than the perils of the forest. One burst, zapping them from left to right, and Blancanales watched them fall.

They finished it with three more high-explosive rounds, one each for the remaining shed and tents. There were no further blasts to rival that produced by

Lyons's first HE round, though Blancanales torched three jeeps with his shot to the motor pool. About that time the burning camo net came loose from its connection to the trees and settled on the clearing like a giant smoking shroud.

They regrouped in the forest, Blancanales waiting for his comrades to arrive and start the hike back to their car.

"Nice cookout," Lyons said to no one in particular. "I should have brought some steaks."

"It isn't party time," said Blancanales.

"Who's up next?" asked Gadgets.

"After this," Pol said, "I think we owe another visit to the FAP."

"It's nice to share," the Ironman said. "They taught me that in Sunday school."

"You miss the rest of it," Schwarz chided him, "or what?"

"Let's get moving," Blancanales said. "We have to keep on stirring if we want the pot to boil."

"You sound like Betty Crocker," Schwarz remarked.

The Politician smiled and said, "One recipe to die for, coming up."

Mataró, Spain

EMILIO SANCHEZ WATCHED his target through a windshield flecked with the remains of suicidal insects, concentrating on the shop across the street. He had been watching for the past five minutes, counting customers who came and went, his nerves on edge.

The hit was one thing, but this waiting was an extra hazard. Anything could happen while they sat there in the car, waiting for Silveira's latest customers to leave.

"We're wasting time," Guillermo Rosa told him from the back seat. "We should kill all three of them and get the hell away from here."

"He's right," Diego Ehrabide said. "We're wasting too much time. The police—"

"*¡Cállate!*" Emilio snapped. "Shut up! Alphonse put *me* in charge, and *I* say we should wait until the women leave."

Jesus Vizcaya, seated at the wheel, took no part in the argument. He smoked a hand-rolled cigarette in silence, staring at the shop across the street. He never seemed to blink, and his flat, reptilian gaze didn't help Emilio's nerves.

The easy thing would certainly have been to rush across the street and burst in on Silveira and his customers, unloading with their submachine guns, killing anything that moved, but Sanchez had a point to make. It had been his idea to kill the brother of the ANE's supreme commander, and he didn't want the message lost in headlines mourning the demise of two old women who had trouble deciding which trinkets to buy.

Sanchez didn't know if they were tourists, but it would be even worse if that were so. He had no love for foreigners, Americans and British least of all, but they made news when they were killed, provoked reactions from their governments, and Sanchez liked to concentrate on one war at a time.

Right now his fight was with Silveira and the ANE. When he had dealt with that specific problem, he could turn his full attention back to killing Spaniards and their lackeys in the Pyrenees.

"They're coming," said Vizcaya, flicking his cigarette into the street.

"Let's do it," Ehrabide urged.

"Another moment," Sanchez ordered, watching as the two old women moved along the sidewalk, chattering like birds. They reached the intersection and began to cross the street. "All right," he snapped. "Come on."

All three of them were armed with Star Z-70s, the compact submachine gun favored by the civil guard and Spanish military. It was less than nineteen inches with the metal stock collapsed, and had forty rounds of ammunition in the magazine. Chambered for the 9 mm Largo cartridge, the Z-70 had a cyclic rate of some 550 rounds per minute in full-auto mode, allowing a gunner to control his bursts with fair precision once he got the hang of it.

But there was no need for precision this time. Sanchez and his comrades shoved through the front door of the shop and leveled their weapons at the man behind the register. Antonio Silveira didn't have his brother's wavy hair or sculpted profile, but their blood was the same, and Sanchez meant to see it for himself.

Silveira glanced up from his register and froze. He didn't recognize the gunmen personally, but he knew what they had come for. Cursing, he stepped to his left and thrust a hand beneath the counter, reaching for a hidden weapon.

He never had a chance.

The three Z-70s cut loose together, firing from a range of less than twenty feet. It seemed impossible to miss, yet a number of their rounds flew wide, peppering the wall behind Silveira, smashing souvenirs that he had carefully arranged on metal shelves.

Silveira still took most of it, his body twitching, jerking to the impact of the bullets, lurching back against the wall. It took less than five seconds to empty the three submachine guns, since the triggers were held down for continuous fire, but the time seemed much longer to Sanchez as he watched his target jump and dance. The triple stream of bullets kept Silveira from collapsing, pinning him against the wall of shelves until they suddenly ran out of ammunition. Then the pull of gravity took over, dropping him behind the counter out of sight.

There was no question of the man surviving, but a leader has his duties. Sanchez ran around the counter, hauling out his Llama automatic as he stood above the prostrate body, bending down to fire the coup de grace.

All done.

He straightened up to find himself alone, Guillermo jogging toward the car, while Ehrabide staked out the sidewalk, prepared to deal with any passersby. In fact, the street was empty as they drove away, the locals wise enough by now to keep their heads down and their eyes closed at the sound of gunfire.

Men who witnessed nothing were not called upon to testify. It was a fact of life that children learned in Spain before they came of age.

Emilio Sanchez had been such a child.

He felt no pity for Antonio Silveira as he stuffed the submachine gun underneath his seat. The execution had been necessary.

He felt only pleasure in a job well done.

Sidon, Lebanon

"MOSSAD, for Christ's sake. What a balls-up."

There was anger in McCarter's voice at being taken by a stranger, more so at the thought of having the Israeli secret service privy to their plans in Lebanon. As far as he could see, security was out the window. They were blown.

It had been bad enough, the walk back to confront his fellow warriors, the Israeli hanging back a pace or two and covering him all the way. McCarter might have tried to take him even then, but he was wise enough to recognize a trained professional and understand that he would stop at least three rounds from the Beretta Model 92 before he turned and closed the gap between them.

Suicide.

He had refused to lead the gunman back at first, but his assailant had a way around that, too. Instead of getting tough, he simply took the walkie-talkie from McCarter's belt and left the frequency alone, transmitting in the clear.

"Whoever's listening," he said, "I've got your man. If anybody wants him back, we need to have a talk."

Katz could have played the silent game and sacrificed McCarter, but he took a chance, and here they were. The gunman's name was Ari Lev, and his affiliation with Mossad had been confirmed by Katzenelenbogen, who had spoken to a mutual acquaintance down in Tel Aviv.

"So here we are," said Ari Lev.

"No, here *you* are," McCarter snapped. "You've barged into the middle of a set you don't begin to understand, and there's a decent chance you've ruined everything."

"I seriously doubt it," the Israeli told him, putting on a mirthless smile. "In fact, if anyone's barged in, it would be you lot. I've been following Jamal Marraq for weeks now, watching every move he makes."

"With what in mind?" Katz asked his fellow countryman.

A shrug from Ari Lev. "Elimination when the time is right. Meanwhile I've managed to identify three dozen of his known associates, all members of As-Sai'qa."

"Making up a yearbook for the class reunion, are you?" asked Calvin James, who was sitting close to the Israeli, covering him in case anything went wrong.

The object of his mocking question kept that smug, infuriating smile in place as he replied. "It never ceases to amaze me, how your country has avoided learning patience in the past three hundred years."

"There's such a thing as waiting too damned long."

"And who would be the judge of that?"

"I will for now," said Yakov Katzenelenbogen.

"I remember you," the younger man replied. "They talk about you sometimes in the training course. It's ancient history, you understand."

"The question we're deciding now," McCarter said, "is whether you have any kind of future."

"Are we? I imagined we were trying to decide if we should all cooperate, or you should simply go back home."

"If anybody's going home—"

"Enough!" Katz stepped between them, cutting off the argument. "We haven't come this far to pack it in without a fight. I'll grant you that it's possible your information might be helpful, but I'm not about to let you dictate terms. This isn't Tel Aviv, and you have no more jurisdiction here than we do."

Ari Lev considered that, deciding he had two alternatives, besides cooperation. He could try to kill five men, in which case he would almost surely die . . . or he could waste the next few days on protests to his chief in Tel Aviv. Assuming that Mossad decided in his favor, breaking precedent by openly defying the Americans, it would already be too late. The strangers would have made their move, and his surveillance of Jamal Marraq would have been entirely in vain.

"What did you have in mind?" he asked.

"We're going for a clean sweep," Katz informed him. "Realistically it's more than we can hope for, but there's no point thinking small. Marraq is next up on our list, to keep As-Sai'qa guessing. After that...well, let's just say we're looking toward the main event."

"To find the leadership," said Ari Lev, "you'll have to penetrate the Bekaa Valley."

There was thinly veiled derision in his tone, but none of them responded to the gibe. He turned from one face to the next, all five, and saw the same thing in their eyes.

"My God, you're serious! You really mean to try it."

"Can you think of any better way to keep Iraq from branching out in Lebanon?" McCarter asked.

"The Bekaa? Five of you?"

"Unless you make it six," Katz said.

And that was something to consider. It appealed to Ari Lev's sense of adventure, his desire to strike a telling blow against the Palestinians who terrorized his homeland. Still...

"It's suicide," he said.

"If you believe that going in," said Calvin James, "I wouldn't be a bit surprised."

"What happened to your confidence?" McCarter asked him, vaguely mocking. "Did you leave it in your other suit?"

It would be childish, worse than lunacy, to do it on a dare. And yet the young Israeli found that he couldn't resist the challenge. In the Bekaa anything was possible. A man could lose his life or find his destiny.

"All right," he said. "When do we leave?"

Katz smiled. "As soon as we dispose of one Jama Marraq," he said.

CHAPTER TEN

Andorra la Vella, Andorra

The principality of Andorra covers 185 square miles, or roughly half the size of New York City. It is the second-smallest sovereign nation on the European continent, surpassing only tiny Liechtenstein, and its capital is the only city in a nation of some fifty-six thousand people. Tourism dominates the Andorran economy, but its location in the Pyrenees, sandwiched between Spain and France, also makes Andorra a favored hiding place for fugitives from one country or the other.

Terrorists, predictably, were no exception to the rule.

Basque fugitives had used Andorra as a hideaway in times of crisis for the past two decades, mostly ducking Spanish officers, occasionally using their retreat to dodge the French. Police in the Andorran capital had no complaints, and neither did the landlords, grocers, restaurants and other merchants who did business with assorted terrorists in hiding.

It was afternoon when Bolan cleared the border checkpoint, with a new stamp in his "Mike Belasko" passport. He would have to add them up sometime, perhaps pick out a wall map of the world that he could fill with colored stick-pins to denote the different countries he had visited or passed through in pursuit of his unending war. There were a few that he had missed, thought Bolan, but the list was getting shorter all the time.

Pablo Lozaro had suggested two stops in Andorra, clearly ill at ease with his decision to cooperate in Bolan's purge of local predators. Still, even grudging help was better than no help at all.

The first address was a nightclub, buttoned up tight in the middle of the day. Bolan passed it by and homed in on his second target, a safehouse on the eastern fringes of the Andorran capital.

The neighborhood was less run-down than simply lived in, showing signs of wear but decently maintained. The residents would never be confused with millionaires, but they were getting by. The hideout masqueraded as a rooming house, but only travelers with the proper terrorist connections were allowed to stay the night. They were not always Basque; some Germans turned up now and then, perhaps a Turk or Palestinian in transit, the occasional Irishman with a price on his head.

The Executioner didn't feel particular this afternoon as he parked his car and walked back to the safehouse. Underneath his lightweight raincoat, he carried a Beretta 93-R and the Mini-Uzi in a shoulder sling. Spare magazines for both filled his pockets. His gray eyes were perfectly inscrutable behind a pair of mirrored shades.

He rang the bell and waited, had the Mini-Uzi in his hand before a balding, red-faced landlord opened the door. His baggy coveralls didn't conceal the pistol at his waist, but he had zipped the garment up too high for him to reach the weapon in a hurry. Bolan shot him in the chest, three silent rounds at point-blank range, and stepped across his prostrate body as he cleared the threshold.

Stairs were on his left, an empty parlor on his right. He walked back toward the kitchen, following his nose. There was a young man working at the stove, two others seated at the kitchen table, playing cards. They all saw Bolan more or less at once, but none of them was fast enough to take him down. The Uzi stuttered, spitting through its custom silencer, as Bolan sprayed the room from left to right.

The cook went down without a whimper, took the steaming saucepan with him, dumping hot stew on his trousers as he fell. The others tried to stand, one reaching for a gun, the other looking hopeless and afraid as Bolan shot them both. The life went out of them in seconds flat, and that made four.

He checked the downstairs bathroom, found it empty, backtracked to the stairs. Four bedrooms on the second floor, a smallish operation, but he reckoned it could handle ten or twelve men in a pinch. Three of the bedroom doors were closed. Bolan checked them each in turn, found tidy rooms apparently belonging to the dead men he had left downstairs. He found no other sign of life until he reached the last room on his left.

The door was open six or seven inches, music emanating from within—Teutonic classical and heavy on the brass. He shouldered through and caught a young man pulling on his slacks, hair wet and tousled from the shower. Scoping out his uninvited visitor, the Mini-Uzi with its silencer, the young man plainly knew that it was Judgment Day.

He threw himself across the bed, intent on scooping up a pistol from the nightstand. Bolan didn't even have to aim for this one, squeezing off a burst that flipped the youthful gunner over on his back. The shooter's outstretched fingers missed their target by a foot and knocked his digital alarm clock to the floor. The clock, in turn, began to buzz and kept it up until the Executioner pulled the plug.

He thought about graffiti, finally decided not to leave a sign. Without clear group affiliations for the five men he had iced, a slogan painted at the scene might be incomprehensible or contradictory. It would be easier and more efficient just to make a phone call when the time was right.

He felt like lunch, decided to check out a restaurant that he had passed on his way into town. A soldier has to eat, and it would put him near the highway, westbound, back to Basqueland.

Where the war was waiting for him.

The war was always waiting for him, everywhere he went.

Cali, Colombia

THE ORDERS HAD COME DOWN from Medellín, and Silvio Ybarra was a man who always followed orders. It was not for him to question the requirements of the high command. There was a reason for the order, and the fact that he would have to risk his life was hardly worth considering.

A soldier did as he was told, never mind the consequences to himself or others. His superiors would ultimately bear responsibility, and Ybarra believed that they were wiser than him.

Still, it was definitely hazardous, a daylight raid against the FAP with only two men to support him. One of those would be the driver, so that Ybarra and Rudy Costa were the two men on the firing line.

Against how many?

Never mind. Ybarra didn't want to think about it at the moment, rolling eastward in the stolen car. He focused on the Ingram MAC-10 submachine gun in his lap, the extra magazines and hand grenades that weighed his pockets down until the jacket felt all strange and lumpy, like a thrift-shop garment.

Focus.

Ybarra couldn't have guessed why his superiors were moving against the FAP. He knew there had been trouble to the north, in Antioquia, but he was vague on details. Men were dead, some of them his compatriots from M-19, some FAP, still others named in radio reports as *narcotraficantes*. It was too confusing for a simple man, so Silvio Ybarra stuck to his specific orders, glad that he had someone else to do his thinking for him in a crunch.

The FAP's main front in Cali was a trucking company that often dealt with the cartel, transporting coca base to various clandestine labs and moving the refined cocaine to private airstrips for the journey north. The truckers also carried weapons for the FAP, and still found time for the occasional legitimate assignment on the side.

On any given day there would be half a dozen workers at the warehouse, all committed neo-fascists, muscle for the drug cartel or both. If they were loading trucks, the drivers would be helping out, more trouble for a two-man task force already outnumbered by the enemy.

The loading dock was empty when Ybarra's driver pulled in close beside the warehouse, drew a sawed-off shotgun from beneath his seat and sat there with the motor running.

Waiting.

Ybarra got out and Rudy Costa followed. They mounted concrete steps to reach the loading bay, where giant doors stood open, revealing the wooden crates and cardboard boxes stacked inside. Immediately on their right as they went in, a smallish office cubicle was walled off from the warehouse proper with partitions made of fiberglass and plywood.

Ybarro saw three men in the office, had them covered with his Ingram as he barged through the open door. The two men facing him were startled into immobility, their tall companion turning in his swivel chair to face the new arrivals with a curious expression.

"Por la revolución," Ybarra told them, triggering a burst that took the tall man's face off, spraying his companions with a soup of blood and brains. Beside him Rudy Costa's CAR-15 cut loose, and they made short work of the others, dropping both before they could rise or reach their weapons.

Ybarra expected more resistance, and he found it as he left the tiny office, ducking as a bullet whispered past his face. Two men were firing from the cover of a forklift across the warehouse, where they had observed the slaughter of their friends. Ybarra ducked behind an upright crate whose labels told him it contained a new refrigerator.

Rudy Costa dodged back toward the office, firing from the hip, but too late. Ybarra was watching as a bullet smacked into Costa's chest. He went down firing, bawling out his pain, until another bullet ricocheted off concrete, clipped his vocal cords and silenced him forever.

Silvio Ybarra knew that he was running out of time. He had a deadline, and the driver would abandon him if he was late. He palmed a hand grenade and dropped the safety pin, crept back around the upright crate to lob it overhand toward the forklift and his enemies.

Surprisingly it worked. The hand grenade fell short, but the concussion of its blast flushed one man out of cover, while the other dropped his pistol, clasping both hands to his ears. Ybarra caught the runner with a rising burst that jerked his legs from under him and dropped him squirming on his face.

Ybarra turned to the second gunner, feeding his Ingram a fresh magazine as he charged. It was madness, something from a movie, but it did the trick. He came in firing, bullets ripping through his adversary's chest and slamming him against the corrugated metal wall.

And that left one.

He came up on the wounded gunner's blind side, standing close enough that there could be no possibility of missing. He fired half a magazine into the twitching enemy and left him in a spreading pool of blood. Then he retrieved Costa's weapon as he retreated from the warehouse to the car.

It was unfortunate to lose a comrade, but Ybarra had the satisfaction of a job completed. He couldn't be criticized for failure to perform upon command.

The driver didn't ask about his missing passenger, accepting Costa's absence as a fact of life. Instead, he stowed the shotgun out of sight and drove Ybarra home with all deliberate speed.

To wait upon more orders from the north.

Sidon, Lebanon

IT WAS UNCOMFORTABLE, going on a raid with strangers—much less foreigners—but Ari Lev would do as he was told. If his superiors in Tel Aviv were satisfied with his companions, it was not for him to second-guess the brass. Still, he would watch his back and be prepared to save himself if anything went wrong.

And it would be a pleasure to eliminate Jamal Marraq.

The scheming bastard had been marked for death as payback for his many crimes against the state of Israel and her people, but the execution of his sentence was delayed while Ari Lev maintained surveillance, fleshing out a list of contacts in the neighborhood. There were undoubtedly a few that he had missed, but if the truth were told, he had been getting tired of simply watching from the sidelines, knowing every day Marraq survived he was a clear and present threat to Lev's homeland.

It was time for him to die, and Lev could only hope that he would be the one to pull the trigger on Marraq.

They had agreed that any strike against the Palestinian's apartment had to be a last resort, considering the risk to neighbors who presumably were not involved with the intended target. Ari Lev was less concerned with ''innocent'' civilians than his new companions, viewing every resident of Lebanon as a potential enemy of Israel, but he found himself outnumbered when it came down to a vote.

The target made it easy for them as the afternoon wore on. Their spotter, the Canadian, reported that Marraq had left his flat and walked three blocks to a tobacco shop, which Lev recognized as an assembly point for members of the Thunderbolt. The owner was a Palestinian and chief lieutenant of Marraq, who let the terrorists convene in his back room from time to time.

Ten minutes put them at the site, and the Canadian reported three more Arabs had arrived within that time. It was impossible to guess how many had shown up before Marraq arrived, but they were limited in terms of space. The shop was closed now, no one visible out front, but Lev knew the meeting room in back was barely large enough to hold a dozen men.

"I'll take the back," said Yakov Katzenelenbogen. "Cal, you've got the car, with Rafael. I don't want any last-minute surprises from the street."

"It's done," the black man said.

"McCarter, come with me," their one-armed chief continued. "Manning, you and Ari—"

"No," said Ari Lev. "I'm going back with you. Marraq is there and he is mine. I haven't spent these weeks in Lebanon to simply hold the door while others do my job."

Katz stared at him, finally nodding. "Fair enough," he said at last. "McCarter, take the front with Manning. We move in two minutes from . . . now."

They crossed the street together, Ari Lev packing his silencer-equipped Uzi SMG in a shopping bag slung over his shoulder. Katz for his part was armed with a Heckler & Koch MP-5 SD-3 submachine gun, carried underneath his jacket on a shoulder sling.

An alley ran behind the small tobacco shop, and Lev was relieved to find no sentries posted there. The back door of the shop was painted blue and badly scuffed below waist level, as if someone was in the habit of kicking it shut. Without a test they knew the door was locked, the men inside well armed.

They took positions in the alley, covering the door, and waited for the action to go down out front. A moment later Ari Lev was rewarded with the crash of glass as Gary Manning lobbed a hand grenade through the shop's front window. Muffled voices reached him through the door, a sound of scuffling feet and scraping chairs...and then all hell broke loose.

The hand grenade exploded in the front room of the shop, inflicting major damage to the building, setting fire to some of the cigars and pipe tobacco on display. Immediately Manning and McCarter opened up with automatic weapons, making it a hopeless task for anyone to slip out through the front.

Marraq and his companions thus were forced to the obvious. The blue door slammed back on its hinges, half a dozen Arabs spilling out into the alley, weapons in hand. They were prepared to fight, at least in theory, but the ambush took them by surprise.

Ari Lev cut loose with his Uzi, dropping the pointman in his tracks, catching the next in line before he could line up a target and fire. Katz took the next three while they stood, dumbfounded, trying to decide which direction to run. They fell together in a bloody heap.

The sixth man was retreating, shouting to a comrade inside the shop, when Ari Lev caught him with a burst between the shoulder blades. His target vaulted forward, flew across the threshold and landed facedown in the back of the shop.

Dark smoke was visible above the roofline from the street, and more was curling from the open doorway. The little shop was clearly doomed, untenable as a defensive outpost for anyone inside.

Such as Marraq.

He had not been among the Palestinians who ran into the waiting crossfire. His flunkies took the risk, as usual, while their commander hung back in relative safety, waiting to check out their fate.

Ari Lev took an incendiary grenade from his bag, pulled the pin and lobbed it through the back door of the shop, while Katz pinned the living occupants inside with short precision bursts. The blast wasn't as loud as that from Manning's frag grenade out front, but it had more spectacular results. Suddenly the back room of the shop became a bright inferno, engulfed in flames.

He heard the screaming well before he saw his targets dodging through the fire, arms flapping in a vain attempt to douse their burning clothes. The first one seemed to be Jamal Marraq—the size and weight were right—but Ari Lev had trouble with the twisted, blackened face. He held the Uzi's trigger down and sent undeserved release to savage souls in torment as the two men lurched and staggered through a roaring wall of flame.

And it was over in a heartbeat, Ari Lev retreating with his one-armed comrade toward their waiting car. If anyone was left inside the small tobacco shop, his fate was sealed. The hungry flames devoured everything, a haze of tart tobacco smoke making the neighborhood smell like an all-night saloon.

"They always tell you smoking kills," said Calvin James when they were under way.

"Bad habits die hard," Gary Manning replied, getting into the mood. Dark humor as sedative in the wake of mortal combat.

Ari Lev cut through the gallows banter with a question. "Shall we try the Bekaa now?"

Beside him, sandwiched between the driver and his younger countryman, Katz thought about it, nodding.

And said, "Why not?"

Medellín, Colombia

THEY HAD DRAWN STRAWS to see who got the high ground, and the Ironman won... if you could call it winning. Still, he would prefer to be the triggerman instead of standing watch downstairs, where Pol and Gadgets had him covered on the street, ensuring his chance to get away.

It was a relatively simple set, all things considered. Lyons on the rooftop with a Walther WA2000 sniper's rifle, sighting through the Schmidt and Bender scope. His target, one block down, was the revolving door of an office building on the far side of the street.

The weapon was a futuristic bullpup model, relatively small and light, chambered for the mighty .300 Winchester Magnum cartridge. It would drop a charging grizzly, if a gunner used it properly, and Lyons's target was a good deal smaller than a bear—though you could make a case for savagery beyond his size.

Specifically the mark was one Antonio Ruiz Aldrete, ranked among the best—or worst—lieutenants of the Gaviria drug cartel. He kept an office in the building, fronting as a travel agent, and a phone call had confirmed that he was in this afternoon. The rest of it was waiting with the rifle, staking out the doorway, waiting for the chosen target to appear.

It was approaching four o'clock when Lyons saw the limo pull up to the curb and fill a red no-parking zone. The men who scrambled out were packing hardware underneath their tailored jackets, ditto with the pair who came out through the glass revolving door a moment later. Lyons had the shot lined up and waiting when Ruiz appeared, his soldiers having checked the street and told him it was clear.

Not quite.

The .300 Winchester Magnum blasts off at 2,680 feet per second, dropping to just under 2,230 feet per second at a range of two hundred yards. Destructive energy is also lost along the way, but the 220-grain projectile still impacts its target with more than 2,400 foot-pounds at a distance of two football fields.

Enough to do the job, and then some.

Lyons took a breath and held it, squeezing off the first shot in his own good time, his cross hairs fixed below Ruiz's chin. There was little or no drop at two hundred yards, the bullet drilling through Ruiz's larynx with the force of a sledgehammer, nearly severing his head before it lifted him completely off his feet.

The dead man landed on his back, blood gushing from his mangled throat. Around him gunners drew their weapons, looking for a target in vain. The Ironman could have dropped them where they stood, but he let it go. No point in giving them a fix on his position when he could use the time to make his getaway.

He broke the rifle down, returned it to the black athletic bag, scooped up the single cartridge case and dropped it in his pocket as he put the roof behind him. Lyons passed by the elevator and took the stairs. More time involved, but there would be less chance of meeting someone.

He found Schwarz waiting for him at the cabstand, in the yellow taxi they had rented for a day. Pol got in at the intersection, still a hundred yards removed from where a crowd had gathered, gawking at Ruiz.

"Eduardo won't be happy," Gadgets said.

"That's the price you pay for fame," said Lyons.

"I'll be interested to see who takes the heat," the Politician said.

Carl Lyons smiled. "I wouldn't be surprised," he said, "if there's enough to go around."

CHAPTER ELEVEN

San Sebastián, Spain

A blood feud knows no boundaries of time or place. The execution of Antonio Silveira in Mataró had unleashed a savage hatred in his brother's heart for the assassins of the ETA. Revenge was sweet, and now Jose Dieguez Silveira meant to eat his fill.

In fact, Manuel Orozco realized, no trigger incident was needed for the leader of the ANE to send his troops against the left-wing ETA. Silveira hated Basques and socialists on principle, as if their mere existence was a personal affront. His father, as a colonel in the fascist army, had conducted numerous interrogations of subversives prior to General Franco's death. More than a few of those were Basque, and their aggressive handling by Colonel Gabriel Silveira had prompted his assassination two months after Franco died.

Jose Silveira had been playing catch-up ever since. His brother's death was the latest in a series of attacks that cried out for retaliation.

That was where Manuel Orozco and his four *pistoleros* came in.

Together they formed a veteran guerrilla unit of Acción Nacional Española, with five assassinations and eleven bombings to their credit in the two years they had operated as a team. Most of their targets had been ETA-related, and the present job was no exception.

Alphonse Gogorza had no brothers, but his second cousin tended bar in San Sebastián, at a tavern where the customers were mostly Basque—and all, in the esteemed opinion of Jose Silveira, dedicated socialists. The tavern was a fitting target for Silveira's first act of grand revenge.

They built the bomb with Semtex smuggled in from France, and packed the satchel all around the charge with nails and bits of jagged, rusty scrap iron. The detonator was a radio-controlled device, and Manuel Orozco armed it only at the final moment, as they sat outside the tavern, drawing lots.

Emilio Reynoso won the honor of delivering the bomb. He took the battered leather satchel when he left the car, and disappeared inside the tavern. If he was asked about the bag, he would pretend to be a traveler, newly arrived in San Sebastián and in need of several drinks before he started looking for a place to stay. Most likely, thought Orozco, no one in the place would give the stranger or his bag a second glance.

Of course, there was an outside chance he would be challenged by the bouncer, known to be an active member of the ETA. In that event, Reynoso had a pistol tucked inside his waistband, at the back. He wouldn't hesitate to use it, drop his adversary where he stood and leave the bomb behind him when he fled.

Orozco sat and watched the tavern with the detonator in his lap.

Ten minutes passed.

Fifteen.

After twenty-two minutes Reynoso left the tavern, casually retraced his steps and climbed into the car. The satchel with the Semtex charge was nowhere to be seen.

"The cousin?" asked Orozco.

"Tending bar, like always," said Reynoso. "I made sure to sit down by the register, where he spends half his time."

"How many others?"

"Besides the bouncer, five or six. It's early yet."

"It's late enough," Orozco said.

He raised the radio transmitter, aimed its short antenna at the tavern and depressed the button with his thumb. The blast was instantaneous, a giant fist that punched up through the ceiling, through the red tiles on the roof. Was that a human torso airborne with the rest of the debris?

Orozco blinked, and it was gone. A pall of smoke had settled on the tavern, bright flames licking from the great hole in the roof. The parking lot was bright with glass from shattered windows, and the door lay thirty feet beyond its frame, the top side black and scorched.

He could hear a woman screaming inside the tavern, while a man competed with her for attention, alternately crying out to God for help and cursing Him. Along the street pedestrians and passing motorists were slowing down to watch the action, several stopping altogether in their morbid curiosity.

A short man staggered out of the tavern, took a few steps in the parking lot before he crumpled, falling on his face. His hair was smoking, and his right arm had been severed at the shoulder, drenching that whole side with blood. The man was not Gogorza's cousin, and Orozco did not recognize his face from any of the ANE's most recent "wanted" bulletins, but he was bound to be an enemy.

Past tense.

A siren began wailing. "Let's go," Orozco said, "before someone starts taking license numbers."

Driving east, they passed the first patrol car, followed by another and another. Inside each car grim-faced officers held automatic weapons.

It was a swift response, but not quite swift enough.

Manuel Orozco lit a cigarette and smiled, imagining his next assignment.

The Bekaa Valley, Lebanon

THE VALLEY HAS A WAY of taking new arrivals by surprise. They come with preconceived ideas, most of them gleaned from media reports and hasty sessions with a Rand McNally atlas. They come expecting craggy peaks and razor wire, scorched earth, a no-man's land where rival warlords fight pitched battles over politics, religion, simple greed.

The Bekaa has all that ... and much, much more.

For openers it is a valley, not a canyon. The topography is more akin to California's fertile San Joaquin than to the rugged cliffs and foaming rapids of an old adventure yarn. The Bekaa has absorbed its share of blood and then some in the past two decades, but its residents still continue farming and raising livestock, living hand-to-mouth as they have always done. The fact that some of them grow opium these days, instead of olives and tobacco, does not represent a basic change in life-style. Palestinians and Shiites build their camps, patrol and train for doomsday, but their raids are typically directed toward the state of Israel or at targets on the coast, in Sidon or Beirut. On balance the occupation troops from Syria have been no more vicious or corrupt than native Lebanese in uniform, but they are more efficient, less concerned with internecine warfare, better armed and better fed.

A casual observer might traverse the Bekaa Valley and dismiss it as another backward farming district where the famous Arab passions sometimes run amok, no worse or better than similar regions in Egypt, Jordan, Syria or Turkey.

The men of Phoenix Force had found two Army-surplus jeeps in Sidon, purchased them for cash, no questions asked. Both the vehicles had seen better days, but had been maintained in decent running order, and the tires were almost new. With three men to a jeep, including Ari Lev, their odds of being trapped and pinned down by the enemy were cut in half.

Their outfits were guerrilla casual, a mix of denim, khaki and traditional. The ethnic mix was not a problem in this valley where Africans, Asians and Latin Americans often dropped in for periods of training at the Palestinian guerrilla camps. If they were stopped and challenged, there were automatic rifles, submachine guns, pistols and grenades within the easy reach of every man, secured with their survival gear and camouflage fatigues.

How many raids against his homeland had begun right here, in the forbidding Bekaa Valley? Yakov Katzenelenbogen wondered. Swift Israeli jets struck back from time to time, but taking out a solitary camp—or several, for that matter—was like spitting on a forest fire. The whole damned valley was a refuge for the kind of terrorists who thrive on hate and live to kill, each faction working overtime to raise a brand-new generation of committed true believers for the cause.

It was a shame, Katz thought, that someone could not stage an "accident," perhaps unload some nerve gas "by mistake," and send the Bekaa's whole damned population straight to Hell. It was a chilling thought—

Katz realized that the innocent would have to suffer with the guilty—but the Bekaa's "innocent" inhabitants were those who fed and sheltered the guerrillas, labored on the opium plantations and betrayed intruders to the execution squads.

So much for innocence.

The roadblock had been thrown up in a hurry, two old flatbeds pulled across the unpaved track, with Arab gunners lounging in the meager shade. It was the kind of ad hoc checkpoint sometimes thrown up in the Bekaa with a specific fugitive in mind, or more often on a whim, by terrorists or bandits looking for a motorist to rob. A pennant drooping from the radio antenna of the flatbed on his left told Katz these thugs were Shiites, members of the armed militia, probably assigned to squeeze a "revolutionary tax" from hapless passersby.

It was too late to turn around without inviting hot pursuit. McCarter slowed the jeep, several members of the Shiite party scrambling to their feet and hoisting weapons as the vehicles approached their checkpoint. Katzenelenbogen slipped a hand between his knees and found the folding-stock Kalashnikov.

As they stopped, a mouthpiece for the Shiites stepped up to scrutinize McCarter and his passengers. The young man held an AK-47 leveled at the empty space between Katz and McCarter, finger on the trigger. It would be a tricky shot to drop him where he stood before he had a chance to open fire.

And that would be McCarter's job.

The Englishman was smiling, leaning forward, covering the double-action Browning automatic in his hand. The Shiite mouthpiece barked an order, waggling the AK-47's snout for emphasis, demanding their ID.

And there would be no better time.

Katz saw it coming, brought his rifle up and twisted to the right, a moving target as McCarter raised the Browning, pumping two quick rounds into the startled Shiite's chest. The young man staggered backward, fell. Katz hit the ground at the same time, the jeep between them, facing toward the enemy.

He didn't realize that he was smiling when it hit the fan and everybody opened fire at once.

Alava Province, Spain

THE CAR WAS TAKING HITS as Bolan slid into the turn and nearly lost it, grappling with the wheel. Behind him came the pop and crack of semiautomatic fire, the high-pitched rattle of a submachine gun, swept away by speed on the erratic downhill run.

A winding highway in the Pyrenees would not have been his first choice for a running battle, but a soldier didn't always have a choice. Sometimes coincidence or fate took over, and you simply had to play the cards as they were dealt.

Like now.

The hit outside Vitoria had come apart almost before it started. Bolan had been cruising for a local captain of the ETA, Juan Gavilan, preparing for a drop-in at the shooter's home, when he was spotted by a scouting team of Basque commandos. There was no way to disguise the Mini-Uzi in his hand, no decent opportunity to stand and fight, so he had opted for retreat, the gunners close behind him all the way.

They were getting closer, running up behind him, peppering his car with bullets, falling back a few lengths when he tapped the brakes or veered around a mountain curve at breakneck speeds. Still, these were local boys, raised in the mountains, and he had no realistic hope of ditching them without a stand-up fight.

The problem was deciding where and when to make his stand.

The mountain road was barely two lanes wide. A compact car could make a U-turn if the driver had sufficient nerve, but there were no convenient turnouts, secondary roads or villages until the highway reached Bilbao. That, in turn, would mean a shoot-out in the streets, with innocent civilians caught up in the cross fire.

No.

He had to lose the tail before it went that far.

At first the gray sedan approaching from the north was simply more bad luck, an obstacle to be avoided. Only when it came abreast did Bolan see the startled faces, half a dozen men, some pointing at the car behind him, weapons heaving into view.

He cursed and took the car around another hairpin curve, the chase car momentarily obscured from view. Now he had *two* cars on his tail, a dozen guns instead of five or six.

He shrugged the anger off, dismissing it as unproductive—suicidal if he let it cloud his thinking. At the moment every ounce of concentration was reserved for staying on the narrow road, avoiding bullets, looking for a place to turn and make his stand.

As if in answer to a silent prayer, the road ahead of him ran arrow straight for something like a quarter of a mile. The grade was still downhill, and steep at that, but anything was better than the winding curves.

In front of him, downrange, there was a scenic turnout on his left, forgotten from his first pass, heading for

Vitoria. It would be close, he realized. Too much momentum, and his car might vault the stone retaining wall and plunge eight thousand feet to rocky crags below.

And if he got it right...what then? The odds were ten or twelve to one, and there would be no cover for the Executioner beyond his ventilated compact. Still...

He saw both cars behind him now, and registered a puff of gun smoke from the second car in line. It was a stupid move on someone's part, trying to shoot past their friends, but maybe he could take advantage of that negligence.

The gravel turnout rushed to meet him. Bolan stepped on the brake and cranked hard left on the steering wheel, putting his car through a screeching half turn, rubber smoking on the asphalt as he slid toward the wall of stone.

And stopped, with something like a yard to spare.

He bailed out on the passenger's side, putting the car between himself and his enemies, dragging the Uzi and gym bag behind him. They might kill him here, but he would not go down without a fight, and some of them were going with him one way or another.

Men in both cars fired as they skidded in to meet him, and Bolan realized that the gunners in the second vehicle had not been firing *past* his Basque pursuers, after all. As they unloaded, bodies scrambling for nonexistent cover, Bolan saw that they were firing on each other, two men falling in the cross fire, then a third.

It clicked for Bolan then, with crystal clarity. The gunners in the second car were ANE, come hunting for a nice Basque target in Vitoria. Their timing was a fluke, however providential it turned out to be for Bolan. They had joined the running fight, assuming any target of the

ETA to be a friend of theirs. Now, as Bolan watched, they seemed intent on wiping out the common enemy.

Both sides were taking hits as Bolan reached inside his gym bag, fishing out a frag grenade. He yanked the pin and pitched it overhand at the farthest vehicle. It struck the hood, spun briefly like a top, then wobbled to the fender, dropping out of sight behind the car.

The three ANE commandos may have seen it coming, but they had no time to run. Three seconds, give or take, before the stunning blast and ripping shrapnel sent them to their just reward.

That left two Basque gunners to contend with, crouching with their backs toward Bolan, momentarily preoccupied. No opportunity for them to readjust their thinking, try to save themselves, before the Uzi cut loose on their flanks, a stream of parabellum shockers ripping flesh and fabric, turning vital organs into lifeless meat.

The cleanup took another forty seconds, Bolan keeping one eye on the road to watch for passing vehicles. He checked each man in turn, found three still breathing, and he gave each one of them a silent mercy round between the eyes.

He would have to ditch the car and find another set of wheels, but he could do that in Bilbao. The rest of it was perfect, rival gunmen slaughtered on the highway, most of the ballistics easily confirmed from weapons scattered at the scene. If anybody stopped to think about the missing Uzi, they would blame the ANE, assuming one or more combatants had escaped.

Sometimes, thought Bolan, you get lucky.

But he could not count on lightning striking twice.

From this point on he had to make his own luck, get it right the first time every time.

The one and only definite alternative was sudden death.

Medellín, Colombia

THE DAY WAS WINDING DOWN, and it couldn't end soon enough to suit Brent Favor. He was tired of taking phone calls from the war zone, turning on the radio and hearing all about the latest massacre of leftists, neo-fascists, narco smugglers.

Twelve years with the DEA, the past two in Colombia, and he had never witnessed anything to match the past twelve hours. It was punch and brutal counter-punch, with twenty-seven dead so far by Favor's count. God only knew how many were missing from the tally or how many more would join the list before the sun rose again in Medellín.

A part of him rebelled at naming targets for the troubleshooters sent by Uncle Sam, but he had come up through the ranks the hard way, taking orders that were sometimes difficult to understand, sometimes illegal to perform, and he had never turned his back on duty yet. Deep down, where his emotions went to hide while he was on the job, he felt a grudging admiration for the trio who had cut through all the red-tape bullshit of the legal system, using deadly force exactly when and where you would expect the optimum results.

It was an atavistic kick to watch them work, no doubt about it, and he also felt a certain brutal satisfaction, knowing in his heart that he had gotten more done in the past twelve hours, taking heavy hitters off the street, than in the past twelve years of operating strictly by the book.

If he had to bend the rules a little—even throw them out the window for a day or two—to put some balance back in the equation, that was fine. So far, the only people harmed were those deserving endless prison time or worse.

Who made the rules, anyway? Politicians. And what politicians knew about reducing crime might fill a pamphlet if you padded it with pompous speeches in the House and Senate. What they did not know and didn't *want* to know would fill a new *Encyclopedia Britannica* from *A* to *Z,* with print so fine you had to read it with a microscope.

They had a "drug czar" now in Washington, and things were worse than last year, infinitely worse than when Brent Favor had taken his job with DEA. There seemed to be no end in sight. Most days he felt as if he were bailing the *Titanic* with a teacup, keeping up a front for no one in particular.

But not today.

Today he felt as if he was fighting back.

The motorcycle came up on his blind side, weaving in and out through traffic, swinging toward the curb with thirty yards to go. The driver of a brand-new taxi saved him, leaning on his horn and cursing the bikers riding double, causing Brent to glance across his shoulder.

Just in time.

He saw the Ingram MAC-10 pointed at his face and sprinted for the nearest doorway, clutching at the Ruger KP91 he carried in an armpit holster. Crouching as the gunner on the pillion opened fire, he tracked the speeding motorcycle, feeling chips of concrete sting his face, and squeezed off two quick rounds while there was time.

A lucky hit. The driver lost it, plowed into a family sedan and vaulted gracefully across the handlebars. He rolled across the trunk of the sedan and dropped off into traffic, vanishing beneath the wheels of a delivery van.

The passenger had gone down with the bike but he recovered swiftly, came up shooting, momentarily disoriented, searching for his target. Favor got there first and put a third round through the gunner's chest from twenty paces.

Done. He didn't feel the rush until he realized it was over. He was still alive, unhurt except for scratches on his cheek and forehead.

Jesus.

Favor tucked his pistol out of sight and sat down in the doorway, listening for sirens.

CHAPTER TWELVE

Tudela, Spain

Grimaldi had grown tired of waiting on the sidelines, and the near miss in Alava Province had confirmed his apprehension. Now, with Bolan safe beside him in their new wheels, rolling through a residential district on the outskirts of Tudela, he felt more at ease.

Not easy yet, but getting there.

They still had far to go before they wrapped up the action in Spain, and it wouldn't be over, in Grimaldi's mind, until they caught the big bird home and put the continent behind them. Bolan had been on a roll so far, but any winning streak could fail, and when your life was riding on the line, one loss was all it took to close the show.

"Lozaro pegged this guy as ETA?" Grimaldi asked as they were pulling out of town, hilly countryside ahead of them.

"Affirmative," said Bolan. "He's low-profile, but the confirmation comes from Interpol. They've marked him as a player in at least three major arms deals that they're sure of. Say another two or three for every one they made, and you'll be closer to the mark."

"Why don't they take him down?"

"The information was delivered by a confidential source inside the ETA," said Bolan. "Think of what it took to find a contact, much less turn him over. No one wants to waste him on a smuggling case when they can bide their time and try to wrap the whole thing up.''

"And he's been working on it how long?" asked Grimaldi.

Bolan smiled. "I didn't ask. You know how these things go. It's never good enough. You're always one brick short of finishing the wall.''

"And they don't mind us playing in the brickyard?"

"Once again I didn't ask.''

"Good thinking.''

Two miles from Tudela, driving west, they found the turnoff for a narrow, unpaved road that wound back toward a farmhouse some three hundred yards removed. Grimaldi drove on past, accelerating for another quarter mile, until he found another side road on the left and took it, bouncing over ruts that made the Volvo rattle.

"This should do it.''

They were well back from the highway, sheltered by a line of trees that had been planted as a windbreak decades earlier. It was approaching dusk when Jack Grimaldi parked and killed the engine, stepping out to stretch his legs. Another moment and he had the trunk lid open, helping Bolan sort the gear.

"He wouldn't normally be guarded,'' Bolan said, "but these days...''

"I'll keep both eyes open,'' said Grimaldi, picking out a SPAS-12 automatic shotgun. He slipped a belt of cartridges around his neck and worked the shotgun's slide to put a live round in the firing chamber. "Ready.''

Bolan took the FA MAS, locked the car and struck off to the east, across an open meadow. By the time they reached a wooden fence and climbed it, night was coming on. Ahead of them the farmhouse had warm lights in the windows, and there was a whiff of wood smoke on the wind.

The guards weren't immediately obvious, but they were present all the same. Grimaldi counted four of them before he finished off his recon and regrouped with Bolan near the barn that had been converted into a garage.

"There could be more inside," he said.

"I'll take the chance."

"So, what's the plan?" Grimaldi asked.

"Straight up the middle," Bolan said. "No fancy footwork."

"Right."

Grimaldi gave the Executioner a lead of several seconds, circling back around the barn to find the perfect vantage point. Two guards were visible from where he stood in shadow, and he had a clear fix on a third. The fourth was on the far side of the house, and Bolan wouldn't meet him going in. Once they had started making noise, however, all the bets were off.

When gunfire sounded from the house, Grimaldi knew what had to be done. The nearest sentry, on his left, was turning toward the sound, unlimbering his submachine gun, when Grimaldi hit him with a charge of buckshot in the chest. At that range it was fatal, and he didn't have to double-check.

Instead, he drew a bead on Number Two and caught him breaking for the house, his concentration broken by the close-range shotgun blast. Another moment and he would have spied his fallen comrade. The SPAS-12 bucked against Grimaldi's shoulder, and a dozen buckshot pellets raked his human target from the chest down to his knees.

Number Three fired a warning shot at no one in particular, and by the time Grimaldi found his mark, the sentry was emerging from a shed behind the house. If he had gone the other way, Grimaldi would have had to chase him. He met him with a single blast from thirty feet and slammed him backward like a scarecrow in a hurricane, his body twitching briefly where it lay before his muscles finally relaxed in death.

It seemed to be all over in the house, and Bolan was retreating when the final lookout showed. They all cut loose at once, two marksmen scoring, while the third pitched over on his side, the AK-47 in his hands unloading one last burst into the spotty lawn.

"All clear?" Grimaldi asked.

"We're done. Let's go."

The fields were dark and silent as they walked back to the car.

The Bekaa Valley, Lebanon

THE SHIITE DIED without a fuss, two bullets in the chest, and down he went as if his bones had turned to jelly. Everything exploded after that, McCarter springing from the jeep, taking the AK-74 with him, ducking as he waddled through the raging cross fire.

On the left side of the road was a ditch. McCarter got there, rolling into brittle, straggling weeds. He risked a glance back at the roadblock, counting heads as best he could, and estimated there were nine or ten Shiite guerrillas still alive and fighting.

One of them was manning a Russian PKB machine gun, firing short, erratic bursts while a companion fed the belted ammunition in by hand. He started off by firing high and wide, but then his fourth burst raked the jeep where Katzenelenbogen crouched, returning fire as best he could with his Kalashnikov.

Rising from a crouch, McCarter braced his Browning double-action pistol in a firm two-handed grip and squeezed off four quick shots. Behind the PKB, he saw his target stiffen, lurching backward, slumping. The heavy weapon followed his direction, hosing down the empty desert for about a second and a half before it started peppering the flatbed's empty cab. About that time the belt jammed in the feed tray, twisted somehow, and the piece fell silent.

Suddenly afraid, the gunner's mate attempted to bail out. McCarter shot him twice between the shoulder blades, an easy double tap from fifty feet, and watched him topple from the truck bed.

McCarter dodged back under cover, holstering his pistol, scooping up his rifle from the weeds. A couple of the Shiites had him spotted now, their bullets raising dust along the berm and whining into empty space as ricochets. McCarter kept his head down, checking out the ditch and wondering how long he had before the opposition recognized a danger on their flank.

The ditch ran on as far as he could see, a small concession to the rains that fell in torrents when they fell at all. By crawling thirty yards or so, McCarter reckoned he could place himself behind the roadblock, bring the Shiites under fire from that direction. He could also kill a few of them at least, and manage to distract the rest while his companions moved out front.

It sounded easy, which immediately told McCarter he would have to watch his ass.

He started creeping through the weeds, no rush about it, trying not to give himself away by raising dust. A scorpion ran in front of him, took one look at Mc-

Carter and retreated to its hole. He let it go, ignoring
thorns and ants and all the other inconveniences that
came with crawling on your belly in a drainage ditch
while bullets whispered overhead.

At least his enemies were firing at the place where he
had started. That was something, an indication that
they had not guessed his plan. The guns were hammering on both sides of the roadblock, someone crying out
in pain, but it wasn't a voice McCarter recognized.

An enemy, in that case. Good enough.

He had to estimate the distance, since he dared not
poke his head above the weeds to check his progress. He
had covered something more than half the distance
necessary when a Shiite gunner dropped into the ditch
about twenty feet in front of him.

The Arab fumbled with his submachine gun but never
had a fighting chance. McCarter hit him with a 3-round
burst that flipped the young man over on his back and
left him sprawling in the weeds.

If anybody on the roadblock noticed the exchange,
they gave no sign. Caught up in dueling with the men of
Phoenix Force, the Shiites concentrated on the targets
they could see, apparently believing that they had
McCarter pinned down at his starting point, afraid to
move.

He reached the body of his fallen adversary, had no
way to move it, so crawled over the inanimate obstruc-
tion. For a heartbeat they were face-to-face, the young
man's sightless eyes fixed on a point no living man
could see. His blood was on McCarter's clothes before
McCarter made it back to clean, dry earth, curled fingers of a lifeless hand snagging briefly on the laces of
McCarter's boot.

A few more feet and he would be there.

Half expecting a grenade or shout of warning at any time, McCarter was relieved when he had finished the distance, estimating he had reached a point some twenty feet behind the Shiite lines. His rifle still had twenty-seven rounds left in the magazine, but he took time to put in a fresh clip in the Browning, just in case.

McCarter chose an arbitrary number in his mind and started counting backward. Five, four, three, two, *one!*

He was smiling as he came up firing from the ditch.

THE ONE THING Ari Lev despised above all else was hiding from his enemies. He had no choice, of course, when it was two-to-one and they were pouring automatic-weapons fire at his position, spraying anything that moved.

He recognized the Shiite banner, knew them as fanatics and disciples of the late and unlamented Ayatollah in Iran. Jew-haters with a vengeance, certainly, and Ari Lev did not object to killing them...if he could only get the chance.

He risked a peek around the jeep, ducked back as bullets swept the road in front of him. The idiots were wasting ammunition, but they probably had lots to spare, supplied at various times by Tehran, Damascus, Tripoli. Wherever money flowed to terrorists, it seemed, the Shiite crazies got their share.

He had a target spotted, creeping to the east in what appeared to be a flanking move. He gave the Arab points for courage, then deducted some for foolishness, considering the open ground that he would have to cross before he reached a decent vantage point.

There was no sport in picking off a fool, but this was not a game, and Ari Lev would take what he could get.

He led the runner with his automatic rifle, tracking to the right, and squeezed out five bullets. Downrange the Shiite seemed to trip on something, jerking like a spastic to the bullets' impact, going down.

Another of the Shiites opened fire on Ari Lev, one of his bullets spanging off the dusty fender of the jeep. Lev had the shooter spotted, but his target ducked behind the truck and out of sight before Lev found the mark.

Across the road McCarter vanished into the ditch, but there was no cut on the side where Ari Lev was pinned. He wished the British soldier well and cursed his own luck, hunkered down behind the jeep. Their point vehicle had been taking solid hits, but so far, Ari's jeep had only suffered a dozen glancing blows. They would be needing vehicles in working order, but if this kept up...

He palmed a frag grenade, released the safety pin and held the spoon in place. The move he had in mind was dangerous, but no more than sitting where he was until a lucky bullet found the gas tank of the jeep that was his only shelter.

On the east, or right, side of the road, there was a jumbled pile of rock approximately forty feet from where the jeeps had stopped. Lev didn't know if he could make it, but he reckoned he was bound to try.

"I'm going for the rocks," he said to Rafael Encizo, crouched beside him in the shadow of the jeep.

"Say what?"

"Just cover me."

Before the Cuban could respond, Lev burst from cover, firing his Kalashnikov with one hand, lobbing the grenade high overhead. Several Shiites tried to bring him down, most of them firing from the hip, not aiming well enough to score, the bullets gobbling up his tracks in spurts of dust.

Lev saw the frag grenade bounce off the nearest flatbed's cab and wobble out of sight. A couple of the Shiites took off running, the others too involved in throwing everything they had at Ari Lev to see the danger they were in.

He reached the pile of rocks as the grenade exploded, diving under cover with a swarm of angry hornets on his heels. Lev could not tell how many Shiites perished in the blast, but fewer guns were firing when he raised his head the next time, and he heard at least two voices raised in warbling cries of agony.

So far, so good.

The action shifted then, but it took Lev a moment to understand exactly what had happened. Guns were going off, but most of them were rattling behind the roadblock now instead of firing toward the jeeps.

McCarter! Obviously he had surfaced on their flank, distracting them with enfilading fire.

No time to waste now. Ari Lev was on his feet and running even as the thought clicked home. He covered thirty feet before the Shiites saw him coming, one of them recoiling from the stream of bullets pouring out of his Kalashnikov.

Too late.

The gunner went down on his face, two others pivoting to face the unexpected danger on their flank. Behind Lev the remaining men of Phoenix Force were charging into battle, firing as they came, but he ignored them, concentrating on his targets. Both men down, another swiveling to face him, when Lev realized his rifle's magazine was empty.

Snarling like an animal, he charged the Shiite gunner, crushed his thick nose with the butt of the Kalashnikov, continuing to club him as the gunner fell. Instead of trying to reload the rifle, Lev drew his Beretta, pumping two rounds through the face of a young Arab with a submachine gun smoking in his hands.

Another moment saw it done, the Phoenix warriors mopping up at point-blank range. Lev counted thirteen dead men once the crimson haze of battle lifted from his eyes, and he began to help his comrades drag the bodies off the road.

The jeep that Katz had driven in was finished, water streaming from its punctured radiator, two tires flattened. The second jeep, to everyone's immense relief, was scarred but functional, its engine turning over on the first attempt.

"We'll take the smaller truck," Katz said when they discovered it was more or less unharmed. "At least it seats three men. Let's clear the rest of this away."

Another seven minutes put them on the road, with Ari Lev inside the flatbed, following McCarter's jeep. The rush of combat had subsided now, replaced by apprehension as he started ticking off the miles.

Round one had gone their way, but it was merely a preliminary bout. The main event was still ahead, and they were likely to be ranged against an army rather than a baker's dozen of excited, poorly trained guerrillas.

Never mind.

It was a soldier's lot to fight one battle at a time, and let the future take care of itself.

For now it was enough for Ari Lev to be alive.

Medellín, Colombia

COCA BASE was normally produced in a jungle lab consisting of a shallow ditch, a plastic liner and some caustic chemicals. But refinement of the crude base into pure cocaine was more an urban art form, practiced in a setting where the temperature and ventilation were controlled and purity assured, armed guards on standby to prevent an interruption of the process that turned poison into gold.

One such facility was operating on the third floor of an aging tenement in Medellín, a mile from police headquarters in the heart of town. The building had been marked for demolition several years ago, but it had yet to face the wrecking ball, and squatters had been warned off by the hard-eyed men who frequented the premises.

The recent move on Favor had convinced Pol Blancanales that the drug cartel deserved some more attention going in. The two dead shooters had been readily identified as members of Eduardo Gaviria's network, though they sometimes free-lanced if the price was right. In this case, it didn't require a rocket scientist to figure out that Gaviria was retaliating for the recent blows against his family and friends, including Favor on his list of targets.

And two could play that game.

Pol took the fire escape, while Schwarz and Lyons went in from the street. All three of them were armed with silenced MP-5 SD-3 submachine guns and their favored side arms, extra magazines tucked into belts and pockets where they would be readily available. Pol also had a flash-bang stun grenade clipped on his belt, to get the enemy's attention when he made his entrance from the fire escape.

The windows had been painted over on the first three floors, but no one bothered with the other three, their altitude eliminating peepers as a matter of concern. The paint helped Blancanales as he scaled the rusty fire escape, no way for guards inside to spot him going up. His friends would have it worse, approaching from the street, six flights of stairs, but they could handle it.

God knows, the two of them had handled worse.

Outside the third-floor window, Blancanales waited another thirty seconds. His comrades should be off the street by now, proceeding up the stairs and dropping any guards they met along the way. No sounds of gunfire yet, which told him that the enemy was either napping or the sentries Schwarz and Lyons met had fallen victim to silent gunfire.

Time.

He primed the stun grenade, reared back and pitched it through the nearest painted window, hastily retreating several paces down the fire escape, well clear of flying glass. The shock of the concussion was pretty much contained by walls of brick and mortar, but Blancanales knew the stunning impact it would have on those inside.

Pol slipped his gas mask into place and vaulted up the stairs, ducked through the open window frame, his submachine gun leading. Dust and smoke were everywhere, white crystals swirling in the murk as mounted floodlights tried to reestablish dominance. He counted four men down, three of them wearing lab coats, one a bruiser in a stylish suit who writhed across the floor, hands clasped against his ears.

The lab was trashed, a wreck of broken glass and scattered plastic baggies, ether and other assorted chemicals unleashed from their containers. The atmosphere was close to toxic now; it would become explosive in a few more moments, as the ether fumes spread.

Pol made the rounds and fired a short burst into each man lying on the floor. A door flew open as he finished the fourth, and two thugs barged in, waving guns, their concentration fading as they gagged on the corrosive atmosphere of plaster dust, cocaine and smoke.

They might have choked to death right there, but Blancanales didn't take the chance. Instead, he shot both gunners and watched them fall together, dying side by side.

Another shadow filled the doorway, and his submachine gun rose to meet the challenge, but Blancanales recognized Carl Lyons through the gas mask, Gadgets close behind him. Lyons took in the scene at a glance, held up his hand, thumb folded, waggling four fingers.

Four dead men downstairs, and they were clear.

Pol joined his comrades for the short trip down. Their gas masks off before they reached the street, they jogged back to their waiting car.

"You think Eduardo's smart enough to read between the lines?" asked Lyons.

"Does it matter?" Blancanales countered.

Lyons thought about it, smiled and said, "Hell no."

CHAPTER THIRTEEN

Washington, D.C.

Brognola dropped the telephone receiver in its cradle, leaned back in his swivel chair and wished the goddamned air-conditioning had not shut down at half past twelve. His office windows didn't open, having been designed apparently with civil-service suicides in mind, and he had sweated through his shirt. A cup of coffee, tepid, sat untouched beside his intercom.

The news from Stony Man wasn't designed to keep Brognola cool and even tempered. None of it was bad exactly, but the action had been heating up to such a point that Hal could feel it slipping out of his control. The drug cartel's attempt to kill a federal agent in Colombia was one suggestion of the crisis yet to come, but he could say the same for late events reported out of Lebanon and Spain.

Control was an illusion, Hal decided. From the moment Bolan and the others left their base at Stony Man, Brognola was reduced to helping with logistics and support, a string pulled here and there. But he was out of touch with action on the ground until reports came in...and by the time that happened, the events were history.

Sometimes Brognola missed the old days, when he had been working in the field, coordinating moves against the Mafia and making arrests himself. It was a different game these days, with all-new rules and players. Few of Hal Brognola's targets went to jail, for one thing. He had gotten used to that part of the job, the killing, and accepted it as necessary. He imagined it was how a military officer must feel, committing men to battle, knowing that his orders would result in violent death for men he knew and others he would never meet in life.

The violence was a part of it, all right, but there was more. Back in the days when he was focused solely on the organized-crime beat, the rip-offs and conspiracies he dealt with had been ninety-eight percent domestic. Foreign mobsters stuck their noses in from time to time, and there was always politics, sometimes involving other nations, but Brognola always felt the battlefield was limited in scope.

Not so today.

The world might be another fellow's oyster, but to Hal it was a ticking time bomb, ready to explode and take him with it if he let his guard down even for a moment. Life and liberty depended on eternal vigilance... and the ability to kick some butt when kicking was required.

He thought about the news from Stony Man and tried to sort it out by theaters of action. Able Team was closest to the nest, locked in a three-way struggle with the drug cartel, a group of homegrown fascists and the troops of M-19. Divide and conquer was the game plan, but a plan could turn around and bite you on the ass in nothing flat if you were careless. Even if you weren't, sometimes things just went against you on the streets.

In Lebanon the men of Phoenix Force had found an unexpected ally in their war against the Thunderbolt. Brognola hoped the new kid on the block didn't turn out to be a handicap when all was said and done. Mossad produced efficient operatives, but you didn't pick up teamwork overnight. Some things were learned only through repetition, experience or trial and error. In the Bekaa Valley's killing fields, he knew, the margin for admissible error was whisper thin.

Six men against an army, and one of them was green in terms of working with the other five, perhaps antagonistic to their goal or jealous of the fact that he would have to share. If Ari Lev became a problem for the mission, Hal would trust in Katz, McCarter and the rest to weed him out before he damaged anything beyond repair.

And that left Spain.

He knew that Striker and Grimaldi had the situation covered going in, but terrorism in the Pyrenees broke all the rules. Instead of clear-cut guidelines, black and white, you had innumerable shades of gray. The Basques had spent long decades fighting to be rid of Franco; then, when he was gone, they pledged unending war against the new democracy before it had a chance to prove itself. Toss in the hard-line fascists who regarded Franco's reign of terror as the good old days, and you had set the stage for internecine warfare on an epic scale, with innocent civilians pinned down in the cross fire, frightened to express themselves on politics, religion and the like.

Behind all three campaigns lay the source of Hal Brognola's tension, festering like a malignant abscess in Iraq. It was beyond the scope of his authority to solve that problem by removal of the man in charge—Brognola had already asked—but he would do the best he could, within the limits set by White House policy.

The limits that civilians placed on soldiers.

Hell, he was all in favor of elected chief executives, and there were few things worse than a police state or a military junta, in Brognola's view. But sometimes, when you had to settle every question by committee, and the members of your panel were a pack of spineless, money-grubbing politicians who could never force themselves to look beyond their own careers or the next election ... well, he understood the impulse toward revolt, armed force, solutions that exploded from the barrel of a gun.

The trick, Brognola thought, was knowing where to draw the line and sticking by your own resolve. At least, that seemed to be the neatest trick in Washington.

Out there, where Bolan and the others were confronting hostile guns right now, the trick was simply getting home alive.

Olot, Spain

ALPHONSE GOGORZA had begun to dread bad news. It was a fact of life for revolutionaries trapped in modern Spain, of course, but he was vain enough to think it should be different. When he planned an operation, sent his best men, he wanted results.

He thought of Sanchez and his people taking out Silveira's brother. That had been a job well done, but it was coming back to haunt Gogorza now. His cousin had been killed in San Sebastián by the ANE, along with six or seven others he had never met. Gogorza would not miss the cousin much, but the inevitable phone call claiming credit for the tavern bombing had been quite specific as to motives, mentioning Gogorza's name and linking him to other outrageous crimes.

The fact that each and every charge was accurate meant nothing to Gogorza. It was the embarrassment that rankled, knowing that the full account would be reprinted in the evening papers, broadcast over radio and television for days. They had the caller's voice on tape, and he was getting air play from Madrid to the Balearic Islands. Anyone in Spain who did not know Gogorza personally would believe he was a savage animal, and there was nothing he could do to shut the bastard up.

But he could still retaliate.

That's how the game was played, when terrorists—or freedom fighters—went to war among themselves. No holds were barred, and the only fair fight was the one you survived, with troops and honor more or less intact.

Gogorza had been working on a death list since Ramon Aguirre brought the news about his cousin and the rest in San Sebastián. His files contained the names of most ANE members in the country, information gleaned from spies and backyard gossip over several years. Beginning with Jose Silveira and descending through the ranks to lowly triggermen, Gogorza reckoned that he could identify some eighty-five percent of the committed neo-fascists operating in the eastern half of Spain.

But he would not stop there.

The ANE was dangerous in terms of individual attacks, but there was still the question of official aid and comfort to the enemy. Gogorza had no doubt that many—most—of the police and military still in uniform were doggedly committed to reviving fascist rule, the glory days when they were free to kill and torture with impunity. To that end, they would certainly encourage private raids against the ETA, relying on a Basque retaliation to inflame the Spanish public, raise a cry for the return of martial law.

Gogorza had a grim surprise in store for all of them.

He would retaliate, all right, but his attacks wouldn't be limited to members of the ANE by any means. His new death list included ranking politicians and policemen, judges, so-called journalists...in short, the cream of the establishment. If martial law was coming—and, in truth, Gogorza would have welcomed it, a crisis that would further unify his people—then, by God, he meant to give the fascists ample cause!

Pablo Lozaro had a place of honor on Gogorza's list. The man was nothing in himself, but he had managed to collect a following of lily-livered pacifists who doted on his every word, forever circulating his petitions, writing to their legislators, even marching in the streets to curb the latest wave of violence in Spain. They couldn't understand that nothing would be settled while the Basques were held as subjects of Madrid and fascist agents carried out attacks upon Gogorza's people.

He had given up on educating idiots, the lot of them in love with platitudes that turned his stomach. Peace and understanding. Love and hope. A bright tomorrow for Iberia.

Gogorza would be happy only when his enemies were dead, his people unified and free. To that end, he suspected that the recent troubles might turn out to be a blessing in disguise.

Before this week he had been holding back, eliminating certain targets from his list in the belief that killing them would start a public backlash, working to the detriment of ETA. But now, when he was being set upon by enemies from every side, Gogorza didn't care.

He felt a sense of liberation from the old restraints, as if a burden had been lifted from his shoulders.

It was curious, Gogorza thought, how grave misfortune could be turned around, transformed into a golden opportunity.

He double-checked his list, crossed out a name that he had written halfway down the page and moved it to the top. Ramon Aguirre cocked an eyebrow, frowning as he took the death list from Gogorza's hand.

"I want the first one brought to me alive," Gogorza said. "As for the rest..."

Instead of finishing, Gogorza raised his chin and drew an index finger straight across his throat, from left to right. Aguirre nodded, folded up the list and put it in his pocket.

As you say, Alphonse."

Gogorza had to smile. "Precisely. As I say."

Antioquia Province, Colombia

HE ALWAYS FELT BETTER with a gun in his hand. Eduardo Gaviria supposed that it went back to his childhood, growing up without a father, running with the lawless street gangs in an era when police shot first and didn't bother asking questions, even with a child of nine or ten years old. A knife was useful as an equalizer, but it always came out second best in confrontations with a gun.

The first time Gaviria killed a man, in the midst of a bungled robbery attempt, he had used an ancient Colt .38 Police Positive. It pulled to the right, and you could feel vibrations from a faulty spring each time the hammer fell, but it had done the job.

Today he could afford a better class of weapon, but the thrill was much the same. It was an atavistic, childlike pleasure in the sound and smell of gunfire, the sensation of ultimate power that came with blasting animal and human targets.

Eduardo needed some explosive therapy this afternoon, when everything he touched had gone awry. His gunmen were unable to complete a simple contract on the *gringo federale,* and within short hours of that fiasco he had lost his largest drug refinery in the heart of Medellín. A lesser man would have been paralyzed with helpless rage, but Gaviria still had plans.

And he still had his guns.

He started out with pistols, firing two at once, an aide reloading for him while he riddled man-size silhouettes at twenty paces. When he tired of handguns, Gaviria shifted to an Uzi, firing off three magazines before he tired of its staccato chatter. Moving to his all-time favorite.

The rifle was a Barrett Model 82, a monster chambered for the .50-caliber Browning machine-gun cartridge. It measured sixty-six inches from muzzle to butt, and weighed thirty-seven pounds with its twelve-power telescopic sight in place. A bipod supported the 37-inch barrel, its ventilated muzzle brake designed to reduce the weapon's savage recoil by some thirty percent. Even so, the Barrett's kick was powerful enough to leave Eduardo's shoulder sore, and he could never keep the muzzle down when firing all eleven rounds in rapid semiautomatic mode.

The dealer lay down on a blanket spread by his subordinate, to save his clothes from grass stains while he fired the Barrett from a prone position. No one he knew could fire the rifle standing up, but he was working out with weights these days and building up his strength to make another try.

A few days after he acquired the Barrett, Gaviria had dispatched a raiding party to a native village north of Bello. They had returned with half a dozen Indians, old men and women whom they thought would be useless to the tribe. Eduardo had them bound to trees and broke his new toy in on living targets, thrilling to its thunderous report and the destruction wrought by .50-caliber projectiles ripping human flesh to shreds.

It was amusing, and Eduardo knew that no one would complain about a few dead Indians.

Today he satisfied himself with plywood targets in the shape of men, their faces clipped from magazines and posters, pasted on. Bill Clinton stood beside George Bush, two members of a rival drug cartel immediately on his left. The other four were ranking politicians, currently at large in Bogotá and Medellín.

All enemies. Gaviria had wished them dead a thousand times.

And some of them were still within his reach.

Eduardo took his time and put the Barrett through its paces, squeezing off the 700-grain projectiles with an estimated muzzle velocity of 3,920 feet per second. George Bush was first to feel his wrath, two bullets through the face that fairly tore his wooden head off, three more to cut him apart at the waist.

Flesh and bone were more resilient than the plywood targets, but Eduardo Gaviria would make do with what he had.

For now.

He thought about the young assassins who had muffed their contract on the *gringo federale*. Gaviria would have loved to stake them out and use the two of them for target practice, but the gringo had disposed of them already at the scene. It was a lucky break for all concerned, as such things go. Dead men could not be forced to testify, and the *sicarios* were spared Eduardo's wrath at their pathetic failure.

Still ...

The dealer knew that he would have to act decisively, and soon, to save himself from losing face with his associates—worse yet, with his competitors. The drug trade was an avaricious business, where survival of the fittest was the one prevailing law. If Gaviria started looking weak to those around him, he would soon be overrun by outside competition, not to mention traitors from the ranks of his own family.

He needed some dramatic lesson for his enemies, and soon.

The Barrett's magazine was empty, Bush and Clinton lying side by side in splintered ruins. Gaviria dropped the empty magazine and snapped a fresh one into place. A third face filled his telescopic sight.

And he experienced a revelation, right there on the lawn.

A lesson for his enemies, and anyone who doubted he was still the ruler of his empire.

It was perfect.

For the first time in three days, the dealer smiled.

Baghdad, Iraq

CONSTRUCTION CREWS were clearing rubble from the compound of the late Iraqi intelligence headquarters when Afif al-Takriti rolled past in his chauffeured Mercedes Benz. The American Tomahawk missiles had done their work with typical efficiency, reducing the nerve center of military intelligence to a slag heap of concrete blocks and twisted I beams jutting upward from a crater that reminded al-Takriti of a lunar photograph.

The bastards simply would not let it rest.

It wasn't adequate for the Kuwaitis to shame the Father-Leader and his Revolutionary Guard, still in disarray. With Operation Desert Storm behind them, the nations of the world retained their economic sanctions, starving thousands of Iraqi citizens, and dared to tell Saddam what he could do with his own subjects in Iraq. The northern no-fly zone was a deliberate insult, manufactured to protect the bastard Kurds from punishment for their innumerable crimes against the state. Inspection of Iraqi military plants and nuclear facilities was simply one more way for the United Nations— that is, the United States—to make the Father-Leader of Iraq seem impotent, a child who could be bullied at a whim.

But they would not succeed. Al-Takriti's life was pledged to the defeat of all their schemes.

As long as he avoided any mortal danger to himself.

The way al-Takriti saw it, he had served his time in front-line combat as a young man in the army, risking death daily against Iran, and later, in the struggle for Kuwait. These days he did his killing with a memo or a telephone, long-distance, and he wanted it to stay that way.

It was, in his opinion, only fair.

The status quo had gone from bad to worse these past few hours in Lebanon, Colombia and Spain. His foreign allies—no, make that associates—were under fire on every side, their enemies unknown or theoretically identified as rival terrorists. Al-Takriti, for his part, preferred to look beyond the obvious.

And what he saw was the United States at work, attempting to subvert his master plan.

It was predictable, of course. The instinct for self-preservation was especially well developed in politicians, regardless of their race or nationality. Politicians were parasites, fattening on the blood of the people, but they knew when it was in their own best interests to stand and fight.

As long as someone else did all the dying.

If al-Takriti had his way, that soon would change. The masters of America would learn that they were not invulnerable to attack from those whom they had wronged.

But first he had to help his various associates abroad before they were wiped out. At the very least he must go through the motions of assisting them, so other freedom fighters would respond affirmatively to his overtures in days to come.

Al-Takriti's master plan was still alive and well, in spite of recent setbacks on the foreign front. It wasn't fair to judge his scheme by the inadequacy of the men selected to participate. A game plan could be valid, even when the team was made of pathetic weaklings hopelessly unsuited to style of play.

Al-Takriti had convinced Saddam of that, or thought he had, but it would not take much to change the Father-Leader's mind. Al-Takriti knew enough to cover all his bases just in case.

He had already purchased open tickets under several different names, departing from Saddam International Airport for his special hideaway. It was another challenge, plotting to evade Saddam's unholy vengeance, even as he tried to save the game in its eleventh hour, but al-Takriti was a versatile performer.

A survivor.

He had feelers out to several different revolutionary groups already. They were second-string, the rejects from his first selection, but they all had lethal records. South Moluccans in the Netherlands. The People's Socialist Movement of Germany. The Executive Committee for the Liberation of Palestine. Action for National Liberation in Brazil. A remnant of the Black Liberation Army in America, its members disguised as innocuous "social workers" in the South Bronx of New York.

Al-Takriti had already planned a second summit conference, this one to convene in Syria, where it would be more difficult for Western agents to detect and track invited guests. He had no doubt that representatives from each and every group would be ecstatic at the prospect of financing from Iraq. They might not love Saddam, per se, but all of them were starved for cash and weapons, languishing in revolutionary limbo.

Waiting for a chance to make that one big score.

Al-Takriti was prepared to let them have their opportunity... assuming they were willing to take orders, choose initial targets in accordance with his will. And once the ball was rolling, with an escalating body count around the world, then he could leave them to their own devices.

Failing that, he was prepared to save himself.

Al-Takriti had considered the alternatives, deciding—quite objectively, he thought—that his demise would not provide Iraq with any benefits. Saddam might feel a little better for it, but al-Takriti's personal commitment to the cause stopped short of senseless sacrifice.

At least, when *he* was chosen as the sacrificial lamb.

It wouldn't come to that, he told himself as the Mercedes Benz pulled into his apartment building's underground garage. He would succeed, and he would reap the full rewards deserved by a hero of the state.

He had no doubts.

It was his destiny.

CHAPTER FOURTEEN

Pamplona, Spain

Mention the name, and everyone immediately thinks of eight days in July, the running of the bulls. Thanks to Ernest Hemingway and some selective coverage from the international media, the Festival de San Fermin has come to define Pamplona for millions of foreigners, the way Mardi Gras defines New Orleans or the Carnival defines Rio de Janeiro. Few of the ignorant tourists look beyond a hectic ritual of manhood, the excitement of the chase, to see Pamplona as it really is, or learn its history.

Few of them know that Charlemagne's army, led by Roland, sacked the city and expelled its Moorish conquerors in A.D. 778... or that the knights were later massacred by vengeful Basques for their intrusion. In 1813, at the end of the bloody Peninsular War, Napoleon's defeated army fought its last battle near Pamplona before fleeing across the Pyrenees and home to France. In the 1930s, during Spain's bitter civil war, Pamplona's Navarre Province became a refuge for diehard Loyalists, who never quite surrendered their resistance to Franco's rule of iron.

The war goes on today, between the ETA and neofascist adversaries, both sides punishing the government for its refusal to adopt a radical position on the left or right. Policemen and officials have been mur-

dered, as have taxi drivers, merchants, innocent civilians on the street.

But it is still the running of the bulls that tourists come to see.

Maria Lozaro had grown up in the Spanish war zone, schooled from birth in her father's view of right and wrong, the inherent evil of violence between human beings. She attended his rallies and signed his petitions, sometimes helped to circulate his pamphlets and editorials...but she also wished there could be more to life somehow.

The past few months Maria had been thinking that a change of scene might help. Not western Spain or even France. She needed *out,* away from all the craziness and killing that had somehow trapped her father and become his life. The violence had not truly damaged her as yet, but Maria knew in her heart that it was only a matter of time. If she lingered too long, she would become her father's clone, an activist who seemed to think of nothing but the cause.

She had not quite decided where to go, but she was making plans and saving money, slowly taking leave of what had been her world for the past twenty-two years. It would be difficult, Maria understood, but it was also necessary. Breaking free was part of growing up, becoming a responsible adult individual.

She would be glad when it was time to leave her day job as a tour guide at Pamplona's fifteenth-century cathedral, with its Gothic cloister and diocesan museum of art, the marble tombs of Carlos II of Navarre and his queen. It had been interesting at first, but that had worn off in a week or two. Maria had been parroting the standard lecture, answering insipid questions, for the better part of eighteen months.

It was definitely time to find a change of scene.

That evening, on the short walk back to her apartment, Maria Lozaro had no good reason to suspect she was in danger. There were constant threats against her father for his editorials and speeches, but he seemed to take them all in stride, as if the peril was illusory. As for Maria, she was unaware of any threats against herself and doubted whether there were many people, friends aside, who even realized she was the daughter of *that* Pablo Lozaro.

She felt a trifle guilty sometimes that she was not more involved, more dedicated to her father's work, but this was her life, damn it! It was not for him to choose a course and trap her in the middle of a movement that, while laudable enough, fell sadly short of a well-rounded life.

Maria wanted more and she would have it.

She didn't see the black sedan until it was upon her, swinging to the curb, its back doors flying open to disgorge a pair of burly thugs. They rushed up on her blind side, seizing her arms, pinning her between them.

She reacted swiftly and instinctively, lashing out with a kick at the man on her left. Her heel struck his instep, evoking a hiss of pain, but instead of releasing her, the man twisted her arm to the small of her back, applying painful pressure to the elbow joint and shoulder while Maria struggled to escape. On her right the second thug clutched her hand in his big, callused fist, squeezing so hard that her knuckles ground together and a bolt of pain shot up her arm.

Unable to resist, Maria was propelled toward their vehicle, banging her head on the door frame as she was forced into the back seat. The man on her right held both arms immobile, without apparent effort, while his crony ran around the other side and scrambled in to sandwich her between them. Doors slammed shut, and the driver took them away with a squeal of rubber on asphalt.

Before they traveled half a block, the bully on Maria's left produced a pillow case and pulled it down over her head like a hood. The kidnappers forced her down toward the floorboard at their feet, one of them punching her hard in the stomach when she resisted.

The fight went out of Maria Lozaro then, and she began to weep. Frustration, fear and pain combined to steal her courage, leaving her with nothing more than tears as a defense.

The dark sedan was lost in traffic, rolling westward toward the setting sun.

Caldas, Colombia

CARL LYONS WAITED for his mark to finish eating, pay his check and tip the waiter, step out into the bruised light of another mountain sunset. Turning east, away from Lyons, the target moved briskly along the sidewalk, sidestepping slower pedestrians, taking no apparent precautions to avoid being followed.

He was cocky, this one, and with reason. Hector de Leon Guerrero had survived two decades as a die-hard revolutionary in Colombia, when a majority of his associates were either killed or sent to prison, some of them condemned to face a firing squad. Guerrero had done time briefly in the early 1980s, serving four months of an eight-year sentence for attempted murder before the victim, terrified by threats from M-19, recanted his description of the man who shot him twice outside the Cali police station.

Guerrero had led a charmed life since that episode, emerging as a hero of sorts to the revolutionary left, but his luck was about to run out. The tab was overdue for ruined and disrupted lives. Carl Lyons was preparing to collect.

He fell into step behind Guerrero, trailing the assassin east, then north as Hector turned a corner, leaving most of the traffic behind. His destination seemed to be a tavern in the middle of the block, La Cucaracha.

Lyons didn't like to think about the clientele that patronized a bar named for a cockroach, but he gave his mark a decent lead, then ducked inside. The atmosphere was dark and smoky, as with saloons the world over. Latin music blared from a jukebox in the corner. Lyons stood by the door for a moment, letting his eyes get used to the murk, picking Guerrero out at the bar.

The Ironman found an empty stool as far away from his intended target as he could, positioned so that Hector wouldn't have to pass him if he tried to leave the tavern. Lyons ordered beer and nursed it from the bottle, watching while Guerrero wolfed three shots of whiskey, with a mug of beer to chase it down.

A quarter of an hour later Guerrero left his stool, proceeding to the men's room. There was no time like the present, Lyons thought, and fell into step behind him, closing up the gap. Guerrero had already disappeared inside a toilet stall as Lyons entered, and they had the men's room to themselves. The whine of third-rate mariachi singers from the jukebox was a trifle less intrusive here, their voices muted by the intervening door and walls.

Carl Lyons washed his hands and dried them on a paper towel, standing with his back to Guerrero's toilet stall, biding his time. There was an element of risk involved, as always, with a takedown in a public place, but Lyons was prepared to take the chance.

Guerrero had been skating long enough, by all accounts. The settlement of his outstanding debt was overdue, and it would serve a double purpose now by sending home a message to his fellow revolutionaries.

Lyons heard the toilet flush, one hand inside his jacket, finding the Beretta with its custom silencer as Hector tucked his shirt in, zipped his pants, prepared to leave the stall. The door swung open, and Guerrero blinked at Lyons, taking in the pistol.

Recognizing death.

He raised one hand as if in protest, while the other slid back toward a holster on his hip. Carl Lyons shot him twice, one bullet drilling through the upraised hand to strike Guerrero in the face, the second nailing him dead center, in the chest. Guerrero staggered backward, falling, and he landed on the toilet with a jolt. There was a loud crack as the toilet separated from the crumbling plaster wall, and rusty-looking water gushed around Guerrero's feet.

The Ironman waded in on tiptoe, leaned across to tuck a business card inside the pocket of Guerrero's dress shirt, crimson soaking through the fabric now. Emblazoned with the name and mailing address of the FAP, the card was one of thousands circulated in Colombia, specifically designed to woo new members, frighten enemies and curry favor with the FAP's assorted friends.

It was an obvious approach, all things considered, but the local atmosphere was such that Lyons felt he had no need for subtlety. Guerrero's M-19 associates would likely blame the FAP without a solid clue to work from; he was merely helping them to reach the logical conclusion, expediting their pursuit of sweet revenge.

It was the very least that he could do for such deserving souls.

A drunk was weaving toward the rest room as he left, and Lyons put on speed without appearing obvious. It was a toss-up whether this one would have sense enough to spot the flood in progress or if he would care enough to check it out. In any case, the Ironman did not plan to wait around and see Guerrero found.

He still had work to do before they put the final icing on the cake.

And time was running out, for all concerned.

Gerona, Spain

MACK BOLAN NEARLY MISSED the news of the abduction in Pamplona. It wasn't reported to police or broadcast by the media. A phone call to the victim's father, in Gerona, warned that he would lose his daughter in a most unpleasant fashion if he failed to follow certain orders from the ETA.

Pablo Lozaro was prepared to do exactly that—give up his life, if necessary, to protect his only child—when Bolan phoned Lozaro to check on his progress with his latest editorial campaign. It took some coaxing, but he got the story of Maria's kidnapping and managed to persuade her father that the best thing he could do for now was nothing. Sit and wait.

The Executioner, meanwhile, would not be sitting still.

He had a list of targets fresh in mind, some ETA, some ANE. He put the neo-fascist fringe on hold for now, and focused solely on the Basque guerrillas who had grabbed Lozaro's daughter off the street. There was a chance that she was already dead, but he didn't think so. A live hostage was always worth more than a corpse, and the gunners could dispose of Maria at leisure, when she had served her purpose.

Which meant, if Bolan's calculations were correct, that he still had a chance to get Maria back. If he was wrong, and the girl was already dead, then he could do no harm.

Gerona struck him as the perfect place to start.

The ETA maintained a local front—Patria Euzkadi, the "Basque Patriots" party—with a storefront office near the heart of town. The party's staff were ETA commandos on a temporary leave of absence from the firing line, detailed to shovel propaganda for public consumption, reviling the Spanish government and any measures aimed at promoting Basque civil rights, while the ETA-Militar continued its campaign of murder and sabotage behind the scenes.

It struck Mack Bolan as a perfect place to leave a message for his enemies.

He breezed in off the street near closing time, all smiles for the receptionist who greeted him with obvious reserve. She spoke sufficient English to make sense of his request, and advised him that the party's local manager was not available for interviews.

A glimpse of the Beretta changed her mind, and she led Bolan past a row of empty cubicles to reach the "private" office space in back. Two men were seated there, both smoking cigarettes and sipping coffee when the Executioner was ushered in to join them.

The receptionist had done her job, but Bolan didn't trust her and he needed an interpreter. The local party boss identified himself with only minor hesitation, sharp eyes darting back repeatedly to the top drawer of his desk.

A weapon there perhaps?

No matter.

The party boss had no more than identified himself when Bolan shot his comrade once between the eyes and dropped him on the carpet, plastic chair and all. The woman flinched but didn't scream, suggesting that she had been close to violent death before. As female shooters in the ETA were not unknown, the Executioner's mistrust of her was clearly justified.

"I have a message for Alphonse Gogorza," Bolan told his captives, trusting the receptionist to translate more or less verbatim. "We can minimize the damage to his cadre if he meets my terms."

The party boss absorbed that much and shrugged, as if to say that he could not speak for Gogorza.

Fair enough.

"A woman named Maria Lozaro was kidnapped by the ETA this afternoon in Pamplona," Bolan went on. "She's Pablo Lozaro's daughter. You know who I mean. I'll be very upset if she is not released, safe and sound, within the next hour."

The smoker blinked at that, checked his wristwatch, and gave a noncommittal nod of understanding.

"I'll be so upset, in fact, that I intend to execute at least one ranking member of the ETA every hour she remains a prisoner, beginning at precisely six o'clock. Your friend—" he waggled the Beretta, pointing with the muzzle "—proves that I mean what I say."

The party boss was listening and nodding, shooting furtive glances toward the top drawer of his desk.

"If that's a pistol," Bolan said, "you may get lucky... or you may get killed. Feel free to try it. I can always send the message back with her."

The tough guy weighed his options and decided it was better to keep breathing for a while. He rocked back in his chair and clasped both hands behind his head, smoke streaming from his nostrils.

"Your choice," said Bolan, backing toward the exit and the street beyond. "When I say six o'clock, I don't mean 6:01 or 6:15. The body count's entirely in Gogorza's hands."

For now, thought Bolan as he hit the street and jogged back to his waiting car. The leader of the ETA could buy himself some time, but there was no such thing as absolution in the slaughterhouse.

Bolan would spend the next fifty-five minutes refining his strategy, spotting his targets and lining up the angles of attack in case Gogorza proved stubborn. It was unlikely that the hostage would be freed without a fight, and Bolan knew that going in.

The Executioner was blitzing on.

The Bekaa Valley, Lebanon

THE PHOENIX WARRIORS left their jeep and stolen flatbed truck two miles from where they planned to meet their enemies in battle, taking care to hide both vehicles from prying eyes. The jeep fit nicely in a smallish cave, brush drawn across the opening. They hid the truck nearby, within a copse of trees. The vehicles might just as easily be found while they were gone, but Katz refused to wire explosives to the starter solenoids without a fix on some specific target.

Hiking over rough terrain, alert to sentries and patrols, night coming on, it took them ninety minutes to complete a trek that should have taken twenty in serene conditions, over level ground. They came up on Zuheir al-Qadi's base camp from the west and found a vantage point from which to scan the compound.

Two wooden towers, north and south, had searchlights mounted in them, but the guards were plainly under orders to reserve the lights for absolute emergencies. Israeli jets still roared across the Bekaa now and then in search of terrorists to kill, and there was no point advertising where the Thunderbolt had pitched its several tents.

The rest of the facilities were fairly standard for a Palestinian guerrilla camp. There were no buildings in the strict sense of the word, unless you were to count the lookout towers. The As-Sai'qa freedom fighters lived in tents, and yards of canvas had been staked out to provide some meager shade for mealtimes. The latrine consisted of an open ditch where lime was sprinkled periodically, but from the smell, Katz reckoned they were saving lime at the expense of hygiene. He imagined sleeping, eating with that smell, and shrugged the notion off.

There was no fence around the camp. The lookout towers were the only obvious security in place, no roving sentries on the ground. Zuheir al-Qadi obviously felt secure within the Bekaa Valley, more concerned about Israeli jets than any foe who might approach on the ground. In spite of late events along the coast, there seemed to be no extra guards on duty to patrol the camp, and that was fine with Katz.

It made a rugged mission that much easier.

The bad news was that after he had counted tents and heads as best he could, Katz estimated forty-five or fifty men inside the camp. That made it roughly eight to one, with Ari Lev along, and while the men of Phoenix Force had dealt with more imposing odds, the present set was bad enough.

Katz passed his glasses to Ari Lev, letting the Israeli scan the camp for several moments. Suddenly he felt Lev stiffen, hissing through clenched teeth.

"There, by the mess tent."

Katz retrieved the glasses, focused, picking out Zuheir al-Qadi and a short man in khaki. They were arguing, from all appearances, the short man waggling a finger in al-Qadi's face and giving him hell.

"Faisal Suwayda," Ari said.

"You know him?"

The Israeli nodded. "He is Syrian. A spokesman for the Baath Party. One of their liaison officers with Palestinian guerrillas."

"Ah."

"We're dealing here with more than the Iranians," said Ari Lev.

"It looks that way."

"What will you do?"

"Right now? Proceed as planned. Surround the camp and move on schedule. Drop as many of them as we can." Katz hesitated, peering through the glasses as he spoke, his stomach turning over slowly. "Damn it all to hell!"

"What is it?"

Ari Lev took the glasses from him. Katzenelenbogen didn't need them as he watched the jeep rev up and leave the camp, scaling a low hill to reach the nearest unpaved access road. He had already glimpsed Zuheir al-

Qadi in the shotgun seat, one of his soldiers at the wheel, another in the back.

The fox was gone, too late for them to spring the trap with him inside.

Katz spat into the sand, a bitter taste of disappointment on his tongue.

"What now?" asked Ari Lev.

"No change," the one-armed warrior told him. "So we miss al-Qadi for the moment. We can still take out his army. Something tells me he isn't going far."

"Faisal Suwayda may have some idea of where he's gone."

"That's not a bad idea. Let's ask him if we get the chance."

Katz issued late instructions to his team and sent the warriors on their way, encircling the campsite. He was far from happy with the new turn of events, but they had come too far to scrub the mission on account of one man slipping through the net.

Zuheir al-Qadi was a mortal. He left tracks like any other man, and they would follow him when they were finished here . . . assuming they were still alive.

And they would have to deal with Syria, as well.

It stood to reason, with the Syrians patrolling widely through the Bekaa, that the ruling Baath Party would have a bloody finger in As-Sai'qa's pie, but Katz had not anticipated finding a party delegate in the compound itself. The new twist called for action on another front, and he would have to clear that move with Stony Man, if possible.

But for the moment Katzenelenbogen had his hands full, counting down the minutes, waiting for his men to finish their encircling maneuver. He was ready for whatever happened next.

As ready as a fighting man can ever be.

Five minutes and the southern tower went up like a rocket, with a thunderclap and leaping flames. One of the tower guards bailed out, a shooting star, his clothes on fire.

Katz pushed off from his hiding place and sprinted toward the killing ground.

CHAPTER FIFTEEN

Medellín, Colombia

Before she took her telephone off the hook, Veronica Guzman had called and instructed her office to page her for only the most extreme emergency. That did not include death threats, of which she had logged seventeen in the space of two days.

It was a record, but not by much. The threats of death and mutilation were routine these days. The callers rang her home and office up from public phone booths, knowing that equipment was in place to trace their calls in seconds flat. Even so, police made no real effort to arrest the callers, and Veronica could hardly blame them. In a country plagued by murders, bombing and abductions, swamped with drugs and taking constant fire from the United States for failure to disrupt the narco traffic, simple threats ranked low on everybody's list of serious offenses.

Still, she worried.

Her immediate predecessor had resigned in fear of his life, citing medical problems as an excuse. *His* predecessor had been killed in office by a car bomb, and the prosecutor before that had been crippled for life in a drive-by shooting two blocks from his downtown office. The pursuit of justice was a deadly business in Colombia—almost as hazardous, in fact, as running drugs to the United States.

Guzman reckoned that the number of dealers and hangers-on murdered each year, per capita, might actually be lower than the death rate for police and prosecutors, judges and civic officials. More gangsters were killed in a year's time, of course, but they also outnumbered justice officials by twenty or thirty to one.

Regrettably some of the judges and local policemen she dealt with were no more than gangsters themselves, addicted to graft and committed to helping the very men they were supposed to be putting in prison.

It seemed hopeless sometimes, and Veronica considered resigning from her post on the average of once every day. She had actually typed the resignation on two occasions, and the latest copy—pointedly undated—was locked in her desk at home. She took it out from time to time and read it through, almost a ritual, drawing marginal peace of mind from the knowledge that she could bail out any time she wanted.

Any time the anger and frustration were too much.

Today had been close, with the attack on Brent Favor, the increased volume of threats to herself and the wild crew of Americans running amok in the countryside. She had given her stamp of approval to their dangerous plan, but she was having second thoughts. It was too late to call them back, but she could still jump ship, send in the "cavalry," as they so quaintly put it.

And to what result?

At the moment the last thing that she needed was more grief from the United States. If these men had been sent from Washington, it meant they had approval from the White House, or the next best thing. Antagonizing one more President wouldn't serve Guzman's needs when she was fighting for her life.

The shower helped a little, steaming water drumming on her head and shoulders, loosening the knotted muscles in her back. A drink would finish the prescription, she decided. Maybe two or three.

It took a lot to get her drunk these days, with so much on her mind. She woke up every morning with a sense of failure, and it dogged her through the day, refusing to be shaken off. Regardless of her victories in court, she always knew that there was more work to be done, the big fish wriggling through her net and going free.

She shut the water off and slid the shower door back far enough to reach a bath towel hanging on the rod. When she had dried her hair a bit and wrapped the towel around herself, she pushed the sliding door back all the way, stepped out . . .

And found herself confronted with a pair of gunmen standing in her bathroom, aiming sawed-off shotguns at her from six or seven feet. She thought about the guard outside her house and wondered briefly whether the *sicarios* had killed or bribed him to effect their entry.

Either way, it all came out the same.

The taller of the gunmen spoke. "Eduardo Gaviria sends his fond regards."

Veronica saw nothing to be gained from courtesy. "Eduardo Gaviria," she replied in level tones, "eats shit for breakfast, and his mother was a two-bit whore."

And she was smiling when the world exploded in her face.

Mataró, Spain

THE ETA HAD BLOWN its deadline, and the Executioner was out for blood.

He had anticipated some defiance from the terrorists, and he had picked out his next mark for maximum effect. At least one ranking member of the ETA per hour, he had promised in the message at Gerona, but he hadn't said the slaughter would be limited to one.

Mataró's chapter of the ETA was led by Maximilian Echeveste, a thug suspected of eleven murders in the past four years. He managed to avoid arrest by terrorizing witnesses and framing alibis with perjured testimony, so secure in his ferocious reputation that he felt no need to hide. He still had bodyguards, of course, but that was fine.

The more the merrier, in Bolan's present state of mind.

He came in from the rear of Echeveste's property, his Mini-Uzi muzzled with the custom silencer. There was a sentry in the yard, but he seemed more concerned with smoking a cigar than standing watch. He never saw grim death approaching, never heard the shot that drove a parabellum slug into his brain at point-blank range.

The Executioner moved on, discovered that the back door of the house was unlocked. Leading with his SMG, he crossed the threshold and found himself inside a kitchen smelling heavily of fish and garlic. With no one to oppose him, he crossed the room, slipped through another door to reach the smallish living room.

Two gunners had the couch staked out, their backs to Bolan as they watched an ancient Western, dubbed in Basque, on television. They were laughing at the dialogue of a pair of Hollywood Indians on-screen.

He could have called to them, announced himself, but Bolan saw no point in raising the alarm. Instead, he shot them where they sat, two rounds per man, and left them slumped together on the couch.

Three down, at least one more to go.

He moved along a narrow hallway toward the bedrooms, stopping at the bathroom. The door was closed, but Bolan tried the knob and felt it turn. He poked his head inside and found a young man seated on the toilet, pants around his ankles, gaping in surprise at the intrusion.

"Don't get up on my account," said Bolan, squeezing off a 3-round burst that pinned the gunner where he sat.

That left two bedrooms, and he found the first one empty, thereby narrowing the field. The master bedroom's door was closed, but light crept underneath to tell him it was occupied. He thought about just barging in, but decided it was more polite to knock.

A gruff voice answered from inside. Without a hint of what the two short syllables might mean, he turned the knob and shouldered through the doorway, leading with his SMG... and almost took a bullet in the face.

The shooter's aim was high, by virtue of excitement, but he did a better job the second time. That bullet tugged at Bolan's sleeve, but he was dodging then, the Mini-Uzi spitting flame, his target jerking and recoiling from the impact of a dozen parabellum slugs.

The master of the house got off another shot before he fell, but it was wasted on the ceiling. Echeveste sprawled across the bed in boxer shorts and undershirt, the latter turning rapidly from white to red. His piggy eyes were open, sightless, fixed on some point overhead that no living man could see.

And that made five. If it wasn't enough to drive his message home, the Executioner was ready to repeat the lesson, time and time again until his enemies gave in or he ran out of targets.

Either way, the ETA had grabbed a tiger by the tail, and letting go would be no simple task.

This tiger was prepared to eat them up alive.

The Bekaa Valley, Lebanon

THE TOWER was their signal, like a beacon burning bright above the compound. Calvin James was ready when the flash of the explosion lit the camp, a nearby sentry lined up in the sights of his Kalashnikov. One squeeze was all it took, a burst of 5.56 mm tumblers ripping through the gunner's chest and blowing him away.

It went chaotic after that, with James and his comrades pressing in from the perimeter, the camp's inhabitants scrambling to repel invaders, to save themselves by any means available. The searchlight in the second lookout tower blazed to life and swept across the camp, a scene that put James in mind of an anthill in panic. Then a second plastic charge went off and brought the tower down, a handful of guerrillas trapped beneath its flaming wreckage.

James came in from the east, behind the mess tent, everything secured now that the evening meal was finished, pots and pans all cleaned and stacked. It was a fairly decent place to hide, and two young gunners clearly had the same idea. He found them huddled near the stove, attempting to become invisible, but unsuccessfully. The unexpected vision of a black man charging toward them with an automatic rifle in his hands brought both guerrillas to their feet, prepared to stand and fight with weapons of their own.

The gunner on the left was closer by a yard or so, and he was carrying a submachine gun while his partner held a rifle balanced in an awkward grasp. James veered off toward the young man with the SMG and hit him with a rising burst that plucked him off his feet and hurled him back against the camp stove in a fair impersonation of an acrobat. The dead man got a burst off as he fell, but it was high and wide.

The other Palestinian was screaming incoherently, his AK-47 swinging into target acquisition just a bit too late. He almost made it, granted, but in combat "almost" isn't good enough.

The Phoenix warrior came in firing, stitched his adversary with a burst across the chest that punched him over backward, out of sight behind a serving table. Double-checking to make sure the guy was finished, James found him twitching like a grounded trout, his fingers clutching empty air, the rifle lost. A mercy round at point-blank range shut off the tremors, leaving James with a pair of stiffs for company and a battle raging in front of him.

The camp was going ape-shit, tracers flying, smacking into bodies, setting tents on fire, while hand grenades provided exclamation points to the erratic sounds of death. It would be near impossible to pick his friends out in the riotous confusion, but he trusted them to keep their heads down and avoid each other's fire.

With that in mind, he palmed a frag grenade, released the pin and lobbed it toward the nearest standing tent. A smoky thunderclap, more dancing flames and he was ready with his rifle when a flaming scarecrow bolted from the heart of the inferno, shrieking unintelligible cries of pain. James dropped him in his tracks, a 3-round burst from twenty feet away, and scanned the camp for other targets.

There! Three young men darting off toward the latrine. It lay in his sector, but the smell had driven him to try another angle of attack. He trailed the moving targets now, some thirty feet behind them, watching every step along the way to keep from winding up a faceless casualty.

He might have taken all three by complete surprise, except that one glanced back over his shoulder in the firelight, saw another figure coming up behind and took him for a friend. He beckoned James on, said something in excited Arabic... and went down like a broken mannequin when James shot him in the chest.

The others recognized their peril now, both turning to confront the enemy. The farthest one from James had reached the brink of the latrine, prepared to leap across it, but he lost his footing and fell into the trench. His exclamation of disgust was smothered by the sound of gunfire from above as James and his adversary dueled from twenty feet apart.

James got there first, and that was all that saved him. Tumblers sheared through the young guerrilla's arm to spoil his aim. Another short burst put him down and out, James edging forward, peering down at the third guerrilla in the latrine.

The Palestinian glared back at him through what appeared to be a mask of mud. His eyes were wide, thin lips drawn back to show his teeth. The gunner's weapon may have fallen underneath him; it was nowhere to be seen.

"You're in the deep shit now," said Calvin James.

And closed those staring eyes forever with a burst from his Kalashnikov.

THE TASK that Ari Lev had set himself was relatively simple, at least in theory. They had missed Zuheir al-Qadi, but Faisal Suwayda still remained within the camp. If Lev could only capture him alive and make him talk, he had no doubt the Syrian could point them toward al-Qadi's destination.

But finding any one man in the smoking, flaming hive of the guerrilla camp was something else again. From the beginning of the Phoenix team's assault, confusion was the order of the day. Explosions, firelight and the desert valley's normal darkness played tricks with vision, and soldiers were running everywhere, some falling, others firing aimlessly at shadows. Ari Lev imagined hell must look a bit like this, if it existed, but he didn't let the reigning chaos hold him back.

Instead, he plunged into the battle, shooting every Palestinian terrorist he met, dodging shrapnel and bullets as best he could, sometimes by the slimmest of margins. In the place of normal fear, he felt a wild exhilaration. Even knowing that he might be shot and killed at any time, he couldn't halt the search.

He knew the Syrian by sight, had glimpsed the khaki uniform Suwayda wore, so different from the limp fatigues favored by the Palestinians. Lev knew that he would recognize Suwayda at a glance, but he was worried that the recognition might not be in time. He had no use for corpses at the moment. He wanted a living man who would give him the information he required.

A jeep came out of nowhere, running dark, the driver swerving madly in an effort to avoid his comrades. All in vain. As Ari Lev watched, one young Arab seemed to throw himself before the juggernaut, as if attempting suicide.

He got his wish. The jeep's momentum would not let the driver stop in time. Destructive impact rolled the young man across the hood, so that his forehead struck the windshield, cracked it in a pattern that reminded Ari Lev of a giant spiderweb. Another heartbeat and the body rolled away, was gone.

And Ari Lev saw the driver. Recognized his prey.

There was no time to think before he lost that single, precious opportunity. He came up firing through the windshield of the jeep, his bullets tearing through the radiator, glancing off the engine block.

The jeep was sputtering and trailing smoke as it swept past, veering toward the ruins of the southern lookout tower. Ari Lev set off in pursuit, knees pumping as he ran, afraid to fire again in case his slugs might find the driver by mistake.

The jeep ran out of steam a few yards past the smoking shambles of the tower, Ari Lev approaching cautiously. He saw his quarry step down from the driver's seat, fists clenched, curses pouring from his lips. The Syrian reached back inside his vehicle to fetch a weapon. Turned. Saw Ari Lev no more than twenty feet away.

They didn't know each other, in the sense of ever having met. Faisal Suwayda was a terrorist "celebrity" of sorts, his name and photograph on file with the Mossad as a potential target if the Syrians required a lesson in decorum. He wouldn't know Ari Lev, no matter how extensive his supply of information on Mossad and Israel.

Still, the Syrian was wise enough to recognize an enemy on sight.

He snarled and brought his AK-47 up, the muzzle rising in a seamless arc. Lev had no choice but to respond in kind. He tried to pick his target, nail Suwayda in the arms and hands, disarm and possibly disable him without a lethal wound.

And it was close.

Six rounds at twenty feet, full-auto mode, and four of them ripped through Faisal Suwayda's forearms. One missed altogether, and the sixth round struck his weapon, split it in two. The larger fragment glanced off and upward, through Suwayda's stomach, liver, clipping the aorta in the middle of his abdomen.

The Syrian was dying as he fell, a dazed expression on his face. He couldn't speak as Ari Lev bent over him, demanding answers in Faisal's own language. Too weak to respond at all, no matter how he longed to curse the enemy and spit in Lev's face.

Too late.

He let the body drop, stood up and kicked it in a sudden fit of rage. The moment passed, and Ari Lev took up his rifle, moving off in search of other terrorists to kill.

THERE IS A POINT in most pitched battles, Yakov Katzenelenbogen knew, when the survivors feel a shift or change in the pervasive atmosphere of death. It doesn't mean the killing is about to stop, by any means, but it announces—to those with the sensitivity to understand—that the tide of combat has turned in favor of one side of the other. This time, when it clicked for Katzenelenbogen in the middle of the Bekaa Valley, he decided it was time to cut and run.

The raid was going well enough, from all appearances—they had reduced the odds from eight or nine to barely four to one—but there was something in the air that made Katz opt for swift withdrawal. Having missed

Zuheir al-Qadi at the start, it hardly mattered if they stayed to mop up every one of his guerrillas, and—

The headlights came in view at that point, rolling down the valley, three large trucks in convoy. It was possible that they were headed somewhere else, of course, but Katz knew in his gut that they were bearing reinforcements for As-Sai'qa at the compound.

Time to go.

He raised the compact walkie-talkie to his face, keyed the transmitter button with his thumb and snapped an order, loud enough to carry over gunfire.

"Break off now! Fall back and regroup on the motor pool. We've got incoming troops."

He didn't bother waiting for the several confirmations, suiting words to action as he ran back toward the motor pool. One flatbed truck and two old jeeps. The vehicles had been among his targets, but he had been sidetracked mopping up at the communications tent, and now he wondered whether it was providence that had spared the vehicles.

No matter. They were still in running shape, and that was all that counted.

Both jeeps had keys in the ignition, ready at a moment's notice, trusting the fanatical guerrillas to refrain from going on a joy ride in the desert. Katz ignored the truck until he finished checking out both jeeps, then doubled back and put a 5.56 mm tumbler into each tire on the right-hand side of the flatbed. His adversaries might have spares, but by the time they got the tires changed, it would be too late for any meaningful pursuit.

They had trouble enough as it was, with three more trucks arriving at any moment, maybe loaded to the max with guns and soldiers, spoiling for a fight. There was no time to waste if they were going to accomplish a withdrawal.

Sixty seconds brought his five companions to the motor pool, and Katz was pleased to note that none was seriously injured. Gary Manning had a cut above one eye, blood leaking down his face, but as with most small cuts around the head and face, it looked worse than it was. Encizo had been grazed across his biceps by a bullet, but again the wound was superficial, nothing that would put him down and out.

"We've got about two minutes if we're lucky," Katz informed them, pointing toward the highway where the headlights were approaching at a steady pace. "Let's hit the road."

Nobody liked the order, least of all Katz himself, but no one argued. It was cut-and-dried survival time. Dead heroes are impressive on memorials, but in the midst of raging combat, they are simply one more obstacle.

The group broke into three-man teams, as they had done for the approach, without the wasted time of drawing lots. Both jeeps responded on the first attempt—a lucky break in Lebanon, where maintenance of vehicles was rarely a priority—and in another moment Katzenelenbogen's team was on the move.

They took fire and returned it, racing south from the camp along the narrow, rutted "highway." Soon the burning camp resembled a miniature stage set, the headlights of the convoy veering off into the camp. Katz kept an eye fixed on the rearview mirror, knowing that it simply could not be that easy.

And it wasn't.

Momentarily the lights came back, three vehicles abandoning the ruined camp and churning southward in a bid to overtake the Phoenix team. The jeeps were faster, but a long pursuit through open Bekaa Valley scenery would surely draw more enemies like flies to feces.

They would have to lose the tail somehow, and that would take some thought. One thing Katz knew for certain: if the trucks had not been full of gunners when they reached the camp, they would be loaded now.

He had a thought and almost smiled.

Instead, he saved the energy and started looking for the high ground that would save their lives.

CHAPTER SIXTEEN

Tarragona, Spain

The Executioner was waiting when his target stepped out of his apartment into darkness. Lying on a roof across the street and six doors down, Bolan had a perfect view through the ten-power infrared scope. If he wanted, he could have counted the pockmarks on his target's face, but he wasn't concerned with physical appearance.

In another moment all the stranger's grooming problems would be solved.

The rifle was a CETME Modelo L, a Spanish weapon built for longer range than the French MA FAS assault rifle. In appearance it closely resembled the Heckler & Koch G3 model, except that the 20-round box magazine was straight rather than curved. A bipod helped him brace the barrel for a distance shot, and Bolan held his breath now, sighting for the kill.

He had been waiting close to half an hour, thrown off schedule by the target's tardiness. He could have scrubbed the mission, gone on to another target from his list, but this one was inviting, too good to pass. Besides, in terms of numbers, Bolan's last raid had put him ahead of the game.

He was keeping his promise and then some. Periodic calls to Pablo Lozaro, in Gerona, confirmed that the ETA still held his daughter hostage.

Fair enough. They would pay the price.

Julian Lazarbal was a prime candidate for an Executioner visitation, even without the added impetus of Bolan's push to liberate Maria Lozaro. An active terrorist since he was old enough to load and aim a weapon, Lazarbal had served eight years in prison prior to his release as part of an ill-conceived government amnesty. Madrid was hoping for a cease-fire when they opened up the prison gates, and it had worked...for all of seven days and thirteen hours. Afterward the government admitted its mistake, but the damage was done. Lazarbal and nineteen others like him were back on the streets, most of them plotting new atrocities with every waking hour.

Bolan tracked the short, barrel-chested man on the walk toward his car, noting the bodyguards that flanked Lazarbal like bookends. A third gun, the driver, was waiting at the vehicle, but none of them was close enough to seriously threaten Bolan once he opened fire.

Not that he meant to give them a chance, when it came down to that.

Lazarbal first, his round face framed in the eyepiece of Bolan's infrared sight, looking sickly green through the night optics. Bolan fixed the cross hairs on his chin, allowing for the range and drop, stroking the trigger with a delicate, almost loving touch.

The CETME recoiled against his shoulder, sending forth a 5.56 mm tumbler. Lazarbal was saying something to his driver when the bullet hit, cutting off the comment in midsyllable, shearing through his larynx in a burst of crimson.

It wasn't enough to take his head off, but the stunning impact slammed him over backward, dark blood pooling on the sidewalk and spreading in all directions while the bodyguards reacted.

Too late.

He took the driver next because the guy was closer to the vehicle, more likely to duck out of sight. Another gentle squeeze, the target pivoting to face the distant sound of rifle fire and getting halfway there before a bullet struck his lower jaw, performing sloppy orthodontics.

The driver went down kicking, maybe a survivor, maybe not. It made no difference to the Executioner, already tracking with his night sight toward the taller of the bodyguards. The man was crouched beside his boss, a pistol in his hand, uncertain how to act when no assailant was to be seen. He knew it was a sniper—that was obvious—but he was losing it on the reaction time.

The third round dropped him on his haunches, spitting blood from ruptured lungs before he toppled over on his side and lay unmoving next to his erstwhile superior. Their blood was mingling on the sidewalk, tributaries streaming toward the gutter.

That left one.

The last surviving gunman may have known his chances, but he had to try regardless. Turning from the vehicle, the bodies at his feet, he sprinted back toward the apartment house, head down.

The broad back made a perfect target, with no evasive moves to spoil the shot. Mack Bolan stroked the trigger twice and watched the man suddenly pitch forward, sliding on his stomach for another six or seven feet before he came to rest, dead, his face pressed against the concrete steps that had eluded him in life.

All done.

He had more calls to make, another message to deliver. Targets to select if there was no word of a hostage's release. The ETA apparently had men to burn, and he would keep on turning up the heat until he got results.

The note he left behind was printed in English. He would trust the ETA or the police to spring for an interpreter. Its message was direct and to the point: "I have more time than you have lives."

To Bolan's mind, that said it all.

The Bekaa Valley, Lebanon

THE HIGH GROUND WAS in fact a narrow cut between two bluffs where someone had decided it was easier to slice a hill in half than go around. Erosion had reduced the jagged lip on either side, and it was overgrown with straggling weeds and a few small trees that sent their taproots deep in search of precious water.

It was perfect.

They concealed the jeeps beyond the ambush site and hiked back to the bluffs, three soldiers on a side. Katz took the left, or western, side, with Encizo and McCarter. On the right, or east, were Gary Manning, Calvin James and Ari Lev.

They brought the whole damned arsenal along, including frag grenades, a Semtex satchel charge and the RPG launcher Manning had used to drop the guard towers at the As-Sai'qa hardsite. Manning had two rockets left, and he would need them both to stop three trucks and pin them in the killing zone.

The bleeding from his facial wound had stopped, and Manning gave it no more thought as he sat waiting in the darkness with the RPG beside him, watching for headlights on the southbound road. The trucks had fallen back a little in the past half hour, but he had no doubt that they were on their way.

Three minutes later Manning saw them coming, and he shouldered the RPG. His first shot would be critical. A miss would give the enemy an exit from the waiting trap. If Manning blew it, he would lose the first two trucks, at least, before he could reload the RPG. It would be touch and go on number three, at that, unless his comrades blocked the way effectively with automatic fire.

The only decent answer was a hit, and Manning had the shot lined up at fifty yards, using the first truck's headlights as his point of reference. It wouldn't be enough to blast the soldiers crouching in the back, not if the truck could still proceed.

He had to take the engine or driver, preferably both. Right now.

The truck reached his imaginary deadline, and Manning squeezed the RPG's trigger, feeling the heat of its back-blast behind him. The nose-heavy rocket struck home on the hood of the truck, ripping steel as it bored toward the engine block. It detonated with a thunderclap that brought the rear end of the truck around, the whole thing going over on its side in dust and smoke and fire.

He had a glimpse of bodies spilling on the roadway, some consumed by flame and tumbling metal as the truck rolled over, ending on its back. Others managed to survive, losing weapons in the process, scrambling to evade the juggernaut, ducking automatic fire that rained upon them from the bluffs on either side.

Manning reloaded his RPG as the second truck screeched to a halt, mere feet from impact with the flaming wreck in front of it. He swung around and sighted on the flatbed bringing up the rear, aware that it would do no good to blow the middle truck and let the third one get away.

His last projectile sped downrange, five pounds of high explosives flying with sufficient speed and force to penetrate 12.6 inches of armor on a direct hit. The tall Canadian was off a fraction on his aim, but it was good enough. The rocket sheared through the upper quadrant of the flatbed's windshield, peeling back a strip of roofing on the cab and detonating in a fireball as it reached the troops huddled behind the driver's seat.

The truck kept rolling, still no damage to its engine, and collided with the second vehicle in line, jolting that truck forward into the burning wreck of the lead truck. The diesel fuel went up a heartbeat later, and the highway cut became a lake of fire, with human figures dashing in and out amid the spreading flames.

Manning dropped the useless RPG and picked up his Kalashnikov. He didn't try to estimate how many soldiers he had killed with two strokes of the trigger. Pinpoint numbers only mattered in the planning stage or afterward, when there was ample time to make a body count, compute the loss on either side.

In mortal combat there was no time for checking off your adversaries, keeping score as if it were a bowling match. You did your best to recognize the enemy and kill him when you had the chance. The killing stopped when there were no more targets left. A fighting man who played by any other rules was doomed before he ever took the field.

With that in mind, Manning started firing down into the highway cut, short bursts conserving ammunition, picking out specific runners in the firelight. Some of those below were now returning fire, but they were scattered, badly shaken, their night vision lost to the bright glow of flames.

In other circumstances Manning might have pitied his opponents.

As it was, he did his best to cut them down.

Medellín, Colombia

CARL LYONS HATED PLAYING catch-up, but he didn't always have a choice. The execution of their contact in the prosecutor's office called for a response, and Able Team had wasted no time.

Brent Favor had been raging on the phone when Lyons spoke to him, and it was all the Ironman could do to prevent Favor's tagging along on the hit. They needed a fourth at the moment like Dolly Parton needed a smaller brassiere. Despite his good intentions and his training at the federal law-enforcement school in Georgia, Favor would have trouble keeping up with Able Team.

And anything that slowed them down right now could get them killed.

The latest play had called for some finesse and yards of nerve. Schwarz made the package, C-4 plastic with a radio-remote detonator, and Lyons won the coin toss for delivery.

The rest came down to planning, luck and guts.

If Eduardo Gaviria ever got around to ranking his subordinates, Bernardo Castelano would have been a colonel at the very least. He stood among no more than three contenders for the throne if Gaviria ever took a fall. Bernardo specialized in managing the transport of cocaine from Medellín to the United States, unhampered by indictments handed down from Washington the year before.

But he was running out of luck tonight.

Brent Favor tipped them to the club where Castelano liked to spend his Friday evenings, and they found his limo outside, the driver lounging at the wheel, smoking a cigar. Bernardo's other bodyguards were in the club, reckoning that one man with the limo was enough.

And this time they were wrong.

Carl Lyons came in from the rear, a casual pedestrian, the nightclub's parking lot a shortcut on his way back home. For the approach he went down on all fours, beyond the driver's line of sight. He wriggled on his belly for twenty feet, then rolled over, scooting on his back to make his way beneath the limo, feeling for the gas tank in the dark.

He found it, taking special care as he attached the plastic charge and armed the detonator. He was easing into his withdrawal when the driver stepped out of the car, walked over to the space between two nearby vehicles and started urinating on the asphalt.

Lyons, huddled underneath the limo with his legs protruding and a pistol on his hand, waited for the guy to finish. If he was spotted when the driver turned around, there would be no choice but to fire, pump lead into the wheelman's ankles, finish him when he was down.

And that would damned near ruin everything.

In fact, the driver's mind was elsewhere as he walked back to the limousine. Perhaps the Ironman's legs were hidden from that angle of approach, or maybe Castelano's man was simply negligent. In any case, he spent a moment on his fly, slid in behind the wheel and slammed the door.

Lyons swallowed a sigh of relief and put his Beretta away, worming out from under the limo an inch at a time, taking care not to make any noise. Once he was clear, he cautiously retraced his movements, crawling well back from the car before he stood and strolled back to his friends.

The rest was waiting, forty minutes altogether, for Bernardo to emerge with guards in tow and strut back to his limousine. The limo pulled out a moment later, Blancanales giving it a lead before he followed in the nondescript sedan. Carl Lyons rode the shotgun seat beside him, the detonator in his hand.

They could have taken Castelano any time, but there was still a solid flow of traffic through the streets of downtown Medellín. Instead of risking innocent civilians, Pol kept on the smuggler's tail for close to half an hour, keeping Castelano's vehicle in sight but never running close enough to give the game away.

And Lyons knew they had him as the limo nosed into a stylish residential neighborhood, the traffic thinning out, then dropping off to zero as they closed in on Castelano's home. His latest digs consisted of the fourth floor in a new apartment house, where he had signed the lease as Juan Valdez.

You had to give him credit, after all. It wasn't every homicidal piece of shit who had a sense of humor.

"Here we go," said Blancanales as their target pulled into the parking lot, rolled past the guard's booth, turning out of sight behind a tall brick fence. The Politician handed Lyons a cordless telephone.

He tapped out Castelano's private mobile number, waiting for the voice that he would recognize immediately.

"Sí."

"Bernardo, how's it hanging?"

Rough English came back at him in answer. "Who the fuck is this?"

"Your nemesis," said Lyons.

"¿Qué?"

"Your people made a bad mistake with Guzman, asshole. Someone has to pay for that, and you're elected."

"How you got this nummer?" Castelano asked.

"A little birdy gave it to me, 'Nardo."

"What the fuck you mean a little birdy?"

"Actually," said Lyons, "I believe it was a vulture. He can't wait to meet you, 'Nardo, and I hate to keep him waiting."

"You not make sense, *pendejo.*"

"Say good-night."

"Good night?"

He pressed the firing button with his thumb, and they were close enough to see the fireball rising from the fenced-off parking lot. Carl Lyons didn't have to see the limousine to know approximately what it looked like. Twisted steel and flaming wreckage, four charred rag dolls trapped inside or strewn around the parking lot like cast-off flotsam from the blast.

"I always hated playing catch-up," Lyons said to no one in particular, and Blancanales took them out of there, in search of other prey.

The Bekaa Valley, Lebanon

IT WAS LIKE spearing minnows in a bucket, no way for the targets to escape, no refuge from the hunters who controlled the high ground. Katzenelenbogen was already weary of the killing, but it didn't pay to leave a job unfinished . . . or to leave armed enemies alive.

The middle truck was burning now, flames licking at its undercarriage, tires deflating as they melted from the heat. Katz had his rifle sights fixed on a pair of gunners crouched beside the flatbed when its fuel tank blew and swamped them both in blazing diesel. They were screaming when he silenced them with two short bursts.

One of the Palestinian thugs was carrying an RPG, and he unloaded on the nearest hillside, hoping for a lucky hit, too frightened and confused to aim his weapon. Katzenelenbogen saw the rocket coming, ducked back with a warning shout to his companions on the bluff and rode the shock wave out as the rocket exploded several yards below him, touching off a minor landslide.

He came up firing, caught the Arab grenadier as he was trying to reload his clumsy weapon, 5.56 mm bullets ripping flesh and fabric with a rising burst. The shooter fell back on the hard-packed surface of the highway, boot heels drumming for an instant, finally lying still.

How many dead so far? How many still alive down there, trapped between the bullets and the flames?

Across the road he caught a glimpse of Calvin James and Ari Lev descending, wary of a trick as they began the gruesome task of mopping up. Katz scanned the killing ground, saw no one but his comrades moving in the firelight. There were bodies scattered everywhere, some of them charred and others burning. None had given up his life without a fight.

Katz tried to hate them, but it wouldn't come. These were his enemies, men pledged to his destruction, the annihilation of his homeland, but he felt no overwhelming urge to see them dead. Annihilating the guerrillas was a job, means to a noble end, but it left Katz with no particular sensation of accomplishment.

He was alive, his comrades likewise. They had done their job successfully, against imposing odds. He felt no guilt or sadness for the Arabs he had killed, but neither was there any triumph in his heart.

Because the job was still not finished.

Zuheir al-Qadi had escaped the trap and remained at large, presumably still anxious for a sweetheart deal with the Iraqis that would subsidize his private war on Israel and America. Beyond that failure, they had also found a link between the Thunderbolt and Syria, in the person of Baath Party spokesman Faisal Suwayda.

That link demanded a response, but Katzenelenbogen wanted to check it out with Stony Man before he launched a foray into Syria. He had no fear of orders to the contrary, but it was only common sense that he should ask.

Yet, on the other hand...

Suppose they were restrained from punishing the Syrians—what then? The job would not be done while any sponsor of the terrorist cartel remained convinced of personal invincibility.

"Let's go," he said to Manning and Encizo, leading them downslope to join the cleanup. Scattered shots rang out as members of the Phoenix team found wounded enemies near death and sped them on their way.

Katz finished one himself, a young man with extensive burns, whose clothing hung in blackened shreds, his body twitching in ungodly pain. For all of that, there was defiance in his eyes as Katz stood over him. He managed to produce a sneer from blistered lips, was working on a curse when Katz squeezed off a point-blank round and banished conscious thought forever.

Done.

They hiked back to the hidden jeeps and huddled for a moment there. The flames and sounds of combat might attract patrols, but they would see the headlights coming from at least a mile away. While they had the time, Katz took a moment to brief them on his plan.

"Suggestions? Comments?"

"Question," Calvin James replied. "You didn't mention anything about reporting this back home. Is there a reason for the cutout?"

"They might tell us not to go," Katz answered. "If it comes to that, I've always found it easier to ask forgiveness than to get permission."

James smiled. "Makes sense to me."

"If anyone objects, we'll put it to a vote," Katz offered. "I'm not drafting anybody for a banzai mission."

No one spoke for several moments. Finally McCarter said, "I reckon it's unanimous. When do we start?"

"We'll need some fresh equipment and intelligence," said Katz.

"That's my department," Ari Lev put in. "If you don't mind a detour into Israel."

"Might as well," McCarter said. "It's almost on our way."

"First thing we ought to do," said Calvin James, "is get the hell away from here before we have more company."

"Agreed," said Katz. "We're heading south, then." Turning back to Ari Lev, he asked the young Israeli, "Have you got a way across the border?"

Moving toward his jeep, the young man smiled and said, "I wouldn't be surprised."

CHAPTER SEVENTEEN

Renteria, Spain

He made the phone call from Alphonse Gogorza's own backyard, spent several moments waiting for an English-speaking aide to reach the telephone.

"Who's calling, please?"

"I have a message for your boss," said Bolan. "Put him on the line."

"Who is my boss?" the houseman asked, deliberately obtuse.

"Gogorza. Do I have to spell it for you? He speaks English, doesn't he? If not, I guess I'll have to shoot a few more of his friends to get my point across."

"A moment."

Bolan waited, unafraid of traces. Rural terrorists were seldom on the cutting edge of high technology, and he had Jack Grimaldi standing watch in case his estimate was wrong.

"Hello?" A new voice on the line, gruff baritone, with just a trace of gravel.

"I hope that's you, Alphonse."

"How do you know this number?"

Bolan smiled. "I've had your number from the start," he said. "Now do you want to talk about the girl, or should I thin your army out a little more?"

"You are American? What brings you here?" There was confusion, mixed with fury, in Gogorza's voice. "We have done nothing to offend America."

"You're an offense to every decent human being on the planet," Bolan told him, "but I didn't call to give you a critique on personality. I want the hostage, safe and sound. Right now that's all it takes to make me go away."

"And if I should refuse?"

"You've had a taste already," Bolan said. "There's plenty more where that came from."

"You are a brave but foolish man," Gogorza said.

"Brave doesn't enter into it," said Bolan, "and my definition of a fool is anyone who takes a beating when he doesn't have to. Shall we talk, or have you got more people tired of living?"

"This is—how you say it?—blackmail."

"I prefer to call it payback," Bolan told him. "Think of it as partial retribution for your sins."

"Are you a priest?" Gogorza's tone was mocking now.

"Not even close," the Executioner replied, "but I can send a few more of your friends to hell if that's your choice."

"How can I trust you?" asked the terrorist.

"The same way I trust you—at arm's length, with a clothespin on my nose."

Gogorza hesitated, making up his mind. "The woman has no further use to me," he said at last. "I let you have her as a gift . . . but I say where and when."

"I'm listening."

"There is a skiing lodge some miles above the town of Renteria," said the ETA commander. He went on to give directions, Bolan listening, committing them to memory. "I meet you there," Gogorza finished. "Midnight. If you want the woman, you will meet me."

Bolan didn't hesitate. "You've got a deal."

He dropped the telephone receiver in its cradle, facing Jack Grimaldi in the car a half block down. He raised one finger, saw the pilot nod.

It was a trap, of course. No killer worth his salt would take the kind of punishment Gogorza had received from Bolan in the past few hours and submit without some effort to repay the suffering in kind. Gogorza's soldiers would be out in force for the occasion, hungry for a chance to win their honor back and spill the blood of an elusive enemy.

The only question left in Bolan's mind concerned the prisoner. Would she be present at the meeting? Was she even still alive?

Not knowing, he would have to take the chance.

But he wouldn't be going in alone, by any means. He had Grimaldi, as it was, and by the time black midnight rolled around, he meant to have an army lined up on his side. The soldiers might not know on whose behalf they were engaged, but it should make no difference in the end.

He lifted the receiver, dropped another coin, tapped out the number. Waited. Went through much the same confusion, waiting for an English-speaker on the other end.

Success at last.

And he was smiling as he told the houseman, "Put Jose Silveira on the line."

Antioquia Province, Colombia

SOME PEOPLE, Lyons thought, just don't know when to quit.

It came with cash and power, the belief that anything was possible upon demand. He had observed the syndrome often, typically in wealthy criminals or politicians who believed themselves to be above the law and common decency. For them, there was no gap between desire and action. If they wanted something, they reached out and took it. If an object or a person irritated them, they snapped their fingers and the problem went away.

Like magic, right.

Except it didn't always work.

Eduardo Gaviria had been playing God in Medellín for so long now that it was second nature to him. He couldn't imagine anyone or anything beyond his power to control or to eliminate. Most politicians and policemen took his bribes without a second thought. When Gaviria told them it was time to jump, they only asked how high.

Veronica Guzman had been a rare exception to the rule, and Gaviria had reacted to her bold defiance in the only way he knew. A simple peasant had defied him, and the peasant had to die.

Eduardo's palace stood dead center in the midst of an estate that sprawled out over several hundred acres. Most of it was forest, though a wide ring had been cleared around the manor house for tennis courts and gardens, heart-shaped swimming pool, garages. On any given day there were at least two dozen guns in residence, protecting Gaviria from the outside world.

They were about to earn their pay... or die in the attempt.

The men of Able Team went in by jeep and left their wheels on Gaviria's land, two klicks from the intended target. Hiking overland, each soldier packed an M-16 A1/M-203, with frag grenades and fighting knives,

Beretta side arms, plus an extra thirty pounds of ammunition and explosives.

They were dressed to kill and looking forward to their showdown with the drug baron.

An hour's walk through the forest brought them to the point where trees gave up and manicured lawn took over. Gaviria's mansion looked marvelous and absolutely out of place in its surroundings. They had studied bird's-eye photos of the house and grounds in Medellín, Brent Favor's special file, so there were no surprises waiting. Five minutes saw them all in place, prepared to move.

Carl Lyons came out of the forest like a creeping shadow, moving up behind the big four-car garage. The manor house showed lights from every downstairs window, with a few more burning on the second floor. He spent another moment in the shadows, fixed a C-4 charge and timer to the western wall of the garage, then moved on.

There was a sentry beside a second car barn, twenty yards away. The punk was young, perhaps a trifle inexperienced, but there was no time left for learning on the job. The Ironman came up on his blind side, cupped a hand across his mouth to stifle any warning cry and slit his throat from ear to ear, retreating into darkness with a dead weight in his arms.

More plastic and another timer, making an allowance for time elapsed since the first charge had been set. He wanted simultaneous explosions, falling on Eduardo's private army like the crack of doom.

Still moving, Lyons reached the tennis court and homed in on the swimming pool. He found two sentries lounging near the deep end, one man planted in a deck chair, his companion on the diving board. Both had submachine guns in their laps, but neither was paying much attention to his job.

Complacency, the Ironman knew, can get you killed.

He drew the sleek Beretta, its muzzle heavy with the silencer, and took the gunners out from thirty feet, before they noticed his approach. Two parabellum rounds for each, one shooter sliding from his chair as if his bones had turned to sand, the other slouching over the board and going for an awkward dive.

The splash was relatively quiet, but it didn't go unnoticed. Moving toward the lifeless goons, berating them in angry Spanish, came a bruiser who would pass for sergeant of the guard. His first sharp question got no answer from the dead, and he was halfway through a double take when he saw Lyons standing by the veranda with a pistol in his hand.

It happened just that swiftly, Lyons squeezing off on instinct, aiming for the heart and coming close enough to take the houseman down. The *pistolero* had his gun in hand, though, and he triggered one round as he fell.

No silencer on that one.

Lyons cursed, reholstered his Beretta and moved in to meet the enemy.

The silent probe was over. It was time to rock and roll.

EDUARDO GAVIRIA WAS in mourning of a sort. The murder of Bernardo Castelano was a bitter blow. The two of them had come up from the streets like brothers, robbed and raped and killed together in their teenage years, staked everything they had or ever hoped to be on the narcotics trade when they were barely old enough to vote. It was unseemly for a man to weep—in truth, Eduardo didn't feel the urge—but he could grieve in other ways.

And he would punish those responsible, no matter what the cost.

But he could only savor sweet revenge if he was still alive, and for the moment that meant hiding out, remaining safe and sound, away from Medellín, until his soldiers brought the enemy to bay.

When that had been accomplished, Gaviria would supply the coup de grace. But in the meantime...

He was lounging in his study, watching television from the States on satellite and sipping brandy from a crystal goblet, when a single shot echoed from outside.

The dealer scrambled to his feet, spilling brandy as he moved toward the tall French doors. He caught himself, thought better of it, thankful that the drapes were closed. Whatever might be happening outside, at least a sniper couldn't glimpse him through the window.

Moving swiftly to the bar, Eduardo set his goblet down and plucked an automatic pistol from its hiding place beside the beer taps. He was never far from weapons in the house, surviving on the theory that it pays to be prepared.

He checked the pistol's load unnecessarily and cocked it, left the safety off. It might be nothing, but Eduardo knew that it was always best to be ready. How many times had he been able to annihilate competitors because they let their guard down at the very moment when they should have been most watchful?

Gaviria wouldn't let it happen to him.

He switched off the lights in his study, moved back toward the sliding doors and peered out through a small crack in the drapes. One of his guards ran past, toward the swimming pool and tennis court, his automatic rifle held chest high.

Eduardo let the curtains fall back into place, retreating. He would have to find out what was happening, take charge before the thing got out of hand. If there was trouble, he could help his soldiers deal with it...or flee and save himself if it came to that.

In either case, he had to take a look outside.

Emerging from the study, Gaviria met Ignacio des Campos, his chief of security, coming to fetch him. "Ignacio, what's going on?" he demanded.

Des Campos, breathing hard, replied, "Some shooting by the pool. We've got at least two people down."

"I only heard one shot."

Des Campos shrugged. "We've got two bodies, maybe more we haven't found."

"But who—"

Eduardo never got the question out. Before his tongue could wrap itself around the words, a powerful explosion rocked the house. He heard the brittle, jagged sound of windows shattering. It sounded like the mother of all sonic booms, but Gaviria knew it must be something worse.

"Goddamnit, what's happening?"

"We need to get you out of here," des Campos said, taking hold of Gaviria's arm and steering him toward the rear of the house. "I've got enough men on the job to handle anything except the fucking army. Once we get you under cover—"

This time the explosion didn't merely rock the house; it sent a wrenching tremor from the roof to the foundation, raining plaster dust on Gaviria's head. The walls and ceiling were suddenly decorated with networks of cracks, as delicate as spiderwebs. Behind him, in the study, Gaviria heard a crash as the Picasso he had purchased from a thief for three-quarters of a million dollars toppled from the wall behind the bar.

The dealer's house was coming down around him, and his first impulse was flight. A braver man would stand and fight perhaps, but first he had to know his enemy and calculate the odds. Gaviria smelled smoke and realized that he had no time left for plotting strategy.

"Let's go!" he told Ignacio des Campos.

And they ran as if their lives depended on it.

HERMANN SCHWARZ was pleased with the impression his explosive charge had made on Gaviria's house. The blast was late, of course, but that couldn't be helped. It took a bit of time, dispatching two armed men without a sound, and he had still been right on schedule when the shooting started near the pool.

The sudden rush of sentries, answering the sounds of gunfire, slowed his progress even more. Schwarz let them pass, proceeding to the house when they were gone, delivering his plastic charge where it was supposed to go. Instead of seven minutes on the timer, though, he made allowances for premature discovery and gave it thirty seconds. Time enough for him to scuttle out of range and make his secondary target, if he had no further problems on the way.

He was almost there, a fleeting shadow, when the Ironman's charges detonated, taking out the two garages. Fuel tanks went up seconds later in a string of secondary blasts, and Schwarz could see flames leaping well above the west wing of the manor house.

There would be other vehicles around the grounds, of course, but taking out Eduardo's precious fleet of six or seven flashy cars would slow the bastards down a little, leaving most of them on foot.

Not that the gunners showed much inclination to escape just now.

His ears picked up the sound of automatic weapons firing from the general direction of the tennis courts. He wished Carl Lyons luck, and would have gone to help him if his orders had not been specific. Blow the northwest corner of the house, then watch the exit on the south. In theory Lyons had the patio and its attendant exits, while Pol Blancanales took the front. If they excluded tunnels and lift-offs from the roof, they had the palace covered, with Gaviria pinned inside.

As long as they could hold.

His plastic charge exploded, caving in a section of the outer wall as if a giant had delivered one hellacious kick with steel-toed boots. A dozen windows blew at once, the shattered glass propelled by pressure from within, while clouds of smoke and dust rose from the site.

Schwarz, meanwhile, was busy covering his post.

The first men through the door were two of Gaviria's flunkies, one armed with an Uzi submachine gun, the other with a pistol. Schwarz gave them room to run, not wishing to obstruct the exit, watching as the gunners turned away from the explosive sounds of combat near the pool and tennis court.

They ran directly toward him, Gadgets rising up to greet them, firing two short bursts that stopped them and left them stretched out in the lawn, bleeding from a dozen wounds to feed the grass.

The house was burning, bright flames licking at the eaves and following the roofline, when another head poked through the door. Schwarz waited, saw the head withdraw. When the man reappeared, Schwarz could see that he held a CAR-15 and wore an automatic in a shoulder holster, no coat to conceal it. Close behind him, ducking through the doorway, came a second figure.

Bingo!

Schwarz knew Gaviria from his photographs at Stony Man and from the file Brent Favor kept in Medellín. He looked a trifle smaller in the flesh, but there was no mistaking that distinctive profile or the "casual" attire that must have set him back at least a grand.

Instead of circling back toward the garages, Gaviria and his sidekick broke to Schwarz's right, or east. He moved to intercept them, swallowing an urge to shout the dealer's name. There was no point in giving him an edge.

Schwarz could have gunned them down at any time, but he was interested in seeing where they were going. On the east side of the house, there was a shed. Eduardo's watchdog opened the door and slipped inside, Gaviria on his heels. A light came on, illumination spilling through the open door and across the grass.

Schwarz was cautiously approaching when he heard the sudden cough of motorcycle engines firing to life. At once he recognized the risk of losing Gaviria if he didn't act without delay.

The M-203 launcher spit a high-explosive round from forty feet away, and Gadgets watched the shed go up like something from those newsreels where a cyclone trashes flimsy mobile homes. The roof went flying like a Frisbee, while the metal walls blew outward in a thunderclap of smoke and flame.

It was incredible, what human beings could absorb sometimes. Eduardo Gaviria was alive when Gadgets reached him, lying twisted at an angle that betrayed his broken spine. His slacks were burning, but he didn't seem to feel it. Over to his left, Eduardo's bodyguard was spread out like a smorgasbord for cannibals, a Kawasaki's handlebars protruding from his open chest.

The dealer may have seen him standing there, but Schwarz was never positive, the way Eduardo's eyes swam in and out of focus. It was over—he was literally going up in smoke—but Gadgets shot him anyway.

He would have done the same for any wounded animal.

Another blast behind him, something in the house this time, and flames were everywhere. He felt a sudden weariness as he turned to join his friends and finish mopping up.

The Syrian Frontier

THEY CROSSED THE BORDER north of Galilee at dawn. Their vehicles and uniforms were Syrian, authentic to a fault. Their weapons, likewise, were authentic standard issue for the Syrian armed forces: Russian-manufactured AKM assault rifles and Helwan 9 mm semiauto pistols, copied from the Beretta design and manufactured in Egypt. A pair of RPGs, plus frag grenades and chunky blocks of Semtex, smelling heavily of marzipan, completed the ensemble.

There had been no R & R in Israel for the men of Phoenix Force. At a hasty conference with a ranking spokesman for Mossad, they were tipped to the report from an informant that Zuheir al-Qadi had been notified of the destruction wreaked upon his camp and reinforcements. Rather than remain and check the damage for himself, As-Sai'qa's leader had already skipped to friendly Syria, a move designed to save him-

self while he awaited orders and relief from the Iraqis
or his contact in Damascus.

If the latest word was true, a meet had been arranged for al-Qadi with a top Baath Party spokesman
at a camp outside Al Sanamayn.

Katz planned to crash that party and remind his enemies that there was nowhere safe on earth for them to
hide.

But first he had to get there, crossing thirty miles of
open desert, dodging Syrian patrols that ran on no set
schedule, maybe spotter aircraft overhead, and approach the camp in daylight, running in the open.

Between them Katz and Ari Lev spoke Arabic, but
there would be no question of a bluff if they met any
natives face-to-face. In that event there would be nothing else for them to do but shoot it out, rely on speed
and sheer audacity to see them through.

The border crossing could have been a problem in itself, but Ari Lev's superiors whipped up an armored
demonstration ten miles to the north, Israeli tanks ma-
neuvering within a stone's throw of the boundary with
Syria, all kinds of traffic on the radio, diverting border
guards and regular patrols to watch the show. It was an
obvious maneuver, but it worked, and Phoenix Force
was three miles into hostile territory when the cruising
tanks withdrew.

And that left twenty-seven miles to go, with the desert temperature already climbing through the seven-
ties, another thirty-odd degrees to climb before it
reached the daily average.

Katz shifted in his seat, the AKM between his knees,
and felt the perspiration soaking through his khaki
shirt. If they were captured in those uniforms, it meant
a firing squad. Katz had no fear of being taken pris-

oner. If it should come to that, he knew that he would go down fighting, take as many of the bastards with him as he could.

The worst of it would not be death, but failure to complete his mission. Katz had gone on many do-or-die assignments since he first put on a uniform for Israel in his teens, but he had never been defeated by an enemy. The day he lost his arm in combat, fighting on the Golan Heights, his sacrifice bought time for the remainder of his troops to score a stunning victory against the opposition.

Yakov Katzenelenbogen had a reputation to protect. And he did not intend to blow it now.

CHAPTER EIGHTEEN

Stony Man Farm

"They're doing *what?*"

"You heard it right the first time," Aaron Kurtzman said. "They missed al-Qadi in the Bekaa, and they've chased him into Syria."

"Katz should have called it in," said Barbara Price, a note of weary resignation in her voice.

"He cut a deal with the Mossad, some guy he used to hang with. Tel Aviv reports the move to us, but only after they were past the point of no return."

"Well, shit."

"We would have sent them anyway," said Kurtzman.

"Maybe. Damnit, that's beside the point."

"I know."

"We get enough surprises from the opposition as it is, without our own team throwing curves."

"It's done, regardless," Kurtzman said. "They're well across the border now."

"Have you told Hal?"

"I thought we'd flip for it."

"No way. You took the call, you tell him."

Kurtzman shrugged. "Okay. I think I'll have some coffee first."

"You want some Valium with that?"

He laughed. "It's not that bad."

"Correction. If they make it, then it's not so bad. If they get caught, we're up shit creek without a paddle."

Kurtzman frowned and nodded, understanding her concern. It had been risky, sending Phoenix Force to Lebanon, but that was very different from invading Syria. Around Beirut, or even in the Bekaa Valley, Katz and company were immersed in a prevailing atmosphere of chaos. Much of the effective government had broken down, and bands of rebels—many of them foreigners—controlled much of the country.

There would be no sideshow of confusion to assist the Phoenix warriors on a probe of Syria. The ruling government was firmly in control, and while Damascus made a show of camaraderie with Washington, the Syrian regime was known for its enthusiastic sponsorship of terrorism in the Middle East and elsewhere. A failure—even a success, if Katz and comrades were identified—could precipitate a major international incident, questions on the floor of the United Nations, no end to embarrassment.

"What kind of backup are they getting from Mossad?" asked Barbara Price.

"They've got an agent with them," Kurtzman said. "We knew about him from before. Equipment, vehicles, intelligence. They weren't all that specific, Barb."

"Okay, so we just sit and wait."

"Unless you've got some viable alternative," the Bear replied.

"We're still on track with Able Team and Striker, though?" she asked. "I mean, they haven't launched a rocket into space or touched off World War III while I was out for coffee?"

"Not that I'm aware of," Kurtzman answered, putting on a weary smile. "They've both got projects in the works. With any kind of luck, they ought to wrap things up within the next few hours."

Barbara knew what that meant, from experience. When Kurtzman started talking luck, it meant her friends—the men she was responsible for guiding through their mission—were embarking on the worst part of the job. When it was over, picking up the pieces in debriefing, she invariably found that luck had less to do with their survival than a blend of guts, audacity and firepower.

"Fill me in," she said.

"Again we're short on operative details," Kurtzman said. "I know that Striker's got some kind of showdown lined up with the ETA. He's using Jack for air support, and they've got something cooking with the far right on the side."

"In other words, he's gone out on a limb again and started juggling chain saws," Barbara said.

"The guy knows what he's doing."

Barbara changed the subject. "Able Team?"

"They're right on program. Gaviria's out, and they've been agitating for a meet between the FAP and Vargas. They've got both sides walking on a razor's edge right now."

Another waiting game.

"Just once," she said, "I'd like to know the answers going in."

"I guess you haven't called the psychic hot line lately."

"Very funny. Have you given any thought to a career change? Stand-up comedy is very big from what I hear."

"I'd have to make it sit-down," Kurtzman answered, with a rueful smile. "It kind of ruins the mystique."

"I'm sorry, Bear."

"For what?"

She shook her head. "Forget it."

"Done, and done. As I recall, we were about to flip for who calls Hal."

"Your memory's short-circuiting again," she said. "You're calling Hal."

"Oh, hell. That's right. I guess I might as well get on it."

Barbara forced a smile. "See you later, Aaron."

"Right."

When he was gone, she poured a steaming cup of coffee, sat down and concentrated on the map in front of her. Three battlefields, the possibilities of failure multiplied in triplicate.

Defeatist thinking.

Barbara concentrated on the positive, remembering that Striker, Able Team and Phoenix Force all shared one trait in common.

They were all adept at kicking ass.

The Pyrenees

THE VILLA HAD BEEN vacant since its owner took his family away from Renteria, into France. He was a manufacturer of sporting goods, but operating costs in Basqueland had become prohibitive with the ETA's oppressive "revolutionary tax." In lieu of payment, his alternatives were death or flight, and he had joined the exodus of citizens who balked at subsidizing terrorism with their hard-earned cash. Alphonse Gogorza viewed him as a traitor, but his absence offered certain benefits.

The villa, for example.

It was on the market, but prospective buyers were discouraged by the tales of bombing and assassination in the province. If they failed to read the headlines, helpful members of the ETA could always phone and remind them of the risks involved with buying in a war zone. Thus, Gogorza punished the elusive owner for his failure to cooperate, while gaining access to a handy home away from home.

The villa made a perfect trap, a single road approaching from the west, with rugged peaks surrounding it on the other three sides. That gave his adversary one way in . . . no way out.

He had regretted picking up the woman almost from the moment she was kidnapped, but the incident was working to his advantage after all. They hadn't managed to secure her father, but Lozaro was a man who thrived on controversy and publicity; he couldn't hide for very long. There would be other chances to remove him from the scene, and in the meantime they were dealing with a larger problem, burying the adversary who had stirred up so much hell in the past two days.

Gogorza still was not entirely sure exactly whom he should expect—the ANE, perhaps, or someone else— but he was ready with a force of fifty men, the cream of those available upon short notice. Armed with modern weapons, they were concealed about the property for maximum effect. It would be a great surprise for anyone approaching on the single winding road.

As for the woman, he had promised to deliver her, and so he would. It was a small thing, dragging her along, and she might come in handy if his enemies demanded proof that she was still alive before they stepped into the trap.

She was alive, all right, if not exactly well. She had resisted questioning and suffered minor damage during the interrogation, but a visit to the hospital should put it right. Several of Gogorza's men had started to amuse themselves with her before he got the call for an exchange, but they had not accomplished much, for all their macho boasting. He would punish the bastards later for the breach of discipline.

As for the Lozaro woman, there could be no question of releasing her. In other kidnap situations, where a ransom was demanded and security maintained, the victim was released with no risk to the ETA. The woman, though, had seen too many faces during her interrogation and the games that followed. She could testify in court—would testify, considering her background and her father's hatred for the movement—and Gogorza couldn't let that happen.

One more death was nothing in the long view. Who would really miss the bitch when she was dead and gone? Her father, certainly...but Pablo would be close behind her, on his way to hell.

Gogorza double-checked his weapons, killing time. He wore the Astra A-80 pistol in a high-ride holster on his hip, fifteen rounds of 9 mm parabellum in the magazine and one in the chamber. His main weapon was the Star Model Z-70 submachine gun, favored by his soldiers for its compact size, light weight and relative concealability.

There would be no need for concealment this time, though. His enemies, when they arrived, would find themselves surrounded and cut off from all escape.

They would defend themselves as best they could, of course, but it should not take long to wipe them out.

It had to be the ANE, and yet ...

The caller was American; he had admitted that. Jose Silveira of the ANE was not noted for his use of foreign mercenaries, but his troops had been depleted by assassinations and arrests. The execution of his brother was enough, perhaps, to make him send for outside help.

What other explanation could there be?

If they were living in the 1970s, he might have blamed the CIA, but the Americans had taken care of that in public hearings, dragging out their dirty laundry for the world to see and laugh at, passing regulations that forbade the Company from using murder as a tool of policy.

But, then again, rules were made to be broken.

Gogorza shrugged the problem off. Whoever his enemies turned out to be, they were definitely on their way by now. The drive from Renteria would take time, on winding mountain roads, and he assumed the opposition would be punctual.

He hoped so.

It would be a shame to keep his soldiers waiting when they so looked forward to a massacre.

Bello, Colombia

MANUEL VARGAS LET his houseman take the phone call, hoping it was something simple for a change. At this point even news from the United States would be welcome—a minor bust, perhaps, or even good news— as a change of pace.

But he had no such luck.

He saw the houseman coming for him, with a dour expression on his face.

"*¿Qué es?*"

"*El teléfono, Jefe.*"

Vargas shook his head in weary disbelief. "Who is it, Paco?"

A confused look from the houseman, followed by a shrug. "He wouldn't say. He told me it's important, though. About the FAP."

"Why must I deal with everything myself?" asked Vargas even as he rose from his chair. The flunkie shrugged.

"Hello?"

A voice he didn't recognize came back at Vargas. "I was thinking that you might be interested in what Otero's people have on tap for you and yours."

"Who is this?"

"What's the difference? Let's just say we have a common interest in Otero being put away for good."

He pictured the police or military agents, crouching in a third-rate office somewhere, tape recorders humming, capturing his every word. If he uttered any statement that could possibly be twisted into evidence of a conspiracy, it would be one more charge against him, if and when he ever went to trial.

"I don't know this Otero you refer to," Vargas said.

The strange voice chuckled in his ear. "I get you. Hell, for all you know this could be the police, the prosecutor's office, even state security. I like a man who thinks fast on his feet."

"I still don't understand—"

The stranger interrupted him, no laughter now. "Suppose I do the talking. You just listen. There'll be nothing anyone could hang you on from that."

A moment's hesitation, then he said, "I'm listening."

"Otero and his people have been taking hits the same as you. His common sense says you're responsible."

"I don't—"

"Just listen for a minute, will you? I'm not laying any blame, and if I was, it wouldn't mean a thing in court without acknowledgment from you. My point is that Otero plans to pay you back in kind. He's got an army shaping up, and job one on their list is nailing you, along with anybody else from M-19 they meet along the way."

"I've never heard of this Otero or the M-19," said Vargas, getting it on tape, but he couldn't disguise the subtle tremor in his voice.

"In that case, it won't matter to you that Otero knows about your secret place. I mean the site ten miles from where you're sitting at the moment. Does it ring a bell?"

"I've no idea—"

The stranger forged ahead, not hearing him. "Otero's people have coordinates and they have muscle. Christ, for all I know, they're on the move right now. You don't have worlds of time."

He had to take a chance. "Assuming that I knew what any of this means, which I do not, why would a stranger call and give me this advice? Who are you? This is an unlisted number. How did you obtain it?"

"Never mind the number. You've got friends you may not even recognize in Medellín and other places who admire your courage and your work. I'm one of them. My job sometimes allows me access to a piece of classified material."

"If you—"

"I don't expect you to believe me," said the stranger. "You'd be foolish to reply, and no one with a shred of common sense mistakes you for a fool. But at the same time, you must recognize at least the possibility that what I've told you is the truth. You can't afford to shut your eyes and just pretend I never called."

"I'm hanging up now," Vargas said.

"Of course. You have important things to do."

The line went dead with that, the dial tone humming in his ear, and Vargas cradled the receiver.

Damn it all!

He was ninety-eight percent convinced the caller must have been a plant, some agent of the Medellín police or military intelligence assigned to play a role, find out if Vargas would betray himself that easily. Well, he had passed the test...but there was still that nagging two percent of doubt.

Suppose the caller *was* a friend of M-19 who shied away from personal involvement? Vargas knew such "closet" revolutionaries numbered in the thousands, and it stood to reason that at least a few of them held jobs in government, where certain files and documents would cross their desks from time to time. Was it so unbelievable that one of them would see a memo or a transcript and be moved to warn his secret idols of disaster in the making? Surely it was not impossible.

He shook his head to clear his mind. It was a trap, no matter how he viewed the phone call. If he totally ignored the warning, and it came to pass that soldiers of the FAP were massing for a raid against his "secret place," he would be sacrificing vital soldiers and supplies. If, on the other hand, he mobilized a force to help defend the jungle site, he would effectively admit complicity in its establishment.

What difference did it make?

The stranger obviously knew about his link to the facility, and while the state might lack sufficient evidence to bring a charge in court, they had enough on Vargas for a firing squad already, come what may. They had to catch him first, before he faced the guns.

And in the meantime, if the caller was correct, he stood to lose a vital portion of his fighting force.

Which left no alternative at all.

He turned to face the houseman, snapping orders in an urgent voice, the stooge repeating them verbatim.

"Do it now."

"*Sí, Jefe.*"

He would take the chance, and if the army lay in wait for him, they would not find him unprepared.

It was time for M-19 to strike in self-defense, and God help anyone who stood in his way.

Baghdad, Iraq

WITH DARKNESS FALLING on the city, Afif al-Takriti decided it was time to leave. He had been hoping that events abroad might stabilize, but that didn't appear to be the case. Instead of lying low or wiping out their enemies, his contacts in the terrorist community continued taking body blows, responding feebly if at all.

The Father-Leader of Iraq was not amused. In fact, his attitude had verged on menacing when he had warned al-Takriti hours earlier that they must have no more bad news.

Since then, the news had all been bad, a litany of woes that would undoubtedly be climaxed with al-Takriti's execution if he didn't slip away. It was providential, thought al-Takriti, that his plans had all been laid out in advance, his hiding place in readiness.

Now all he had to do was slip away from Baghdad unobserved, no small task in itself.

Al-Takriti didn't think Saddam was watching him— at least no more than he watched everyone around him—but precautions would be taken all the same. A borrowed car to reach the airport, a disguise of sorts to match the photos in his bogus passport, and he could be on his way before the next sunrise.

Away and safe from harm…unless the Father-Leader tracked him down.

Al-Takriti shuddered but he held to his resolve. One problem at a time was adequate for any man to pon-der. He would take care to cover his tracks, and by the time Saddam could trace him—if a trace were even possible—al-Takriti would have claimed his cash, set off for some new destination faraway.

It was a shame, he thought, to leave great work un-done, but a survivor didn't linger in the face of danger when the opportunity for victory was plainly gone. Self-preservation was the prime directive, and al-Takriti meant to save himself at any cost.

A reputation could be built from scratch, but once the man was dead, all efforts were in vain.

He took some time with the disguise, applying spirit gum and fastening the mustache to his upper lip. It wasn't one of those ridiculous mustaches like the Groucho Marx impersonators wore, but rather a de-vice of quality, prepared with a professional in mind. Real hair, and no expense spared in the preparation, artists making sure it was exactly right.

When he was finished with the mustache, he went on to fix the artificial scar that ran from his right eyebrow to the corner of his mouth. Again he used professional materials, applying them as he had been instructed by his acting coach. The man was dead now, sad to say, an unsolved stabbing in the street. Al-Takriti's little secret had gone with him to the grave.

A change of clothes, an outfit that he wore only at home, before the mirror, and his task was nearly done. No living man had ever seen him wear this suit, these shoes. The items had been purchased for him by an aide in the belief they would be used in covert operations. Not a total lie, at that. The aide, as if it mattered, had been lately detailed to assist UN inspectors in their tour of Iraqi power plants.

Al-Takriti saved the most unpleasant portion of the ritual for last. The all-white contact lens was large, uncomfortable and opaque. It had required no end of practice just for him to put it in and take it out successfully. Al-Takriti still despised it, with the chafing pain, the blinding of his right eye that was automatic with the lens in place, but it was part of his disguise.

In truth, the most effective part.

He wedged the contact lens in place, allowed himself a few choice oaths, then scrutinized his image in the mirror. It was quite a different man, he thought. His mother might have known him, given time and opportunity for a minute inspection, but his closest friends would pass him on the street without a second look. The white eye and the scar, on top of everything, were obvious enough to make most strangers glance away, afraid of the embarrassment that came with staring at the handicapped.

Exactly the reaction he was hoping for.

Al-Takriti's bag was packed and ready. In the parking lot of his apartment house, a borrowed vehicle was waiting. Any lookouts of Saddam's would certainly have seen al-Takriti coming home. The subsequent appearance of a strange man in a strange car should not stir them from their posts.

And by the time they recognized the gravity of their mistake, al-Takriti would be gone. Saddam could vent his wrath on them instead of a disciple who had served him faithfully for years.

It was poetic justice.

And al-Takriti was making up the verses as he went along.

CHAPTER NINETEEN

The Pyrenees

"We're getting there," Grimaldi said, his soft voice sounding scratchy in Bolan's earpiece. "Five minutes, give or take."

The Executioner was more than ready, leaning forward in his seat to scrutinize the rugged peaks around them. Jack Grimaldi flew the helicopter down as low as safety would permit, some of the crags like looming giants overhead, all of them seeming close enough to touch.

The warrior checked his watch and found that they were doing well in terms of time. The plan required an indirect approach, with Bolan unobserved on touchdown, coming up behind his enemies—and that meant extra time for scrambling over rocks and ledges, making like a mountain goat. It was a game the Basques grew up with, and he could not let himself be second best.

"You think Silveira's people will be there on time?" Grimaldi asked.

"No way to tell," said Bolan. "I'm just hoping they show up at all."

"You stirred them up, all right," said Jack. "They hate Gogorza's guts. Too bad we can't sit back and let them do each other in."

"That wouldn't help the lady," Bolan said.

Grimaldi nodded. "Right. Assuming she's along."

"It's in Gogorza's interest to produce her," Bolan said. "He's still not sure exactly where I'm coming from, what tricks I might have up my sleeve. He gets a call to put the lady on, and she's not there, he blows it. My bet is he won't leave anything to chance."

"So all you have to do is stroll in there and take her out, the both of you alive and well."

"That's it," said Bolan, grinning despite himself at the irony in his friend's voice.

"And you're the one who doesn't go for miracles."

"Right now," the Executioner replied, "I'll take whatever I can get."

They flew for several moments without speaking.

"So anyway," said Grimaldi, "I hang back out of sight and give you ten before I crash the party. Any problems going in, you've got an open channel. Say the word, I'll lift you out of there and give the bastards hell."

"I'm counting on it," Bolan said.

Bolan wished it were safe to double back and check the winding road that climbed from Renteria to the higher elevations. Confirmation of Silveira's movements would have put his mind at ease, but in the last analysis it hardly mattered.

Bolan was committed to a meeting with Alphonse Gogorza and his men. Whatever happened in regard to the diversion, whether the arrival of Gogorza's enemies made Bolan's work a little easier or not, he would proceed.

A woman he had never seen before was waiting for him, even though she didn't know it yet. More to the point, the Executioner had pledged to do a job, regard-

less of the odds, and he would not—could not—turn
back.

"Here goes."

It wasn't quite a meadow, more a sloping stretch of
grass against the mountainside, but it would have to do.
Grimaldi swung the Cobra gunship in a tight half circle, settling down, while Bolan disengaged his headset
and his safety harness, making ready to go EVA.

He turned and flashed a smile at Jack, the thumbs-up
signal passed between them. Bolan tucked the FA MAS
beneath his arm and ducked out through the hatch, bent
low to run beneath the whirling rotor blades. Grimaldi
lifted off once more, and he was on his own.

The Cobra rose and circled out of sight. Inside the
cockpit, Jack Grimaldi would be counting down the
numbers even now... which meant that Bolan had no
time to waste.

He checked his compass, got his bearings and began
to hike across the mountainside. He matched his pace
to the terrain, his breathing to the altitude, pushing
himself as his body began to adapt.

He could feel time slipping through his fingers as he
stalked across the mountainside, homing in on his still-
invisible target. Time for Maria Lozaro. Time for Jack
Grimaldi. For his enemies.

Perhaps, the Executioner admitted, for himself.

Western Syria

THE SUN WAS three hands high and blistering the desert
floor when Katz first glimpsed their destination dead
ahead. He didn't use the walkie-talkie, instead signal-
ing to Calvin James and company behind him with a
simple wave of his arm. The lookouts would have spot-

ted them by now, and any extraordinary maneuvers would betray them instantly, before they came in firing range.

Easy does it, he thought, and McCarter obviously felt the same, holding a steady speed with the jeep, reaching down with his right hand and hoisting the folding-stock AKM into his lap. Behind Katz, Rafael Encizo had his weapon cocked and ready, resting on his knees.

Two hundred yards and closing.

Katzenelenbogen didn't bother double-checking his Kalashnikov. It had been cocked since he got in the staff car, with the safety off, prepared for any unforeseen emergency. He kept the rifle close now, with the fingers of his good left hand wrapped tight around the pistol grip.

One hundred yards.

Stick figures blossomed into full-blown human beings, armed with automatic weapons, staking out the fenced perimeter of an extensive compound. At a guess Katz thought the camp must stretch at least two hundred yards, north to south, approximately one hundred yards east to west. Inside the chain-link fence with tangled razor wire on top, he made out tents and huts constructed of corrugated metal, painted desert camouflage to frustrate aerial surveillance and attack.

The gate was roughly fifteen feet across and set on wheels, three gunmen stationed there in readiness to fend off an assault or grant admittance to expected guests. Katz wondered what they must be thinking, checking out the dust trail of the staff cars drawing closer by the moment, but he couldn't place himself inside their minds.

The next best thing was getting in their faces, and another moment put him there, McCarter braking slowly into the approach. One guard was watching from inside the gate, his two companions moving forward to inspect the new arrivals. The familiar vehicles and uniforms had lulled their first suspicion, but a close look would demolish the illusion. They were bound to blow the whistle any second now....

Katz and McCarter fired together, one on either side, their human targets going down like rag dolls in a windstorm. On the far side of the gate, the third man shouted something unintelligible to the camp at large and grappled with the AK-47 that was hanging, muzzle down, across one shoulder.

Katz unleashed a short burst from his AKM that put the Arab gunner on his back, legs twitching in the dust. McCarter stood on the accelerator then, and they surged forward, smashing through the gate with some resistance from the chain-link fencing, but the razor wire came down behind them, in the space between the vehicles, and Gary Manning ground it underneath his wheels.

They went in firing, Syrians and Palestinians in disarray on every side, some armed, while others scrambled for weapons they had briefly laid aside. There had been no way for them to establish targets, beyond Mossad's prediction that Zuheir al-Qadi would be present with at least one ranking member of the Baath Party, and Katz had decided to take things as they came.

A lookout tower on his right was spitting bullets, one rebounding off the staff car's fender. Katz fired back, momentum and the swerving of the vehicle a handicap, spent brass erupting from the AKM's ejection port.

Somehow he hit the tower guard. It may have been a flesh wound or a graze—Katz never knew—but he could witness the results. The guard lurched backward, tried to save himself by hanging on to his machine gun. The weapon broke free of its mount, the recoil adding new momentum to the Arab's backward sprawl. The crow's nest had a waist-high railing, with a roof on wooden posts to offer shade. The gunman toppled over, plunged thirty feet, the machine gun firing all the way.

Unlike a movie stunt man, this one didn't rise and walk away.

Katz ducked as bullets whispered past him, and McCarter put the staff car through a zigzag, racing toward a hut that seemed to be the base command post. It was worth a shot, at least, and they had to start somewhere.

The question for Katz at the moment was where it would end.

Antioquia Province, Colombia

THE LONG HIKE in had taken ninety minutes, watching out for traps and sentries on the way. But it was worth the effort, Blancanales thought, to put them on the firing line without a chance of having been observed. The downside, when he thought about it, was the absence of a swift escape route.

Once the battle started, it would all come down to do or die.

The Able warriors fanned out in accordance with the strategy they had arranged before departing Medellín. Encirclement was difficult, with only three men on the site, but they avoided covering the access road on the west side of the camp, and thereby saved themselves some ground.

If anyone was coming from the city, Blancanales didn't want to keep them from their destination. Right now letting people *in* was part and parcel of the plan.

He had already caught a glimpse of Manuel Vargas moving restlessly around the compound, an inspection tour of sorts. The rebel leader seemed distinctly out of place in slacks and sport shirt, while his men wore olive drab fatigues or jungle camouflage, but he was clearly in control. He wore an automatic pistol on his hip and had a submachine gun slung over his shoulder, looking more like an undercover cop than one of Colombia's ten most-wanted fugitives.

It would have been a relatively simple thing to snipe him from the trees, rain fire and steel upon the camp, but Blancanales and his warriors had agreed to wait. Another hour, maybe more, to find out if Luis Otero and his gunners from the FAP were really on their way.

Ten minutes later Blancanales had his answer. Sudden turmoil erupted in the camp, a chopping sound of rotors as the helicopter came in overhead. A gunner in the open cargo bay cut loose with automatic fire to scatter and distract the M-19 guerrillas, keep their heads down.

Show time!

There was no need to alert his comrades. Schwarz and Lyons both had ringside seats, and both of them would know exactly what was happening. The FAP had showed, all right, and they were coming in with no holds barred, no quarter asked or offered.

Blancanales braced himself for action as the helicopter gunship swung away and out of sight, its mission finished. On his left wild firing had erupted at ground level, M-19 defenders standing fast against the spearhead of Otero's charging troops. They held at first, but it was difficult, the jungle offering concealment to their enemies, while members of the forest garrison were more or less exposed.

As the pointmen for Otero's column fought their way into the camp, Blancanales's own approach was hardly noticed, save by one young rebel he surprised as he emerged from the trees. The young man raised his submachine gun, finger on the trigger. Then Blancanales hit him with a 3-round burst that opened up his chest and dumped him over backward in the dirt.

It was a three-way race, of sorts, from that point on. The men of Able Team were heavily outnumbered, but that made it easier, at least in principle, for them to move among the rival soldiers, pausing here and there to wreak some havoc of their own. In fact, the air was thick with flying bullets that couldn't discriminate between one target and another, drilling tents and prefab buildings, tearing flesh and stripping greenery from the surrounding trees. The Able warriors had no special magic that would keep them safe, aside from sheer audacity.

In front of Blancanales stood an open shed with fifty-gallon oil drums stacked inside. He guessed that something in the drums was probably combustible, his finger tightening around the trigger of the M-203 launcher mounted underneath the barrel of his M-16 A1.

The high-explosive round went in on target, touching off a firestorm as the drums of fuel were ruptured, set afire, the vapors from their contents burning under pressure. Blancanales shrank back from the heat, recoiling, dropping prone as smoking shrapnel waffled overhead.

A secondary blast, and several of the drums took flight like great, unwieldy rockets, wobbling off at different angles, dragging tails of fire. They came down in their own good time, incinerating tents, collapsing Quonset huts, flattening the runners who attempted to escape.

A little glimpse of hell on earth.

And Pol felt right at home.

The Pyrenees

JOSE DIEGUEZ SILVEIRA had been waging war against the ETA for so long now that it was easy for him to forget exactly how the conflict started. At the moment, though, he needed no reminders. From the instant of his brother's death, he had been pledged to slaughter every Basque insurgent he could find.

And now he had his chance.

There were risks, of course, but Silveira had taken every possible precaution. He had friends with the police and military intelligence, still loyal to the Falangist principles of the Franco years, and they had all assured him that the phone call was not part of an official scheme to crush his organization. That left unofficial rivals of the left or right, and Silveira believed that his shock troops were well enough armed to cope with any challenge they would meet.

The ETA was foremost in his thoughts, of course. It seemed unlikely that Gogorza's people would invite him to attack their sanctuary in the Pyrenees, but there was no end to the treachery of Basque guerrillas in their endless war to amputate a vital part of Spain. Whatever their intentions, if the ETA had placed the call, they would regret it soon enough.

The mountain road was narrow, switching back upon itself each hundred yards or so, as if the engineers had done their best to carve a giant serpent on the mountainside. Jose Silveira occupied the front seat of the third car in the caravan, four more behind him, close to forty guns in all. He could have doubled that by calling in his troops from other provinces, but that meant waiting past the deadline, and he didn't plan to miss his golden opportunity.

Before the sun went down this day, Alphonse Gogorza and his soldiers would become statistics.

He had never seen the villa that the nameless caller had described, but there were hundreds like it in the nearby mountains. Most were summer homes or weekend hideouts for the wealthy, but a growing number had been rented to tourists or converted into minilodges for the skiing season. He could picture it already, the pastoral setting, hardly evocative of a battlefield.

But that would change, and quickly, once Silveira and his men arrived.

Their first glimpse of the villa came when they were still at least two hundred yards distant. Just a peek, but it confirmed Silveira's notion of the place: a rambling house, outbuildings, planted in the middle of a smallish meadow, rugged slopes surrounding the property on three sides.

They were approaching from the fourth side, coming from the west, and it was probable that spotters had already seen their convoy on the road. Silveira used his hand-held radio to urge the point car on to greater speed, prodding his driver with an elbow as the vehicles in front of them began to pull away.

Surprise was out of the question now, unless his adversaries were asleep at their posts. And in the absence of surprise, audacity was normally the next best thing.

How long before they started taking fire? Silveira's car was armored, purchased with donations from a sympathetic millionaire in Majorca, but the other vehicles were standard factory issue. It would not take much to stall a car on the narrow mountain road, block those behind it and create a two-lane slaughter pen.

Still, he had faith in the commandos he had handpicked for the point cars. Each and every one of them was a killer, tested and proven, and none of them had ever let him down.

Not yet.

No firing from the villa as they reached the final curve and powered into the approach. Silveira felt a sudden apprehension that the villa would be empty, the phone call a ruse to lure him away from home while the ETA struck on his flank. But he would fool them, even then, for he had left a trusted security force behind to deal with any problems in his absence.

No. If the insurgents wanted to destroy him, they would have to do it face-to-face.

As if in answer to his thoughts, a sheet of automatic fire descended from the villa, bullets rattling off Silveira's armored vehicle like pellets in a sudden hailstorm. Up ahead he saw the point cars taking hits, the second driver swerving out of line in an attempt to gain more ground before his engine took a fatal hit.

Initiative, by God! The courage of a born crusader!

"Hurry! Faster, man!" Silveira snapped.

His driver grunted, stood on the accelerator, speeding forward.

Into the jaws of the storm.

Western Syria

IT WOULD HAVE BEEN more pleasant, Ari Lev decided, to sit back and watch Israeli jets destroy the desert compound with their cluster bombs and napalm . . . but he didn't have a choice. The battle had been joined, and there was no time now for second thoughts on strategy.

The spacious compound had become a shooting gallery, confusion Ari Lev's one ally as he bailed out of the staff car, sprinting for the cover of a nearby Quonset hut. The "borrowed" vehicles and uniforms had given them an edge to start with, and the costume still worked in his favor, with soldiers running everywhere, almost hysterical in their pursuit of fleeting targets.

They were looking for the enemy, but common uniforms and drifting battle smoke made spotting doubly difficult. Only close inspection could determine whether any given individual was friend or foe, and hesitation on the battleground was tantamount to suicide.

The sound of footsteps at his back brought Ari Lev around. Two Syrians were moving toward him, neither leveling his weapon, the pointman looking visibly relieved to see a friendly face . . . until he realized the face was strange to him, an infiltrator staring at him down the barrel of an AKM.

One burst was all it took to drop both soldiers in their tracks, the sound of gunfire blending with combat noises from the camp at large. Lev checked his flank, made certain there were no more adversaries close enough to surprise him, then turned back to the main event.

One of the lookout towers took a hit from Rafael Encizo's RPG. The crow's nest seemed to vaporize on impact, wooden planks reduced to flying slivers, all of it consumed by fire. The tower was a giant smoking torch and starting to disintegrate. The ladder fell away and smashed to the ground, its huge legs blown away by the blast. One leg came down across the shoulders of a Palestinian guerrilla, flattened him and pinned his body to the earth. Another fell across the mess tent, rupturing a line that fed the stoves with liquid propane gas. A spark caught underneath the flapping tent, and the resultant fiery blast consumed the propane tank, the tent and half a dozen soldiers sheltered there.

It was a slaughterhouse out there, but Ari Lev knew it could still go either way. His team was heavily outnumbered, and he could see nothing of the targets that had drawn him here. Zuheir al-Qadi, for the Thunderbolt. Issam Moshin representing the Baath Party, from Damascus.

Both of them were marked for death, but Ari Lev had to find them first.

He circled back to the Quonset hut. It's door was open, beckoning to the unwary with a slice of darkness. Ari Lev went through the doorway in a graceful shoulder roll and came up with his rifle braced against his hip, prepared for anything.

A solitary soldier sat between two bunks, legs folded, trying to become invisible. It didn't work, and he was working on Plan B—armed self-defense—when Ari shot him in the forehead.

He swiftly checked the other bunks, found no more hidden stragglers, and left a fist-size Semtex charge behind. His calling card. The timer gave him ninety seconds to evacuate, and Lev wasted no time bailing out.

He hit the hard ground running, shoulders hunched and ready to receive a bullet. It could come from anywhere. In front of him, behind, from either side. The shot that killed him might come from a Syrian, a Palestinian or even one of his companions, suddenly disoriented in the battle murk. A bullet had no loyalty; it could not discriminate.

And so he ran as if his life depended on it.

Knowing that it did.

Behind him the explosion tore his recent hiding place apart, the fireball chasing Ari Lev like dragon's breath.

CHAPTER TWENTY

The Pyrenees

Mack Bolan heard the gunfire from a distance as he cleared the final mountain pass that separated him from his intended destination. He was running late, impeded by a rock slide, but from what he saw below, he wasn't *too* late.

Not yet.

The warrior picked up speed, moving with greater confidence now that he had solid ground beneath his feet instead of shifting rock and sliding shale. The villa and its smaller buildings lay some eighty yards below him, with the winding mountain road another fifty yards or so beyond. The arrival of Silveira's troops had drawn away whatever sentries had been assigned to watch the back of the house, and Bolan met no opposition going in.

He still had time before Grimaldi made his strike, but it was running short. No time at all to waste on doubts or second guesses. He would have to do it right the first time or forget about the whole damned thing.

And cutting loose was not an option.

Not with Maria Lozaro a hostage, caught up in the cross fire.

He ran across the meadow, praying that Gogorza wasn't paranoid enough to sew the field with mines or trip wires. Sliding into cover beside a small garage, he caught his breath and listened to the battle heating up a few yards distant, just beyond his line of sight.

It seemed as if the ANE was out in force. He counted seven cars, with two of them apparently disabled, passengers unloading on the house and yard with everything they had. And it was plenty, including automatic rifles, submachine guns, riot shotguns, side arms. All they needed now was Arnold Schwarzenegger striding through the battle smoke, immune to bullets, and the scene could easily have fit with any action movie coming out of Hollywood.

Except that it was real.

The bodies stretched out on the ground were leaking real blood from their wounds, and they wouldn't jump up to fetch a cup of coffee if you shouted "Cut!" A gunner died before his eyes, and Bolan watched as buckshot ripped off the guy's scalp, a crimson halo spurting as he fell.

Time to move.

Approximately sixty feet separated the villa and the small garage. An easy stroll in normal circumstances, but it turned into a bloody gauntlet with so many bullets in the air. One shot would do the job; they didn't even have to aim. A stray would take him down as well as any expert marksman's bullet could have done.

But Bolan had no choice.

He broke from cover, sprinting for the house, heard angry hornets sizzle past him as he ran. One nicked the stock of Bolan's FA MAS and slapped the piece against his hip, but Bolan held the rifle fast and concentrated on his destination. Reached it. Paused just long enough to catch his breath.

Lozaro's daughter would be somewhere in the house, he knew, and getting in was the priority. He worked along the eastern wall, crouched low to slip beneath the windows unobserved, until he reached a door.

And found it locked.

He hadn't brought the picks along and had no time to fool with them in any case. Instead, he rose, stepped back a pace and blew the lock apart with three rounds from his automatic rifle. Stealth went out the window in pursuit of urgency.

He barged across the threshold, cleared the entryway in two long strides, moved through the vacant pantry, kitchen, dining room. Now there were choices to be made. The house branched into wings, a staircase on his left providing access to the second floor.

Outside, a hand grenade exploded, its shrapnel clearing several downstairs window frames.

He took a chance and started up the stairs.

Antioquia Province, Colombia

SCHWARZ WAS ABOUT TO LOB a frag grenade at the motor pool when death crept up behind him, reaching out with strangler's arms. He never knew exactly how the FAP guerrilla lost his weapon, but the guy was bent on killing someone, anyone, and Schwarz's camouflage fatigues made him resemble any other M-19 commando in the camp.

He nearly dropped the lethal egg when he was tackled from behind, a slip that would have cost his life, but Schwarz maintained his grip somehow, kicked back and dropped his chin to keep one hairy arm from cutting off his air.

It was a strange sensation, grappling with a stranger on his back and both hands full. He dared not drop the frag grenade, and if he lost the M-16 A1, there was at least a chance his enemy could pick it up and fire before Schwarz had an opportunity to counter his attack.

He struggled for a moment silently, his enemy a dead weight on the Able warrior's shoulders, one arm wrapped around his neck, the other scrabbling at his ammo belt for any weapon it could find. Schwarz kicked back sharply, hoping for a shin or instep, fanning empty air.

Goddamn it!

Clutching fingers found his Ka-bar fighting knife and tried to yank it from its sheath. A strap around the pommel held it fast, but not for long. Schwarz lashed out with the butt of his assault piece, feeling stupid in his awkwardness.

How long before his sweaty palm lost touch with the grenade? Five seconds after that, he could expect a clap of thunder, jagged shrapnel ripping through his legs and entrails, little satisfaction in the knowledge that his enemy would almost certainly die with him in the clinch.

The world was spinning, getting hazy, but he had a sudden inspiration. It would call for strength, agility, precision timing, but he just might pull it off.

And he had nothing more to lose by the attempt.

Schwarz braced himself, feet wide apart, and reached behind him with his right hand, wedging it between his own back and the belly of his tormentor. The strangler's shirt had worked loose from his pants, and Schwarz felt hairy, naked skin against his knuckles.

Perfect.

With a mighty twist and shove, he plunged his hand inside the waistband of his adversary's pants, released the frag grenade and yanked his hand out. Before the movement was completed, Schwarz was bending forward at the waist, knees flexing, letting gravity take over for a classic judo toss.

Three seconds left and counting, as his enemy sailed overhead and came down in front of Schwarz with force enough to steal his breath away. Schwarz could have kicked his teeth in, but there was no time.

He turned and bolted, flung himself headlong toward a nearby tent. Poor shelter, but he took what he could get, relying on the laws of physics to protect him from the main brunt of the blast.

And when it blew, the frag grenade was muted, partly smothered by the nameless gunner's body as he tried to rise, still dazed. There was no question of surviving a grenade at skin-touch range, both legs sheared off, his torso shredded from the breastbone downward.

Jesus.

Schwarz avoided looking at the mess he'd made. It was a sloppy way to kill, extravagant by any standards, but he didn't make the rules. If there had been a way to save himself by juggling chain saws while he whistled "Yankee Doodle," Gadgets would have tried that, too.

Unlike his latest enemy, the compound's motor pool was still intact. A couple of the vehicles had taken hits from random fire, but nothing serious. A broken windshield here, a dimpled fender there.

Schwarz meant to take the rebels' rolling stock and turn it into so much scrap iron, but his last grenade had gone into the dead man's shorts. Instead, he fed the M-203 launcher with a high-explosive round and lined his sights on the middle vehicle of five parked in a row.

It was a relatively easy shot, but Gadgets took his time. He still heard ringing in his ears from the traumatic pressure on his throat a moment earlier, and he hadn't entirely overcome the minute trembling of his hands. Schwarz took perhaps a heartbeat longer than he would have under normal circumstances, nothing that a casual observer could identify as hesitation, squeezing off when he was sure he had it right.

The target was a vintage panel truck, all primer gray, with rust spots showing on the undercarriage. Schwarz's HE round made a clean hit on the nose, erupting into brilliant flames. The gas tank blew a moment later, finishing the vehicles on either side. When they in turn exploded, Gadgets watched a flaming tire and wheel pop out of the inferno, rolling arrow straight across the camp.

He followed it toward the CP hut to see what he could find.

The Pyrenees

MARIA LOZARO had no clear grasp of what was happening outside her room, but she was frightened by the sounds of combat echoing around the villa. She couldn't begin to guess how many guns and machine guns were firing. An explosion rocked the villa, followed moments later by a second blast that sounded closer than the first.

Her little room was on the second floor. Maria knew that much because she had been forced to climb the stairs, a gunman hanging on to her left arm, using the excuse to let his greasy fingers rub against her breast. The blindfold had not been removed until they had her safe inside the room that she now occupied. It had no windows, and the furniture consisted of a cot and folding chair. She thought of using one or both to barricade the door, but it wouldn't be possible with hands cuffed tight behind her back.

At least her legs were free, allowing her to pace the floor and work off nervous energy, but since the shooting started, she had huddled in the corner farthest from the door and impotently wished herself away to any other spot on earth.

Maria was certain that she was marked for death. She had already seen too many faces, heard too many names in careless conversation, for her kidnappers to let her go. On top of that, as long as she survived, Gogorza and his cronies could be sure Maria would continue with her father's work.

It was ironic, that. A few more hours, days at most, and she would have been gone. Abduction by the ETA had changed her mind about an old man's personal crusade, and now the enemy would have to kill her for her newfound principles.

Unless *their* enemies broke in and killed her first.

Whatever was happening outside, Maria knew Gogorza's men were not engaged in idle target practice. Rather, they were fighting for their lives, but she could only guess at the identity of their assailants. Right-wing thugs, perhaps?

A statement overheard in passing came back to her. Someone was putting fierce heat on the ETA, though she couldn't have said exactly who or why. Gogorza's sudden urge to move her was at least an indirect result of those attacks, but it provided nothing in the way of explanation.

Even if her father had believed in violence, he couldn't have done such things alone, and who was there to help him?

Who could save her now?

A sound of footsteps in the hallway brought Maria to her feet. They would be coming back to finish it, she thought, and hoped the bastards would be merciful at least. A simple bullet in the brain.

Alphonse Gogorza entered, a pair of gunmen on his heels. "It's time for us to go," he said.

"Go where?" Maria asked.

"No questions! You should count your blessings that you're still alive, with all the trouble you've caused."

She didn't reply to that in words, but there was an immediate response, a spark of triumph in her mind at the idea she might have caused her captors even more inconvenience. To bring about their deaths would be—

Maria caught herself, astounded at the turn her thoughts had taken, wishing strangers dead. Except that these men were not strangers; they were sadistic predators, befouling everything they touched, and all the peaceful protest marches in the world would never purge their taint of evil from the land without a fight.

"I will not go," she said. And stood her ground.

Gogorza drew a pistol, thumbed the hammer back and aimed it at her face. "Your choice," he said. "With me, you live. If I must leave you here..."

He left the rest of it unspoken, but Maria got the message loud and clear. At least while she survived there was a slender thread of hope for rescue, something she could focus on, distract herself from fear.

"No blindfold, then?"

Gogorza's laugh was harsh and brief. "No blindfold, little bitch. I don't want you to miss the show."

Western Syria

SEEING THE ROCKET COMING, McCarter hit the deck in time to save himself, grimaced as it singed his hair. Somewhere behind him, near the fence, it found a target and exploded, spraying shrapnel in a killing radius of fifty feet.

It was sheer madness, firing off an RPG like that inside the camp, but discipline had gone to hell in nothing flat, the Syrians unhinged by fighting almost hand-to-hand with enemies they could not readily identify. The staff cars had been shot to hell, of course, but they were empty, smoking hulks.

No help at all.

Still lying prone, McCarter shot the Syrian before he could reload his RPG. A short burst to the chest, and he was down on all fours, yelping like a wounded dog before he toppled over on his side.

For God's sake, thought McCarter, let them die like men.

And when it's my turn, let me do the same.

He had a glimpse of Gary Manning, twenty paces distant, pumping slugs into a pair of Palestinian guerrillas. Never mind how young they were. The submachine guns in their hands made all the difference in the world. Fanatics had no age, no gender. They were killers without conscience, and it made no difference to McCarter that their murders were committed in a holy cause.

If anything, that only made it worse.

He scrambled to his feet and bolted for the open door of the communications hut. Inside, a Syrian with sergeant's stripes was fiddling with a shortwave radio, intent on beaming out an urgent SOS. McCarter shot him in the back and kept on firing after he had fallen, taking out the radio transceiver in the most effective way he knew.

Had any message gotten out before McCarter tagged the operator? It didn't appear so, but he had no way of being sure. In any case, no further summons for the cavalry would be sent out from this particular location.

He left a smallish Semtex charge behind as he departed from the hut, its timer counting down to doomsday. Thirty seconds was a lifetime in the hellgrounds, but it gave him ample room to duck outside and sprint for cover. Squeezing off short bursts at several targets on his way, he reached the burned-out shambles of a Quonset hut and threw himself behind the smoking pile.

The Semtex blew a heartbeat later, punching out the walls of the communications hut, hurling its flat metal roof sixty feet in the air. It caught a draft of wind there, wobbled into its descent and came down spinning like the blade of a giant rotary saw.

One of the Syrians looked up in time to see it coming, but he wasn't quick enough to save himself. Instead, he raised his pistol, firing at the giant piece of shrapnel, treating it like some unwieldy bird of prey, a thing of flesh and blood.

It struck him underneath the chin and kept on going, taking the gunner's skull for an abbreviated magic carpet ride. His headless body stood there for an instant, stubbornly defying gravity before toppling.

McCarter scanned the compound, searching for his friends, and caught a glimpse of Calvin James, his uniform in sooty tatters, pumping rounds from his Kalashnikov into a tent where several Syrians had gone to ground. Some eighty yards away Encizo had another target lined up for his RPG, the heavy rocket rattling toward another barracks hut. The blast sent shrapnel flying, body parts of several Syrians airborne with the remainder of the trash.

The others would be out there somewhere, screened from his position by a pall of drifting smoke or huddled under cover like himself.

Provided all of them were still alive.

He concentrated on his agenda. On his left two barracks buildings stood unscathed, with automatic weapons firing through the open doors and windows. There was no way he could estimate how many soldiers were inside each hut, aside from counting muzzle-flashes. Eight or nine at least, between the two, perhaps with other timid stragglers hiding out to save themselves.

He chose his moment, bolted from his makeshift hiding place and ran toward the nearest barracks. With Semtex charges on the rear wall, just to capture their attention, he would be waiting for survivors when they bolted from the ruins.

Simple.

All he had to do was pull it off like clockwork—twice, no less—and keep himself from getting snuffed in the attempt.

Antioquia Province, Colombia

CARL LYONS TRACKED the flaming oil drum through its arc and grimaced as it came down just behind two running members of the FAP. Their clothing was immediately drenched with burning fuel. Their screams were wild, unearthly, and seemed to last forever while the human torches ran around in circles, bumping into one another, nearly falling. Their high-pitched cries of pain went on forever, voices merging into one long shriek from Hades.

Lyons shot them, two rounds each, and left them smoking where they fell. He went in search of other targets, found two warring groups of M-19 and FAP commandos dueling from respective corners at the east end of the camp. He made it five or six guns on a side, the rebels fighting from a slit trench, while their neo-Nazi adversaries ranged themselves behind the smoking ruins of the motor pool.

They didn't see him coming, wrapped up as they were in an exchange of automatic-weapons fire. The Ironman slipped into a vacant barracks tent, still more or less undamaged, moving to the side that faced his would-be targets. Slicing through the canvas with his Ka-bar, Lyons had a field of fire including both positions and the open ground between.

He primed his M-203 launcher with a high-explosive round and cupped another in his palm where it would be in instant readiness. The hasty plan owed everything to pinpoint timing. A delay would surely blow it, leave him open to attack by one or both contingents, nothing but a sheet of canvas to protect him from incoming fire.

A mental coin toss put the FAP on top, and Lyons sighted quickly, triggered the grenade. Before it reached the target, he was already reloading, tracking toward his secondary mark. The muffled thud of Lyons's second shot was covered by the detonation of his first grenade, and number two went up a moment later, spewing dirt and shrapnel, flesh and blood.

On each side of the firefight, dazed survivors lurched from cover, several of them losing blood from shrapnel wounds, some thirty feet between them as they straightened up and started stretching muscles cramped by awkward immobility.

The gunners opened up on both sides of their private no-man's land, some of their bullets going high and wide, others scoring hits. The Ironman could have let them work it out between themselves, but war had never much appealed to Lyons as a bland spectator sport.

He worked both sides, a short burst to the left, immediately followed by another to the right. In seconds there was no one standing, several of the fallen twitching in their death throes, and he left them to it, saving ammunition for the hostiles who were still alive and well.

Western Syria

HOW MANY LEFT?

McCarter had no way of knowing, but Zuheir al-Qadi's corpse was not among the several he had seen so far. Until the leader of As-Sai'qa was accounted for, McCarter's work in the camp would not be finished.

He chose a new direction, moving through the battle smoke in search of targets, passing bodies stretched out on the ground. He checked each face in turn—where there were faces to be found—hoping that al-Qadi would be one of them, praying that his Phoenix comrades would not be among the dead.

McCarter struck out all the way around, and kept on searching, dropping three more Syrians who crossed his path and saw the error of their ways too late to save themselves. No VIPs among them, and he left them where they lay, blood soaking deep into the arid soil.

CHAPTER TWENTY-ONE

The Pyrenees

Grimaldi's warship was the Cobra AH-1S, manufactured by Bell. A two-man crew was optimum, but Jack experienced no difficulty flying by himself. The Cobra's 1,400 SHP Avco Lycoming engine gave him a maximum cruising speed of 172 miles per hour with the chopper fully loaded, but Grimaldi was dawdling now, killing time and waiting for his scripted moment to appear and crash Gogorza's little party.

They might be short on numbers, but the whirlybird had firepower to spare. The TAT nose turret sported a 7.62 mm Minigun in tandem with a 40 mm grenade launcher, both weapons operable by the pilot in the absence of his forward gunner. On the Cobra's stubby wings, Grimaldi packed an M157 launcher with seven 2.75-inch rockets, a double pod with Stingers, and dual M35 mounts with 20 mm Gatling guns prepared to lay down fire at the imposing rate of some 6,000 rounds per minute.

Death from above, bet your ass.

But it would take only one lucky shot, maybe two, to bring him down.

With that in mind, Grimaldi checked his watch and reckoned it was close enough to start his indirect approach. Once more around the mountain, Jeeves, and by the time he reached Gogorza's village, he would be in time for the festivities.

Coming into the approach some ninety seconds later, he could see smoke rising from the highway leading to the villa, one car definitely burning, possibly a second. Tiny figures ducked and dodged across the killing ground, elastic lines that might or might not hold, depending on the circumstances.

Time to stir things up.

Grimaldi knew that Bolan would be making for the house to find a way inside and free Gogorza's hostage. For his own part, Jack wasn't convinced the woman would be present, but he bowed to Bolan's instinct when it came to plotting strategy.

And when it came to killing from the air, he bowed to no one.

Coming in low from the north, he unloaded a couple of the 2.75-inch rockets on his first pass, lighting up another of Silveira's vehicles and scattering the gunmen who were using it for cover.

Simple.

It would cheer Gogorza's people to see him strafing members of the ANE, some of them reckoning their fearless leader had a neat trick up his sleeve. An air force they had never heard of, and here it was to save their asses in the nick of time.

Not quite.

He circled back and made a beeline for the ETA contingent, triggering the Minigun and 40 mm launcher in the nose assembly. He had a glimpse of bodies flying, some of them disintegrating, but a strafing run with hostile weapons blasting at him from below left no time for a body count.

He skimmed above the villa, close enough to put a Stinger down the chimney, but Grimaldi made no hostile move against the house. Not yet. If Bolan was inside, he needed time—to find the hostage, deal with any guards and drag her out of there. They had a signal prearranged, with deadlines, and Grimaldi didn't plan to jump the gun.

Not when he had so many targets in the open, begging for attention.

On his third pass he came in behind Silveira's stalled caravan and fired off three more of the 2.75-inch rockets. Twisted steel and flaming gasoline filled both lanes of the narrow mountain highway, cutting off the one sure avenue of flight. More bodies scattered on the pavement, some of them on fire, and he pulled out before the scattered, ineffective ack-ack fire could reach him.

Circling over hell, Grimaldi checked his watch and then his fuel gauge. Both informed him that his time was running short, the deadline fast approaching when, if Bolan had not shown himself or beamed their designated signal skyward, Jack was under orders to destroy the house and everyone inside.

Meanwhile, he owed the grunts downstairs another rattle, just to keep them on their toes.

Western Syria

THE NEXT SUMBITCH gets in my face, thought Calvin James, I take his freaking head off, and I don't care who it is.

In fact, it was a Palestinian. Late twenties by the look of him, except he had an old man's worn, discolored teeth. He bared them in a snarl, a submachine gun rising in his hands, and James rearranged those choppers for him with a butt stroke from the AKM. The guy went down like so much dirty laundry, one hand rising to his ruined mouth. James pumped two rounds through the hand.

The fight had come down to a bloody battle of attrition, no precision tactics to it. They had scattered on arrival in the compound, each man with a job in mind, alternative assignments ready if the first fell through, and it was all downhill from there. Through the chaos, smoke, explosions, running men and sprawling bodies, bullets whispered on every side.

His fellow Phoenix warriors had a sizable advantage over Calvin. They might not pass for Arabs under close inspection, but a black man had no chance at all. The borrowed uniform helped out, of course, and it was better now, with many of the men around him filthy from the battle, faces blotched with dirt and soot. Still, any fool could spot him if they took the least amount of time, and that made James a special target in the killing ground.

He passed the motor pool, where half a dozen vehicles had been reduced to flaming scrap iron. There had been no helicopter in the camp when they arrived, and that would mean al-Qadi and his Syrian associates were still inside.

Or were they?

It was going on nine minutes since they had crashed the gates and got the party rolling. Anything could happen in that length of time, including one or two intended targets slipping unobserved out some secret exit.

If that turned out to be the case, then it was all a ghastly waste of time and effort, and they had risked their lives for nothing.

Calvin James caught himself before the mood could run away with him. He came up on the CP hut, already pocked with bullet holes, and was about to check it out when someone cleared the threshold in a rush, boots crunching on the sand. James took a heartbeat to persuade himself the runner was not one of his companions, swinging up the AKM and firing off a 6-round burst that pitched the poor dumb bastard over on his face.

No uniform, for what it might be worth.

The black Phoenix pro checked his flanks, made certain he was clear and crouched beside the body. Turned it over, smiling as he recognized the face from photographs displayed to him by agents of Mossad the night before.

Issam Moshin stared back at James with lifeless eyes, sand clinging to the lashes from his fall. He might be hot stuff in Damascus when his cronies from the great Baath Party gathered to discuss their strategy for crushing Israel, but he didn't look like much to Calvin James right now.

Another stiff, with plenty more for company.

And if Moshin was still around, they had a decent chance of finding Zuheir al-Qadi on the premises, as well.

The dead man had been carrying a briefcase. James retrieved it on a whim and took it, thinking he could always ditch it if it got to be a burden. On the flip side, if Moshin had risked his life to save it, then the contents might be worth a look at Stony Man.

It was a hoot, how things worked out.

One minute he was in the dumps, afraid that they had blown it with their mission, let the big fish wriggle through their net. Now he was packing God-knows-what around the hellgrounds in a briefcase, if you please, and looking for the VIP who still eluded him.

Zuheir al-Qadi.

The leader of the Thunderbolt would hear some thunder of his own, if Calvin James found him. An umbrella wouldn't keep him from the storm, once James began to rain on his parade.

Sometimes, James thought, the sound of thunder could be music to the ears.

Antioquia Province, Colombia

IT HAD OCCURRED to Pol Blancanales that Manuel Vargas might attempt to flee the camp if it appeared his men were giving ground before the onslaught of Luis Otero's FAP assault. The tide of battle had not turned per se, but with some help from Able Team, both sides were catching hell, and it occurred to Pol that Vargas might regard this as an advantageous time to cut and run.

It all came down to logic, second-guessing an opponent Blancanales only knew from files and photographs, as a chaotic battle raged. It stood to reason that his quarry would not make directly for the road, Otero's soldiers having sealed it off. That left the jungle, pressing close around the camp on every side, but it didn't make sense to Blancanales that his enemy would strike off aimlessly.

There was another road, Pol knew, located some miles to the south. It was a dirt track, used at different times by timber companies and coca growers carrying their harvest to the labs, but it could also serve as an escape route. A long march through the jungle—seven hours minimum—would put a traveler within ten miles of Bello. It was doubtful that Otero would have spotters waiting there, and if he did, the force would probably be small, relaxed, anticipating no real action so far from the battle site.

Pol chose a point where he would leave the camp if he was fleeing southward toward the Bello road, and worked his way around in that direction, dodging confrontations where he could, conserving ammunition. Picking out his vantage point, he knew there was a chance that Vargas had already slipped away—or that he might be lying dead somewhere in the confusion of the killing ground—but Pol would give the plan some time, an opportunity to see if it bore fruit.

Three minutes later, when the battle showed no signs of winding down, he saw three men advancing cautiously, shooting frequent glances back toward the heart of the action, making sure they had not been observed. Two gunners in the standard camouflage fatigues, one in street clothes.

Vargas.

Blancanales was already sighting down the barrel of his M-16 A1 when someone called to Vargas from the sidelines in a harsh, demanding voice.

"I knew you'd run away, *pendejo.*"

Rising from the undergrowth, Luis Otero faced his enemy, an automatic rifle in his hands, three soldiers stepping up to back his play. That made it seven guns, and Blancanales waited, watching from the shadows on Otero's flank.

"This treachery is what I would expect from one like you," said Vargas, checking out the hostile weapons, weighing odds and angles of attack.

"You mean, because I do not wait for you to stab me in the back?" Otero answered mockingly. "A wise man does not wait to feel the blade between his shoulders."

"This is all your doing," Vargas countered. "You and your alliance with the *narcotraficantes*."

"Jealousy will be the death of you, Manuel. Today, in fact."

Pol didn't catch the signal, but he witnessed the results. All seven guns went off at once, or nearly so, their racket merging into one hellacious din that momentarily eclipsed the sounds of combat farther back, inside the camp. A storm of bullets whipped the trees and shrubbery, stripping leaves from branches, gouging divots in the larger trunks.

In front of Pol the rival thugs were also taking hits, their bodies jerking, spouting crimson. Dying index fingers locked on triggers, firing even as they fell. Eight seconds, give or take, and there was one man standing when the racket faded.

Vargas.

He was not unscathed, however. Blancanales saw blood soaking through his shirt beneath one arm, and there was more dribbling down his face and neck, where a bullet had shredded one ear. He might have other wounds, for all the Politician knew, but tattered ferns concealed his body from the waist down.

Vargas was reloading his submachine gun, fumbling awkwardly with the replacement magazine, when Blancanales showed himself.

"You almost made it," he informed the chief of M-19.

Vargas blinked at him, wobbling a bit on his feet. "Who are you?"

"Does it matter?"

Vargas thought about it. "No," he said at last. "Otero could not stop me. Neither can you."

"I already have," Pol informed him, taking up slack on the M-16's trigger while Vargas tried to raise his SMG.

Pol fired off half a magazine, no misses at a range of less than twenty feet. The 5.56 mm rounds punched Vargas through a jerky little dance step, one complete rotation, and he finally toppled over backward in the weeds.

Pol stood among the corpses, listening to sounds of battle from the camp. They were slackening a bit, but some of the combatants still had ample fight left in them yet. He took the compact walkie-talkie from his belt and pressed the black transmitter button with his thumb.

"We have a touchdown," he announced. "Fall back and disengage."

Lyons's familiar voice came back to him from the radio. "Affirmative."

"Roger that," said Schwarz.

Pol left the dead to keep each other company and faded back in the direction of the preselected rendezvous. With the FAP and M-19 now neutralized, Able Team's mission was complete. They would return to Stony Man Farm, hoping that their colleagues enjoyed similar success with their targets.

Western Syria

IT ALL CAME DOWN to this, Zuheir al-Qadi realized. Defeat, abject humiliation, and he didn't even know his adversaries. Someone sent from Israel, he had little doubt, and he would gladly pay them back in kind.

But first he had to save himself.

The base camp's motor pool had been destroyed, the vehicles converted into flaming scrap, but he had taken care to note the other means of transportation stationed around the camp.

The motorcycles, for example.

They would not have been his first choice, since he had not driven any two-wheeled vehicle in several years, but lack of practice and a risk of minor injury were small things in comparison with death. A motorbike would give him speed and greater flexibility in terms of tackling the desert and avoiding roads until he was sure that he wasn't pursued.

Zuheir al-Qadi made his way across the camp by fits and starts, first sprinting, then collapsing on the ground and playing dead, repeating the procedure time and time again before he reached the site where several motorcycles sat beneath a tarp set up to shield them from the desert sun.

He spent a precious moment peering into gas tanks, picking out the cycle that appeared to have a near-full complement of fuel. He dragged the motorcycle off its kickstand, rolled it out from under the tarpaulin and was settling on the driver's seat when someone close behind him spoke his name.

Zuheir al-Qadi turned and saw a young man in a Syrian uniform aiming a Kalashnikov rifle at his face. He didn't recognize the soldier from his interaction with camp personnel, but he was about to pull rank, demand that the rifleman leave him alone...when it hit him.

His enemies had come in through the front gates of the camp in Syrian staff cars, wearing Syrian uniforms. Zuheir al-Qadi felt his scrotum shrivel as he realized this must be one of them, a stranger pledged to kill him in the name of Israel or some other hostile government.

"Who are you?" he demanded. Stalling.

"Ari Lev," the young man told him, circling cautiously until he stood before al-Qadi with his rifle pointed at the Arab's chest.

"A Jew." Of course. It had to be.

"You are condemned for crimes against the state of Israel and her people," said the youngster, sounding very solemn.

"Get on with it," the Palestinian replied, still arrogant despite his fear. "You Zionists would rather talk a man to death than shoot him, I suppose."

"You're in a hurry, then," said Ari Lev. "I won't detain you."

He was braced to fire when a bedraggled Palestinian appeared behind him, sizing up the situation at a glance and firing two shots at the Jew from twenty feet. He rushed it, and the first round missed its mark, but number two struck Ari Lev above the belt line and to the left.

The young Israeli spun to face his unseen adversary, firing as he turned. The ragged Palestinian got off another pistol shot, but it was wasted, slugs from the Kalashnikov already ripping through his chest.

Zuheir al-Qadi wasted no time reaching for his own side arm, the automatic bucking four times in his fist. All four rounds found their target, ripping through the young man's back with stunning force. Ari Lev tried to stand, but it demanded too much from his dying body, and he slowly toppled forward.

Zuheir al-Qadi switched the pistol to his left hand, gripped the motorcycle's throttle in his right and rose to kick the starter. He was halfway there when something like a giant fist struck home, below his heart, and dumped him off the bike. It fell across his left leg, pinning him. His automatic clattered on the ground, just out of reach.

Another man in Syrian battle dress stood over him, smoke curling from the muzzle of his AKM. It took a moment for Zuheir al-Qadi to realize that the gunman had only one hand. In place of the right, he wore a metal claw that gripped his rifle, held the muzzle steady on Zuheir al-Qadi's face.

"You're done," the large man said in Arabic.

"Another Jew," al-Qadi sneered. "Go on and kill me, then. You think that it will save your precious Israel? Never! You will never win!"

Zuheir al-Qadi never heard the shot that split his skull and spilled his brains into the sand.

The Pyrenees

HE MET THEM on the landing, two guns out in front, Gogorza and the woman coming up behind. The gunners saw death coming, peeling off to either side, but they had little room to work with, nowhere to hide.

Mack Bolan took them with a rapid one-two punch, short bursts of 5.56 mm tumblers blasting from his FA MAS. The shooter on his left went down without a whimper, sprawling on his face, arms splayed as if to catch the floor in an embrace. His comrade on the right absorbed four rounds and did a sloppy backward somersault across the banister, head over heels and screaming as he fell.

That left Alphonse Gogorza and his human shield.

The ETA commander had a pistol pressed against Maria's head, its hammer cocked, his finger on the trigger. How much pull would it require to decorate the landing with her brains? Three pounds? No more than four.

"You have a choice," said Bolan, carefully enunciating every word. "You kill the woman, I kill you. Or I can take her out of here and walk away."

"Am I supposed to trust you?" Even in the tension of the moment, Bolan thought Gogorza was about to laugh out loud.

"You don't have all that many options," he replied.

"Perhaps," Gogorza said, "but I can still choose how I wish to die."

"And take a woman with you? Where's the honor in that kind of death?"

"You are American," Gogorza said. "You understand my war no better than the Spaniards who sit back and pray for Franco to return."

"I understand enough to know it ends right here for one of us. You make the call."

Gogorza stared at Bolan, then he snarled in rage and shoved Maria clear. She stumbled, fell against the banister, then caught herself. Gogorza raised his pistol, sighting on the Executioner, and he was almost fast enough.

Almost.

A rising burst from Bolan's FA MAS ripped through Gogorza's slacks, his shirt, his throat and face. The rippling impact drove him backward, airborne, boot heels skimming over carpet. Where he struck the wall, Gogorza left a crimson smear, then slouched to a seated posture on the floor.

"Come on," said Bolan, reaching for the woman's hand, uncertain whether she would understand his words. They had no time to waste, regardless. If he didn't signal Jack Grimaldi soon, it would all be over, with the Cobra raining hellfire on the house.

He led Maria down the stairs, met two more gunners just emerging from the dining room and killed them where they stood. The woman followed him without a word of protest, realizing that her life was in this stranger's hands. Out through the back, they ran toward the mountain slope as Bolan palmed his walkie-talkie, thumbing the transmitter button.

"Striker clear!" he told Grimaldi, who was circling somewhere on the far side of the villa, giving the combatants hell. "Clean sweep!"

They ran another hundred yards, then Bolan turned to watch the grand finale. The Cobra hovered just off the east wing of the villa, firing its two Stingers and the last few smaller rockets, 20 mm guns unloading on the house with some 6,000 rounds per minute.

Doomsday.

Half a dozen rapid-fire explosions rocked the villa, lifting off a massive portion of the roof, bright flames erupting from the opening. The east wall crumpled inward, smoke obscuring the shattered remnant of the house as Jack Grimaldi put his Cobra through a looping turn and thundered overhead, abandoning the field.

He would be waiting for them on the far side of the mountain, at the chosen pickup point. Maria didn't hesitate as Bolan pointed toward the pass above them and began to walk in that direction, leaving her to make the choice. She fell in step behind him, never glancing back to see the final ruin of the men who had abducted her and who would certainly have claimed her life without the intervention of a warrior she had never met.

It felt good, walking briskly in the clear, cool mountain air. She would have many questions for the stranger who had saved her life, but they could wait awhile.

Right now it was enough to be alive.

CHAPTER TWENTY-TWO

Jura Mountains, Switzerland

The villa north of Neuchâtel was perfect as a hideaway. It might have been designed and built to order, from the way it met al-Takriti's needs.

Relaxing in the sunshine while a cool breeze played across his skin, the fugitive Iraqi knew he was a lucky man. It could have been much worse if he had waited at his post in Baghdad for the bad news to arrive. Six days, and European commentators still broke into scheduled programming from time to time, reporting progress in the search for certain terrorists in Spain and Syria who were believed to be survivors of the recent carnage in those countries.

So they said, at any rate, but it was one thing to report a story, quite another to examine what was said and read between the lines.

Al-Takriti had no doubt that members of the ANE had clashed with ETA supporters in the Pyrenees, but there was much that went before their great, climactic battle that the media had overlooked . . . deliberately or otherwise. It was the same in Syria, where the official charges flying back and forth between Damascus and the Jews in Tel Aviv fell short of answering the many questions in al-Takriti's mind.

Somehow, somewhere, he knew the damned Americans had been behind all this . . . but it wasn't his problem anymore. Al-Takriti was retired, albeit prematurely, from the service of his government. There would be no official pension, no gold watch or medal for his years of service, but he would survive quite nicely all the same.

The money he had siphoned from his ministry would see to that. If he should ever feel the pinch of rising prices, he could always buy another set of bogus papers, relocate to Africa or South America and start from scratch.

The Third World always needed killers, more particularly killers with a talent for administration. Someone who could plot a coup or brutally suppress one, build a prison camp or foment armed revolt among the inmates. Versatility had always been al-Takriti's trademark, and it wouldn't fail him in the future if he kept his wits about him.

Guards for the estate had been a minor problem, solved with ingenuity. Al-Takriti had been forced to leave his loyal subordinates behind in Baghdad, never knowing which of them would sell him out in favor of a bonus from the Father-Leader. Not that he could blame them for their avarice... but he was looking out for number one this time, and that meant all dead wood must go.

He had considered hiring Swiss, but they were not a race of fighters. Switzerland had cherished its neutrality so long, supported by the mountainous terrain that made invasion prohibitive, that they had softened, lost the killing edge found in certain other races on the continent. If they were unsurpassed as bankers, watchmakers, mechanics, they left much to be desired in their devotion to the martial arts.

Al-Takriti's final choice of German skinheads for his bodyguard was predicated on several decisive factors. First and foremost they despised the Jews enough to overcome their initial misgivings at the thought of working for a "raghead" from the Middle East. The thought of clashing with Israelis visibly excited them the way most men become excited by a lovely woman. They were also young, athletic and proficient with a wide variety of weapons. Finally, their price was well below the going rate for mercenary bodyguards.

Al-Takriti had selected nineteen of the best from forty-seven who showed interest in his offer. One of them, the oldest, was appointed to command the rest and see that none of them got out of line. Al-Takriti made no effort to dispel the rumor that he was a close friend of Saddam Hussein.

In fact, he started it himself.

What better way to keep the Germans in their place than with a subtle threat of retribution from the Father-Leader should they fail in their sworn duty to protect al-Takriti's life and limbs?

Conversely he had let it slip that certain members of Saddam's regime were traitors, anxious to eliminate al-Takriti for his loyalty to the Father-Leader. Raised on paranoia and delusions of conspiracy, the skinheads never got around to asking why he was in Switzerland instead of sticking close beside Saddam.

Al-Takriti paid the bills, he was despised by the Israelis . . . what more could an up-and-coming neo-Nazi ask for in a temporary boss?

He couldn't hide forever in the Jura Mountains, that was obvious, but it would still be safe for several months. Saddam would seek al-Takriti somewhere closer to his home—in Syria, perhaps, or Lebanon. It would take time for the accountants to discover various discrepancies in his financial records, longer still to trace the money back to Switzerland. They might not make the link at all, in fact, but he was ready with a backup plan just in case.

It was huge world, when he thought about it, filled with countless places for a fugitive to hide. Some of the hideouts were admittedly inferior to others, but a man with ready cash on hand could pick and choose.

Al-Takriti closed his eyes and felt the warm sun on his skin.

He would enjoy retirement, he decided.

Living well was still the best revenge.

Stony Man Farm

THE FLIGHT from Washington took twenty minutes once Brognola finally got clearance to take off. A jeep was waiting on the airstrip when he reached the Farm, the driver one he recognized, a soldier wise enough to keep the conversation minimal. Another moment brought him to the farmhouse, Kurtzman there to greet him on the porch.

"Barb's double-checking," Kurtzman said in lieu of small talk, "but we're sure it's him. Surveillance photos were a little tricky, but they're ninety-five percent conclusive. Put it all together with the rest, and I'd say it's a go."

Inside, Hal took a right to the computer room, stood back and waited while the Bear tapped buttons on the keypad for the coded access door. A nod from Akira Tokaido, crunching data at his terminal, the earphones of a Walkman pumping nonstop heavy metal to his brain. The screen in front of him kept shifting images:

a mug shot, followed by a map, a spread sheet filled
with numbers, yet another photograph.

They rode the elevator down, emerged into the basement War Room. Barbara Price was on the speaker-
phone, just winding up her conversation with a man
who sounded vaguely French. A fax machine beside her
elbow beeped and whirred, expelling what appeared to
be a legal document. She broke the long-distance connection and turned to Hal.

"It's a wrap," she informed him. "Al-Takriti's in
Switzerland. A villa in the Juras, north of Neuchâtel."

"How firm is that?" Brognola asked.

"I'd stake my reputation on it," Price replied. "But
it will take an on-site visit if you want a guarantee."

"So tell me what you have."

"We came up empty, looking for him in Iraq," said
Kurtzman. "By itself that doesn't prove a thing, but
then the Company got word Saddam was looking for
him, too. The Revolutionary Guards have trashed his
house and pulled his mistress in for questioning. I'll be
surprised if anybody hears from her again."

"He pulled a fade?"

"And then some," Barbara said. "We're still not sure
exactly how he wriggled out of Baghdad, but he wasn't
waiting for the other shoe to drop. The way it looks, he
left before the final SOS went out in Lebanon and
Spain."

"A man who plans ahead."

"And then some," Kurtzman said. "According to a
friendly source in Baghdad, there's a hefty stack of
dinars missing from al-Takriti's budget. He's been
shorting some of their connections overseas, investing
on his own in projects that would bring a high return."

"And burying the profits," Hal surmised.

"In Switzerland," said Barbara Price. "We haven't cracked the banking code, of course, but we've been on the line to Interpol. They checked flight information for the period in question, and we got three possibles in Zurich, two more in Lucerne. They all flew in from Middle Eastern or Mediterranean points of origin, easy to reach from Iraq."

"Surveillance?" asked Brognola.

"That's affirmative. We weren't in time to catch them getting off the plane, you understand, but playing catch-up is our specialty. Four of the five were traced to various hotels and eliminated on the basis of a visual comparison to CIA surveillance photographs."

"And Number Five?"

"He calls himself Mahomet Bey. Flew in from Istanbul on Tuesday night. He had plenty of time to meet with his bankers in Zurich before he was traced yesterday. I've just received a copy of the paperwork he filled out seven months ago, when he picked out his villa in the Juras. Word is that he ticked off the locals, recruiting all his staff from Germany. The neo-Nazi crowd."

"Expensive," said Brognola.

"He can swing it," Barbara Price replied. "According to the narco boys at Interpol, Mahomet Bey has been suspected of involvement with the Turkish heroin traffic for over a year. Three guesses where he got his buy-in money."

"Something tells me that Saddam is not amused," Brognola said.

"We ought to drop a dime and let the bastard sweep his own trash off the street," said Kurtzman.

"It's a thought," Brognola conceded, "but it wouldn't send the message that I had in mind."

"Which is?"

"You play, you pay. No sanctuary anywhere on earth."

"Does that include Saddam?" asked Kurtzman.

"Don't I wish." Brognola's tone was gruff. "He spends so much time in the spotlight that we'd need an order from the Man, in writing. If it ever comes to that, my guess would be they'll send a Tomahawk to do the job."

"The marvels of technology," said Barbara Price.

"More likely," Kurtzman said, "our various elected representatives will sit around and shoot the shit until Saddam keels over from old age."

"It's not our call," Brognola said. "And that's a quote, directly from the top."

"And what about al-Takriti?" Kurtzman asked.

"He's ours," Brognola answered. "Make the calls."

Athens, Greece

THE CHOICE of staging areas had been left up to Katz, as long as he selected someplace quiet and convenient. Athens seemed to fit the bill, a decent launching pad for any target city in the Middle East or Europe, even northern Africa.

The problem was, they had no way of knowing where al-Takriti would turn up... or if he would be found at all. Common sense dictated he would try to find a place where cash was readily available and Arabs were familiar visitors. Those broad requirements didn't narrow down the field to any great degree, but Katz had tentatively ruled out the Caribbean and South America on the strength of a hunch.

Al-Takriti would be running for his life when he abandoned Baghdad. That meant running from Saddam, and every moment spent in transit to his destination was a risk. The sooner he touched down and went to ground, the greater were his chances of surviving the initial hunt.

To Katz that meant a Western European destination, someplace where the rich could find a happy medium of luxury and privacy. Forget about the strife-torn Balkans and the former Soviet republics, one short step removed from civil war. No wealthy fugitive would willingly subject himself to those conditions when he had Saddam's headhunters on his trail already.

Still, the narrowed playing field left several possibilities, with Greece among them. Spain would be too hot, in Katzenelenbogen's estimation, but he couldn't rule out France, Italy, Switzerland, Austria, even Scandinavia. If he was wrong, and the Iraqi had been brave enough to risk a longer run from Baghdad, then al-Takriti could be anywhere.

It galled Katz, being forced to sit and wait for someone else to do the work instead of tracking down the target on his own. His recent brush with death in Lebanon and Syria, together with the loss of Ari Lev, had left him with the need to punish someone. Even after finishing Zuheir al-Qadi, Katz had known their task wasn't complete.

Not while the brains behind the terror network was at large.

It finally came down to Baghdad, and he understood the reasons why a strike against Saddam himself was not considered feasible. There was a yawning gulf between that understanding and agreement, but a life in military service had accustomed Katz to following the orders he was given.

Most of them, at any rate.

The call he had been waiting for came through at 2:18 p.m. Katz took it in his hotel room and put it on the scrambler when he recognized the voice of Barbara Price at Stony Man. Three minutes later he had all the information he required. He made four more calls in swift succession, summoning the other members of his Phoenix team.

Ten minutes brought the last of them to Katzenelenbogen's room. He had three chairs, which left two of them sitting on the bed. They wrapped up the small talk in record time and listened while he ran through the latest information.

"It's Switzerland," he told them. "Confirmation through a visual ID. Al-Takriti calls himself Mahomet Bey, pretends to be a Turk. His paperwork's in order, which should come as no surprise. We work on the assumption that he has at least one Swiss account to help him make it through a premature retirement."

"Where in Switzerland?" McCarter asked.

"The Jura Mountains, north of Neuchâtel," Katz said. "We'll get specifics on arrival. All I know right now is that our target has a villa staffed with German skinhead types, Jew-haters, most of them on file with GSG-9 for suspicion of terrorist acts against tourists and foreign refugees."

"Delightful." Gary Manning made a sour face.

"It's par for the course," Katz replied. "We've also got a rumble that al-Takriti, as Mahomet Bey, has been investing heavily in Turkish heroin. That tells me he's got cash to burn and criminal connections who can get weapons, documents, whatever he may need to slip away a second time."

"That's if he gets the chance," said Calvin James.

"Affirmative. We're booked for Zurich on the four-fifteen, so don't waste lots of time selecting wardrobe. Anything we need, as far as hardware, will be waiting for us on the ground."

"And Striker?" Rafael Encizo asked.

Katz nodded. "That's my understanding. With the goons al-Takriti has on hand, we should have decent odds. Say, three or four to one."

"We're sure about the Germans?" asked McCarter.

"All except the numbers," Katz replied. "GSG-9 is missing fifteen, maybe twenty skinheads from their normal haunts, but I'm not sure how tight they are on head counts. Let's be safe and call it twenty-five. No point in being overconfident. Assume that all of them are armed."

"I've gotta tell you," Calvin James said, grinning. "It always cheers me up to butt head with the redneck crowd."

"That's good," Katz said. "I like to see a man who's happy in his work."

"You bet."

Katz checked his watch. "We fly in eighty-seven minutes. Meet me downstairs in fifteen. We should just make the flight."

They filed out silently, no jokes in parting, each man occupied with private thoughts. Another battlefield ahead of them, and when would it finally be over?

Katz put the question out of mind and started packing. He chose the bare essentials, left the rest behind, a warrior long accustomed to departures and the fact that no return was guaranteed.

If it turned out to be a one-way flight, so be it. But the gruff Israeli could be sure of one thing.

He would not be going down alone.

Monaco

IT HAD BEEN INADVISABLE for Bolan to remain in Spanish territory once the smoke cleared in the Pyrenees. Officially the government was blaming most of the fatalities on a guerrilla war between the ETA and ANE. It satisfied the tabloid press and made the paperwork a great deal simpler for the police, but there would still be questions asked behind the scenes, polite inquiries in the diplomatic circles, ripples spreading in a dark and deadly pond.

He had selected Monaco for all the same reasons that led Phoenix Force into Athens...plus the added factor of nostalgia. Monaco had been on Bolan's hit parade a lifetime earlier, when he was waging his one-man war against the Mafia from New York and Chicago to its European outposts. He had lingered only long enough to kill a man and nearly die himself, but there were pleasant memories among the others.

Sun and sand. A woman. The casinos.

He was not a gambler in the normal sense, but he enjoyed a little of the sideshow atmosphere from time to time. Atlantic City and Las Vegas were like cheap bordellos in comparison to Monaco, where diplomats and royalty came to play. The atmosphere was different somehow. More sophisticated than the hurly-burly of American casino towns. New Jersey and Nevada offered all the trimmings: deep-shag carpeting, Jacuzzis in the suites, free drinks and limousines and showgirls for the heavy hitters. But beneath the neon flash, they were a vestige of the wild frontier. The owners doled out money, tried their best to buy respectability, but they would never learn that cash and flash sometimes add up to trash.

In Monaco it was a different story. More laid-back, without the desperate atmosphere that brought bag ladies into the American casinos, wearing gloves to save their hands from chafing on the one-armed bandits, urinating where they stood in lieu of giving up the one hot slot machine that might pay off at any time.

His room faced the casino, and he liked to watch the wealthy guests arriving in their limousines, the men in evening jackets, women draped in furs and diamonds. It was quite a show, but Bolan didn't venture any closer.

He was waiting for a call to start the game anew.

It came through at 2:37 p.m. Bolan had the scrambler waiting, pictured Barbara tapping buttons in the Farm's computer room while he completed his connection at the other end. The message, finally, was short, concise, devoid of any personal entanglements.

The way war ought to be.

He listened, memorized his orders, severed the connection. Packed his meager personal belongings and the scrambler that would pass a cursory inspection as a compact radio. He had an hour, give or take, to catch the flight for Zurich. There was no time to be wasted in departing the hotel.

Grimaldi had been peeved about returning to the States alone, but he was needed for a loan-out to the DEA, the kind of reciprocity that kept Brognola's Stony team in touch with everything that happened in the federal sphere of law enforcement. Bolan had been left behind to wait and rendezvous with Phoenix Force once the Iraqi runner had been found.

He thought of Switzerland, the last stop on a trail of death that covered half the globe. It was a hopeless task to try to count the bodies strewn along that trail, from the beginning of his quest to its conclusion. Terrorists and tyrants, spies and soldiers, volunteers and hostages of fate.

Whatever lay ahead of him in Switzerland, the Jura Mountains, it would be the end of a campaign. Whichever way it went, the game was winding down.

He finished packing, paid his bill and caught a taxi to the airport. Showed his bogus passport at the immigration desk and took a seat in the departure lounge until his flight was called. When they were airborne, winging over France, the warrior let himself relax.

Al-Takriti might not be the evil heart behind the terrorist cabal, but he had been its brains. Removing him would send a message to Saddam, regardless of al-Takriti's current status on the Father-Leader's hit list. When Saddam decreed a person's death, he wanted the event to flow directly from his order, carried out by agents under his control. To be preempted, cut out of the loop, would be a grievous insult.

And the message underlying it would still get back to Baghdad, loud and clear.

When pushing the United States, it was a grave mistake to push too far. Saddam had seen that lesson driven home on more than one occasion, but he still refused to learn.

Would this time make a difference?

Bolan doubted it, but no one asked for his opinion on the fine points of diplomacy. So much of politics came down to public relations, the triumph of style over substance, that Bolan was happy to remain aloof from that domain.

And if the order came one day to hit Saddam or someone like him, would the Executioner respond?

He fell asleep, still pondering the question, and was dreaming fitfully before his flight reached Switzerland.

CHAPTER TWENTY-THREE

Jura Mountains, Switzerland

McCarter did the honors in Grimaldi's absence, handling the big Sikorsky UH-60 Black Hawk helicopter like a pro. He was exactly that, of course. He was qualified to fly any British or American prop aircraft up to four engines, with a sideline in choppers.

Bolan had the utmost faith in his ability to place them at the target site and bring them back again.

The Black Hawk's sliding doors were closed, but it was still a challenge to speak above the noise from a pair of GE T700 turboshaft engines running flat out at some 167 miles per hour. Shouting was the only way to go, but they had done their talking on the ground, rehearsed their strategy in detail, and the Executioner was silent now.

They had an edge of sorts, arriving out of nowhere with the sun behind them, but a helicopter made itself apparent going in, despite the IR jet-pipe noise suppressors for hovering flight. There was no such thing as a silent, invisible chopper, and Bolan knew there was no way on earth that al-Takriti's pet skinheads could miss their arrival.

As for an effective response...well, that was a whole other ball game.

They would command at least some measure of surprise. The rest of it came down to speed, sheer unadulterated nerve and airborne fire support from McCarter in the Black Hawk. Five men on the ground and one perched overhead, the latter with a wide array of heavy armaments at his disposal.

Versus . . . what?

Brognola and the GSG-9 analysts had estimated twenty skinheads, give or take a handful. There would be no Arabs on the site besides al-Takriti; he couldn't afford the possibility of any leak that would betray him to Saddam. Say twenty-one opposing guns, and add another five or six for safety's sake, to keep from getting overconfident.

The easy way would be to blast them from the air, unleash McCarter's arsenal and turn the villa into smoking hell of Earth before the enemy could scramble to their vehicles and race off down the mountainside. Unless one of the skinheads made a very lucky shot indeed, it was the safest way, as well.

And Bolan ruled it out.

He wanted to be sure this time. No slipups, oversights or errors of omission. Only soldiers on the ground could verify a given kill, and he was bound to see al-Takriti dead before he left the mountaintop this afternoon.

"Two minutes," said McCarter, sounding flat and distant in the earphone Bolan wore.

The Executioner alerted his companions, holding up two fingers, watching as they began to double-check their weapons, cinch their webbing tighter for the drop into a hot LZ. Four men that he would trust with everything he had.

Reconnaissance had shown McCarter where to land, the safest angle of approach, and he spent no time circling around the target. He was hovering, reducing altitude, as Bolan caught the sliding door and rolled it back. The Black Hawk's miniguns cut loose on someone Bolan could not see from where he sat.

He wished the poor dumb bastards luck.

All bad.

When they were six or seven feet above the sloping lawn, he led the way outside. Knees bent to bear his weight on impact, Bolan powered toward the villa, ready with his Steyr 5.56 mm AUG. He heard a crack of gunfire, spun to find the source and caught a tall, anemic-looking skinhead just emerging from behind a corner of the house.

The Nazi had an Uzi in his hands, and Bolan registered the irony without a break in stride. He didn't have to aim the AUG at this range, merely stroke the trigger lightly for a 3-round burst that stitched neat holes across the skinhead's bony chest and punched him over backward, out of sight.

One down.

The villa loomed in front of him, and Bolan went in firing, charging toward a set of tall glass doors.

AFIF AL-TAKRITI WAS a man who placed less faith in destiny than in strategic planning. He had known the Father-Leader would attempt to find and punish him, but he believed the various precautions he had taken in his flight would be sufficient to provide some breathing room. If he was wrong on that point, he had bodyguards in place, provisions for escape in an emergency.

But he hadn't believed the dogs could sniff him out so soon.

Al-Takriti recognized disaster in the sound of helicopter engines, knew the worst was happening as automatic weapons opened fire outside the house. One helicopter, by the sound of it, but that was bad enough. It took only one bullet to erase a life, one man to pull the trigger. If Saddam had found him out this quickly, where on earth could he presume to hide?

And what if it wasn't Saddam?

Al-Takriti wasted no more time on speculation. Every second counted now, and logic told him he was swiftly running out of time. He had been sipping Turkish coffee in his study with his shoes off when his ears picked up the sound of helicopter engines. Quickly putting on his shoes, he wished the black Italian loafers had been combat boots, but they would have to do.

Al-Takriti crossed the room in three long strides and opened up a cabinet constructed out of highly polished oak. He reached inside and chose a black Beretta automatic, checked the pistol's load and tucked it in his belt. Two extra magazines went in a pocket on the left. His next choice was a compact MP-5K submachine gun, loaded with a curved box magazine. The extra clips for that piece stuffed a pocket on al-Takriti's right.

The money next.

He couldn't leave the villa empty-handed, even though the bulk of his purloined reserve was still in Zurich, safe and sound. Assuming he could escape the villa, he might be forced to hide for days on end before he dared approach the bank in Zurich. Even cryptic phone calls were a risk when you were being hunted by Saddam.

Or someone else?

Al-Takriti left his study, found the houseman known as Erik waiting for him as he crossed the threshold. Erik had a pistol in his hand, a grim expression on his face.

"You're leaving, then," he said.

"And what would you suggest?" al-Takriti asked. "That we remain and have a chat with the police when they arrive?"

His choice of pronouns was not lost on Erik. "We?"

Al-Takriti frowned, as if the question was a personal affront. "Do I appear so foolish as to leave without my trusted aide?"

"I thought you might decide that it was quicker on your own."

"We're wasting precious time," al-Takriti said. "We have to reach the car before—"

A loud explosion rocked the villa, close enough to rattle Erik's nerves, yet far enough removed to spare them any but the faintest whiff of smoke. The east side of the house, al-Takriti thought. It would not interfere with his escape.

"Come on!" snapped Erik, leading him along a hallway toward the north, or rear, end of the villa. Past the staircase, where another skinhead met them, brandishing a shotgun, questioning his leader in their native German. Erik shut him up with two curt syllables and shouldered past him, with al-Takriti on his heels.

The car was risky, granted, but the only other option was a hike across the Juras, with al-Takriti in Italian loafers and a flimsy dress shirt, trained assassins bringing up the rear.

It never once occurred to him that they were being raided by police. The Swiss were very sensible in matters that pertained to privacy, neutrality... and cash. If the authorities had any questions for him, which was very doubtful, they would telephone or drop by in their own good time, with ample warning to the master of the house.

These were assassins on his doorstep, and in view of that, it hardly mattered whether they were working for Saddam or someone else. Al-Takriti would be just as dead, no matter who paid for the bullets, and he didn't mean to let that happen.

Not without a fight.

He understood there was a chance that he might fail in his escape attempt, but it would never be for lack of trying. Anyone who tried to stop him now must be an enemy, and enemies were only fit to die.

They reached the exit, Erik cracked the door to take a peek outside, then threw it open, charging toward the car. Al-Takriti followed, impressed despite himself with the dramatic vista of the sky and mountains all around.

He thought that he had never seen another day so beautiful, and never would again.

KATZ LIKED THE STEYR AUG. It's short bullpup design was perfect for a skilled, one-handed shooter in a hurry, and the built-on launcher for grenades cut down on bulk and weight. The plastic magazines were clear, allowing him to check the rifle's load any time he liked, and the design surrendered nothing in terms of firepower, giving Katz the same 5.56 mm punch he would have expected from an M-16 A1.

The weapon's standard optic sight was yet another bonus, but Katz didn't need it as he bailed out of the Black Hawk, veering wide of Bolan's track and running for his life around the east side of the villa. Scattered shots were audible, the rattle of a submachine gun, answered by an AUG, and it would only be another moment now before the skinhead sentries came in force.

How many?

Katz dismissed the question. As far as he could tell, there were no innocent civilians on the premises, no cooks or washerwomen to avoid when spraying automatic fire around the house and grounds. No half-assed war of watch and wait, when there were neo-Nazis and depraved Iraqui terror-mongers to be killed.

His first live target was a young man dressed in denim jeans and jacket, spit-shined boots with crimson laces, and a SPAS-12 riot shotgun in his hands. He did not flinch at the sight of Katz, but rather stood his ground and braced the shotgun at his hip, prepared to fire.

The Steyr AUG spit half a dozen rounds, and four of them at least were dead on target. Katzenelenbogen saw the young man's jacket pop and ripple with the impact of the 5.56 mm tumblers, blood the color of his bright bootlaces spurting forth to taste the mountain air. The skinhead staggered backward, time enough to fire one blast before his legs got tangled up in each other, and he fell.

Still moving, that one, but a single round between his ears at something close to point-blank range put paid to any risk of resurrection. Katz jogged past him, using his shiny claw to pluck a rifle grenade from the pouch at his waist, snapping it into place on the AUG's launcher.

He came around the corner of the house and met two skinheads running in the opposite direction, closing on a hard collision course. They both cut loose with automatic weapons at the first sight of their enemy, Katz diving to his right, a shoulder roll that could have used a bit more planning to alleviate the jolt of impact.

Even so, he came up with the AUG more or less on target. He squeezed the trigger and sent the sleek grenade downrange. It clipped one skinhead's temple, staggered him and wobbled off to detonate beneath the

villa's eaves. A six-foot section of the canted roof flew
back, spewing smoke and flame.

One target reeling, he concentrated on the other,
nailing three rounds in a fist-sized pattern at the center
of the young man's chest. Before the dead youth hit the
turf, Katz had his partner lined up in the Steyr's sights,
blood streaming down the skinhead's pasty face from
a gash at the hairline, where he had been scraped by one
of the rifle grenade's fins.

Too late, the fledgling Nazi realized his danger,
bringing up his SMG to meet the challenge. Katzenelenbogen shot him once between the eyes and watched
him topple forward.

The gruff Israeli scrambled to his feet, hooked free a
new grenade and mounted it. No interruptions this time
as he sighted on the house and fired his missile through
the picture window of a spacious living room. The blast
was partially contained by solid walls, but flame gushed
through the window for an instant, catching on the
drapes and flowing up the window frame in arrogant
defiance of gravity. Katz had a glimpse of smoking
furniture inside, no movement that would indicate a
living presence in the room.

Move on.

So many men to kill, so little time.

THE GLASS DOORS shattered with a burst from Bolan's
AUG, cascading like the remnants of a frozen water-
fall, the larger fragments bursting as they struck the
concrete patio. He plunged through the gap, still firing, picking out a skinhead in the doorway opposite and
nailing him with three rounds to the chest.

They seemed to have a lot in common, these disciples of the Fourth Reich's "master race." Besides the

buzz cuts, they were slender, wiry, some of them anemic looking, pale skin latticed with tattoos. Whatever else they might be, in their fantasies of Aryan supremacy, the skinheads were not bulletproof.

The room in which he stood appeared to be some kind of recreation hall, complete with billiard table, dart boards on the wall, a Nautilus machine, a large-screen television standing in the corner, ringed by easy chairs. The lifeless skinhead was its only occupant just now, and Bolan put the place behind him, seeking other prey.

Outside he heard the sounds of battle echoing around the villa. Two explosions shook the house, some seconds in between them, but they weren't close enough to hamper Bolan's movements. Plaster dust came down in rivers from the ceiling, long cracks showing here and there, but Bolan paid little attention to the minor inconvenience.

Time to hunt.

Al-Takriti would be somewhere in the house, perhaps attempting to get out, but that left ample space for him to cover in his search. Two floors, perhaps a dozen rooms on each, with several different exits to the grounds.

Where should he start?

He let the villa's floor plan guide him, moving through the only exit from the game room, past the fallen skinhead with his slack expression, blood spreading from beneath him in a slick four feet wide and growing. Down a corridor, past stairs, where Bolan paused and listened for the sound of voices, footsteps, hearing neither.

Moving on.

A bathroom on his left, the door ajar. He kicked it open, scanned the room, its shower stall, found no one to oppose him there. Next up, a pantry on the right. He was approaching it with quick but cautious strides when suddenly the door flew open and a skinhead burst into the hallway, gun in hand.

The young man glanced in both directions, wary of an ambush, but the small precaution was too little and too late. He spied the Executioner, spat out a curse in German, pivoting to aim and fire his pistol in a single fluid movement.

He was good . . . but not quite good enough.

The bullet passed a foot from Bolan's head, the Executioner already fading to his left and dropping to a crouch, his finger tightening around the automatic rifle's trigger. Squeezing off a second round before he died, the skinhead did no better than with the previous round. He recoiled with a shudder as a stream of 5.56 mm tumblers ripped his chest and abdomen apart.

He went down kicking, took a moment more to wriggle through his death throes, then finally lay still. As a precaution, knowing it was wasted effort, Bolan kicked the side arm well beyond the dead man's reach as he passed.

As far as Bolan knew, no fighting man had ever died from taking too many precautions on the battlefield. It always seemed to go the other way, and those who lived to wear their medals home got lucky...or else they took the time to guard their flanks.

The kitchen was on his right. Bolan poked his head through a swinging door, saw movement in the corner of his eye and ducked back out. A shotgun blast ripped through the wooden door where he had stood a heartbeat earlier, a second charge of buckshot peppering the wall opposite.

He palmed a frag grenade and dropped the safety pin. Edged forward, knowing that a lucky shot might nail him through the plaster wall if his assailant took the chance. He made the pitch a simple backhand with a snap, retreating as another shotgun blast ripped through the door and smashed the jamb.

Too close for comfort, but the Executioner was prone when the frag grenade went off, a few stray bits of shrapnel punching through the wall perhaps three feet above his head. Another second found him on his feet and charging through the tattered remnants of the swinging door, the reek of cordite in his nostrils.

He found his adversary seated with his back against a stainless-steel refrigerator, broad doors pocked with shrapnel scars. The kid was dying, gutted by the frag grenade, but he was still alert enough to recognize his enemy. He tried to find the shotgun, but his hand was missing several fingers and the weapon lay beyond his reach.

The next best thing was cursing at his killer, but the neo-Nazi's throat was full of blood, obstructing speech. He blew some crimson bubbles, started gagging on it, and the Executioner had seen enough. A mercy round between the hateful eyes released the skinhead to Valhalla or wherever he was bound.

Not finished yet. He still had twenty rooms to check, or thereabouts, and he was running out of time.

The Executioner moved on in search of larger prey.

"COME OUT AND PLAY, you redneck sons of bitches!"

Calvin James was flying on adrenaline, the rush of battle he had first experienced on mean streets in Chi-

cago, learning all about it as a Navy SEAL in Vietnam.
There were occasions when he took to martial tasks with
grim determination, lacking any pleasure in the hunt,
but that was not the case today.

"I'm waiting, Adolf! Come and get it!"

Darting like a wraith in front of him, a skinhead
broke from cover, making off toward the garage, firing
as he ran. James tracked him with the Steyr AUG, remembering to lead a moving target, squeezing off a
careful 5-round burst from twenty yards away.

The runner seemed to trip on something, lurching,
suddenly off balance, and a tiny burst of crimson appeared around his throat as he fell. James went to check
his kill, make sure the skinhead was not merely
wounded, but a bullet snapping past his face distracted
him.

He hit the deck and brought his AUG around to face
the house. A door was standing open, a shadow behind
it, sighting down an automatic pistol. James fired a
short burst, but lost his target as the skinhead leaped
back out of sight.

The Phoenix warrior switched the AUG's selector
lever into semiauto and mounted a rifle grenade on the
Steyr's built-in launcher. He considered waiting for the
gunman, deciding instead to fire directly at the door, no
recoil to speak of as the missile flew downrange.

The door's solid core provided enough resistance for
the impact fuse to detonate, spewing shards of wood
and twisted shrapnel. When James's eyes pierced the
veil of smoke, he saw the door was gone except for one
odd piece still bolted to the bottom hinge. It formed a
gate of sorts across the opening, no more than ankle
high ... but it was tall enough to trip you if you didn't
watch where you were going.

James never really understood what happened next. The skinhead could have found another way out, through the house. Instead, he came out firing through the shattered doorway, didn't check his footing, tripped and went sprawling on his face.

James waited, let the young man scramble to his hands and knees, eyes wide with fear as he lunged for his pistol. That was when the 5.56 mm bullets ripped his left side open, from the armpit to his hip, flipping him over.

"Like shooting Kluxers in a pigpen," James muttered, rising from the grass and moving toward the doorway.

Caution was in order here. The house was everybody's target, one way or another, as they scoured the villa for al-Takriti. It wouldn't do for the Phoenix warrior to engage Mack Bolan or another of his friends in combat as they roamed aimlessly through empty rooms. But he had just seen evidence that enemies remained inside the house. The place wasn't secure by any means, and taking care of that was part of his job.

He hesitated on the smoky threshold, then stepped over it and went to work.

Spring-cleaning with a vengeance. All human trash must go.

"I'm waiting, Heinrich." Calling to the enemy, a game that also served to hedge his bets against a friendly ambush. "Any of you skinhead motherfuckers want to rock and roll?"

CHAPTER TWENTY-FOUR

Bolan reached another staircase, this one near the spacious living room, where one of the Phoenix warriors had already unloaded a rifle grenade. The curtains and carpet were burning, and an overturned couch was smoldering. But the house was clearly in no immediate danger of going up in flames.

Should he check out a hallway leading to his left or scout the second floor? He decided to move up the stairs. The Steyr had a fresh mag snug in place, his finger on the trigger, ready for a challenge.

The second floor was getting smoky, but the air was breathable so far. He started checking bedrooms left and right, two empties on his first two tries. The third room had a brand-new skylight that the architect had never planned on, a substantial portion of the ceiling blown away by high explosives. There was no one in the room, and Bolan turned away.

The next door on his left was standing partly open, furtive noises coming from inside the room. When Bolan entered with a high kick and a shoulder roll, the occupant laid down a burst of submachine-gun fire.

And missed the Executioner by inches, knocking holes in plaster, gouging polished woodwork on the chest of drawers. He kept on firing, bullets rippling through the sheets and blankets on an unmade bed, lost in the mattress.

It was risky, second-guessing an opponent, but he knew approximately when the SMG had used the last rounds in its magazine. There was an outside chance that it could be a trick, but Bolan didn't care for waiting, lying pinned down in a corner with a bed and nightstand as his only cover, waiting for the skinhead to reload.

He came up firing, and to hell with consequences, tracking on the memory of sound at first, the visuals arriving microseconds later to confirm his judgment. Standing on the far side of the room, an Uzi clutched in one hand and a fresh mag in the other, Bolan's adversary took the burst between his chin and pelvis, slamming back against the wall. The crimson skid marks of his passing were like abstract artwork on the plaster as he slumped into a boneless seated posture on the floor.

How many dead was that? He started counting on his way back to the corridor, then gave it up. With Phoenix Force in action, and McCarter hunting from the sky, he had no way of estimating casualties. It was a futile game as long as al-Takriti was at large, somewhere inside the house or on the grounds.

He finished checking out the bedrooms, meeting no more skinheads. Doubling back, he checked the west wing of the house. The last room on his right, in that wing, had a window facing on the yard, and he was drawn there by the sounds of combat emanating from outside. A peek would do no harm before he started back downstairs and resumed the hunt.

But what he saw outside and below made Bolan catch his breath.

Al-Takriti and a skinhead, racing across the lawn without a backward glance.

He couldn't see where they were going, but they were not dressed for mountain climbing, and their obvious determination told him the Iraqi still had one trick up his sleeve at least.

The window had a little balcony outside, with a low railing, clearly not intended as a functional appendage to the house. No matter. It should hold his weight, and if it didn't... well, then Bolan would be on the ground just that much sooner.

Hoisting up the sash, he ducked outside and peered across the railing of the balcony. Some twelve or thirteen feet to reach the grass below, and Bolan made the leap without a second's hesitation. Landing in a crouch, he checked his flank for skinheads, found himself alone and set off in pursuit of the Iraqi he had come so far to kill.

DUMB LUCK and careless marksmanship saved Gary Manning's life as he approached the east face of the villa, moving across the lawn at a determined, loping pace. Three skinheads saw him coming and opened up with submachine guns at the limit of effective range, too hasty in their nervous agitation for a decent shot.

The Phoenix warrior veered off course and went to ground behind a wooden toolshed. It was taking hits, the bullets punching through one wall and rattling around inside before they spent their force and wound up in the dirt. On either side stray rounds cut divots in the turf or sizzled past like hornets looking for an enemy to strike.

It seemed to be a standoff, but the tall Canadian wasn't about to spend his afternoon pinned down behind a shed while neo-Nazis used him to perfect their aim. They might get lucky, given time, and Manning had much better things to do than hang around the backyard playing games.

He fixed a rifle grenade to the muzzle of his Steyr AUG and set the fire selector switch to semiauto mode. He needed a diversion now to give himself a little combat stretch and draw the hostile fire to one side of the shed.

A sack of fertilizer stood against the shed, unopened, waiting to be moved inside or slit and sprinkled on the villa's several flower beds. His Ka-bar slit the heavy paper, left to right, and Manning tipped the bag, three-quarters of its contents spilling in a dusty, aromatic pile. The rest would do for ballast, he decided as his left hand closed around the bag and hoisted it to test the weight.

Okay.

It wouldn't fool his enemies for long—mere seconds, at the most—but Manning didn't need a lot of time. Coordination was the key, and if he blew it...well, then he would never know the difference.

He flung the leaking bag of fertilizer toward the house, heard automatic weapons open at once and wasted no time lunging in the opposite direction. He was airborne as he cleared the shed, his AUG already angling toward the skinheads, squeezing off a round to launch the sleek grenade before he touched down on the grass.

It helped that Manning's adversaries stood together, almost like a firing squad, drawing comfort from numbers. His grenade was slightly off the mark, touching earth a yard or so in front of the intended targets, but it came close enough to knock them sprawling with the shock wave, pepper them with shrapnel as they fell.

Two of the skinheads wound up sprawling on the grass, their comrade on his knees, one hand pressed flat against his bleeding cheek, the other wrapped around an Uzi SMG. The neo-Nazi's one good eye was open, blinking grit from off the lashes, homing in on Manning as the tall Canadian stood up.

They fired together, but the skinhead's aim was worse than ever, doubtless owing to his pain and shock. The Steyr AUG was still in semiauto mode, and Manning used the optic sight to fire three bullets at a range of fifty yards. The dead man stayed there another moment, upright, kneeling on the grass, then toppled slowly forward.

The other two were breathing when he reached them, but each breath was clearly being drawn on borrowed time. Another round for each, at point-blank range, and they lay still.

He glanced up at the house and saw smoke rising somewhere on the other side. The Black Hawk circled overhead, its rotors slapping at the air, McCarter riding herd on his companions.

And the clock was definitely running.

He could make out other bodies on the ground in each direction, but it was impossible for him to guess how many skinheads still remained to fight for their Iraqi boss. A futile exercise, in any case, since he had not been sent to count them but to take them down.

He thumbed the AUG's selector switch to automatic fire and started for the house. Al-Takriti might not be there, Manning thought, but it would do no harm for him to have a look inside. There was a chance he might get lucky, after all.

Somebody had to bag the fox, it stood to reason, and the bullet might as well be his.

He started jogging, reached the east wall of the house in seconds flat and smashed a window to make his way inside.

THE BEST PART of this property, al-Takriti thought, had always been the scenery. A child of arid flats and brooding, rocky foothills, he still marveled at the peaks around him, snowcapped during nine months of the year, with sheer rock cliffs on every side. The villa occupied a kind of natural plateau, the access road on one face, winding up the mountainside, but you could literally parachute from any of a dozen different points on the perimeter to north and west.

The smaller of al-Takriti's two garages lay due north, some thirty yards beyond the house. It held one vehicle, two others quartered in the larger building on the west side of the house. Yet two more cars were parked in front, unsheltered from the elements.

Al-Takriti understood that he would need a car to make his getaway. Aside from lacking any kind of mountaineer's equipment, he could never hope to outrun a pursuing helicopter in such wild terrain. The pilot could sit back and run him till he dropped, or make it quick and shoot him from the air.

The two cars out in front were lost to him. Al-Takriti knew that much the moment he heard helicopter engines and the sound of gunfire. If the vehicles weren't disabled instantly, they would be sitting targets in the middle of the curving driveway.

Al-Takriti shunned the double-car garage for similar reasons, knowing that the larger structure was more likely to become a target from the air and for attackers on the ground. It also meant a run halfway around the house on open ground, exposed to hostile fire from every side.

A last resort, perhaps, but he would try the compact first and double back should his luck run out.

In fact, he thought, his luck was running short enough right now.

Behind him, all around the grounds, the sound of automatic-weapons fire and shotguns echoed, battered back and forth between the peaks that rimmed al-Takriti's mountain hideaway. For all he knew, the Germans might be holding fast, but he couldn't afford to take the chance. Police would certainly become involved, no matter which side won the fight, and killing time with Swiss detectives was not high on Afif al-Takriti's list of things to do.

They reached the building, Erik tugging at a ring of keys that jangled on his hip. The ring was on some kind of cord or cable, manufactured like a carpenter's measuring tape, to be pulled out some distance, then snap back on its own when it was released. The leader of al-Takriti's skinhead bodyguards thumbed through the keys and found what he was looking for, unlocked the wide garage door, raised it on its hidden tracks.

"We go," he said, and if the German was concerned at all about his fellow neo-Nazis, he deserved a prize for acting self-absorbed. He started for the driver's side, al-Takriti stepping up to intercept him.

"No. I'll drive."

The skinhead looked confused at first, then nodded, reaching for the key ring on his belt. Before he could remove it, though, al-Takriti raised his little SMG and fired a burst directly into Erik's chest, at nearly skin-touch range.

The impact drove his human target backward, arms outflung, and dropped him on the lawn like some outlandish caricature of the crucifixion scene.

"I have my own keys," said al-Takriti to the dead man, fishing them from his pocket. He slid behind the steering wheel and pushed them into the ignition slot.

The Germans were expendable, and taking one of them along when he was running for his life would be a terrible mistake. Two mouths to feed, risks multiplied on every side, all for the benefit of someone he despised as an accursed Westerner.

It had been good to have a guard beside him on the short run from the house to the garage, but Erik had outlived his usefulness.

The compact's engine started on his first attempt. Al-Takriti eased the gearshift into first, released the parking brake, eased out of the garage. There was a jostling thump as he ran over Erik's legs, but nothing that would slow him down.

The rest of it depended on his skill and luck, in almost equal measure. There was still a decent chance that he would die, al-Takriti realized, but if it happened, he would not be hiding in a closet, pleading with his enemies to spare his life.

Whatever his attackers wanted from al-Takriti, they would have to take.

McCARTER HAD the larger of the two garages in his sights, a pair of denim-clad defenders crouched behind it, popping out from time to time to fire hasty bursts of submachine-gun fire in his direction. It was wasted effort, but it made them feel like men, creating the illusion that they had a chance.

In fact, McCarter knew, they had no hope at all.

The average Black Hawk helicopter carried no offensive armament, but was designed to serve the U.S. military as a flying workhorse, hauling troops and cargo into combat zones. A pair of pintle-mounted miniguns or light machine guns was the standard complement for self-defense, but it wasn't the only way to go.

Another option, utilized on the Sikorsky that McCarter flew, was the addition of an external stores support system, anhedralled wings attached above the cabin, with four pylons plumbed for fuel tanks that gave the Black Hawk an extended range of 1,380 miles. The tanks could likewise be detached, replaced with armament including Hellfire missiles, mine dispensers, gun and rocket pods or Stingers.

McCarter had opted for quad-mounted Hellfires on one wing, the air-to-ground missiles guided by reflections from a laser carried on the Black Hawk and directed by McCarter at the target of his choice. The starboard wing supported Stingers and a 12-round pod of 68 mm SNEB rockets. Designed for killing armor on the battlefield, the latter rockets served as well against such lesser targets as civilian vehicles and houses...or a nice two-car garage.

McCarter was fed up with playing watchdog for his comrades on the ground. The fight was winding down, and while he would not strike the house while any member of the Stony team remained inside, he knew damned well that he had no friends in the neighborhood of the garage.

Sighting was a simple matter, lining up the radar-guided rockets, sending half a dozen on their way like airborne furies in a tale from Greek mythology. McCarter watched the white garage disintegrate, transformed into a rolling fireball, secondary blasts from fuel tanks adding extra smoke and heat. One of the skinheads made a break for daylight, trailing flames behind him like a superhero's cape until his legs gave out and he collapsed to smolder on the grass.

McCarter circled back to overfly the driveway and the broad front lawn. The two cars parked outside al-Takriti's villa had absorbed their share of rifle fire at the start of the battle, but another trio of defenders was entrenched there, using the bullet-pocked hulks as a shield while they dueled with Rafael Encizo, pinning him down at the edge of a decorative flower bed.

McCarter came in on their flank and reached out with his optics from a range of sixty yards, the laser sights locked on and activated. When he fired the first two Hellfire missiles, it was over. There was nothing for his enemies to do but stand and die.

Not that it required much in the way of effort, crouching in the shadow of a limousine one moment, vanishing in smoke and flame the next. You didn't need a turn in acting school to play that part, and it was just as well.

Regardless of the rave reviews, there would be no way on God's earth for those two walk-on players to return and do the sequel.

Encizo was on his feet and moving as McCarter lifted off, a thumbs-up signal to the Black Hawk as he stormed the front porch of the villa, sprayed the door with bullets from his AUG and bulled his way inside.

And through it all, where had al-Takriti gone?

McCarter practiced lining up the Arab's villa in his sights and waited for the word to burn it down.

THE EXECUTIONER was gaining on al-Takriti when he saw the Arab shoot his bodyguard at point-blank range and duck inside the car. Another moment and the compact had begun to move, across the skinhead's prostrate body, gaining speed along the curving driveway. At this rate it would pass within a few feet of him, and he didn't mean to let it go.

Instead of firing from the sidelines, Bolan stepped into al-Takriti's path, the Steyr AUG unloading half a magazine in automatic fire. He saw the bullets striking headlights, grille, hood, windshield, but the driver saved himself by ducking to his right, below the dashboard.

He was relatively safe in that position, but he couldn't see where he was going, and the car began to swerve hard right, in the direction of al-Takriti's lunge for cover. Well off course and still accelerating, it was making close to thirty miles per hour when it clipped a shade tree on the driver's side, then veered even farther to the right.

The villa was behind al-Takriti now, and he was steering, unintentionally, for the nearest cliff that marked the boundary of his estate. Another hundred yards or so, and he would have to pray for flying lessons on the long trip down.

Al-Takriti risked a glance above the dash and recognized his peril, hauling on the wheel for all his strength, hard left. He stood on the brakes at the same instant, plowing long furrows in the manicured lawn as his tires found traction, locked, dug in.

And so he saved himself, but only from the cliff.

Bolan was watching when al-Takriti bailed out of his car on the passenger's side, keeping the vehicle between them. Moving in on him was bound to be a problem, since al-Takriti had his SMG and God knew what else. Standing at the edge of his effective range, the Executioner prepared another rifle grenade, using the Steyr's optic sight this time as he drew a bead on the rear half of the compact.

In the old days, with the M-1 Garand, riflemen were taught to fire grenades with the butt of their weapon braced on mother earth, an arching mortar shot that was often long on altitude and short on accuracy. With the Steyr, Bolan picked his target, made a slight adjustment for the weight of the grenade and let it rip.

The compact shuddered, belching smoke and fire, the trunk lid sprang open, gaping like an open mouth. The fuel tank would be blowing any second, but al-Takriti didn't wait around to feel the heat.

He came out firing with the submachine gun, still beyond effective range, a full mag wasted by the time he covered fifty feet. Bolan tracked him, maintaining the distance between them, and watched him reload. He marked the runner's course and saw where it was taking him.

Back toward the cliff.

It was an easy stalk, all things considered. Bolan's prey had nothing in the way of cover, and mobility was limited by geography. Al-Takriti could have run back toward the house, but Bolan never would have let him get there. Almost as an afterthought, the Stony warrior palmed his compact walkie-talkie, speaking to his allies.

"This is Striker. Clear the house ASAP. Confirm positions when you're clear. Air One, reduce the target when you've verified no friendlies left inside."

They came back with acknowledgments, and Bolan waited, following al-Takriti on a run to nowhere, roughly circling the property. A moment later Bolan heard the sound of heavy metal thunder at his back and paused to watch the Black Hawk finishing al-Takriti's dream house in the Juras, razing it with high-tech thunderbolts.

Al-Takriti saw it, too, the image of destruction beaten home by one blast following another, like the roll of doomsday drums. He veered off course again, turned back in the direction of the nearest cliff and ran until he reached the precipice.

Mack Bolan overtook him there, approaching cautiously, the Steyr AUG set for full-auto fire. Al-Takriti faced the mountains, standing with arms slack at his sides, still clutching the small submachine gun. When he turned to face the Executioner at last, his eyes betrayed a beaten man.

"Who are you?" he demanded.

"Just a soldier."

"An American."

"That's right ."

"You punish me because I served Saddam."

The tall man shook his head. "Because you murdered total strangers, and you would have murdered hundreds more."

"I murdered no one, sir."

"Semantics. You devised the plan, arranged liaison with the triggermen. I didn't come out here to argue definitions. You know what you've done as well as I do."

"And are you so innocent?" al-Takriti asked.

"I'll take my chances when the time comes. This is your day in the spotlight."

"So, an executioner."

"Give that man a cigar."

"It doesn't matter that I've left Saddam?"

"Not even close."

Al-Takriti glanced across his shoulder, toward the chasm at his back. "I cannot kill myself," he said.

"Nobody asked you to."

The Arab nodded, smiled and raised his submachine gun, with the muzzle aimed in Bolan's general direction. Was his finger on the trigger? Bolan didn't know or care. The AUG spit out a stream of 5.56 mm tumblers, pummeling al-Takriti backward, toward the cliff's edge and beyond.

One moment he was there, a jerking pupped spouting crimson from at least a dozen wounds, and then he vanished. Bolan walked up to the precipice in time to see a tiny rag-doll figure far below him, caroming off jagged rocks, soon dwindling out of sight in the bottomless void.

The warrior raised his head and scanned the mountains, found them grim and silent witnesses to one more transient sideshow in the game of life and death. The Juras had been ancient when the first man left his cave in Europe to pursue game on the plains. They would be standing when the Executioner and his companions had returned to dust and vanished out of living memory.

He raised the walkie-talkie, turned to face the circling Black Hawk as he spoke.

"Let's wrap this up," said Bolan, speaking to the team at large. "We're going home."

**Bolan's fury is unleashed against
an evil empire reborn**

Gold Eagle presents a special
three-book in-line continuity

Beginning in March 1995, Gold Eagle brings you another action-packed three-book in-line continuity, THE ARMS TRILOGY.

In THE ARMS TRILOGY, the men of Stony Man Farm target Hayden Thone, powerful head of an illicit weapons empire. Thone, CEO of Fortress Arms, is orchestrating illegal arms deals and secretly directing the worldwide activities of terrorist groups for his own purposes.

Be sure to catch all the action featuring the ever-popular THE EXECUTIONER starting in March, continuing through to May.

Available at your favorite retail outlet, or order your copy now:

Book I:	March	SELECT FIRE	$3.50 U.S.	☐
		(The Executioner #195)	$3.99 CAN.	☐
Book II:	April	TRIBURST	$3.50 U.S.	☐
		(The Executioner #196)	$3.99 CAN.	☐
Book III:	May	ARMED FORCE	$3.50 U.S.	☐
		(The Executioner #197)	$3.99 CAN.	☐

Total amount	$_____
Plus 75¢ postage ($1.00 in Canada)	$_____
Canadian residents add applicable federal and provincial taxes	
Total payable	$_____

To order, please send this form, along with your name, address, zip or postal code, and a check or money order for the total above, payable to Gold Eagle Books, to:

In the U.S.	In Canada
Gold Eagle Books	Gold Eagle Books
3010 Walden Avenue	P. O. Box 636
P. O. Box 9077	Fort Erie, Ontario
Buffalo, NY 14269-9077	L2A 5X3

AT95-2

Don't miss out on the action in these titles featuring
THE EXECUTIONER®, ABLE TEAM® and PHOENIX FORCE®!

SuperBolan

#61436	**HELLGROUND**	$4.99	☐
	In this business, you get what you pay for. Iberra's tab is running high—and the Executioner has come to collect.		
#61438	**AMBUSH**	$4.99 U.S.	☐
	Bolan delivers his scorched-earth remedy—the	$5.50 CAN.	☐
	only answer for those who deal in blood and terror.		

Stony Man™

#61894	**STONY MAN #10 SECRET ARSENAL**	$4.99	☐
	A biochemical weapons conspiracy puts America in the hot seat.		
#61895	**STONY MAN #11 TARGET AMERICA**	$4.99	☐
	A terrorist strike calls America's top commandos to the firing line.		

(limited quantities available on certain titles)

TOTAL AMOUNT	$
POSTAGE & HANDLING	$
($1.00 for one book, 50¢ for each additional)	
APPLICABLE TAXES*	$_____
TOTAL PAYABLE	$_____
(check or money order—please do not send cash)	

To order, complete this form and send it, along with a check or money order for the total above, payable to Gold Eagle Books, to: **In the U.S.:** 3010 Walden Avenue, P.O. Box 9077, Buffalo, NY 14269-9077; **In Canada:** P.O. Box 636, Fort Erie, Ontario, L2A 5X3.

Name:_____

Address:_____ City:_____

State/Prov.:_____ Zip/Postal Code: _____

*New York residents remit applicable sales taxes.
 Canadian residents remit applicable GST and provincial taxes.

GEBACK9A